PRAISE FOR CLIVE BARKER

AND

Abarat

"A blend of *Alice in Wonderland* and *The Lion, the Witch and the Wardrobe*." —*Entertainment Weekly*

"Keeps you effortlessly turning the pages." —*The New York Times Magazine*

"A writer of stunning imagination." —*Atlanta Journal-Constitution*

"A fantastic read, with the right amount of suspense and humor." —*Chicago Tribune*

"Above all, this is a deeply lovely catalogue of the strange. Islands carved into colossal heads, giant moths made of coloured ether, words that turn into aeroplanes, tentacled maggot-monsters: they dance past like a carnival, a true surrender to the weird." —*The Guardian*

"Clever, but oh so creepy." —*People*

"Barker throws plenty of chills at readers." —*Publishers Weekly*

"Always creating and always pushing into the farthest reaches of the human mind, [Barker] is an artist in every sense of the word. He is the great imaginer of our time."
—Quentin Tarantino

"Abarat is an intriguing creation, deserving of comparison to Oz. Barker pours out an utter phantasmagoria, ruled by the logic of dreams. . . ." —*Kirkus Reviews*

"Barker imbues the traditional conventions of fantasy with a whimsical Wonderland quality, providing a host of bizarre characters, a fabulous landscape, and a coherent underlying mythology."

—ALA *Booklist* (starred review)

"The most imaginative of the macabre novelists, and he just keeps getting better." —*Kansas City Star*

"*Abarat* is a story that will capture the imaginations of all readers, offering a limitless landscape to visit and revisit."
—*Outsmart*

"Clive Barker is a magician of the first order."
—*New York Daily News*

ALSO BY CLIVE BARKER

CLIVE BARKER

Abarat

JOANNA COTLER BOOKS

An Imprint of HarperCollins*Publishers*

Printed in the U.S.A. For information address HarperCollins Children's
Books, a division of HarperCollins Publishers,
1350 Avenue of the Americas, New York, NY 10019.
www.harpercollins.com

Library of Congress Cataloging-in-Publication Data
Barker, Clive, date.
Abarat / Clive Barker. — 1st ed.
p. cm. — (Abarat)
    Summary: Candy Quackenbush of Chickentown, Minnesota, one day finds
herself on the edge of a foreign world that is populated by strange creatures, and
her life is forever changed.
ISBN 0-06-028092-1 — ISBN 0-06-059637-6 (pbk.) — ISBN 0-06-440733-0 (pbk.)
[1. Fantasy.] I. Title. II. Series.
PZ7.B25046 Ab 2002   2002001299
[Fic]—dc21   CIP
                                                                 AC

Typography by Alicia Mikles
❖
First Harper Trophy edition, 2003
First rack edition, 2004

To Emilian David Armstrong

I dreamed a limitless book,
A book unbound,
Its leaves scattered in fantastic abundance.

On every line there was a new horizon drawn,
New heavens supposed;
New states, new souls.

One of those souls,
Dozing through some imagined afternoon,
Dreamed these words.
And needing a hand to set them down,
Made mine.

C. B.

CONTENTS

PART FOUR: WICKED STRANGE

PROLOGUE

THE MISSION

Three is the number of those who do holy work;
Two is the number of those who do lover's work;
One is the number of those who do perfect evil
Or perfect good.

—From the notes of a monk
of the Order of St. Oco;
his name unknown

THE STORM CAME UP out of the southwest like a fiend, stalking its prey on legs of lightning.

The wind it brought with it was as foul as the devil's own breath and it stirred up the peaceful waters of the sea. By the time the little red boat that the three women had chosen for their perilous voyage had emerged from the shelter of the islands, and was out in the open waters, the waves were as steep as cliffs, twenty-five, thirty feet tall.

"Somebody sent this storm," said Joephi, who was doing her best to steer the boat, which was called *The Lyre*. The sail shook like a leaf in a tempest, swinging back and forth wildly, nearly impossible to hold down. "I swear, Diamanda, this is no natural storm!"

Diamanda, the oldest of the three women, sat in the center of the tiny vessel with her dark blue robes gathered around her and their precious cargo pressed to her bosom.

"Let's not get hysterical," she told Joephi and Mespa. She wiped a long piece of white hair out of her eyes. "Nobody saw us leave the Palace of Bowers. We escaped unseen, I'm certain of it."

"So why this storm?" said Mespa, who was a black

woman, renowned for her resilience, but who now looked close to being washed away by the rain beating down on the women's heads.

"Why are you so surprised that the heavens complain?" Diamanda said. "Didn't we know the world would be turned upside down by what just happened?"

Joephi fought with the sail, cursing it.

"Indeed, isn't this the way it *should* be?" Diamanda went on. "Isn't it right that the sky is torn to tatters and the sea put in a frenzy? Would we prefer it if the world did not care?"

"No, no of course not," said Mespa, holding on to the edge of the pitching boat, her face as white as her close-cropped hair was black. "I just wish we weren't out in the middle of it all."

"Well, we are!" said the old woman. "And there's not a thing any of us can do about it. So I suggest you finish emptying your stomach, Mespa—"

"It *is* empty," the sick woman said. "I have nothing left to bring up."

"—and you Joephi, handle the sail—"

"Oh, Goddesses . . ." Joephi murmured. "*Look.*"

"What is it?" said Diamanda.

Joephi pointed up into the sky.

Several stars had been shaken down from the firmament—great white cobs of fire piercing the clouds and falling seaward. One of them was heading directly toward *The Lyre*.

"Down!" Joephi yelled, catching hold of the back of Diamanda's robes and pushing the old woman off her seat.

Diamanda hated to be touched; *manhandling*, she called it. She started to berate Joephi roundly for what she'd done, but she was drowned out by the roaring sound of the falling star as it rushed toward the vessel. It burst the billowing sail of *The Lyre*, burning a hole right through the canvas, and then plunged into the sea, where it was extinguished with a great hissing sound.

"I swear that was meant for us," Mespa said when they had all raised their heads from the boards. She helped Diamanda to her feet.

"All right," the old lady replied, yelling over the din of the seething waters, "that was closer than I would have liked."

"So you think we *are* targets?"

"I don't know and I don't care," Diamanda said. "We just have to trust to the holiness of our mission."

Mespa licked her pale lips before she chanced her next words.

"Are we *sure* it's holy?" she said. "Perhaps what we're doing is sacrilegious. Perhaps she should be left to—"

"*Rest in peace?*" said Joephi.

"Yes," Mespa replied.

"She was barely more than a girl, Mespa," Joephi said. "She had a life of perfect love ahead of her, and it was stolen."

"Joephi's right," said Diamanda. "Do you think a soul like hers would sleep quietly, with so much life left to live? So many dreams that she never saw come true?"

Mespa nodded. "You're right, of course," she conceded. "We must do this work, whatever the cost."

The thunderhead that had followed them from the islands was now directly overhead. It threw down a vile, icy rain, thick as phlegm, which struck the boards of *The Lyre* like drumming. The lightning came down around the trembling vessel on every side, its lurid light throwing the curling waves into silhouette as they rose to break over the boat.

"The sail's no use to us now," said Joephi, looking up at the tattered canvas.

"Then we must find other means," said Diamanda. "Mespa. Take hold of our cargo for a few moments. And be careful."

With great reverence Mespa took the small box, its sides and lid decorated with the closely etched lines of talismans. Relieved of her burden, Diamanda walked down to the stern of *The Lyre*, the pitching of the boat threatening several times to throw her over the side before she reached the safety of the little seat. There she knelt and leaned forward, plunging her arthritic hands into the icy waters.

"You'd best be careful," Mespa warned her. "There's a fifty-foot mantizac that's been following us for the last half hour. I saw it when I was throwing up."

"No self-respecting fish is going to want my old bones," Diamanda said.

She'd no sooner spoken than the mottled head of a mantizac—not quite the size Mespa had described, but still huge—broke the surface. Its vast maw gaped not more than a foot from Diamanda's outstretched arms.

"Goddess!" the old lady yelled, withdrawing her hands and sitting up sharply.

The frustrated fish pushed against the back of the boat, as if to nudge one of the human morsels on board into its own element.

"So . . ." said Diamanda. "I think this calls for some moon-magic."

"Wait," said Joephi. "You said if we used magic, we would risk drawing attention to ourselves."

"So I did," Diamanda replied. "But in our present state we risk drowning or being eaten by that *thing*." The mantizac was now moving up the side of *The Lyre*, turning up its enormous head and fixing the women with its silver-and-scarlet eye.

Mespa clutched the little box even closer to her bosom. "It won't take me," she said, a profound terror in her voice.

"No," said Diamanda reassuringly. *"It won't."*

She raised her aged hands. Dark threads of energy moved through her veins and leaped from her fingertips, forming delicate shapes on the air, and then fled heavenward.

"Lady Moon," she called. "You know we would not call on you unless we needed your intervention. So we do. Lady, we three are of no consequence. We ask this boon not for ourselves but for the soul of one who was taken from among us before she was ready to leave. Please, Lady, bear us all safely through this storm, so that her life may find continuance . . ."

"Name our destination!" Joephi yelled over the roar of the water.

"She knows our minds," Diamanda said.

"Even so," Joephi replied. *"Name it!"*

Diamanda glanced back at her companion, faintly irritated. "If you insist," she said. Then, reaching toward the sky again, she said: *"Take us to the Hereafter."*

"Good," said Joephi.

"Lady, hear us—" Diamanda started to say.

But she was interrupted by Mespa.

"She heard, Diamanda."

"What?"

"She heard."

The three women looked up. The roiling storm clouds were parting, as though pressed aside by titanic hands. Through the widening slit there came a shaft of moonlight: the purest white, yet somehow warm. It illuminated the trough between the waves where the women's boat was buried. It covered the vessel from end to end with light.

"Thank you, Lady . . ." Diamanda murmured.

The moonlight was *moving* over the boat, searching out every part of the tiny vessel, even to the shadowy keel that lay beneath the water. It blessed every nail and board from prow to stern, every grommet, every oar, every pivot, every fleck of paint, every inch of rope.

It touched the women too, inspiring fresh life in their weary bones and warming their icy skin.

All of this took perhaps ten seconds.

Then the clouds began to close again, cutting the moonlight off. Just as abruptly as it had begun, the blessing was over.

The sea seemed doubly dark when the light had passed away, the wind keener. But the timbers of the boat had acquired a subtle luminescence from the appearance of the moon, and they were stronger for the benediction they had received. The boat no longer creaked when it was broad-sided. Instead it seemed to rise effortlessly up the steep sides of the waves.

"That's better," said Diamanda.

She reached out to reclaim their precious cargo.

"I can take care of it," Mespa protested.

"I'm sure you can," said Diamanda. "But the responsibility lies with me. I know the world we're going to, remember? You don't."

"You remember the way it *was*," Joephi reminded her. "But it will have changed."

"Very possibly," Diamanda agreed. "But I still have a better idea of what lies ahead of us than you two do. Now give me the box, Mespa."

Mespa handed the treasure over, and the women's vessel carved its way through the lightless sea, picking up speed as it went, the bow lifting a little way above the waters.

The rain continued to beat down on the women's heads, gathering in the bottom of the boat until it was four inches deep. But the voyagers took no notice of its assault. They simply sat together in grateful silence, as the magic of the moon hurried them toward their destination.

"There!" said Joephi. She pointed off toward the distant shore. "I see the Hereafter."

"I see it too!" said Mespa. "Oh, thank the Goddess! I see it! I see it!"

"Hush yourselves," Diamanda said. "We don't want to draw attention."

"It looks empty," Joephi said, scanning the landscape ahead. "You said there was a town."

"There *is* a town. But it's a little distance from the harbor."

"I see no harbor."

"Well, there's not much of it left," Diamanda said. "It was burned down, long before my time."

The keel of *The Lyre* was grating on the shore of the Hereafter. Joephi was first out, hauling on the rope and securing it to a piece of aged timber that was driven into the ground. Mespa helped Diamanda out, and the three of them stood side by side assessing the unpromising landscape spread before them. The storm had followed them across the divide between the two worlds, its fury undimmed.

"Now, let's remember," said Diamanda, "we're here to do one thing and one thing only. We get our business done and then we leave. Remember: *we should not be here.*"

"We know that," said Mespa.

"But let's not be hasty and make a mistake," Joephi said, glancing at the box Diamanda carried. "For *her* sake we have to do this right. We carry the hopes of the Abarat with us."

Even Diamanda was quieted by this remark. She

seemed to meditate on it for a long moment, her head downturned, the rain washing her white hair into curtains that framed the box she held. Then she said: "Are you both ready?"

The other women murmured that yes, they were; and with Diamanda leading the way, they left the shore and headed through the rain-lashed grass, to find the place where providence had arranged they would do their holy work.

PART ONE

MORNINGTIDE

Life is short,
And pleasures few,
And holed the ship,
And drowned the crew,
But o! But o!
How very blue
The sea is!

—The last poem written by
Righteous Bandy, the
nomad Poet of Abarat

1

ROOM NINETEEN

THE PROJECT MISS SCHWARTZ had set for Candy's class was simple enough. Everyone had a week to bring into school ten interesting facts about the town in which they all lived. Something about the history of Chickentown would be fine, she said, or, if students preferred, facts about the way the town was today, which meant, of course, the same old stuff about chicken farming in modern Minnesota.

Candy had done her best. She'd visited the school library and scoured its shelves for something, *anything*, about the town that to her sounded vaguely *interesting*. There was nothing. Nada, zero, zip. There was a library on Naughton Street that was ten times the size of the school library; so she went there. Again, she scanned the shelves. There were a few books about Minnesota that mentioned the town, but the same boring facts were repeated in volume after volume. Chickentown had a population of 36,793 and it was the biggest producer of chicken meat in the state. One of the books, having mentioned the chickens, described the town as "otherwise undistinguished."

Perfect, Candy thought. *I live in a town that is* otherwise undistinguished. Well, that was Fact Number One. She needed only nine more.

"We live in the most boring town in the country," she complained to her mother, Melissa, when she returned home. "I can't find anything worth writing about for Miss Schwartz."

Melissa Quackenbush was in the kitchen, making meatloaf. The kitchen door was closed, so as not to disturb Candy's father, Bill. He was in a beer-induced slumber in front of the television, and Candy's mother wanted to keep it that way. The longer he stayed unconscious, the easier it was for everyone in the house—including Candy's brothers, Don and Ricky—to get on with their lives. Nobody ever mentioned this aloud. It was a silent understanding between the members of the household. Life was more pleasant for everyone when Bill Quackenbush was asleep.

"Why do you say it's *boring*?" Melissa asked, as she seasoned the meatloaf.

"Just take a look out there," Candy said.

Melissa didn't bother, but that was only because she knew the scene outside the window all too well. Beyond the grimy glass was the family's chaotic backyard: the shin-high grass browned by the heat wave that had come unexpectedly in the middle of May, the inflatable pool they'd bought the previous summer and had never deflated and stowed away, now a dirty circle of red-and-white plastic at the far end of the yard. Beyond the collapsed pool was the broken fence. And beyond the fence? Another yard in not much better shape, and another, and another, until eventually the yards ended, and the streets too, and the empty grasslands began.

"I know what you want for your project," she said.

"Oh?" said Candy, going to the fridge and taking out a soda. "What do I want?"

"You want something *weird*," Melissa said, putting the meat into the baking tin and thumbing it down. "You've got a little morbid streak in you, just like your grandma Frances. She used to go to the funerals of complete strangers—"

"She did not," Candy said with a laugh.

"She did. I swear. She loved anything like that. You get it from her. You certainly don't get it from me or your dad."

"Oh well, that really makes me feel welcome."

"You know what I mean," Candy's mother protested.

"So you don't think Chickentown is boring?" Candy said.

"There are worse places, believe me," Melissa said. "At least it's got a bit of history . . ."

"Not much of one. Not according to the books I looked at," Candy said.

"You know who you should talk to?" Melissa said.

"Who?"

"Norma Lipnik. You remember Norma? She and I used to work at the Comfort Tree Hotel together?"

"Vaguely," Candy said.

"All kinds of strange things happen at hotels. And

the Comfort Tree has been around since . . . oh, I don't know. You ask Norma, she'll tell you."

"Is she the one with the white-blond hair, who always wore too much lipstick?"

Melissa looked up at her daughter with a little smile. "Don't you go saying anything rude to her now."

"I wouldn't do a thing like that."

"I know how these things slip out with you."

"*Mom*. I'll be really polite."

"Good. You do that. She's the assistant manager there now, so if you're real nice to her, and you ask the right questions, I bet you she'll give you something for your project that nobody else in class will have."

"Like what?"

"You go over there and ask her. She'll remember you. Ask her to tell you about Henry Murkitt."

"Who's Henry Murkitt?"

"You go and ask her. It's your project. You should get out there and do some legwork. Like a detective."

"Is there much to detect?" Candy said.

"You'd be surprised."

She was. The first surprise was Norma Lipnik herself, who was no longer the tacky woman that Candy remembered: her hair teased high and her dress too short. In the eight years or so since Candy had seen Norma, she had let her hair go naturally gray. The bright red lipstick was a thing of the past, as were the short dresses. But once Candy had introduced herself, Norma's new professional reserve was soon cast to the winds, and the warm gossipy woman Candy remembered emerged.

"Lord, how you have grown, Candy," she said. "I never see you around; you or your mother. Is she doing okay?"

"Yeah, I guess."

"I heard your dad lost his job at the chicken factory. Had a little problem with the beer, so I was told?" Candy didn't have time to agree or deny this. "You know what? I think that sometimes people should be given second chances. If you don't give people second chances, how are they ever going to change?"

"I don't know," Candy said, feeling uncomfortable.

"*Men*." Norma said, "You stay away from them, darlin'. They are more trouble than they're worth. I'm on my third marriage, and I don't give that more than two months."

"Oh—"

"Anyway, you didn't come over here to listen to me chattering on. So how can I help you?"

"I've got this project to do, about Chickentown," Candy explained. "It was set by Miss Schwartz, who always gives us these projects that are only fit for sixth graders. Besides, she doesn't like me very much—"

"Oh, don't let her get you down, honey. There's always one who makes your life hell. You'll be out of school soon enough. What are you going to do then? Work over at the factory?"

Candy felt a great weight settle on her shoulders, imagining that horrendous prospect.

"I hope not," she said. "I want to do something more with my life."

"But you don't know what?"

Candy shook her head.

"Don't worry, it'll come to you," Norma said. "I hope it does, because you don't want to get stuck here."

"No, I don't. I really don't."

"So you've got a project about Chickentown—"

"Yes. And Mom said there were some things that went on in the hotel I should find out about. She said you'd know what she was talking about."

"Did she indeed?" said Norma, with a teasing little smile.

"She said to ask you about Henry—"

"—Murkitt."

"Yes. Henry Murkitt."

"Poor old Henry. What else did she say? Did she tell you about Room Nineteen?"

"No. She didn't mention anything about a room. She just gave me the name."

"Well, I can tell you the tale," Norma said. "But I don't know if Murkitt's story is the kind of thing your Miss Schwartz will be looking for."

"Why not?"

"Well, because it's rather *dark*," Norma said. "Tragic, in fact."

Candy smiled. "Well, Mom says I'm morbid, so I'll probably like it."

"Morbid, huh? All right," said Norma. "I guess I should tell you the whole darn thing. You see,

Chickentown used to be called Murkitt."

"Really? That wasn't in any of the books about Minnesota."

"You know how it is. There's the history that finds its way into the books and there's the history that doesn't."

"And Henry Murkitt—?"

"—is part of the history that doesn't."

"Huh."

Candy was fascinated. Remembering what her mother had said about doing some detective work, she took out her notebook and began to write in it. *Murkitt. History we don't know.*

"So the town was named after Henry Murkitt?"

"No," said Norma. "It was named after his grand-father Wallace Murkitt."

"Why did they change it?"

"I guess Chickentown fits, doesn't it? This place has got more damn chickens in it than it has people. And sometimes I think folks care more about the chickens than they do about each other. My husband works over at the factory, so that's all I ever hear from him and his friends—"

"Chicken talk?"

"Chickens, chickens and more darn chickens." Norma glanced at her watch. "You know I don't have much time to show you Room Nineteen today. I've got a big party of folks coming in. Can we do this another day?"

"I've got to have the report in by tomorrow morning."

"You kids, always leaving things to the last minute,"

Norma said. "Well, okay. We'll do this quickly. But you be sure to jot it all down, because I won't have time to say anything twice."

"I'm ready," said Candy.

Norma took her passkey from her pocket. "Linda?" she said to the woman working at the front desk, "I'm just going up to Room Nineteen."

The woman frowned. "Really? What for?"

The question went unanswered.

"I won't be more than ten minutes," Norma said.

She led Candy away from the reception area, talking as she went. "This is the new part of the hotel we're in right now," she explained. "It was built in 1964. But once we step through *here*"—she led Candy through a pair of double doors—"we're in the old hotel. It used to be called the High Seas Hotel. Don't ask me why."

Even if Candy hadn't been told that there was a difference between the portion of the hotel she'd been in and the part that Norma had brought her into, she would have known it. The passageways were narrower here and less well lit. There was a sour smell of age in the air, as if somebody had left the gas on.

"We only put people up in the old part of the hotel if all the other rooms are full. And that only happens when there's a Chicken Buyer's Conference. Even then, we try never to put people in Room Nineteen."

"Why's that?"

"Well, it's not that it's *haunted*, exactly. Though there have been stories. Personally, I think all that stuff about the afterlife is nonsense. You get one life and you'd better make the best of it. My sister got religion last year and she's shaping up for a sainthood, I swear."

Norma had led Candy to the end of a passageway where there was a narrow staircase, illuminated by a single lamp. It cast a yellowish light that did nothing to flatter the charmless wallpaper and the cracking paintwork.

Candy almost remarked that it was no wonder the management kept this part of the hotel out of the sight of guests, but she bit her tongue, remembering what her mother had said about keeping less courteous thoughts to herself.

Up the creaking stairs they went. They were steep.

"I should stop smoking," Norma remarked. "It'll be the death of me."

There were two doors at the top. One was Room Seventeen. The other was Room Nineteen.

Norma handed the passkey to Candy.

"You want to open it?" Norma said.

"Sure."

Candy took the key and put it in the lock.

"You have to jiggle it around a little."

Candy jiggled. And after a little work, the key turned, and Candy opened the ill-oiled door of Room Nineteen.

2

WHAT HENRY MURKITT
LEFT BEHIND

IT WAS DARK INSIDE the room; the air still and stale.

"Why don't you go ahead and open the drapes, honey?" Norma said, taking the key back from Candy.

Candy waited a moment for her eyes to become accustomed to the gloom, then she tentatively made her way across the room to the window. The thick fabric of the drapes felt greasy against her palms, as though they hadn't been cleaned in a very long time. She pulled. The drapes moved reluctantly along dust-and dirt-clogged rails. The glass Candy found herself looking through was as filthy as the fabric.

"How long is it since anybody rented the room?" Candy said.

"Actually I can't remember if there's been anybody in it since I've been at the hotel," Norma said.

Candy looked out of the window. The view was no more inspiring to the senses or the soul than the view out of the kitchen window of 34 Followell Street, her home. Immediately below the window was a small courtyard at the back of the hotel, which contained five or six garbage cans, filled to over-brimming, and the skeletal remains of last year's Christmas tree, still wearing its shabby display of tinsel and artificial snow. Beyond the yard was Lincoln Street (or so Candy guessed; the journey through the hotel had completely disoriented her). She could see the tops of cars above the wall of the yard, and a Discount Drug Store on the opposite side of the street, its doors chained and padlocked, its shelves bare.

"So," said Norma, calling Candy's attention back into Room Nineteen. "This is where Henry Murkitt stayed."

"Did he come to the hotel often?"

"To my knowledge," Norma said, "he came only once. But I'm not really sure about that, so don't quote me."

Candy could understand why Henry would not have been a repeat visitor. The room was tiny. There was a narrow bed against the far wall and a chair in the corner with a small black television perched on it. In front of it was a second chair, on which was perched an over-filled ashtray.

"Some of our employees come up here when they have half an hour to spare to catch up on the soap operas," Norma said, by way of explanation.

"So they don't believe the room's haunted?"

"Put it this way, honey," Norma said. "Whatever they believe it doesn't put them off coming up here."

"What's through there?" Candy said, pointing to a door.

"Look for yourself," Norma said.

Candy opened the door and stepped into a minuscule bathroom that had not been cleaned in a very long time. In the mirror above the filthy sink she met her own reflection. Her eyes looked almost black in the murk of this little cell, and her dark hair needed a cut. But she liked her own face, even in such an unpromising light. She had her mother's smile, open and easy, and her father's frown; the deep, troubled frown that Bill Quackenbush wore in his beer-dreams. And of course her odd eyes: the left dark brown, the right blue; though the mirror reversed them.

"When you've quite finished admiring yourself . . ." Norma said.

Candy closed the bathroom door and went back to her note-taking to cover her embarrassment. *There is no wallpaper on the walls of Room Nineteen*, she wrote, *just plaster painted a dirty white*. One of the four walls had a curious abstract pattern on it, which was faintly pink. All in all, she could not have imagined a grimmer or more uncomfortable place.

"So what can you tell me about Henry Murkitt?" she asked Norma.

"Not that much," the woman replied. "His grandfather was the founding father of the town. In fact, we're all of us here because Wallace Murkitt decided he'd had enough of life on the trail. The story goes that his horse upped and died on him in the middle of the night, so they had no choice but to settle down right here in the middle of nowhere."

Candy smiled. There was something about this little detail which absolutely fit with all she knew about her hometown. "So Chickentown exists because Wallace Murkitt's horse died?" she said.

Norma seemed to get the bitter joke. "Yeah," she said. "I guess that about sums things up, doesn't it? But apparently Henry Murkitt was very proud of having his family's name on the town. It was something he used to boast about."

"Then they changed it—"

"Yes, well, I'll get to that in a moment. Really, poor Henry's life was a series of calamities toward the end. First his wife, Diamanda, left him. Nobody knows where she went. And then sometime in December 1947, the town council decided to change the name of the town. Henry took it very badly. On Christmas Eve he checked into the hotel, and the poor man never checked out again."

Candy had guessed something like this was coming, but even so it made the little hairs on the nape of her neck prickle to hear Norma say it.

"He died in this room?" Candy said softly.

"Yes."

"How? A heart attack?"

Norma shook her head.

"Oh, no . . ." said Candy, beginning to put the pieces together. "He killed himself?"

"Yes. I'm afraid so."

The room suddenly felt a little smaller, if that were possible, the corners—despite the sun that found its way through the dirtied glass—a little darker.

"That's horrible," Candy said.

"You'll learn, honey," Norma said. "Love can be the best thing in life. And it can be the worst. The absolute worst."

Candy kept her silence. For the first time she saw how sad Norma's face had become in the years since they'd last met. How the corners of her mouth were drawn down and her brow deeply etched with lines.

"But it wasn't just love that broke Henry Murkitt's heart," Norma said. "It was—"

"—the fact that they changed the name of the town?" Candy said.

"Yes. That's right. After all it was his family name. *His* name. His claim to a little bit of immortality, if you like. When that was gone, I guess he didn't think he had anything left to live for."

"Poor man," Candy said, echoing Norma's earlier sentiments. "Did he leave a note? I mean, a suicide note?"

"Yes. Of a kind. As far as I can gather he said something about waiting for his ship to come in."

"What did he mean by that?" Candy said, jotting the phrase down.

"Well, he was probably drunk, and a little crazy. But he had something in the back of his head about ships and the sea."

"That's strange," Candy said.

"It gets stranger," Norma said.

She went to the small table beside the bed and opened the drawer. In it was a copy of Gideon's Bible and a strange object made of what looked like brass. She took it out.

"According to the stories," she said, "this is the only object of any worth he had with him."

"What is it?"

Norma handed it to Candy. It was heavy and etched with numbers. There was a moving part that was designed to line up with the numbers.

"It's a sextant," Norma said.

Candy looked blank. "What's a sextant?"

"It's something sailors use to find out where they are when they're out at sea. I don't exactly know how it works, but you line it up with the stars somehow and . . ." She shrugged. "You find out where you are."

"And he had this with him?"

"As I say: according to the stories. This very one."

"Wouldn't the police have taken it?" Candy said.

"You would think so. But as long as I've been working in the hotel that thing has been here in that drawer, beside the Gideon's Bible. Henry Murkitt's sextant."

"Huh," said Candy, not at all sure what to make of any of this now. She handed the object back to Norma, who carefully—even a little reverently—returned it to its place and slid the drawer closed. "So that and the note were all he left?" Candy asked.

"No," said Norma. "He left something else."

"What?"

"Look around you," Norma replied.

Candy looked. What was there here that could have belonged to Henry Murkitt? The furniture? Surely not? The age-worn rug under her feet? Perhaps, but it was unlikely. The lamp? No. What did that leave? There weren't any pictures on the walls, so—

"Oh, wait a minute," she said, looking at the stains on the wall. "Not those?"

Norma just looked at her, raising a perfectly plucked eyebrow.

"Those?" Candy said.

"No matter how many coats of paint the workmen put on that wall, the stains show through."

Candy went closer to the wall, examining the marks. A part of her—the part that her morbid grandmother could take credit for—wanted to ask Norma the obvious question: how had the stains got up there? Had he shot himself, or used a razor? But there was another part that preferred not to know.

"Horrible," she said.

"That's what happens when people realize their lives aren't what they dreamed they'd be," Norma said. She glanced at her watch. "Oh Lord, look at the time. I've got to get going. That's the story of Henry Murkitt."

"What a sad man," Candy said.

"Well, I guess all of us are waiting for our ships to come in, one way or another," Norma said, going to the door and letting Candy out onto the gloomy landing. "Some of us still live in hope," she said with a half-hearted smile. "But you have to, don't you?"

And with that she closed the door on the room where Henry Murkitt had breathed his last.

3

DOODLE

MISS SCHWARTZ, CANDY'S HISTORY teacher, was not in a pleasant mood at the best of times, but today her mood was fouler than usual. As she went around the classroom, returning the project papers on Chickentown, only her few favorite students (who were usually boys) earned anything close to good marks. Everyone else was being criticized.

But nothing the rest of the class had faced compared with Miss Schwartz's attack on Candy's paper.

"*Facts*, Candy Quackenbush," the woman said, tossing Candy's paper about Henry Murkitt's demise down on her desk. "I asked for facts. And what do you give me—?"

"Those *are* facts, Miss—"

"Don't answer back," Miss Schwartz snapped. "These are *not* facts. They are morbid pieces of gossip. Nothing more. This work—like most of your work—is worthless."

"But I was in that room in the Comfort Tree Hotel," she said. "I saw Henry Murkitt's sextant."

"Are you hopelessly gullible?" said Schwartz. "Or are you just plain stupid? Every hotel has *some* kind of ridiculous ghost story. Can't you tell the difference between fact and fiction?"

"But, Miss Schwartz, I swear these are facts."

"You get an 'F,' Candy."

"That's not fair," Candy protested.

Miss Schwartz's upper lip began to twitch, a sure sign that she was going to start yelling soon.

"Don't talk back to me!" she said, her volume rising. "If you don't stop indulging in these dim-witted fantasies of yours, and start doing some *real* work, you're going to fail this class completely. And I'll personally see you held back a year for your laziness and your insolence."

There was a lot of tittering from the back of the class, where the coven of Candy's enemies, led by Deborah Hackbarth, all sat. Miss Schwartz threw them a silencing look, which worked; but Candy knew they were smiling behind their hands, passing notes back and forth about Candy's humiliation.

"Why can't you be *normal*?" Miss Schwartz said. "Give me work like this from Ruth Ferris." She leafed through the pages.

Miss Schwartz held up the paper, so that everybody could see what an exemplary piece of work Ruth had done. "You see these graphs?" Miss Schwartz was flicking through the pages of colored graphs Ruth had thoughtfully provided as appendices to her paper. "You know what they're about? Well, do you, Candy?"

"Let me guess," said Candy. "Chickens?"

"Yes. Chickens. Ruth wrote about the number one industry in our community: chickens."

"Maybe that's because her father is the factory manager," Candy said, throwing the perfect Miss R. Ferris a sour look. She knew—*everybody* knew, including Miss Schwartz—that Ruth's pretty little charts and flow diagrams ("From Egg to Chicken Nugget") had been copied out of her father's glossy brochures for Applebaum's Farms.

"Who cares about chickens?" Candy said.

"Chickens are the lifeblood of this town, Candy Quackenbush. Without chickens, your father wouldn't have a job."

"He doesn't have a job, Miss Schwartz," said Deborah.

"Oh. Well—"

"He likes his beer too much."

"All right, that's enough Deborah," said Miss Schwartz, sensing that things were getting out of hand. "You see how disruptive you are, Candy?"

"What did I do?" Candy protested.

"We waste far too much time on you in class. Far too much—"

She stopped speaking because her eyes had alighted on Candy's workbook. She snatched it up off the desk. For some reason Candy had started drawing wavy patterns on the cover of her book a couple of days before, her hand simply making the marks without her mind consciously instructing it to do so.

"What is this?" Miss Schwartz demanded, flipping through the pages of the workbook.

The interior was decorated in the same way as the cover: tightly set lines, hundreds of them, waving up and down all over the page.

"It's bad enough you bring these morbid stories of yours into school," Miss Schwartz was saying. "Now you're defacing school property?"

"It's just a doodle," Candy said.

"Good Lord, are you going crazy? There are *pages* and *pages* of this rubbish." Miss Schwartz held the workbook at arm's length as though it might infect her. "What do you think you're doing? What *are* these?"

For some reason, as Miss Schwartz stared down at her, Candy thought of Henry Murkitt, sitting in Room Nineteen on that distant Christmas Eve, waiting for his ship to come in.

Thinking of him, she realized what she'd been drawing so obsessively in her workbook.

"It's the sea," she said quietly.

"It's *what*?" said Miss Schwartz, her voice oozing contempt.

"It's the sea. I was drawing the sea."

"Were you indeed? Well, it may look like the sea to *you*, but it looks like two weeks in detention to *me*."

There was a little eruption of laughter from the back of the class. This time Miss Schwartz didn't hush it. She simply tossed the defaced workbook onto Candy's desk. It was a bad throw. Instead of landing neatly in front of the disgraced Candy, it skimmed across the desk, taking the paper about Henry Murkitt, along with several pens, pencils and a blue plastic ruler, off the other side and onto the floor.

The laughter halted. There was a hush while one of the pens rolled to a halt. Then Miss Schwartz said: "I want you to pick all that *trash* up."

Candy didn't reply, at least not at first. She remained in her seat, not moving a muscle.

"Did you *hear* me, Candy Quackenbush?"

The Hackbarth clique was in hog heaven. They watched with smirks on their faces as Candy sat in her seat, still refusing to move.

"Candy?" Miss Schwartz.

"I heard you, Miss Schwartz."

"Then pick them up."

"I didn't knock them off the desk, Miss Schwartz."

"I *beg your pardon*?"

"I said: I didn't knock them off the desk. You did. So I think you should pick them up."

All the blood had drained from Miss Schwartz's face. The only color that remained was the purple of the shadows under her eyes.

"Get up," she said.

"Miss Schwartz?"

"You heard me. I said *get* up. I want you down at the principal's office *right now*."

Candy's heart was beating furiously and her hands were clammy. But she wasn't going to let Miss Schwartz or any of her enemies in class see that she was nervous.

She was irritated with herself for letting Miss Schwartz escalate this stupid showdown. Maybe the principal would be more sympathetic to Candy's researches than Miss Schwartz, but Candy doubted that she'd even get to show him her paper. All Miss Schwartz would want to talk about was Candy's insolence.

Unfortunately it was a subject the principal took very seriously. Only a month ago he had talked to the whole school about that very subject. There would be a policy of zero tolerance, he told everyone, toward pupils who were disrespectful to teachers. Any student who crossed the line, he'd said, between civility and rudeness of any kind could expect serious consequences. He had meant what he said. Two weeks ago he had expelled two students for what he had called "extreme discourtesy" toward a teacher.

Candy half wondered if there was still time to apologize; but she knew it was a lost cause. Miss Schwartz wanted to see Candy squirming in front of the principal, and she wasn't going to let anything keep her from witnessing that.

"You're still sitting down, Quackenbush," the woman said. "What did I tell you? Well?"

"Go to the principal's office, Miss Schwartz."

"So move your lazy behind."

Candy bit her tongue and got up. Her chair made an ugly squeal as she pushed it back. There was more nervous laughter from one or two places around the class, but mostly there was silence, even from the loquacious Deborah Hackbarth. Nobody wanted to draw Miss Schwartz's venomous attention in their direction right now.

"And pick up your workbook, Quackenbush," Miss Schwartz said. "I want you to explain your defacing of school property to the principal."

Candy didn't argue. She dutifully went down on her haunches and gathered up all the things that Miss Schwartz had knocked off her desk: the pencils, the pens, the workbook and the paper on Henry Murkitt.

"Give that stupid paper *and* the workbook to me," Miss Schwartz said.

"I'm not going to destroy them," Candy protested.

"Just *give them to me*," Miss Schwartz demanded, her voice almost cracking with rage.

Candy put the pens and pencils down on her desk and gave the book and paper to Miss Schwartz. Then—without looking around at the rest of the class—she made her way to the door.

Once she was outside the classroom in the eerie hush of the corridor, she felt a peculiar sense of *relief*. She knew she should be feeling full of regret and self-recrimination, but the truth was that a significant part of her was glad she'd said what she'd said. Miss Schwartz had picked on her one too many times.

She was a ridiculous woman anyway, with her endless snide remarks and her ludicrous obsession with chickens.

"Who cares about chickens?" Candy said, her voice echoing down the empty passageway.

The door at the end of the corridor was open. Through it she could see the sunlit yard, and beyond the yard the school gate and the street. It would be so easy, she thought, just to walk out of here right now and never have to hear Miss Schwartz pontificate on the Glories of Chicken Farming ever again.

What was she thinking? She couldn't do that. She'd be expelled for certain.

So what? said a voice at the back of her head. *Just walk out. Go on. Walk out.*

For some reason, the doodles that she had drawn in her workbook came back into her mind. Only this time, instead of being black lines on gray, recycled paper, they were bright in her mind; very bright. And all kinds of colors, the way the sun appeared in your mind if you looked at it for a moment and then closed your eyes. Dozens of little suns: green and red and gold; then colors, too, that you couldn't even name. That was the way the lines looked in Candy's mind's eye.

And they were *moving*. The wavy lines were rolling across the darkness inside her skull, rolling and breaking, the brilliant colors bursting into arabesques of white and silver.

Behind her she heard a familiar sound: the *click, click, click* of Miss Schwartz's heels.

"What are you still doing in the corridor, Candy Quackenbush?" she yelled down the corridor. "I told you to report to the principal's office."

Everyone in the classes along the passage had heard the woman, Candy knew. Tomorrow she'd be the butt of every idiotic joke. Candy glanced over her shoulder. Miss Schwartz was gaining on her, her arms crossed in front of her bosom. Held captive behind them was the evidence for the prosecution: Candy's workbook and the paper on Henry Murkitt. Poor Henry Murkitt, sitting in that cold little room in the hotel, waiting with his sextant for a ship to come and find him. Checking the stars, consulting his watch. Waiting and waiting until he could stand the wait no longer.

Candy looked away from Miss Schwartz, her gaze returning to the rectangle of brightness at the end of the corridor.

And still the lines rolled on in her mind's eye. Rolled and broke. Rolled and broke.

"Where do you think you're going?" Miss Schwartz demanded.

Candy's feet knew, even if her brain was a little slow at catching up with the idea. They were taking her out of here.

"You head right back to the principal's office!" Miss Schwartz called after her.

Candy didn't really hear the woman's words very clearly now. The lines in her head were making a *sound*, like the din of white noise on an untuned television. It washed away Miss Schwartz's demands.

"Candy Quackenbush! Come back here!"

Her shrill voice was being heard from one end of the school to the other, but the person to whom they were directed was deaf to them.

Out she went, with Miss Schwartz pursuing her, inventing new threats and demands to throw in Candy's direction. Candy took no notice of them.

She stepped over the threshold and out into the bright morning.

A little portion of her mind still said: *Candy, turn around. What are you doing? They'll expel you for certain,* but the voice was too small to convince her feet.

At the threshold, she broke into a run. It took her thirty seconds to reach the school gate and get out into the street.

A few students caught sight of her as she made her departure. Those who knew her said they'd never seen Candy Quackenbush looking happier.

4

"STREET ENDS"

Tнε ввιGнT ROLLING DOODLE stayed in Candy's mind's eye, even though her feet had obeyed its instruction and carried her out through the school gates and into the street. She briefly thought about going home, but the notion didn't stay in her head for long. She had no desire to be back in Followell Street. Though her mom would be at work, her father would be up and about by now, and he'd want to know why she had returned from school in the middle of the morning.

So she walked in the opposite direction: down Spalding Street to the intersection with Lennox; over Lennox and on toward the Comfort Tree Hotel on Stillman Street. She had half a thought to call in at the hotel and tell Norma Lipnik exactly what had happened when she'd tried to tell the sad story of Henry Murkitt. Perhaps she could even persuade Norma to lend her the passkey so that she could go back up to Room Nineteen and look at the sextant again. Hold it in her hands and examine it; see if she got a clearer picture of poor Henry's last hours when she did so.

But once she got to the hotel, she found the desire to see the sextant was not as important as another desire, one which she could not name or comprehend, but which kept her going, on past the hotel to the intersection of Stillman and Lincoln.

Here, for a moment, she stopped. The streets were busy in both directions, at least busy for Chickentown. There were four or five cars waiting at the lights every time they turned red. One of the drivers was Frank Wrightson, who had been a drinking buddy of her father's until six months before, when they'd had a big falling-out. It had ended in a shouting match outside the house and a few blows half-heartedly exchanged. The men had not spoken to each other since.

"Hey, Candy!" Frank yelled as he drove by.

She waved, trying not to look too guilty for being out in the street in the middle of a Thursday morning.

"No school today?" Frank yelled.

Candy was just trying to figure out a way to answer this without lying to Frank Wrightson, when the woman in the car behind his truck honked her horn to hurry him on his way. Returning Candy's wave, he drove off.

Which way now? she thought. She couldn't wait at the intersection forever.

And then the decision was made for her. A gust of wind came down Stillman Street from the direction of the chicken factory. It stank of chicken excrement and worse. *I'm not going to take Stillman Street,* she thought to herself. So that left Lincoln. Without another thought, she turned the corner, and as soon as she'd done so she knew that was the decision she was supposed to make.

Not only did the foul smell disappear almost completely, but there—at the far end of the street, where Lincoln ran out of houses and gave way to the prairie—was a cloud, vast and shaped like some enormous flower, blossoming as the wind carried it south, away from town.

For some reason the sight of it—its golden color, its shape, its sheer size—put everything she'd left behind—Miss Schwartz and her stupidities, Deborah Hackbarth and the rest, even the smell on Stillman Street—out of her head.

Smiling as she walked, she headed on past the hotel and on down Lincoln Street toward the cloud.

The wavy lines in her head began to fade now, as though they had done their job by getting her out wandering until she came in sight of this blossom-cloud. She'd seen it; she had her destination.

The houses were thinning out now as she approached the end of Lincoln Street. She could remember venturing so far in this direction only once before, and that was because Patti Gibson, who'd been her best friend three years ago, had brought her down here to show her one of the few memorable front lawns in Chickentown. It had belonged to an old woman by the name of Lavinia White, known to all as the Widow White. In place of flowers, Lavinia had "planted" plastic pinwheels in the grass, the kind constructed of brightly colored plastic that made a whirring sound when the wind spun them. No doubt the Widow White was a little bit crazy, because she hadn't simply put three or four of these things in her garden; she'd planted hundreds, in place of ordinary flowers. Some bright scarlet, some eye-pricking green, some striped or spiraled. It had been quite a sight, Candy remembered.

To her astonishment she found that they were still there. She heard them before she saw them, the massed noise of their whirring coming to meet her down Lincoln Street. When she came in sight of them, she found that they were all rather the worse for wear. Clearly the Widow White had not replaced the pinwheels with new ones over the last few seasons, and many had been knocked over by the wind, or had lost their plastic blooms, and she'd simply left the sticks in the dirt. But perhaps one in three of them remained operational, and that still provided a bizarre spectacle.

Candy glanced up at the house itself as she passed, and there in the upper window, sitting in a wheelchair watching the world go by (or as much of the world as would pass by the last house in the street before the grasslands began) was old Widow White herself. She had her eyes on Candy, so Candy gave her a wave and a smile. The Widow White returned neither.

There was no barricade or fence at the end of the street. Just a sign, placed at the limit of the asphalt that stated, with absurd redundancy:

STREET ENDS

"Oh really?" said Candy, looking up at the sign. Beyond it, there was just rolling prairie and the cloud.

It had grown in size in the time that Candy had taken to walk the length of Lincoln Street, and it was no longer moving away from town. The wind had changed direction, and now seemed to be coming from the north. It had a curious tang to it, which was not the smell of the factory and its clotted drains. She didn't know what it was.

She glanced back over her shoulder down the length of Lincoln Street. From here it was a half-hour walk home, at least. If the great gilded cloud was bringing rain, then she was going to get wet on her way back to Followell Street. But she had no desire to start the homeward trek, not for a little while, at least. She had no idea of what lay ahead of her besides the wild hills and the long grass, and the orange milkweed, the larkspur, and prairie lilies in among the grass.

But walking for a while where nobody (except the Widow White) knew she'd gone was better than going home to listen to her father in the first stages of the day's drinking, raging on about the injustices of his life.

Without another thought she walked on past the STREET ENDS sign, catching it with her palm as she went so that it rocked in the shallow hole some lazy workman had made for it, and headed out into the gently swaying grass.

Butterflies and bees wove ahead of her, as if they were showing her the way. She followed them, happily. When next she looked back, the shoulder-high grass had almost obscured Chickentown from sight. She didn't care. She had a good sense of direction. When the time came for her to find her way back, she'd be able to do just that.

Her eyes glued to the great swelling mass of the cloud, she walked on, her griefs and humiliations left somewhere behind her, where the road ended and the ocean of grass and flowers began.

5

A SHORE WITHOUT A SEA

AFTER PERHAPS TEN MINUTES of walking, Candy glanced back over her shoulder to see that the gentle swells and gullies she'd crossed to get to her present position had put Chickentown out of sight completely. Even the spire on the church on Hawthorne Street and the five stories of the town hall had vanished.

She took a moment and turned on the spot, three hundred and sixty degrees. In every direction the landscape presented the same unremarkable vista of wind-blown grass, with two exceptions. Some way off to her right lay a small copse of trees, and nearly dead ahead of her was a much more curious sight: a kind of skeletal tower, set in the middle of this wilderness of grass and flowers.

What was it? Some kind of watchtower? If it had been a watchtower then those who'd occupied it must have been very bored, with nothing to watch.

Though it promised to be nothing more than a near ruin, she decided to make it her destination. She'd get there, sit for a while, and then head back. She was getting thirsty, for one thing. She wanted a glass of water. Maybe on the return journey she'd pick up some soda from Niles' Drug Store. She dug in her pocket, just to see what she had. Two singles, one five- and one ten-dollar bill. She pushed them down to the very bottom of her pocket, so they wouldn't slip out.

The wind had become stronger in the time since she'd left the limits of Chickentown, and a little more bracing. There was still the smell of spring green in the air, but there was something else besides, something Candy couldn't quite name, but which teased her nevertheless.

She walked toward the tower, her mind becoming pleasantly devoid of troubling thoughts. Miss Schwartz; letters threatening expulsion; her father in his drinking chair, staring up at her with that look of his, the look she knew meant trouble: all of it was left behind, where the street ended.

Then her toe caught some object so that it skipped ahead of her through the grass. Just a stone, surely. Nevertheless, she bent down to take a closer look, and to her surprise she saw that it was not a stone at all, but a shell. It was large too: about the size of her balled fist, and there were a number of short spikes on it. It wasn't, she knew, a snail's shell. For one thing it was too big, and she had never seen a snail's shell with spikes. No, this was a *sea* shell, and it was clearly old. Its colors had faded, but she could still see an elaborate pattern upon it: a design that followed its diminishing spiral.

She turned it over, brushed what looked suspiciously like sand out of its crevice, and put it to her ear. It was a trick her grandfather had first taught her, listening to the sea in a shell. And though she knew it was just an illusion—the subtle reverberations of the air in the shell's interior—she was still half persuaded by it; half certain she heard the sound of waves, as if the shell still had some memory of its life in the ocean.

She listened. There it was.

But what was a seashell doing out here?

Had somebody dropped it while walking here? That seemed highly unlikely. Who went walking with seashells in their pocket?

She looked down, wondering if anything else had been dropped in the vicinity. To her surprise, the answer was yes: there were a number of odd items scattered under her feet. More shells, for one thing, dozens of them. No, hundreds; some small, a few even larger than the one she'd picked up. Most were cracked or broken, but some were still intact, their shapes and designs more beautiful, more bizarre, than anything she'd ever seen in a book.

And there was more besides, a lot more. As she studied the ground, her eyes becoming accustomed to picking out curiosities, the curiosities multiplied. There were pieces of wood scattered among the shells, most smoothed into little abstract sculptures by the pale, freckled sand that was mingled with the dark Minnesota dirt. As she bent to pick one of the sculptures up, she saw that there was glass here too: countless fragments—green, blue and white—turned into smoky jewels. She picked up three or four and examined them in the palm of her hand, walking a little way as she did so.

There were more mysteries underfoot with every step she took. A large fish—its flesh pecked away by birds, and the remains baked by the sun. And even a piece of pottery, on which a fragment of an exquisite design remained: a blue figure staring at her with almost hypnotic intensity.

Fascinated by all this, she paused to examine her finds more closely. As she did so, she caught a movement in the long grass out of the corner of her eye. She dropped down onto her haunches, below the level of the tallest grass stalks, and there she stayed, suddenly and unaccountably nervous.

She brushed the last of the sand off her fingers and watched for whatever had moved to move again.

A hard gust of wind came through the grass, making it hiss as the stalks rubbed against one another.

After perhaps a minute, during which the only motion was the bending of the grass, she decided to chance standing up.

As she did so the thing she'd seen moving chose precisely the same moment to also stand upright, so that the pair of them, Candy and the stranger, rose like two swimmers emerging from a shallow sea.

Candy let out a yelp of shock at the sight of the stranger. And then, once the shock had worn off, she started to laugh. The man—whoever he was—was wearing some kind of Halloween mask, or so it seemed. What other explanation could there be for his freakish appearance? His left eye was round and wild, while his right was narrow and sly, and his mouth, framed by a black mustache and beard, was down-turned in misery.

But none of this was as odd as what sprouted from the top of his head. There were large downy ears, and above them two enormous antlers, which would have resembled those of a stag except that there were seven heads (four on the left horn, three on the right) growing from them. Heads with eyes, noses and mouths.

They weren't, she realized now, static, nor were they made of rubber and papier-mâché. In short, it was not a mask the man was wearing. These heads sprouting from the antlers were *alive*, and they were all staring at Candy the way their owner was staring at her: eight pairs of eyes all studying her with the same manic intensity.

She was speechless. But they were not. After a moment of silence the heads erupted into wild chatter, their manner highly agitated. Candy had no doubt about the subject of conversation. One minute the heads were looking at her, then they were facing one another, their volume rising as they attempted to out-talk one another.

The only mouth that wasn't moving was that of the man himself. He simply studied Candy, his wild and sly expression slowly becoming one of tentative enquiry.

Finally, he decided to approach her. Candy let out a little gasp of fear, and in response he raised his long-fingered hands as though to keep her from running away. The heads, meanwhile, were still chattering to one another.

"*Be quiet!*" he ordered them. "You're frightening the lady!"

All but one of the heads (the middle of the two on his right horn, a round-faced, sour individual) responded to his order. But this one kept talking.

"Keep your distance from her, John Mischief," the head advised its big brother. "She may *look* harmless, but you can't trust them. Any of them."

"I said *hush up*, John Serpent," the man said. "And I mean it."

The head made a face and muttered something under its breath. But it finally stopped talking.

"What's your name?" John Mischief asked Candy.

"Me?" Candy said, as though there was anybody else in the vicinity to whom the question might be directed.

"Oh Lordy Lou!" another of the heads remarked. "Yes, *you, girl.*"

"Be polite, John Sallow," John Mischief said, reaching up (without taking his eyes off Candy) and lightly slapping the short-tempered head for its offense.

Then, having hushed his companion, John Mischief said: "I do apologize for my brother, lady."

Then—of all things—he *bowed* to her.

It was not a deep bow. But there was something about the simple courtesy of the gesture that completely won Candy over. So what if John Mischief had seven extra heads; he'd bowed to her and called her *lady*. Nobody had ever done that to her before.

She smiled with improbable delight.

And the impish man called John Mischief, along with five of his seven siblings, smiled back.

"Please," he said. "I don't wish to alarm you, lady. Believe me, that is the very last thing I wish to do. But there is somebody in this vicinity by the name of Shape."

"Mendelson Shape," the smallest of the heads said.

"As John Moot says: *Mendelson Shape.*"

Before Candy could deal with any more information she needed a question answered. So she asked it.

"Are you all called John?" she said.

"Oh yes," said Mischief. "Tell her, brothers, left to right. Tell her what we are called."

So they did.

"John Fillet."

"John Sallow."

"John Moot."

"John Drowze."

"John Pluckitt."

"John Serpent."

"John Slop."

"And I'm the head brother," the eighth wonder replied. "John Mischief."

"Yes, I heard that part. I'm Candy Quackenbush."

"I am extremely pleased to make your acquaintance," John Mischief said.

He sounded completely sincere in this, and with good reason. To judge by his appearance, things had not gone well for him—*or them*—of late.

Mischief's striped blue shirt was full of holes and

there were stains on his loosely knotted tie, which were either food or blood; she guessed the latter. Then there was his smell. He was less than sweet, to say the least. His shirt clung to his chest, soaked with pungent sweat.

"Have you been *running* from this man Shape?" Candy said.

"She's observant," John Pluckitt said appreciatively. "I like that. And young, which is good. She can help us, Mischief."

"Either that or she can get us in even deeper trouble," said John Serpent.

"We're as deep as we can get," John Slop observed. "I say we trust the girl, Mischief. We've got absolutely nothing to lose."

"What are they all talking about?" Candy asked Mischief. "Besides me."

"The harbor," he replied.

"What harbor?" Candy said. "There's no harbor here. This is Minnesota. We're *hundreds* of miles from the ocean. No, thousands."

"Perhaps we're thousands of miles from any ocean you are familiar with, lady," said John Fillet, with a gap-toothed smile. "But there are oceans and oceans. Seas and seas."

"What on earth is he talking about?" Candy asked Mischief.

John Mischief pointed toward the tower that stood sixty or seventy yards from where they stood.

"That, lady, is a lighthouse," he said.

"No," said Candy, with a smile. The idea was preposterous. "Why would anybody—"

"Look at it," said John Drowze. *"It is a lighthouse."*

Candy studied the odd tower again.

Yes, she could see that indeed it could have been designed as a lighthouse. There were the rotted remains of a staircase, spiraling up the middle of it, leading to a room at the top, which might have housed a lamp. But so what?

"Somebody was crazy," she remarked.

"Why?" said John Slop.

"Oh, come on," said Candy. "We've been through this. We're in Minnesota. There is no sea in—"

Candy stopped mid-sentence. Mischief had put his hand to his mouth, hushing her.

As he did so all of his brothers looked off in one direction or another. A few were sniffing the air, others tasting it on their lips. Whatever they did and wherever they looked, they all came to the same conclusion, and together they murmured two words.

"Shape's here," they said.

6

THE LADY ASCENDS

MISCHIEF INSTANTLY GRABBED Candy's arm and pulled her down into the long grass. His eyes were neither wild nor sly now. They were simply afraid. His brothers, meanwhile, were peering over the top of the grass in every direction, and now and then exchanging their own fearful looks. It was most peculiar for Candy to be with one person, and yet be in the company of a small crowd.

"Lady," Mischief said, very softly, "I wonder if you would *dare* something for me?"

"Dare?"

"I would quite understand if you preferred not. This isn't your battle. But perhaps Providence put you here for a reason."

"Go on," Candy said.

Given how unhappy and purposeless she'd been feeling in the last few hours (no, not hours: months, even years), she was happy to listen to anybody with a theory about why she was here.

"If I could distract Mendelson Shape's attention away

from you for long enough, maybe you could get to the lighthouse, and climb the stairs? You carry far less weight than I, and the stairs may support you better."

"What for?"

"What do you mean: what for?"

"Well, once I've climbed the stairs—"

"She wants to know what she does next," John Slop said.

"That's simple enough, lady," said John Fillet.

"When you get to the top," said John Pluckitt, "you must *light the light*."

Candy glanced up at the ruined tower: at the spiraling spire of its staircase, and the rotting boards of its upper floor. She couldn't imagine the place was in working order, not in its present state.

"Doesn't it need electricity?" she said. "I mean, I can't even see a lamp."

"There's one up there, we swear," said John Moot. "Please trust us. We may be desperate, but we're not stupid. We wouldn't send you on a suicide mission."

"So how do I make this lamp work?" Candy asked. "Is there an on-off switch?"

"You'll know how to use it the moment you set eyes on it," Mischief said. *"Light's the oldest game in the world."*

She looked at them, her gaze going from face to face. They looked so frightened, so exhausted. "Please, lady," said Mischief. "You're our only chance now."

"Just one more question—" Candy said.

"No time," said Drowze. "I see Shape."

"Where?" said Fillet, turning to follow his brother's gaze. He didn't need any further direction. He simply said. "Oh Lordy Lou, there he is."

Candy raised her head six inches and looked in the same direction that Fillet and Drowze were looking. The rest of the brothers—Mischief included—followed that stare.

And there, no more than a stone's throw from the spot where Candy and the brothers were crouched in the grass, was the object of their fear: Mendelson Shape.

The sight of him made Candy shudder. He was twice the height of Mischief, and there was something spiderish about his grotesque anatomy. His almost fleshless limbs were so long, she could readily imagine him walking up a wall. On his back there was a curious arrangement of cruciform rods that almost looked like four swords which had been fused to his bony body. He was naked but for a pair of striped shorts, and he walked with a pronounced limp. But there was nothing frail about him. Despite the lack of muscle, and that limp of his, he looked like a creature born to do harm. His expression was joyless and sour, filled with hatred toward the world.

Having got herself a glimpse of him, Candy ducked down quickly, before Shape's wrathful gaze came her way.

Curiously, it was only now, seeing this *second* freakish creature, that she wondered if perhaps she wasn't having some kind of hallucination. How could such beings be here in the world with her? The same world as Chickentown, as Miss Schwartz and Deborah Hackbarth?

"Before we go any further," she said to the brothers, "I need an answer to something."

"Ask away," said John Swallow.

"Am I dreaming this?"

By way of reply, all eight brothers shook their heads, their faces for once expressing the same thing. *No, this is no dream*, those faces said.

Nor, deep in her bones, had she expected the answer to be any different. They were all awake together, she and the brothers, and all in terrible jeopardy.

Mischief saw the sequence of thoughts crossing her face. The doubt that she was even awake, and then the fear that indeed she was.

"This is all Providence, I swear," he said to her. "You're here because you can light the light. You and only you."

She did her best to put the fear out of her head and to concentrate on what John Mischief had just said. In a curious way it made sense that she was here because she *had* to be here. She thought of the doodle she'd made on her workbook; the way it had seemed to brighten in her mind's eye, inspiring her limbs to *move*. It was almost as though the doodle had been a sign, a ticket to this adventure. Why else, after living all her life in Chickentown, should she be here—in a place she'd never been before—today?

This must be what John Mischief meant by Providence.

"So, lady?" Mischief said. "What is your decision?"

"If I'm not dreaming this, then perhaps it is Providence."

"So you'll go?"

"Yes, I'll go," Candy said simply.

Mischief smiled again, only this time, they *all* smiled with him. Eight grateful faces, smiling at her for being here, and ready to chance her life. That was what was at stake right now, she didn't doubt it. The monster moving through the grass nearby would kill them all if he got his claws into them.

"Good luck," Mischief whispered. "We'll see you again when you come down."

And without offering any further instruction, he and his brothers darted off through the grass, bent double to keep out of Shape's sight until they were clear of her.

Candy's heart was thumping so hard she could hear her pulse in her head. Ten, fifteen seconds passed. She listened. The grass hissed all around her. Strangely enough, she'd never felt so alive in her life.

Another half minute went by. She was tempted to chance another peep above the surface of the swaying grass, to see whether Mendelson Shape was limping in her direction, but she was afraid to do so in case he was almost upon her.

Then, to her infinite relief, she heard eight voices all yelling at the same time:

"Hey, you! Mendelson Shmendelson! Looking for us? We're over here!"

Candy waited a heartbeat, then she chanced a look. Shape, it seemed, had indeed been looking in her direction, and had she raised her head a second earlier would have seen her. But now he was swinging around, following the sound of the brothers' voices.

At that moment, Mischief leaped up out of the grass and began racing away from the lighthouse, diverting Shape's attention.

Shape threw open his arms, his huge, iron-taloned claws spread as wide as five-fingered fans.

"There. You. Are!" he roared.

His voice was as ugly as his anatomy: a guttural din that made Candy's stomach churn.

As he spoke, the configuration of crosses on his back shifted, rising up like featherless, metallic wings. He reached over his shoulders and grabbed two of the blades, pulling them out of the scabbards in his leathery flesh. Then he started through the grass toward his prey.

Candy knew she could not afford to delay. The brothers were chancing their lives so that she could attempt to reach the lighthouse unseen. She had to go *now*, or their courage would be entirely in vain.

Candy didn't watch the pursuit a moment longer. Instead, she set her eyes on the lighthouse and she began to *run*, not even bothering to try and conceal herself by staying below the level of the grass. Simply depending for distraction upon Shape's terrible appetite to have the John brothers in his grasp.

As she raced through the grass, she became aware that the great rain cloud that had first caught her eye was now directly above the lighthouse, hovering like a golden curtain over the drama below.

Was this part of the makings of Providence too? she wondered as she ran. *Did clouds also have their place in the shape of things?*

By the time the thought had passed through her head, she had reached the threshold of the lighthouse. She chanced a quick look over her shoulder at Mischief and his pursuer.

Much to her horror she saw that her brief period of protection was over. Shape had given up chasing the brothers—realizing perhaps that the pursuit was just a diversion—and he had now turned his attention back toward the lighthouse.

His eyes fixed upon Candy, and he let out a blood-curdling cry at the sight of her. He spread his arms wide, and with swords in hand, he began to move toward her.

He didn't run; he simply strode through the grass with terrible confidence in his uneven step, as if to say: *I don't have to hurry. I've got all the time in the world. I've got you cornered, and there's no escape for you. You're mine.*

She turned away from the sight of his approach and pushed on the broken door. The hinges creaked, and there were a few moments of resistance, when she feared that fallen timbers on the other side might have blocked it. Then, with a deep grating sound, the door opened and Candy slipped inside.

Though there were plenty of holes in the walls, and the sun came through in solid shafts, it was still far chillier inside than it was out. The cold air stank of rotting wood. Large fungi had prospered in the damp murk, and the boards beneath her feet were slick with mildew. She slipped twice before she had even reached the bottom of the stairs.

The prospect before her looked dangerous. No doubt once upon a time the spiral wooden stairs had been perfectly safe to climb, but that was decades ago. Now all but a few of the railings had collapsed, and the structure which had supported the staircase had been devoured by woodworm and rot, so that it seemed the stairs themselves had virtually nothing to depend on for their solidity.

She peered through one of the holes in the wall, just to confirm what she already knew: Mendelson Shape was still advancing toward the lighthouse.

Unlikely as a safe ascent seemed, there was no way back now. Shape would be at the front door in just a few seconds. She had no choice but to try the stairs. She put her hand on the shaky bannister and began her cautious ascent.

Outside in the long grass, the John brothers watched the silhouetted form of the lady Quackenbush as she started up the stairs.

"She's something special, that one," Drowze murmured.

"What makes you say that?" Moot remarked.

"Look at her!" Drowze said. "Not many creatures of this wretched Hereafter would be so brave."

"She's half mad," said Serpent, "that's why. I saw it in her eyes, right from the beginning. She's a little bit crazy."

"So we send a crazy girl to do our handiwork for us?" Pluckitt said. "That's not very heroic."

"Will you just shut your *cake-holes*, all of you?" Mischief snapped. "Drowze is right. There *is* something about the lady. When we first laid eyes on her, didn't anybody think they'd maybe seen her *before*?" There was silence from above. "Well?"

"You told us to shut our cake-holes," Sallow reminded him airily. "We're just obeying instructions."

"Well, I think she's got a touch of magic about her," Mischief said, ignoring Sallow's riposte. He went to his belt and unsheathed the little knife that hung there. "And we have to protect her."

"You're not . . ." Moot began.

". . . intending to attack . . ." Pluckitt continued.

". . . Mendelson Shape?" Slop went on.

"Not with *that* pitiful excuse for a weapon?" Fillet concluded.

"Well—" said Mischief. "Unless somebody has a better idea?"

"He's twice our size!" said Sallow.

"Three times!" said Moot.

"He'll tear out our heart," said Slop.

"Well, we can't leave the lady Quackenbush undefended," Mischief replied.

"I vote we *run*," Moot said. "This is a lost cause, Mischief. At least if we get away now, the Key's safe with us. If we throw ourselves into the fray we're not just endangering our lives—"

"—which are *very* valuable—" John Serpent remarked.

"—we're endangering the Key," Moot reasoned. "We can't afford to do that."

"Moot's right," said John Sallow. "We've got a chance to run. I vote we take it."

"Out of the question," Mischief remarked. "She's risking her life for us."

"As I observed," Sallow replied. "The creature's half mad."

"And as *I* said," Mischief replied. "You can all shut your cake-holes, because you're wasting your breath. We're going to keep Shape away from her as long as we can."

So saying, Mischief set off running through the grass toward Mendelson, his little knife at the ready.

As he came within six or seven strides of his target, Shape sensed his presence and swung around, the swords whining through the air. His mouth was wide and foamy, as though he was working up an appetite as he approached the tower. The pupils of his eyes had gone to pinpricks, giving him an even more monstrous expression. His aim was poor. The blades missed the brothers by a foot or more, simply lopping off the feathery heads of the prairie grass.

Mischief just ducked down and doubled his speed, running at the enemy.

"Everybody—" he said. "Give the *Warriors' Yell*!"

At which point all the Johns loosed a cry so discordant, so insane; so bestial—

"*EEEIIIGGGGGORRRAAARRGUU—*"

—that even Shape hesitated, and for a moment looked as though he might retreat.

Then he seemed to remember the absurdity of his enemy, and instead of backing away he came at them again with the swords. But the Johns were swift. Mischief darted under Shape's vast hand and pushed his little blade into Shape's thigh. The knife went in three or four inches and lodged there, blood spurting over Mischief's hand and arm. It was enough to make the monster let out a cry of rage and pain. He dropped the blades and clutched the wound, gritting his teeth as he pulled the knife out.

Inside the lighthouse, Candy had climbed fifteen steps when she heard Mendelson's shout. She carefully ascended another three, until she could see through a hole in the wall. She had quite a good view. She could see that Mischief was playing David to Shape's Goliath out there.

The sight gave her courage. Instead of advancing up the stairs tentatively, as she'd been doing, she picked up her speed. With every step she took, the whole structure rocked and groaned, but she reached the top of the flight without incident and found herself in a round room, perhaps eight or nine feet across.

She'd reached the top of the lighthouse. But now that she was actually *up* here, where was the light? It was just as she'd feared. If there'd ever *been* a light up here (which she strongly doubted: this place was more folly than functional), then it had been stolen long ago, leaving just one strange item in the middle of the room: an inverted pyramid, perhaps three feet high and carefully balanced on its tip, its three sides decorated with a number of designs, like hieroglyphics. On the top of the pyramid (or rather on what had been its base) was a small, simple bowl. The purpose to which any of this obscure arrangement might have been put escaped Candy entirely.

Then she recalled what Mischief had said, when she'd remarked that she couldn't even see a lamp up at the top of the tower. What was it exactly? He'd said something about *light being the oldest game in the world? Perhaps this odd creation represented some kind of game,* she thought. The problem was that she had no idea how to play it.

And now, as if matters weren't bad enough, she heard the din of Shape beating down the lighthouse door; smashing it to smithereens in his fury. The noise reached a chaotic climax, followed by a few seconds of silence.

Then came the limping footfall of the monster himself, as he climbed the lighthouse stairs to find her.

7

LIGHT AND WATER

"*WHERE ARE YOU, CHILD?*" Shape growled as he ascended.

The sound of his voice, and the thump and drag of his limping step, froze Candy for a moment. This was like something from a nightmare: being hunted down by some hellish beast; some vile creature that wanted to eat her alive, limb by limb, finger by finger.

No!

She shook herself from her trance of terror. She wasn't going to let this abomination take her!

She looked around the room for a door that led out onto the narrow balcony that encircled the room. The door in question was directly behind her. She went over to it and turned the handle. It was locked, but that presented no problem to her, not in her present panicked state. She put her shoulder to the rotted wood and forced it open quite easily. Then she stepped out onto the balcony. The boards had been more exposed to the extremes of Minnesota's summers and winters than the interior floors—and they instantly gave way beneath her weight. She threw herself forward and grabbed hold of the rusted iron railing. Her speed probably saved her life, because two heartbeats later the whole patch of floorboards beneath her right foot crumbled away. Had she not had the support of the railing, she would have surely fallen through the hole and probably dropped to her death.

Very gingerly, she hauled her foot out of the hole and sought out a more reliable place to stand. She could still hear Shape in the tower behind her, calling out singsong threats to her as he climbed. It was some horrible little nursery song he was singing. The kind only a monster like Shape would have had sung to him in his cradle.

> *"O little one,*
> *My little one,*
> *Come with me,*
> *Your life is done.*
> *Forget the future,*
> *Forget the past.*
> *Life is over:*
> *Breathe your last."*

Doing her best to blot out the sound of Shape's obscene little lullaby, she scanned the landscape around the lighthouse.

"Mischief!" she yelled. "Where did you go?"

She only had to call once. Then he was there, racing toward the tower through the grass. There was blood on his hands, she saw. Had he wounded Shape? She dared hope so.

"Lady Candy? Are you all right?"

"I can't find any light up here, Mischief! I'm sorry."

"He's coming, lady!"

"I know, Mischief. Believe me: I know. *But there's no light—*"

"There should be a cup and ball up there. Isn't there a cup and ball?"

"What?"

"The oldest game, Candy. *Light is the oldest game —*"

Candy glanced back inside. Yes, there was a cup, of sorts, sitting on top of the inverted pyramid.

"Yes! There's a cup!" she yelled back down to the brothers.

"Put the ball in it!" Mischief replied.

"What ball? There isn't any ball."

"There should be a ball."

"Well there isn't one!"

"So *look*!" yelled John Serpent.

Candy didn't waste time telling Serpent to be more polite. She had only seconds to spare before Shape made an entrance into the round room, she knew. So she stopped talking and did as Mischief suggested, stepping over the hole she'd made in the platform and returning to look for the ball.

She listened as she scoured the room. To judge by the sound of his feet, Shape was close to the top of the stairs. Then—just as she was certain he was about to open the door—she heard the welcome sound of splintering timber, and her pursuer loosed a shout of alarm. His weight had apparently been too much for the staircase. She heard a series of crashes as broken portions of the steps fell away into the stairwell. A moment of silence followed, when she dared hope that perhaps Shape had fallen down the stairwell along with the broken stairs and was lying at the bottom of the flight. But instead of the distant moans she'd hoped to hear, there came an outburst of words in a language she had never heard before. She didn't need a translator to recognize them as curses.

She crossed to the door and glanced down, just to see what had happened. A large portion of the staircase—five or six stairs—had indeed collapsed under Mendelson Shape's weight. But he had somehow managed to avoid the full fall by jumping back down the stairs before they had collapsed beneath him. This left a sizeable gap for him to get across before he could continue his ascent. She was disappointed that he wasn't dead or comatose at the bottom, but this was better than nothing.

Looking up at her, he made horns of his forefinger and smallest finger, which he jabbed threateningly in Candy's direction. No doubt had he possessed the power to strike her dead on the spot, dead she would have been. But all he could do was curse and point, so she left him to it and went back to search for the missing ball.

As she did so, she heard Mischief yelling up at her from outside. Obviously he'd heard the din.

"I'm coming in, Lady Candy!"

She went to the outer door and called down to him.

"*No!* Stay where you are. You can't get up here anyway. The stairs have collapsed!"

She saw him looking through the holes in the tower wall to confirm what she'd told him. He was aghast.

"How will you get down?" he said, apparently more concerned with her safety now than with the oldest game in the world.

"I'll find a way when the time comes," Candy said. "First I'm going to find this stupid ball."

"We're coming in!" he said again.

"Wait!" she told him. "You just stay there. *Please*."

Without waiting for an answer, she went down on her haunches and started a systematic search of the floor, looking for the missing part of this bizarre puzzle. It was not immediately visible, but there were several places where the boards had rotted completely, leaving holes in the floor. She went to each one, pulling up the worm-eaten boards to get a better look at what lay beneath. They came away easily, in showers of splinters, dust and dried beetle corpses.

The first hole revealed nothing. The second, the same. But the third was the charm. There it was: rolled away under the boards. A small turquoise-and-silver ball. She had to tear away a little more of the rotted boards before she could fish it out between her fingers. When she finally succeeded, she discovered that it was surprisingly heavy for its size. It wasn't wood or plastic; it was metal. And elegantly engraved on its blue-green surface was a design she knew! There it was, etched into the metal: the doodle she'd drawn so obsessively in her workbook.

She didn't have any time to wonder at this. Behind her she heard a series of fierce grunts from the stairwell, followed by another crash. She knew in an instant what was going on. In his ambition to get to her, Shape had dared to try and jump the gap in the stairs.

She glanced up at the door, which stood open a few inches. Through it she could see Shape. He had succeeded in leaping over the gap, and he was coming up the remaining stairs two at a time, his razor claws making a horrid squeal on the timbers that lined the stairwell.

Candy looked at the small, simple cup that sat on the pyramid. Mischief's words echoed in her head.

Light's the oldest game in the world—

Shape was at the door, staring with one pinprick pupil through the crack at Candy, his jaws wide, dripping foam like the maw of a mad dog. He started to sing his lullaby, again, but more softly now, more liltingly.

> *"Forget the future,*
> *Forget the past,*
> *Life is over:*
> *Breathe your last."*

As he sang he pushed the door, slowly, as though this was some game.

Candy didn't have time to cross to the pyramid and put the ball in the cup. If she wasted those three or four seconds then Shape would be through the door and tearing out her throat, no doubt of it.

She had no choice: she had to play the game.

She took a deep breath and threw the ball. It wasn't

a good throw. The ball hit the edge of the cup instead of landing in it, and for several seconds it circled the rim, threatening to topple out.

"Please," she willed it quietly, staring at the ball like a gambler watching a roulette wheel, knowing she had this throw and only this throw; there would be no second chance.

And still the ball rolled around the rim of the cup, undecided where to fall.

"Go on," she murmured, trying to ignore the creak of the door behind her.

The ball made one last, lazy circle of the rim, and then rocked back and forth for a moment and toppled into the cup, rattling around for a few seconds, before finally settling.

Shape let out a sound that was as far from human as any throat that was fashioned like his could make: a profound din that rose from a hiss to the noise of a creature tormented to the edge of madness. As he loosed this unearthly sound, he pushed open the door, threw Candy aside and reached for the ball so as to snatch it out of the cup.

But the tower was having none of that. Some process beyond Candy's comprehension had begun with that simple throw of hers. An invisible force was in the air, and it pitched Shape back, its power sufficient to carry him out through the door.

Outside, Candy heard Mischief and his brothers whooping like a pack of ecstatic dogs. Though they couldn't possibly see what she'd done, they knew she'd succeeded. Nor was it hard for Candy to understand *how* they knew. There was a wave of pure energy emanating from the pyramid. She felt the fine hairs at the base of her skull starting to prickle, and behind her eyes the design of the ball burned blue and green and gold.

She retreated a step, then another, her eyes fixed on the ball, cup, and pyramid.

And then, to her astonishment, the pyramid began to *move* on its pinpoint axis. It quickly gathered speed, and as it did so a fire seemed to be ignited in its heart, and a silvery luminescence—flickering tentatively at first but quickly becoming solid and strong—flowed out through the designs on the sides of the device.

It was just before noon in Minnesota; even with a thin cloud layer covering the sun, the day was still bright. But the light that now began to spill through the hieroglyphics on the spinning pyramid was brighter still. They were brilliant streams, pouring out in all directions.

She heard a soft, almost mournful, noise from Mendelson Shape. She glanced over at him. He was staring at the device with all the malice, all the intent to do harm, drained from his face. He was apparently resigned to whatever happened next. He could do nothing about the phenomenon except watch it.

"Now look what you've done," he said, very, very softly.

"What exactly *have* I done?" she said.

"See for yourself," he replied, and for a moment he unhooked his gaze from the spinning pyramid so as to nod out at the world, beyond the lighthouse.

She didn't have any fear of turning her back on him now. At least until this miraculous process was over, it seemed, he was pacified.

She went to the door and stepped out, over the hole she'd made, to stand on the platform and see what she, and the game of ball and cup, had brought into being.

The first thing she noticed was the blossom-cloud. It was no longer moving slowly, responding to the gentle dictates of the wind. It was moving speedily overhead, like an immense golden wheel with the tower in which she stood as its axis.

She stood and admired the sight for a few moments, amazed at it. Then she looked down at the John brothers, who had turned their faces from the tower and were all looking out across the wide expanse of open prairie. *What were they looking at?* she wondered. She knew there was nothing out there for many miles, not so much as a house. For some reason, though the suburbs of Chickentown had spread in every other direction from the heart of the town, they had never spread northwest beyond Widow White's house. This was empty land; unused, unwanted.

And yet, there was something out there that John Mischief and his siblings wanted to see. Mischief was cupping his hands over his eyes as he stared into the faraway.

Candy could feel the light from the pyramid like a physical presence, pressing against her back. It wasn't an unpleasant sensation. In fact, it was quite pleasurable. She imagined that she could sense the power of the light passing through her body, lending her its strength. She seemed to feel it being carried through her veins, spilling out of her pores and out on her breath. It was just a trick her mind was playing, she suspected. But then, perhaps not. Today she couldn't be certain of anything.

Behind her, Mendelson Shape let out a plaintive moan, and a moment later, eight throats loosed a chorus of shouts from below.

"What is it?" she called down to them.

"Look, lady! Look!"

She looked, following the brothers' collective gaze, and all that she'd seen today—all, in fact, that she'd ever seen in her life up to this extraordinary moment— became a kind of overture: *and the astonishments began.*

There, in the distance, approaching over the rock and grass of Minnesota, rolling out of nowhere, there came a glittering sea.

Candy's eyes had always been good (nobody in her family wore glasses); she knew her gaze didn't deceive her. There were *waves* coming, foaming as they rolled and broke and rolled again.

Now she knew what she'd done up in the tower. She had called this sea out of the air, and like a dog answering the summons of its master, the waters were coming.

"You did it!" Mischief was hollering, jumping up and down and twisting full circle in the air. *"You did it, lady! Oh, look! Look!"* He turned to stare up at her, his tears of bliss pouring down his face. *"You see the waters?"*

"I see them!" she shouted down to him, smiling at his joy. Then more quietly, she said: "Murkitt was right."

The grasslands were still visible beneath the approaching tide, but the closer the sea came, the less solid the real world appeared to be, and the more the power of the waves took precedence.

It wasn't just her sight that confirmed the reality of the approaching tide. She could smell the tang of the salt water on the wind; she could hear the draw and boom of the waves as they came closer, eroding the world she'd thought until now was the only one that existed, drowning it beneath the surf.

"It's called the Sea of Izabella . . ." Mendelson Shape said behind her. Did she hear yearning in his voice? She thought she did.

"That's where you come from?"

"Not from the sea. From the islands. From the Abarat."

"Abarat?"

The word was completely foreign to her, but he spoke of it so confidently, how could she believe it did not exist?

The Islands of the Abarat.

"But you'll never see them," Shape said, the expression on his face losing its dreaminess, becoming threatening again. "The Abarat isn't for human eyes. You belong in this world, the Hereafter. I won't let you go into the water. I *won't*, you hear me?"

The brief moment of gentility had apparently passed. He was once again his old, savage self. He pulled himself to his feet, blood running freely from the wound Mischief had made in his leg, and started toward her—

Candy took a stumbling step backward, out of the door onto the broken platform. The wind had suddenly become chillier and stronger, its gusts carrying drops of moisture against her face. It wasn't rain that the wind carried, it was flecks of sea surf. She could taste their salt on her lips.

"*Mischief!*" she yelled, taking a careful step back over the hole in the platform, and grabbing hold of the iron railing to keep herself from slipping.

Shape was ducking through the door, his arms so long he was able to reach over the hole. One hand snatched hold of her belt with his fingers, his nails slicing the fabric of her blouse. The other went up to her throat, which it immediately encircled.

She attempted to call for Mischief a second time, and at the same time tried to turn and look for him. But she could do neither. Shape had too tight a stranglehold upon her. She tried again to call out, but seeing what she was attempting to do, Shape tightened his grip still further, till tears of pain sprang into Candy's eyes and blotches of whiteness appeared at the corners of her vision.

Desperate now, she reached up and grabbed at his vast hand, trying to tear it away from her throat. She was going to pass out very quickly if she couldn't get him to loosen his grip. But she didn't have the strength to pry so much as a single finger loose. And now the whiteness was spreading, threatening to blot out the world.

She had one tiny hope. As the incident on the stairs had proved, the tower's rotting structure wasn't strong enough to support a creature of Shape's size and weight. If she could just pull him out from the doorway onto the boards of the platform, which her *own* weight had cracked, then maybe there was a chance that the boards would collapse beneath him, as the stairs had.

She knew she had seconds, at best, to do something to save herself. His grip was like a vise, steadily closing. Her head was throbbing as though it was going to explode.

She grabbed hold of the railing again, and inched her way along it, in the hope of pulling him after her, but even that was a lost cause. Her body was almost drained of strength.

She looked into Shape's face as he continued to tighten his grasp on her neck. He was grinning with satisfaction, his eyes reflecting the bright waters that were assembling behind her; his teeth a grotesque parade of gray points, like the arrowheads she'd found sometimes lying in the long grass as a child.

That was the last thought that passed through her head before unconsciousness overtook her: Shape had a mouthful of chiseled arrowheads—

Then she seemed to feel the world crack beneath her and his hand slid off her throat as the platform folded up beneath them. There was a great eruption of splintered wood and a shout of alarm from Shape. His hand slipped off her neck. And suddenly she was falling through the broken platform, dropping to the ground in a rain of broken planks.

Had she been conscious when she fell, she would have done herself very considerable damage. But luckily she passed out as she fell, and thus landed with every muscle in her body relaxed.

And there she lay, lost to the world, sprawled in the grass at the foot of the lighthouse, while the waters of the Sea of Izabella came rolling in to meet their summoning light.

8

A MOMENT WITH MELISSA

SEVERAL MILES AWAY FROM the place where her daughter lay unconscious in the grass, Melissa Quackenbush was out in the backyard of 34 Followell Street, cleaning the barbecue after work. It was a task she hated: scraping pieces of burned-to-charcoal chicken meat off the grill, while the armies of ants that had been devouring the remains scattered in all directions.

Of course, it was always her job, never her husband's. The Lump, she called him behind his back, and not fondly. Right now he was sitting inside, slumped in front of some game show that he was only half watching through a haze of beer. In the early days after his being laid off, his lack of motivation to get up and find himself a new job had angered her. But now she was resigned to it, just as she was resigned to scraping off the remains of last week's barbecue from the grill. It was her life. It was not what she'd wanted, nor what she'd dreamed for herself—not remotely—but it was all she had: the Lump, and the kids, and a barbecue grill caked with carbonized chicken.

And then, just as she was finishing with the task, she felt a gust of wind coming from somewhere far, far off. She'd worked up quite a sweat as she scraped at the caked meat, and the wind was welcome, cooling the beads of perspiration on her forehead and the back of her neck, where her graying hair had stuck to her skin.

But it wasn't the temperature of the wind that made her close her eyes and luxuriate in it. No, it was the smell that it carried on its back.

Absurd as it was, she could smell the sea. It was impossible, of course—how could the wind be carrying a smell over a thousand miles? But even as half her mind was saying: *This can't possibly be the sea that I'm smelling,* the other half was murmuring: *But it is, it is*.

Another gust came against her face, and this time the smell it brought, and the feelings the smell evoked, were so strong they almost overwhelmed her.

She dropped the can of cleaning spray. She dropped the metal spatula she'd been using to scrape off the meat.

As they hit the paving stones, a memory came into her head from some long ago. It was a memory she wasn't even sure she was pleased to be conjuring up. But she had no choice in the matter. It came into her mind's eye so powerfully, so clearly, that it might have happened yesterday.

She remembered rain, battering down on the top of the old Ford truck she and Bill had owned when they'd first been married. They'd run out of gas in the middle of the rainstorm and Bill had gone off to fetch enough gas to get them running again, leaving her alone in the middle of the downpour that had come out of nowhere. Alone in the dark and the cold.

Well, no, that wasn't altogether true. She hadn't been completely alone. There'd been a baby in her belly. As Melissa had sat in that cold truck waiting for Bill to come back, Candy Francesca Quackenbush had been just an hour from being born. It was two in the morning and Melissa's water had just broken, and so, it seemed, had the waters of heaven itself, because to this day she could not remember being in a rainstorm so sudden and so intense.

But it wasn't the rain or the cold or the kicking of the unborn child in her womb that she was remembering now. Something else had happened; something that the smell of seawater now pricking her nostrils had brought back into her head. The trouble was, she couldn't remember precisely *what* that something had been.

She stepped away from the barbecue—away from the smell of burned chicken and cleaning fluid—to get a breath of purer air.

And as she did so—as she inhaled the sea air that could not *be* sea air—another piece of the vision snapped into focus in her mind's eye.

She'd been sitting there in the truck, with the rain beating a crazy tattoo on the roof, and suddenly, without warning, there had been light *everywhere*, flooding the old Ford's interior.

Melissa didn't know why, but this memory—the vehicle filling up with pure white light—was somehow connected to the smell in the air. It didn't make any sense. Clearly her mind was playing tricks with her. Was she going crazy? Crazy with sadness and disappointment. Her eyes had started to sting, and tears now ran down her cheeks; ran and ran. She told herself not to be silly. What was she crying about?

"I'm not crazy," she said to herself softly. Nevertheless, she felt suddenly lost, unanchored.

There was an explanation for this, somewhere in her memory. The trouble was that she couldn't quite reach it.

"Come on . . ." she said to herself.

It was like having a name on the tip of her tongue, but not being able to bring it to mind.

Frustrated with herself, and more than a little unnerved (maybe there was something wrong with her, smelling the ocean in the middle of Minnesota; maybe her life was making her nuts), she turned her back on the open sky and returned rather deliberately to the cloud of sour but familiar smells that hung around the barbecue. They weren't pleasant, but at least she understood them. Wiping her tears away with the back of her hand, she told herself to forget what she thought she was smelling, because it was a trick her nose was playing on her, no more nor less than that.

Then she picked up the spatula and the can of cleaning fluid that she'd dropped, and she went back to her weary and unhappy work.

9

EVENTS ON THE JETTY

CANDY HEARD A CHORUS of voices, all speaking the same word.

Lady, they were saying; *lady, lady, lady . . .*

It took her several moments to realize that these many voices were all addressing *her*.

It was the Johns speaking: Mischief, Fillet, Sallow, Moot, Drowze, Pluckitt, Serpent and Slop. They were all calling to her, trying to get her to wake up. She felt herself tentatively shaken. And—just as tentatively—she opened her eyes.

Eight concerned faces were looking down at her: one large one and seven smaller.

"Anything broken?" John Fillet said.

Candy made a very cautious attempt to sit up. The back of her neck hurt, but it was no worse than the ache she sometimes woke with when she'd been sleeping in an odd position. She moved her legs and her arms. She wriggled her fingers.

"No," she said, somewhat surprised at her good fortune, given the distance she'd fallen. "I don't think anything's broken."

"Good," said John Sallow. "Then we can get moving."

"Wait!" said Mischief. "She's only just—"

"Sallow's right!" said John Fillet. "We haven't got time to wait. That damnable creep Shape is going to be down here in a few seconds."

Shape! The sound of his name was enough to make Candy seize Mischief's arm and haul herself to her feet. The last thing she wanted was Mendelson Shape's claws around her throat a second time.

"Where are we off to?" she wanted to know.

"We're going home, lady," Mischief said. "You're going to yours. And we're going to ours." He put his hand into his inside pocket. "But before I go," he said, dropping his voice to a whisper as he spoke, "I wonder if you could possibly do something for me—for us all—until we meet again?"

"What do you need?" Candy said.

"I just need you to carry something for us. Something very precious."

From the interior of his jacket he brought an object wrapped up in a little piece of coarsely woven cloth and secured with a brown leather thong that had been wrapped around it several times.

"There's no need for you to know what it is," he said. "In fact, if you don't mind, it's better you don't. Just *take* it and keep it safe for us, will you? We'll be back, I promise you, when Carrion's forgotten about us, and we can chance the return trip."

"Carrion?"

"Christopher Carrion," John Serpent said, his voice laden with anxiety. "The Lord of Midnight."

"Will you take it for us?" said John Mischief, proffering the little parcel.

"I think if I'm going to carry something," Candy said, "I should at least know what it is. Especially if it's important."

"What did I tell you?" Serpent said. "I *knew* she wouldn't be content with that '*It's better if you don't know*' line. She's entirely too inquisitive, this one."

"Well, if I'm going to be a messenger girl," Candy said, addressing John Serpent, "I think I have a right—"

"Of course you do," Mischief said. "Open it up. Go on. It's all yours."

Curiously enough the little parcel seemed to have almost no weight, except for that of the wrapping and the cord. Candy pulled at the large knot, which although it looked hard to undo seemed to solve itself the moment she began to pick at it. She felt something move in the parcel. The next moment there was a rush of light out of the bag, which momentarily filled her gaze. She saw several points of brightness appear before her, joined by darting lines of luminescence. They hovered for a moment, then the lights sank away into her unconscious and were gone.

The whole spectacle—which couldn't have taken more than three seconds—left her speechless.

"You have the Key now," John Mischief told her gravely. "I beg you to tell *nobody* you have it. Do you understand? *Nobody*."

"Whatever you say," she replied, looking at the

empty bag, mystified. Then, after a moment: "I don't suppose you're going to tell me what door this key opens?"

"Truly, lady; better not."

He kissed her hand, bowing as he did so, and began to retreat from her. "Good-bye, lady," he said. "We have to go."

Candy had been facing the tower throughout this conversation. Only now, as Mischief retreated from her, did she realize what a change had come over the world in the brief time in which she'd been unconscious.

A ramshackle jetty had appeared out of the ground, and at its far end large waves were breaking, their weight sufficient to make the structure creak and shake down its entire length. Beyond the breaking waves the Sea of Izabella stretched off toward a misty blue horizon. Minnesota—at least as Candy had known it—had apparently disappeared, overwhelmed by this great expanse of invading water.

"How . . ." Candy said, staring at the panorama slack-jawed with astonishment. "How is this possible?"

"You called the waters, lady. You remember? With the cup and ball?"

"I remember," she said.

"Now I must go home on those waters," Mischief said. "And you must go back home to Chickentown. I'll return, I promise, when it's safe to do so. And I'll claim the Key. In the meanwhile, you cannot imagine what service you do to freedom throughout the islands by being the keeper of that Key."

He bowed to her again and then—politely but firmly—he nodded toward Chickentown.

"Go home, lady," he said, like a man attempting to send home a dog that didn't want to leave his side. "Go back where you're safe, before Shape gets down from the tower. *Please.* What you carry is of great significance. It can't be allowed to fall into Shape's hands. Or rather, into the hands of his master."

"Why not? What happens if it does?"

"I beg you, lady," Mischief said, the urgency in his voice mounting, "ask no more questions. The less you know, the better for you. If things go wrong in the Abarat and they come looking for you, you can claim ignorance. Now there's no more time for conversation—"

He had reason for his urgency. There was a loud noise from out of the tower behind them, as Shape attempted to clamber back down the broken staircase. Judging by the din from within, it wasn't an easy job. His weight was causing yet more of the structure to collapse. But it would only be a matter of time, Candy knew, before he navigated the remnants of the staircase and was out through the door in pursuit of them all.

"All right," she said, reluctantly conceding the urgency of her departure. "I'll go. But before I go, I *have* to have one proper look."

"At what?"

"The sea!" Candy said, pointing off down the jetty toward the open expanse of bright blue water.

"She'll be the death of us," Serpent growled.

"No," said Mischief. "She has a perfect right."

Mischief grabbed hold of Candy's hand and helped her up onto the jetty. It creaked and swayed beneath them. But having dared the tower's stairs and balcony, Candy wasn't in the least intimidated by a little rotten wood. The jetty shook violently with every wave that struck it, but she was determined to get to the end of it and see the Sea of Izabella for herself.

"It's amazing . . ." she said, as they proceeded down the length of the jetty. She'd never seen the sea before.

All thought of Shape and his claws had vanished from her head. She was entranced by the spectacle before her.

"I still don't see how it can have happened," she said. "A sea coming out of *nowhere*."

"Oh, this is the least of it, lady," Mischief said. "Out there, far off from here, are the twenty-five islands of the Abarat."

"Twenty-five?"

"One for every hour of the day. Plus the Twenty-Fifth Hour, which is called Odom's Spire, which is a Time Out of Time."

It all sounded too strange and preposterous. But then here she was standing on a jetty looking out over a sea that hadn't existed ten minutes before. If the sea was real (and real it was, or else why was her face cold and wet?), then why not the islands too, waiting where the Sea of Izabella met the sky?

They had come to the end of the jetty. She gazed out over the waters. Fish leaped up, silver and green; the wind carried sea birds the likes of which she had never seen or heard before.

In just a few seconds Mischief and his brothers were going to be gone into these mysterious waters, and she was going to be left to return to her boring, suffocating life in Chickentown.

Oh, God! Chickentown! After all this, these wonders, these miracles: *Chickentown!* The thought was unbearable.

"When will you come back?" she said to Mischief.

"Wait, lady," Mischief replied.

"What?"

"Stay . . . very . . . still."

As he spoke, he went into the outer pocket of his jacket and he pulled out—of all things—an old-fashioned pistol. It was a small weapon, and it looked as though it was made of brass.

"What are you doing?" she said, dropping her voice to a whisper.

"Doing what I can," he said softly, "to save our lives."

She saw his eyes flicker over his shoulder, in the direction of somebody on the jetty behind her.

"Shape?" she murmured.

"Shape," he replied. "Please, lady. Don't move."

So saying, he suddenly stepped to the side of her and he fired.

There was a loud crack, and a plume of purple-blue smoke erupted from the barrel of the pistol. A moment later there was a second sound, much less loud, as the bullet struck its intended target.

Candy knew immediately what John Mischief had done. He hadn't shot Shape. He'd fired at the cup on the top of the pyramid, and the ball had jumped out of it. She could instantly sense the massive change in the air around them.

"Nice shot!" said Sallow. "Though why you couldn't have put a bullet through Shape's eye defeats me."

"I take no pleasure in putting holes in living things," Mischief said, pocketing the gun.

Candy glanced over her shoulder. Shape was standing about halfway along the jetty, glancing back toward the tower. It was clear that he too knew what Mischief had done. How could he doubt it? The air was vibrating with the news.

"The tide's changing, lady," Mischief said. "And I have to go with it. Shape will follow me, all being well, because he believes I have the Key."

"No, *wait*!" Candy said, seizing hold of Mischief's arm. "Don't do this!"

"Don't do what?" said John Moot.

"I don't want to go back to Chickentown."

"Where else can you go?" said John Sallow.

"With you!"

"No," said John Serpent.

"Yes," said Candy. "Please. I want to go into the water."

"You have no idea of the risks you'd be taking."

"I don't care," Candy said. "I *hate* where I live. I hate it with all my heart."

As she spoke she felt the wind change direction. The waters around the jetty had become highly agitated now; almost frenzied, in fact. The tide was turning on itself, and in the process making the antiquated boards of the jetty rattle and shake. She knew she only had a few seconds to persuade Mischief and his brothers. Then they'd be gone, into the water and away with the tide; away to Abarat, wherever that was.

And what chance did she have of ever seeing them again, once they'd gone? Sure, they'd tell her they'd come back again, but what was a promise worth? Not much, in her experience. How many times had her father promised never to slap her again? How many times had she heard him swear to her mother that he was going to give up drink forever? None of it meant anything.

No, once they were gone, she might very well never see them again. And what would she be left with? A memory, and a life in Chickentown.

"You can't do this to me," she told Mischief. "You can't leave me here, not knowing if you'll ever come back."

As she spoke she heard the jetty creak behind her. She looked around, already knowing what she would see. Mendelson Shape was coming down the jetty toward them. For the first time she saw quite clearly why he limped (and perhaps why he hadn't been quite agile enough to catch hold of her). He was missing his right foot. It was severed at the ankle, and he walked on the stump as though it were a peg leg. If it gave him any pain he didn't display it. He wore his arrowhead tooth grin as he approached his victims, spreading his arms like an old-style preacher welcoming them into his lethal flock.

Candy knew that she still had a chance to escape, but she had no desire to turn back.

Even if it meant risking life and limb to stay here on

the jetty with Mischief, it was worth the risk. She grabbed a fierce hold of Mischief's hand and said:

"Wherever you all go, I go."

Eight faces looked at her wearing eight different expressions. Fillet looked perplexed, Sallow blinked, Moot feigned indifference, Drowze laughed, Pluckitt sucked in his cheeks, Serpent scowled, and Slop blew out his lips in exasperation. Oh, and Mischief? He gave her a wide, but unquestionably desperate, smile.

"You mean it?" he said.

Shape was thirty yards from them, closing fast.

"Yes, I mean it."

"Then it seems we have no choice," he said. "We have to trust to the tide. Can you swim?"

"Not very well."

"Oh Lordy Lou," Mischief said, and this time all eight faces did the same thing: they rolled their eyes. "I suppose not very well will have to do."

"Then what are we waiting for?" Candy said.

In the time it had taken them to have this short conversation, Shape had halved the distance between his claws and their throats.

"Can we please *go*?" Drowze said, yelling louder than a head so small had any business yelling.

Hand in hand, Candy and Mischief raced to the end of the jetty.

"One—" said Fillet.

"Two—" said Pluckitt.

"Jump!" said Slop.

And together they leaped into the air, committing their lives to the frenzied waters of the Sea of Izabella.

PART TWO

TWILIGHT AND BEYOND

"Believe me, when I say:
There are two powers
That command the soul.
One is God.
The other is the tide."

—Anon.

10

THE WATERS

THE SEA OF IZABELLA was considerably colder than Candy had expected. It was gaspingly cold; iced-to-the-marrow cold. But it was too late for her to change her mind now. With the ball knocked out of the cup by Mischief's bullet, the Sea of Izabella was retreating from the jetty at the same extraordinary speed at which it had first appeared. And it was carrying Candy and the John brothers along with it.

The waters seemed to have a life of their own; several times the sheer force of their energies threatened to pull her under. But Mischief had the trick of it.

"Don't try to swim," he yelled to her over the roar of the retreating seas. "Just trust to Mama Izabella to take us where She wants to take us."

Candy had little choice, she quickly realized. The sea was an irresistible power. So why not just lie back and enjoy the ride?

She did so, and it worked like a charm. The moment Candy stopped flailing, and trusted the sea not to harm her, the Izabella buoyed her up, the waves lifting her so high that on occasion she caught sight of the jetty and the lighthouse. They were already very far off, left behind in another world.

She scanned the waters looking for Shape, but she couldn't see him.

"You're looking for Mr. Shape?" said John Slop.

He didn't need to yell any longer. Now that they were a good distance from the shore, the waves were no longer so noisy.

"Yes, I was," Candy said, spitting out water every five or six words. "But I don't see him."

"He has a *glyph*," Mischief said, by way of explanation.

"A glyph? What's a glyph?"

"It's a craft; a flying machine. Well, actually it's *words* that turn into a flying machine."

"She doesn't understand what you're saying, Mischief," John Sallow said.

Sallow was right. Candy was completely confused by what Mischief was telling her. Words that turn into vehicles? Despite the look of incomprehension on her face, Mischief pressed on with his explanation.

"The better you are at magic, the more quickly you can conjure a glyph. For the really expert magician, someone who knows his summonings, it can be almost instantaneous. Two or three words and you've got a flying machine. But it will take Shape several minutes to conjure it. He's not a bright fellow. And if you get the conjuration wrong, it can be very messy."

"Messy? Why?"

"Because glyphs get you up in the air," Mischief said,

pointing skyward. "But if they fail for some reason—"

"You fall," said Candy.

"You fall," Mischief said. "One of my sisters died in a decaying glyph."

"Oh, I'm sorry," Candy said.

"She was being abducted at the time," he said rather matter-of-factly.

"That's terrible."

"We later found out she'd arranged it all."

"I don't understand. Arranged to be abducted?"

"Yes. She was in love with this fellow, you see, who did not love her. So she arranged to be abducted so that he would come after her and save her."

"And did he?"

"No."

"So she died for love."

"It happens," said John Fillet.

"And what of you, lady?" said John Drowze. "Do you have any sisters?"

"No."

"Brothers? Mother? Father?"

"Yes. Yes. And yes."

"I don't see you mourning the fact that you may never see them again," John Serpent said, rather sharply.

"Be quiet, John," Mischief snapped.

"She may as well hear the truth," John Serpent replied. "There's a very good chance she will never see her home again."

Something about the expression on his face suggested to Candy that he was taking pleasure in attempting to scare her. "We're going to the Abarat, girl," Serpent went on. "It's a very unpredictable place."

"So's the Hereafter," Candy said, not about to be intimidated by Serpent.

"Nothing to compare!" Serpent said. "A few tornadoes? A few poxes? Inconsequential stuff. The Abarat has terrors that will turn your hair white! That's even assuming we reach the islands."

"What do you mean?"

"I mean that Mama Izabella contains a wide variety of beasts that will have you as an appetizer."

"*Enough*, Serpent," Mischief said.

"Does he mean sharks?" Candy said, not wishing to exhibit too much nervousness, but already scanning the waters for a telltale dorsal fin.

"Sharks I'm not familiar with," Mischief replied. "But the Great Green Mantizac would certainly swallow us whole. We're not red, you see."

"Red?"

"The creatures in the Izabella leave the color red alone. That's why all the ships and boats and ferries on the Sea of Izabella—every single one—are painted red."

Candy was listening to this, but in truth she was only half hearing it. The flurry of events on the jetty hadn't given her time to properly think through the consequences of what she was doing. Now she had committed herself to the waters, and there was no way back. Perhaps she might never see her family again.

What would it be like in the house, when the family

realized that she'd gone? They would surely assume the worst: think she'd been abducted or simply run away.

It was her mother she was most concerned about, because she'd take it the hardest. Hopefully there'd be some way to get a message to her when she reached their destination.

"You're not regretting that you came, I hope?" Mischief said, his expression suggesting he was feeling a little guilty for his own part in this.

"No," Candy replied firmly. "Absolutely not."

The words had no sooner escaped her lips than a big wave lifted her up and wrenched her away from the John brothers. In just a couple of seconds, she and Mischief were carried away from one another. She heard three or four of the brothers yelling to her, but she couldn't make sense of what they were saying. She caught sight of them in the dip between the waves, but the glimpse was brief. The next moment they were gone.

"I'm over here!" she yelled, hoping that Mischief was a stronger swimmer than she was and would be able to make his way back to her. But the words were no sooner out of her mouth than another wave of substantial size came along and carried her even farther away from the spot where they'd been parted.

A little twitch of fear clutched her stomach.

"Don't panic," she told herself. "Whatever you do, don't panic."

But her own advice was hard to take. The waves were getting larger all the time, each one carrying her a little higher than the one that preceded it and then delivering her into an even deeper trough. However much she told herself not to be afraid, there was no escaping from the facts. She was suddenly alone in an alien sea, filled with all kinds of—

Her panic stopped in its tracks, shocked out of her by a sight of such peculiarity all other concerns were forgotten.

There, squatting around a small table at the bottom of the next wave were four card players. The table around which they were sitting was apparently floating freely a couple of inches above the surface of the water, and the players were squatted around it, the very picture of nonchalance.

Candy just had time to think, *I've seen everything now*.

Then another wave caught her, and she was carried down its steep blue slope into the midst of the game.

11

THE CARD PLAYERS

THE FOUR PLAYERS WERE a mixture of species. Their skin was scaly and had a silvery-green gleam to it, while their hands, in which they held fans of very battered playing cards, were webbed. Their faces, however, possessed all the features of a human face but seasoned with a hint of fish. The game they were immersed in seemed to be demanding their full attention, because not one of the four noticed Candy until she came barreling down the flank of the wave and all but collided with their table.

"Hey! Watch out!" a female among the quartet complained. "And keep your distance. No spectators!"

Three of the players were looking up at Candy now, while the fourth took the opportunity to take a surreptitious peek at the cards held by the players to his left and right. As soon as he'd done so, he concealed his cheating by feigning a great deal of interest in Candy.

"You look lost," said the cheat, who was a male of this hybrid species. His accent seemed vaguely French.

"Yes, I suppose I am," said Candy, spitting out

water. "Actually, I suppose I'm *very* lost."

"Help her, Deaux-Deaux," the cheat casually said to the player on his left. "You're going to lose this game anyway."

"How do you know?"

It was the fourth player, a female, who offered up the answer. "Because you *always* lose, my dear," she said, patting his shoulder. "Now go and help the girl."

Deaux-Deaux glanced at his hand of cards, and seeming to realize that he was indeed going to lose, tossed them down onto the table.

"I don't see why we can't play water polo like everybody else," he complained, with more than a hint of piscatorial pout.

Then he drained the liquor glass that was sitting on the table in front of him and did something that defied all expectation. He got up from the table, and using his enormous feet, he skipped over the water to Candy, then squatted down again in the sea beside her. The smell of his breath was potent, and he seemed to have some difficulty fixing his focus on her.

She was familiar with people in this condition, and it irritated her, but she was happier to have company in the water than to be alone.

"I'm Deaux-Deaux," the creature said.

"Yes, I heard," Candy said. "I'm Candy Quackenbush."

"You're from the Hereafter, aren't you?" he said as they bobbed up and down together.

"Yes, I am."

"If you're thinking of going back, it's going to be a long trip."

"No, no, I don't want to go back," Candy said. "I'm headed for the Abarat."

"You are?"

At the mention of the Abarat, there was a show of interest from the rest of the table. Two of the three other players threw in their hands, leaving the cheat protesting that this was unfair because he had the winning hand.

"That's because you cheated, Pux," one of the females said, and getting up in the same casual fashion as Deaux-Deaux, skipped over to Candy. Unlike her partner, she was not drunk. Indeed she studied their human visitor with a curious intensity, which put Candy in mind of the look Mischief had first given her.

"Are you by any chance responsible for this occurrence?"

"Which occurrence would that be?" Candy said.

"You are, aren't you?" the female said. "I'm Tropella, by the way."

"I'm very pleased—"

"Yes, yes," Tropella said impatiently. "You called the Izabella, didn't you?"

Candy saw no reason not to tell the truth. "Yes," she admitted. "I called the sea. I didn't realize what I was doing when—"

Again, rather rudely, she was cut off. "Yes, yes. But why? It is forbidden."

"Oh, let the girl alone," Deaux-Deaux said.

"No, but this is not to be taken lightly. The waters

were never to go back to the Hereafter. We all know that. So why—"

"Look," said Candy, interrupting her questioner with the same curtness she'd received from Tropella. "Can we have this conversation later? I have a friend somewhere in the sea. And I've lost him."

"Oh Lordy Lou," said Deaux-Deaux. "What's his name?"

"Well, there're eight of them. He has these brothers and they live—"

"On his head?" Deaux-Deaux said, leaning closer to Candy, his eyes wide.

"Yes. You know him?"

"That can only be John Mischief," Tropella said.

"Yes, that's him."

At the mention of John Mischief's presence hereabouts, the remaining card player abandoned their table and skipped over to Candy. She had all their attention now.

"You know John Mischief?" Tropella said.

"A little."

"He's a master criminal," Pux chimed in. "Wanted on several Hours for grand larceny and the Lord alone knows what else."

"Really? He didn't seem like a criminal to me. In fact, he was very polite."

"Oh, we don't care if he's a criminal," said Tropella. "The laws of the land aren't like the laws of the sea. We don't have courts and prisons."

"We don't have a lot of thieves," Pux said, "because we don't have much to steal."

"We're all Sea-Skippers, by the way," Deaux-Deaux explained.

"And you?" Tropella said, still studying Candy with that odd intensity of hers. "You were not wanted there, perhaps?"

"I'm sorry?"

"You weren't wanted in your world. *Your business is in the Abarat.*"

Tropella didn't seem to require Candy to confirm or deny this; she was simply informing her of something she'd already decided.

"I wonder if we could *do* something about finding Mischief?" Candy said, looking from face to face.

"Deaux-Deaux," Pux said, "you have the largest voice."

"Oh. My pleasure," said Deaux-Deaux.

He clambered somewhat unsteadily onto the surface of the water and skipped up the side of the next large wave. Having reached the top, he stood there and hollered, confirming the fact that he did indeed have a voice of operatic proportions.

"Mister Mischief!" he yelled. *"We have your girlfriend and we will eat her in two minutes with a small side salad, unless you come here and save her."* He grinned at Candy. "Just kidding," he said. *"Well, Mister Mischief?"* he yelled again. *"Where are you?"*

"He *is* joking?" Candy said to Pux.

"Oh yes," said Pux. "We wouldn't eat an important person like you. Sometimes we'll take a sailor, but—" He shrugged. "—so would you if it was always fish. Yellow fish, green fish, blue fish. Fish with funny little eyes that go pop in your mouth. It gets so boring, eating fish. So yes, we eat a sailor now and then. But not you. You we will see safely to your destination. On that you may rely."

Deaux-Deaux was still hollering, running up waves like a man running up a down escalator so as to stay at the top.

"Hey, Mischief! We are very, very hungry."

"I think the joke's—"

Candy was about to say *over*. But she never finished the sentence. Before she could do so, John Mischief erupted out of the water behind Deaux-Deaux and grabbed him around the waist. Deaux-Deaux toppled backwards, and the two of them flailed wildly in the water for half a minute—the brothers hollering all manner of threats—until Pux and Tropella were able to skip over and bring the altercation to a halt.

"Hey, hey," Deaux-Deaux said, climbing back onto the water to retreat from a furious Mischief. He held his webbed hands up palms out, to keep his attacker at bay. "It was a joke. A little joke. I was just trying to get your attention. We mean your cutie-pie no harm. I mean, what kind of fish-folk do you think we are? Tell him, Candy."

"They've all been very kind to me," Candy confirmed. "Nobody's laid a finger on me."

The Johns were not convinced. They were all exchanging fiercely suspicious glances.

"If it was a joke," John Drowze said fiercely, "then it was an extremely asinine joke."

"I would have drowned without their help," Candy

said, attempting to cool the situation down. "I swear. I was starting to panic."

"But you're right," Pux said. "It *was* an imbecilic stupid joke. So, please, in the name of peace let us carry you both to the Abarat. The Izabella can be rough, and we would not wish to see two such significant personages drown."

"You would carry us?" said John Mischief, smiling his unruly smile. "Truly?"

"Truly," said Tropella. "It's the least we can do."

It certainly sounded like a good idea to Candy. Despite the fact that she'd done as John Mischief had suggested, and relied on Mama Izabella to bear her up, she was still extremely tired. The icy water and the pummeling of the waves—not to mention the pursuits that had preceded this aquatic adventure—had taken their toll.

"What do you think?" Candy said to the Johns. "Should we accept the ride?"

"I think it's up to you," Mischief said.

"Good," Candy said. "Then I say *yes*."

"Yes?" Pux said to Mischief.

"If the lady says yes, then yes it is," Mischief replied.

"Splendid," said the fourth card player. "I'm Kocono, by the way. And I just want to say what a delight it is to meet Mr. Mischief. Tropella was right, we don't care about the law of the land. So they say you're a criminal, so what? You're a *master*. That's what counts."

The Johns erupted into a chaotic din of denials and explanations at Kocono's little speech. Candy only caught fragments of their defenses in the uproar, but they sounded distinctly contradictory. She was very amused.

"Is it true?" she said, laughing, as the protestations grew wilder. "Are you all master criminals?"

"Put it this way . . ." John Slop began.

"Be careful now," John Moot warned his brother.

"We're not saints."

"So it *is* true," Candy replied.

Mischief nodded. "It's true," he conceded. "You're in the company of eight world-class thieves," he said, not without a little touch of pride. "Saints we are not."

"But then," said Deaux-Deaux, "who is?" He thought on this. "Besides saints."

With this matter settled, Candy and Mischief were each lifted up between two of the Sea-Skippers, their legs propped up on the creature skipping ahead of them, and supported by those skipping behind. If it wasn't the most comfortable way to travel, it was certainly preferable to being immersed in the cold water, in fear of drowning or being nibbled at by Great Green Mantizacs.

"Which island are you going to?" Pux asked Candy.

"I don't know," she replied. "This is my first visit."

The Sea-Skippers looked at the Johns for an answer.

It was John Drowze who replied. "I say we go to the Yebba Dim Day, in the Straits of Dusk."

There was a general consensus from the brothers.

"The Yebba Dim Day it is," Kocono announced.

"Wait," Candy said. "Don't forget your table."

"Oh, Mizza will find her own way home," Kocono said. "Mizza!"

A head with large, rather woebegone features—and a square cranium almost as flat as the shell on which the Sea-Skippers' cards and liquor glass still stood—appeared from the water.

"You want me to wait for you at Tazmagor?" the creature said.

"Yes, please," said Kocono.

"It was nice playing on you," Deaux-Deaux said. "As always."

"Oh, think nothing of it," the Card Table replied, and paddled off through the swell.

Candy shook her head. For some reason, out of the back of her skull came the memory of her beloved uncle Fred, her mother's elder brother, who'd worked in a zoo in Chicago, cleaning up after the animals. Once, he'd been taking her around the place, pointing out his favorite animals, who were all oddities. The two-toed sloths, the anteaters, the mules.

"If you ever doubted that God had a sense of humor, all you'd have to do is look at some of these guys," he'd remarked.

Candy smiled to herself, picturing Uncle Fred's round, bald face as he looked fondly down at her. No doubt the sight of Mizza the Floating Card Table would have had him laughing until the tears trickled down his face.

"What are you smiling at, lady?" Mischief asked Candy.

But before she had a chance to explain, the Sea-Skippers took off at a breath-snatching speed, and they were on their way to the Yebba Dim Day.

12

A TALK ON THE TIDE

IT WAS A BIZARRE journey for Candy. For John Mischief too, she suspected. Even though the noise of the sea and the slap of the Sea-Skippers' feet on the waters prevented them from conversing, Mischief and his brothers would occasionally erupt in laughter, as though they were revisiting their recent adventures and were suddenly hugely amused by the fact that it was ending in this comfortable but faintly absurd fashion.

For her part, Candy found the rhythm of the travel quite relaxing after a while and was so lulled that she let her eyes close. Sleep quickly overtook her strangely fatigued body. When she opened her eyes, an hour and twenty minutes later, according to her watch, the sky was darkening overhead.

She was by habit a great sky watcher, and she knew the names of many of the stars and constellations. But though a sprinkling of stars had appeared as the darkness deepened, she found she could recognize none of the configurations ranged above her. At first she assumed she was simply looking at the sky from a different angle, and so was failing to recognize what was in fact a perfectly obvious constellation. But as she continued to study the heavens as they darkened to night (an unnatural night, by Minnesotan standards: it was barely two in the afternoon), she realized that she was not mistaken. There were no recognizable arrangements of stars up there.

This was not the same heaven that hung over Minnesota.

For some reason she found this much more disquieting than the fact of the Sea of Izabella appearing from nowhere, or the prospect of some hitherto unvisited archipelago of islands awaiting her somewhere ahead.

She had assumed (naïvely, perhaps) that at least the *stars* would be constant. After all, hadn't the same stars she knew by name hung over all the other fantastic worlds that had existed on earth? Over Atlantis, over El Dorado, over Avalon? How could something so eternal, so immutable, be so *altered*?

It distressed her, and yes, it made her a little afraid of what lay ahead. Apparently the Abarat wasn't just another part of the planet she knew, simply hidden from the sight of ordinary eyes. It was a different world entirely. Perhaps it had different religions, different ideas about good and evil, about what was real and what wasn't.

But it was too late to turn her back on all of this. After all, something here had *called* her, hadn't it? Wasn't that why she'd been drawing on her workbook the same design she'd found on the ball in the lighthouse: because for some urgent reason the ball had been sending out a portion of its power (a power to summon seas), and her mind had been ready to receive it? She'd done so without any conscious thought: drawn, and redrawn the design in a dreamy state. She'd even walked away from the principal's office without giving what she was doing any deep thought, simply going where her feet and her instincts had led her.

Though this all had looked accidental at the time, perhaps none of it was. Perhaps, as Tropella had said, *Candy had business in the Abarat.*

Was it possible?

She was just a schoolgirl from Chickentown. What business could she have in a world she hadn't even seen?

But then was the idea any less likely than the fact that the sky over her head was now filled with stars from the heavens of another universe? Even the darkness between those stars—the darkness of space itself—was not like space as she saw it from her bedroom window. There were subtle colors pulsing through it: shades of deepest purple and rich royal blue, moving like tides across the sky, ready to be swum or sailed.

In the time that she'd been turning all these wild ideas over, the Sea of Izabella had quieted down considerably. The waters were virtually flat now, and the step of the Sea-Skippers more hushed because it was easier going. It was even possible for Candy and the Johns to chat normally, as their bearers skipped side by side.

"We're moving through the Ring of Darkness right now," John Drowze explained. "That light you see ahead of us"—Candy had not seen any light before, but now that it was pointed out, she saw a distinct paling of the sky close to the horizon—"the light at Efreet—"

"—one of the Unfettered Islands," Sallow broke in to add.

"What does that mean?"

"It means they govern themselves," said John Slop. "They don't pay taxes to the Abaratian government, nor are they part of the Commexo Company."

"Oh, don't get political on us, Slop," John Drowze complained.

"I just wanted her to understand the complexities of—"

"Nobody *understands* the complexities of the islands anymore," John Mischief said despairingly. "It used to be so simple. You had the Islands of Night and the Islands of Day—"

"And almost constant war," John Serpent interjected.

"At least everybody knew where they stood. You had your allegiances and you lived and died by them. But now?" He made a noise of profound disgust. "Now who knows?"

"Oh, do stop," said John Drowze wearily.

If there was more to be said on the subject (and undoubtedly there was) nobody got to say it, because at that moment Pux whispered—

"*Quiet, everyone.*"

"What's the problem?" said Serpent.

"Look up."

Everybody turned their gazes skyward. There were dark forms, like those of huge birds with the bodies of men, circling around, blotting out the stars.

"Vlitters," said Deaux-Deaux.

"They won't touch us," Sallow opined.

"Maybe not," said Pux. "But if they see us, they can report us to Inflixia Grueskin. We're in her waters."

Candy didn't ask for the details on Inflixia Grueskin; the name was descriptive enough.

"Are you going under the Gilholly Bridge?" Mischief whispered.

"It's the quickest way," said Tropella. "And we're all getting tired. Trust us. We know what we're doing."

Mischief duly fell silent. By degrees the travelers approached the bridge in question, which spanned perhaps half a mile's width of glacial water between two islands. On one side the light was still embryonic, barely delineating the shapes of the cliffs and the immense buildings that were perched on top of them. On the other side, the light was noticeably brighter. Candy could see a temple of some kind, or perhaps the ruins of a temple, and beside it a row of pillars.

One of the creatures Pux had referred to as Vlitters swooped down and skimmed the shining water, its lower jaw cutting through the reflection of the starlit heavens. Candy caught only a glimpse as it dived, skimmed and rose again. It was an odd-looking beast: a cross between a bat and a human being. Though it had failed to see the Sea-Skippers and their passengers, the Vlitter *did* see something edible. It scooped up a fish the size of a baby, which let out a furious doglike yelping as it was taken, and continued to yelp until the Vlitter consumed it, mercifully somewhere too high up to be seen.

They moved on, with the yelping of the doomed dog-fish still echoing off the walls of the temple and the cliffs, away from the calm waters beneath the bridge. The sea became steadily rougher as they cleared the protection of the islands, and Candy was glad for all their sakes that the journey's end was close at hand. What would she have done, she wondered, if she hadn't the good fortune to meet the card players at their game? She would surely have drowned, despite all that Mischief had told her about relying on the kind arms of Mama Izabella.

They moved off to the left now, and what Candy saw ahead was yet another puzzlement. The sky, which had seemed to be growing lighter, was darkening once again. There was an immense bank of blue-gray mist filling the panorama ahead of them, and there were more stars showing through the mist. No doubt of it, the glimpse of day she'd seen had been only that: a glimpse. Now night was approaching again.

The sight of this murky vista was clearly a welcome one for the Sea-Skippers.

Pux was so happy he broke out into song as he skipped. The ditty was sung to the familiar tune of "O Christmas Tree," but the words were unexpected.

> *"O woe is me!*
> *O woe is me!*
> *I used to have a Hamster Tree!*
> *But it was eaten by a newt,*
> *And now I have no cuddly fruit!*
> *O woe is me!*
> *O woe is me!*
> *I used to have a Hamster Treeee!*

"You like my song?" Pux said, when he was done.

"It wasn't quite what I was expecting," Candy said. "But yes. It was certainly . . . um . . . unusual."

"I'll teach it to you!" Pux said. "Then you'll have something to sing as you go around the Yebba Dim Day and people will think, *Oh she's one of us*."

"Is this a very well-known song?"

"Believe it or not," said John Serpent, his expression one of profound distaste, as usual, "yes."

"Then I *should* learn it," Candy said, secretly glad to be causing the condescending John Serpent a little discomfort.

"So," said Mischief. "From the top. Altogether now."

Everybody joined in with the song this time (except Serpent and Moot), and Candy quickly picked it up. By the time they came to the fourth rendition, Pux said:

"This time a solo, from Miss Quackenbush."

"Oh no . . ."

"Oh *yes*," said Deaux-Deaux. "We've carried you all this way. The least you can do is sing us a song."

It was a reasonable request. So Candy sang out her first Abaratian song as the mist ahead began to thin, and they skipped their way into the Straits of Dusk.

"Nice. Very nice," said Pux when she was done. "Now I'll teach you another."

"No, I think one's enough, for now. Maybe another time."

"I don't imagine there will *be* another time," said Tropella. "We very rarely come into the shipping routes. It's not safe. If we go to sleep on the waves, we risk getting mown down by a ferry. That's why we head back out to the Ring of Darkness. It's safer there."

"Don't be so sure you won't meet this lady again," Mischief said to the company. "I believe she's in your lives forever now. And we're in hers. There are some people, you know, who are too important to ever be forgotten. I think she's one of them."

Candy smiled; it was a sweet speech, even if she didn't quite believe it.

Nobody seemed to know what to say when Mischief had finished, so there was just a thoughtful silence for a minute or two as the mists ahead of them continued to part.

"Ah . . ." said John Sallow. "I do believe I see the Yebba Dim Day."

The last scraps of mist parted now, and their destination came into view. It was not an island in any sense that Candy understood the word. It seemed to be a huge stone-and-metal head, with towers built on top of its cranium, all filled with pinprick windows, from which beams of light emerged to pierce the mist.

"Set your watch to Eight," Mischief said to Candy.

"I don't understand," Candy said. "One minute it looks like it's dawn, the next it's night, and now you're saying set my watch to eight o'clock."

"That's because we're now in the Straits of Dusk," said John Sallow, as though the matter were simplicity itself. "It's always Eight in the Evening here."

Candy looked well and truly confused.

"Don't worry," said Deaux-Deaux. "Eventually you'll get the knack of it. For now just *go with the flow*. It's easier that way."

While Candy set her watch to eight o'clock, the Sea-Skippers brought them around the front of the immense head of the Yebba Dim Day.

A steep staircase ran like a vein up the side of the place, and more light poured from a host of windows and doors. There was a great riotous commotion coming out of the head, the din of voices shouting and singing and crying and laughing, all echoing across the water.

"So, lady," said Deaux-Deaux, "here we are."

The Sea-Skippers brought them to a tiny harbor in the nook where the titan's chest met his arm. There were a number of small red boats in the harbor, many of which were in the process of entering or leaving—and a sizeable crowd on the quayside. The entrance of the four Sea-Skippers—along with their passengers—caused a good deal of confusion and comment.

Very soon people were appearing from inside the

Great Head to see what all the brouhaha was about. Among these newcomers were several people in uniforms.

"Police!" said John Sallow sharply.

The word was echoed among his brothers.

"Police?"

"Police!"

"*Police!*"

Mischief turned to Candy and swiftly caught hold of her arm.

"So quickly—" he said.

"What do you mean?"

"I have to go. So quickly."

"Because of the police?"

"Keep your voice down," said John Serpent; his usual charmless self.

"*Hush!*" Mischief said to him. "Don't you ever talk to my lady that way again!"

"Your lady!" Serpent snorted, as though in these final snatched moments he wanted to express his contempt for Mischief's respectful handling of Candy. But there was no time. Not for Serpent; nor for Mischief; not even for Candy to say more than a hurried: "Good-bye!"

The police were coming down the dock, parting the crowd as they advanced. Candy doubted that they'd recognized the criminals yet (though Mischief's antlers made him exceptionally easy to spot); but they were interested in these new arrivals, and Mischief wasn't going to allow their general curiosity to turn into an arrest scene.

"Do you have a permit for those Sea-Skippers?" one of the policemen hollered.

"This is where we part, lady," Mischief said. "We'll meet again, I know we will."

He took her hand, turned it over, and lightly kissed the palm. Then he jumped into the water.

"*Hey, you!*" a second policeman yelled, barging through the crowd to make his way to the end of the quayside. "*It's him!*" he yelled.

"Oh no," Candy heard Deaux-Deaux say. "This is a pleasant introduction to the Yebba Dim Day."

"We should have gone to Speckle Frew," said Tropella. "It would have been a sight quieter."

"Well, it's too late now," said Pux.

"He's getting away!" the second policeman was shouting.

"*Who?*" came the reply from one of his companions.

"Whatshisname! The one who cleared out Malleus Nyce's house in Tazmagor! *Him!* Whatshisface!" He was steadily becoming redder and redder as his frustration mounted. "*The master criminal!*"

At which point about seven people in the crowd said: "John Mischief!" at the same time.

"Yeah! That's what I said," the policeman replied lamely. "*John Mischief!*"

Now all eyes, both those of the crowd and of the officers, were fixed on the patch of turbulent water where John Mischief had last been seen.

One of the policemen, a huge blue-skinned man with a square-cut orange beard, now attempted to commandeer one of the faster-looking boats in the little harbor, apparently intending to give chase in it. But its owner—who was almost as big as the officer, and had the advantage of being six or seven yards away, across a span of grimy dock water—wasn't playing.

"You! Get that boat over here!" the officer yelled.

The man deliberately neglected to look in the officer's direction and proceeded to maneuver his vessel out through the knot of boats. Clearly the idea of losing his precious boat to a belligerent officer with more testosterone than sea-sense had made him nervous. The attempted retreat enraged the officer even more.

"Come back!" he yelled. "Your vessel is commandeered!"

"Let it be, Branx!" one of the other officers called. "There are plenty of other boats."

But Officer Branx wasn't going to have his authority disregarded. Pulling off his jacket and boots, he jumped into the dirty water and began to swim toward the retreating vessel, yelling as he went.

"You bring that boat right back here! Do you hear me? *Right back here!*"

His absurd behavior had trebled the crowd on the dock. The wooden structure was creaking, sending up a warning to those perched on it that it would not be wise to perch there much longer. The warning was, however, ignored. And the noisier the crowd became, the more people emerged from the Great Head to see what was going on.

"You know, Candy," Tropella said, "I don't want

another hurried good-bye—"

"But if I'm going to go without being noticed, this would be a smart time to do it?"

"Don't you agree?"

"Absolutely," Candy said.

Everybody's attention was on the swimming policeman, who had managed to reach the escapee in the boat and had hauled himself onboard where—despite cries from his fellow officers that he should desist—he proceeded to harangue the boat owner, who promptly hit the policeman with an oar. The oar broke, and Officer Branx toppled over the edge of the boat like a silent comedian, sinking into the filthy water.

Consternation! Now it was the boat owner who dived in to drag the unconscious man up out of the water, mindful, no doubt, of what the penalty would be if the overzealous officer drowned. The dowsing had shocked Policeman Branx out of his unconscious state however, and as soon as he surfaced, the altercation began afresh. The two men struggled and flailed in the water for a while, during which time Candy—having exchanged the very briefest of farewells with the Sea-Skippers—slipped away through the crowd toward the door of the Yebba Dim Day.

As she went she glanced over her shoulder, so as to have one last glimpse of her friends to fix in her head; just in case Mischief was overly optimistic in his beliefs, and none of them ever met again.

But Mischief had long gone, and all four Skippers had already leaped into the water and dived down under the boats so as to escape the harbor undetected.

Candy experienced a sudden and acute sense of loss. She felt utterly and painfully alone. Without John Mischief, how would she get by in this strange world?

It wasn't that she felt the need to turn around and go home. There was nothing for her back in Chickentown, or at least nothing that she wanted. She hated her father. And her mother, well, she just made her feel empty. No, there was nothing for her there. But coming here, entering this strange New World, was like being born again.

A new life, under new stars.

So it was with a curious mingling of anticipation and heavy heart that she pressed against the flow of the crowd and eventually brought herself through the doors and into the city that stood on the Straits of Dusk.

13

IN THE GREAT HEAD

CANDY HAD ALWAYS PRIDED herself upon having a vivid imagination. When, for instance, she privately compared her dreams with those her brothers described over the breakfast table, or her friends at school exchanged at break, she always discovered her own night visions were a lot wilder and weirder than anybody else's. But there was nothing she could remember dreaming—by day or night—that came close to the sight that greeted her in The Great Head of the Yebba Dim Day.

It was a city, a city built from the litter of the sea. The street beneath her feet was made from timbers that had clearly been in the water for a long time, and the walls were lined with barnacle-encrusted stone. There were three columns supporting the roof, made of coral fragments cemented together. They were buzzing hives of life unto themselves; their elaborately constructed walls pierced with dozens of windows, from which light poured.

There were three main streets that wound up and

around these coral hives, and they were all lined with habitations and thronged with the Yebba Dim Day's citizens.

As far as Candy could see there were plenty of people who resembled folks she might have expected to see on the streets of Chickentown, give or take a sartorial detail: a hat, a coat, a wooden snout. But for every one person that looked perfectly human, there were two who looked perfectly *other* than human. The children of a thousand marriages between humankind and the great bestiary of the Abarat were abroad on the streets of the city.

Among those who passed her as she ventured up the street were creatures which seemed related to fish, to birds, to cats and dogs and lions and toads. And those were just the species she recognized. There were many more she did not; forms of face that her dream-life had never come near to showing her.

Though she was cold, she didn't care. Though she was weary to her marrow, and lost—oh so very lost— she didn't care. This was a New World rising before her, and it was filled with every kind of diversity.

A beautiful woman walked by wearing a hat like an aquarium. In it was a large fish whose poignant expression bore an uncanny resemblance to the woman on whose head it was balanced. A man half Candy's size ran by with a second man half the first fellow's size sitting in the hood of his robe, throwing nuts into the air. A creature with red ladders for legs was stalking its way through the crowd farther up the street, its enormous coxcomb bright orange. A cloud of blue smoke blew by, and as it passed a foggy face appeared in the cloud and smiled at Candy before the wind dispersed it.

Everywhere she looked there was something to amaze. Besides the citizens there were countless animals in the city, wild and domesticated. White-faced monkeys, like troupes of clowns, were on the roofs baring their scarlet bottoms to passersby. Beasts the size of chinchillas but resembling golden lions ran back and forth along the power cables looped between the houses, while a snake, pure white but for its turquoise eyes, wove cunningly between the feet of the crowd, chattering like an excited parrot. To her left a thing that might have had a lobster for a mother and Picasso for a father was clinging to a wall, drawing a flattering self-portrait on the white plaster with a stick of charcoal. To her right a man with a firebrand was trying to persuade a cow with an infestation of yellow grasshoppers leaping over its body to get out of his house.

The grasshoppers weren't the only insects in the city. Far from it. The air was filled with buzzing life. High overhead birds dined on clouds of mites that blazed like pinpricks of fire. Butterflies the size of Candy's hand moved just above the heads of the crowd, and now and then alighted on a favored head, as though it were a flower. Some were transparent, their veins running with brilliant blue blood. Others were fleshy and fat; these the preferred food of a creature that was as decadently designed as a peacock, its body vestigial, its tail vast, painted with colors for which Candy had no name.

And on all sides—among these astonishments—were things that were absurdly recognizable. Televisions were on in many of the houses, their screens visible through undraped windows. A cartoon boy was tap-dancing on one screen, singing some sentimental song on another, and on a third a number of wrestlers fought: humans matched with enormous striped insects that looked thoroughly bored with the proceedings. There was much else that Candy recognized. The smell of burned meat and spilled beer. The sound of boys fighting. Laughter, like any other laughter. Tears, like any other tears.

To her amazement, she heard English spoken everywhere, though there were dozens of dialects. And of course the mouth parts that delivered the words also went some way to shape the nature of the English that was being spoken: some of it was high and nasal, a singsong variation that almost seemed about to become music. From other directions came a guttural version that descended at times into growls and yappings.

All this, and she had advanced perhaps fifty yards in the Yebba Dim Day.

The houses at the lower end of The Great Head, where she was presently walking, were all red, their fronts bowed. She quickly grasped why. They were made of boats, or the remains of boats. To judge by the nets that were hung as makeshift doors, the occupants of these houses were the families of fishermen who'd settled here. They'd dragged their vessels out of the cool evening air, and taken a hammer and crowbar to the cabins and the deck and hold, peeling apart the boards, so as to make some kind of habitation on land. There was no order to any of this; people just seemed to take whatever space was available. How else to explain the chaotic arrangement of vessels, one on top of the other?

As for power, it seemed to be nakedly stolen from those higher up in the city (and therefore, presumably, more wealthy). Cables ran down the walls, entering houses and exiting again, to provide service for the next house.

It was not a foolproof system by any means. At any one moment, looking up at the hundreds, perhaps thousands, of heaped-up houses, *somebody's* lights were flickering, or there was an argument going on about the cables. No doubt the presence of monkeys and birds, pecking at the cables, or simply swinging from them, did not improve matters.

It was a wonder, Candy thought, that this outlandish collection of people, animals and habitations worked at all. She could not imagine the people of Chickentown putting up with such chaotic diversity. What would they think of the ladder-legged creature or the smoke creature, or the baby beast throwing nuts in the air?

I need to remember as many details as I can, so when I get back home I can tell everybody what it was like, down to the last brick, the last butterfly. I wonder, she thought to herself, *if they make cameras here? If they have televisions,* she reasoned, *then surely they have cameras.*

Of course she'd first have to find out if the few

soaked and screwed-up dollars she had in the bottom of her pocket were worth anything here. If they were, and she could find somewhere to purchase a camera, then she could make a proper record of what she was seeing. Then she'd have proof, absolute proof that this place, with all its wonders, existed.

"Are you cold?"

The woman who had addressed her looked as though she might have some Sea-Skipper in her heritage. Vestigial gills ran from the lower half of her cheek into her neck, and there was a faintly mottled quality to her skin. Her eyes had a subtle cast of silver about them.

"Actually I am a little," Candy said.

"Come with me. I'm Izarith."

"I'm Candy Quackenbush. I'm new here."

"Yes, I could tell," Izarith said. "It's cold today; the water gets up through the stones. One day this place is just going to rot and collapse on itself."

"That would be a pity," Candy said.

"You don't live here," Izarith said, with a trace of bitterness.

She led Candy to one of the houses made from fishing boats. As she followed the woman to the threshold, Candy felt just a little pang of doubt. Why was she being invited into Izarith's house so quickly, without any real reason, beyond that of a stranger's generosity?

Izarith seemed to sense her unease. "Don't come in if you don't want to," she said. "I just thought you looked in need of a fire to warm you through."

Before Candy could reply there was a series of

crashes from outside the Head, accompanied by a din of yells and screams.

"The dock!" Candy said, looking back toward the door.

Obviously the jetty had finally given out beneath the weight of the crowd. There was a great rush of people out to see the calamity, which was of course only going to make matters worse out there. Izarith showed no desire to go and see what had happened. She just said: "Are you coming?"

"Yes," said Candy, offering the woman a smile of thanks and following her inside.

Just as Izarith had promised there was a fire in the little hearth, which the woman fueled with a handful of what looked like dried seaweed. The kindling was consumed quickly and brightly. A soothing wave of warmth hit Candy. "Oh, that's nice," she said, warming her hands.

On the floor in front of the fire was a child of perhaps two, her features one generation further removed from the sea-dwelling origins of her grandparents, or perhaps her great-great-grandparents.

"This is Maiza. Maiza, this is Candy. Say *hello*."

"Hell. O," said Maiza.

With her duty to courtesy done, Maiza returned to playing with her toys, which were little more than painted blocks of wood. One of them was a boat, painted red; a crude copy, perhaps, of the vessel whose boards had built these walls.

Izarith went to check on the other child in the room; a baby, asleep in a cot.

"That's Nazré," she said. "He's been sick since we came here. He was born at sea, and I believe he wants to go back there."

She bent low, talking softly to the baby.

"That's what you want, isn't it, dearling? You want to be out away from here."

"You want that too?" Candy said.

"With all my heart. I hate this place."

"Can't you leave?"

Izarith shook her head. "My husband, Ruthus, had a boat, and we used to fish around the Outer Islands, where the shoals are still good. But the boat was getting old. So we came here to trade it in for a new one. We had some money from the season's fishing and we thought we'd be able to get a good boat. But there were no new boats to be had. Nobody's building anymore. And now we're almost out of money. So my husband's working putting in toilets for the folks in the towers, and I'm stuck down here with the children."

As she told her tale, she pulled back a makeshift curtain which divided the little room in two and, sorting through a box of garments, she selected a simple dress, which she gave to Candy.

"Here," she said. "Put this on. If you wear those wet clothes much longer you'll get phlegmatic."

Gratefully, Candy put it on, feeling secretly ashamed of her initial suspicion. Izarith obviously had a good heart. She had very little to share, but what she had, she was offering.

"It suits you," Izarith said, as Candy tied a simple rope belt around her waist. The fabric of the dress was brown, but it had a subtle iridescence to it; a hint of blue and silver in its weave.

"What's the currency here?" Candy asked.

Plainly Izarith was surprised by the question; understandably so. But she answered anyway. "It's a zem," she said. "Or a paterzem, which is a hundred zem note."

"Oh."

"Why do you ask this question?"

Candy dug in the pocket of her jeans. "It's just that I have some dollars," she said.

"You have *dollars*?" Izarith replied, her mouth wide in astonishment.

"Yes. A few."

Candy pulled the sodden notes out and carefully spread them on the hearth, where they steamed in front of the fire.

Izarith's eyes didn't leave the bills from the moment they appeared. It was almost as though she was witnessing a miracle.

"Where did you get those . . . ?" she said, her voice breathless with astonishment. Finally she tore her gaze from the hearth and looked up at Candy.

"Wait," she said. "Is it possible?"

"Is *what* possible?"

"Do you . . . come from the Hereafter?"

Candy nodded. "Actually I come from a place called America."

"America." Izarith spoke the word like a prayer. "You have dollars, and you come from America." She shook her head in disbelief.

Candy went down on her haunches before the fire and peeled the now almost dried dollars off the hearth. "Here," she said, offering them to Izarith. "You have them."

Izarith shook her head, her expression one of almost religious awe.

"No, no I couldn't. Not dollars. Angels use dollars, not Skizmut like me."

"Take it from me," Candy said, "I'm not an angel. Very far from it. And what's a Skizmut?"

"My people are Skizmut. Or they were, generations ago. The bloodline's been diluted, over the years. You have to go back to my great-grandfather for a pure Skizmut."

She looked melancholy; an expression which suited the form of her face better than any other.

"Why so sad?"

"I just wish I could go back into the deeps and make my home there, away from all this . . ."

Izarith cast her sad eyes toward the window, which was without frames or panes. The crowd outside moved like a relentless parade. Candy could see how hard it would be to exist in this tiny hovel, with the twilight throng moving up and down the street outside, all the hours that God sent.

"When you say the deeps," Candy replied, "do you mean the sea?"

"Yes. Mama Izabella. The Skizmut had cities down there. Deep in the ocean. Beautiful cities, made of white stone."

"Have you ever seen them?"

"No, of course not. After two generations, you lose the way of the fish. I would drown, like you."

"So what can you do?"

"Live on a boat, as close as we can to the deeps. Live with the rhythm of Mother Izabella beneath us."

"Well, perhaps the dollars will help you and Ruthus buy a boat," Candy said.

Candy handed Izarith a ten and one single, keeping six for herself.

Izarith laughed out loud, the music in her laughter so infectious that her daughter, Maiza, started laughing too.

"Eleven dollars? *Eleven*. It would buy *two* boats! *Three* boats! It's like eleven paterzem! More, I think!" She looked up, suddenly anxious. "And this is *really* for me?" she said, as though she was afraid the gift would be reclaimed.

"It's all yours," Candy said, feeling a little odd about sounding too magnanimous. After all, it was only eleven bucks.

"I'm going to spend a little piece of this one," Izarith said, selecting a single, and pocketing the rest. "I'm going to buy some food. The children haven't eaten this day. I think you haven't either." Her eyes were shining; their joy increased by the silvery luster that was the gift of her Skizmut breeding. "Will you stay with them, while I go out?" she said.

"Of course," Candy said. She suddenly realized she was starving.

"And Maiza?"

"Yes, Muma?"

"Will you be kind to the lady from the Hereafter, while I fetch bread and milk?"

"Grish fritters!" said Maiza.

"Is that what you want? Grish fritters with noga seeds?"

"Grish fritter with noga seeds! Grish fritter with noga seeds!"

"I won't be long," Izarith said.

"We'll be fine," Candy said, sitting down beside the child in front of the fire. "Won't we, Maiza?"

The child smiled again, her tiny teeth semitranslucent, carrying a hint of blue.

"Grish fritters with noga seeds!" she said. "All for me!"

14

CARRION

OVER HIS MANY YEARS of service to Christopher Carrion, Mendelson Shape had come to know the geography of the Twelfth Tower on the island of Gorgossium very well. He knew his way around the kitchens and the scrying rooms, he knew his way down through the vaults and the Black Chapel and through the Rooms of Tears.

But today when he returned to the Tower with the news that he had lost everything (the Key, Mischief *and* his accomplice in his theft, the girl called Candy), Shape was told by Carrion's lumpen-headed servant Naw that he was to report to a chamber he had never visited before: the Great Library close to the top of the Tower.

Dutifully he did so. It was the largest room he had ever entered in his life: a vast, round, windowless chamber, with stacks of books rising perhaps forty feet into the air.

Waiting there for his master to arrive, Mendelson was not a happy man. He was dressed in a long shabby coat that was lined with werewolf baby wool, but it didn't keep the cold from his marrow. His teeth wanted to chatter, but he kept them from doing so. It would not be good to show fear, he knew. Carrion would only be inspired to cruelty if he sensed that the creature he was talking to was afraid.

Mendelson had witnessed Carrion's cruelties many times. Sometimes he'd come to this Tower and it seemed there'd been somebody weeping or screaming or begging for mercy behind every door: all Carrion's handiwork. Even today, climbing the stairs to the Great Library, he'd heard somebody behind the stones, sealed in forever in some dark narrow space in the walls, calling out to him, sobbing for light, a piece of bread, mercy.

But this was the wrong place to look for mercy, Mendelson knew. The vaulted ceilings of the Twelfth Tower, which were painted with scenes designed to terrify, had looked down on many a dreadful scene, and none had ended—Mendelson was certain—with the granting of mercy.

His footless leg was aching, but he did not dare sit down, in case Carrion entered and caught him lounging. Instead, to pass the time, he went to one of the many tables in the Library, stacked with books that had presumably been brought down from the shelves because they had caught Carrion's eye.

One, set on a little lectern for easy reading, was a book Shape remembered from his childhood: *Pincoffin's Rhymes and Nonsenses*. The book had been a favorite of his, containing many a rhyme and lullaby he still knew by heart, including the one he'd sung to the girl from the Hereafter. It was open to a grim little nursery song he had forgotten. But now, reading it, he was enchanted anew.

> *Scarebaby, scarebaby,*
> *Where do you run?*
> *Out in the graveyard,*
> *To have you some fun?*
> *Dancing with skeletons*
> *Up from the ground?*
> *Doing a jig*
> *On the burial mound?*

His lips moved as he scanned the words and it brought back a distant memory of his mother, Miasma Shape, sitting with her three boys—Nizz, Naught and Mendelson—reading aloud from Pincoffin's opus. Oh, how he'd idolized his mother!

He read on.

> *Scarebaby, scarebaby,*
> *Horrid you are!*
> *With the wings of a bat,*
> *And a face with a scar,*
> *The fangs of a vampire,*
> *The tail of a snake;*
> *You open your mouth*
> *And the noise that you make*
> *Is a song that the Devil sings,*
> *Bitter and loud.*

Tell me, my baby,
Was your mother proud?

"*A song that the Devil sings.*" That was a phrase that had lingered in his head over the years, though he had forgotten, until now, its source. He had many times wondered if he could ever hope to make such a song.

He let a sound escape his throat now. A low, menacing growl that was magnified by the circular chamber. Oh yes, that sounded like something to put fear into the hearts of his enemies. That was the noise, he thought to himself, that he would make when he found that wretched girl again: a sound so horrible, her wits would crumble.

He made a louder noise still, and from the top of the stacks of books, disturbed by the din, there swooped two winged creatures that descended to a point about three feet over his head and there hovered. They were the size of vultures and they had ashen, bloated faces, like monstrous cherubs.

"What do you want?" he said, staring up at them.

Their tiny whiteless eyes fixed on him for a moment, then they seemed to decide that he was nothing of importance and returned to their roosts, climbing in wide spirals to the top of the stacks.

Mendelson returned to the final verse of the poem.

Scarebaby, scarebaby,
Where do you run?
Not out to the morning,

Not out in the sun.
You live in my nightmares,
You hide from the day;
And there, little—

"Shape?"

The one-footed man turned.

The voice had come out of the shadows, across the room. No door had opened to let the speaker in. He'd been here all the time, watching Mendelson. Listening to him practice his growls.

Mendelson didn't move. He simply studied the shadows, waiting for the appearance of the person who had addressed him. He knew of course, who that somebody was. It was the Lord of Midnight himself: Christopher Carrion.

"Sit," the voice said. "Please, Shape, sit. Are you fond of books?"

The voice was deep and—even in the simplest of questions—was somehow tinged with despair. It was the voice of someone who had walked in the abyss.

Mendelson could see him now, faintly. He was an imposing figure, six foot six or more, his long robes black, which was why he had blended so well with the shadows.

He walked toward Shape, and the candles on the table illuminated him a little.

He had the most piercing eyes of any man Mendelson had met. They glistened in his bald, pale head. As always, he wore a collar of translucent mate-rial that resembled glass, which had been devised to cover the lower half of his head. It was filled with a blue fluid, which was now suddenly lit up by the presence of several snaking forms. They flickered in their fluid—some white as summer lightning, some yellow as sliced fat—weaving bright patterns around the Lord of Midnight's head. Plainly he took pleasure in their proximity, perhaps even a kind of comfort. When one of them brushed against his skin, he smiled, and that smile was so ghastly it made Mendelson want to run from the room.

He knew from what Naw had told him why Carrion smiled that smile, and what those bright shapes were. Carrion had found a way to channel every nightmarish thought and image out of the coils of his brain and bring them into this semiphysical form. He breathed the fluid, the flickering forms ran in and out of his mouth and nostrils, soaking his soul in his own nightmares.

His voice, reverberating through this soup of dark visions, was tinged with the power of those nightmares; their terror touched every syllable he spoke.

"The books, Shape . . ."

"Yes? Oh yes, the books. I have books. A few."

"And what else do you have?" Carrion said.

The serpentine lights flickered around Midnight's head. His eyes fixed on Mendelson.

"Or *don't* have?"

"You mean the Key?"

"Yes, of course. The Key. What else would I mean?"

"Lord, please forgive me. I don't have the Key."

Mendelson waited, fearing that Carrion would come at him; strike him, perhaps. But no. He just stood there, piercing Shape with his hollow gaze.

"Go on," he said quietly.

"I . . . I found the men who stole it from you."

"John Mischief and his brothers."

"Yes."

"He escaped with the Key to Efreet and took a boat to the Hereafter. I went after him, and I sank the boat, and thought I would have him—"

"But?"

"The tide was with him. It carried him all the way to the other side."

"All the way to the Hereafter?" Carrion said, with a little touch of yearning in his voice.

"Yes."

"How is it there?" he said, almost conversationally.

"I saw very little of it. I was trying to catch Mischief."

"Of course you were. You were doing your honest best, but he kept avoiding you. Eight heads are better than one, eh? You were outnumbered."

"I was, Lord," Mendelson said, beginning to dare think that his master understood the hazards his servant Shape had endured to get all the way to the Hereafter and back.

Carrion went to the largest of the chairs in the Chamber. He sat down in it and knitted his hands together lightly in front of him, as if in prayer.

"So?" he said.

"So . . . ?"

"Tell me what happened."

"Oh. Well . . . I almost caught up with him, at Hark's Harbor."

"The Harbor? I thought it was destroyed."

"There are some minor portions remaining, Lord. A lighthouse. A jetty."

"No ships?"

"No ships. I think those that were scuttled are buried in the earth. Anyway, I saw none."

"So, go on. You went to the Harbor and—"

"He had an accomplice."

"Besides his brothers?"

"Yes. A girl. A girl from the Hereafter."

"Ah! He had an accomplice. And a girl, to boot. Poor Shape. You didn't stand a chance."

"No, Lord."

"So he gave her the Key?"

"Did he? I don't know. Yes. Possibly."

"Did he or did he not give her the Key?" Carrion asked, his voice subtly gaining in volume and menace.

Mendelson looked at the floor. His teeth had begun to chatter, though he'd promised himself he would not let them.

"Look at me, Shape."

Mendelson was afraid to do so. He kept his eyes downcast, like a man confronted by an enraged animal.

"I said: *look at me!*"

Shape seemed to feel something catch hold of his head and jerk it back, so that he was forced to look at the man sitting before him. An instant later that same power pressed on his shoulders, driving him down onto the mosaic floor with such force that his knee bones cracked like whips.

Carrion's face looked skeletal, the marks around his mouth (where, according to rumor, his grandmother Mater Motley had once sewn up his lips) like the teeth of a skull; the arid flesh above the line of the fluid close to mummified. Only his eyes had any real life. And that was an insane life, crazed beyond recall.

There was nothing in the world Mendelson Shape wanted more than to be out of the Library at that moment.

"You failed me," Carrion said.

His voice seemed to resonate in Mendelson's head, so that Shape was suddenly and sickeningly aware of the form of his own skull, of the death's head he carried just out of sight behind his skin.

"I'm sorry. I did all I could. I swear."

"What was the name of this girl?"

"I heard only one name. Candy."

Carrion's upper lip curled at the very idea of sweetness. "Would you know her again if you saw her?"

"Yes. Of course."

"Then it seems I must let you live, Mendelson. You have dealt with this girl. Presumably you know something of her nature?"

"Yes. I believe I do," Shape said, through his chattering teeth. He wanted desperately to look away from Carrion's face, but the Lord of Midnight held him there.

"I think she probably has the Key, don't you?"

"But Mischief—"

"Gave it to her."

"I didn't see such a thing, Lord."

"But he will have done so."

"If I may ask . . . what makes you so sure?"

"Because he's like you. He's tired of the chase. He wants somebody else to be the object of my eye, at least for a while." Carrion paused for a moment and looked up at the ceiling. The cherubic beasts, roused from their roosts by the sound of the torment below were circling in the Library vault, enjoying the spectacle.

Finally, Carrion said: "You have to go back and find me this girl."

"But, Lord—"

"Yes?"

"She came here."

Carrion rose from his seat. "You saw her, *here*?"

"No. I saw the tide carry her away."

"So she could have drowned! She could be in the belly of a mantizac!"

He came at Mendelson finally, his hands raised. Filled with a kind of terrible relief that he was getting what he deserved, Shape felt himself lifted up, though Carrion made no contact with him. He was thrown across the nearest table and the books—including *Pincoffin's Rhymes*—went flying. Mendelson was held down by an invisible force, so strong it kept his breath from coming freely. He heard his breastbone creak.

"Listen to me, Shape," Carrion said. *"Your brothers are dead for their failures, and you will join them in the lime pit if you do not succeed in this last venture.*

Do you understand?"

Mendelson could barely manage a nod.

"Find me this . . . Candy. If she's dead, find me her body. I can interrogate the dead if I need to. I want to know what kind of creature she is. The tide carried her, you say?"

"It seemed that way," Mendelson said.

"That's strange. After all that happened, I'm sure Our Lady Izabella would drown most souls, rather than carry them here."

Carrion took his eyes off Shape for the first time in several minutes, and Shape felt the weight of the power upon him relax somewhat. "There is something *strange* here," Carrion said, half to himself. "Something mysterious."

"How will I find her, Lord, in all the islands?"

"You will have help for that," Carrion said, his wrath apparently quenched. "Go down to the kitchens. Eat. Wait for word from Naw. I will see you again when I have some clue . . ."

"Yes, Lord."

"A *girl*, eh?" Carrion said, as though amused at the notion.

Then he moved away, and was enveloped by the darkness.

The bone-cracking weight removed from his chest, Shape rolled off the table, gasping for breath.

In the vaulted ceiling above, the vile cherubs were still circling, chattering to one another as they went, excited by the violence they'd just witnessed.

Mendelson ignored them. He hauled himself up to

his foot and stump, and waited a few moments until the ache in his chest subsided.

Then he hobbled to the door and headed away down to the kitchens, promising to himself he would burn his few books when he went home, for fear they would put him in mind of the terrors he had just endured.

PART THREE

WHERE IS WHEN?

"The Day is words and rage.
The Day is order, earth and gold.
It is the philosophers in their cities;
It is the map-makers in their wastelands.
It is roads and milestones,
It is panic, laughter and sobriety;
White, and all enumerated things.
It is flesh; it is revenge; it is visibility.

The Night is blue and black.
The Night is silence, poetry and love.
It is the dancers in their grove of bones,
It is all transforming things.
It is fate, it is freedom.
It is masks and silver and ambiguity,
It is blood; it is forgiveness;
It is the invisible music of instinct."

—Fasher Demerondo
The Division of the Hours

15

BUG

MAYBE IT WAS THE warmth of the fire, maybe it was the strange scent of the dress she'd been given, maybe it was simply the fact that she was exhausted; whatever the reason, Candy slipped into a pleasant doze in front of Izarith's fire, while little Maiza played singsong games beside her. It wasn't a deep enough sleep to bring dreams, just a few flickering memories of sights she'd seen in the last few hours. The lighthouse, in all its ragged glory, standing in the long grass, neglected, but waiting. The turquoise ball, etched with the very same design she'd drawn on her workbook. The Sea of Izabella rolling out of nowhere, like a foaming miracle—

She opened her eyes suddenly, her heart jumping. Maiza had suddenly stopped her singing and had gone from the spot on the ragged rug beside her. She had retreated to the corner of the room, close to her brother's cot, her eyes fearful.

Behind her, Candy heard a whirring sound. Something told her to move very cautiously, which she did, turning her head oh-so-slowly to discover what was making such a peculiar noise.

Hovering in the middle of the room was a creature that looked to Candy like a cross between a very large locust and a dragonfly. Its wings were bright green, and it had uncannily large eyes, beneath which lay a design on its head that looked at first glance like a smile.

She glanced back at Maiza. Plainly the poor child didn't know what to make of this thing any more than Candy. She was gripping hold of the edge of the cot as though she was ready to climb in and hide with her brother if the creature made a move toward her.

Candy didn't have any time for bugs, big or small. Back in Chickentown they often had plagues of flies, because of the factories, and there was nothing she hated more than to go into the kitchen and find a host of big blue insects crawling on the dishes her mother had left caked with food in the sink before she went to work. Candy had no sentimentality about flies. She'd take a cloth and whip at them, catching them in mid-flight and killing them when they hit the ground.

She knew where they'd been: in the coops, eating chicken excrement, or feeding on the caked blood that stank in the gutters around the slaughterhouse. They were flying diseases as far as she was concerned. The only good fly was a dead fly. The same with roaches, which periodically invaded the Quackenbush house on Followell Street. Again, no mercy.

But this was a bug of a different order, and Candy wasn't sure how to treat it. For one thing, it was so *big*; more like a bird than an insect. She wasn't afraid of it stinging or biting her; she was quite ready to risk that. But she was afraid of enraging it and then having it turn on the children. She decided rather than swatting it like a very large wasp, she'd treat it as if it *were* a bird and try to coax it out it through the door.

"Maiza?"

"I want Muma."

"She's coming back soon. I want you to sit *very* still, yes?"

"Yes."

Having instructed the child, Candy tried to position herself so that she could shoo the insect through the door. But wherever she moved around the room, the creature repositioned itself, so that it was always staring directly at her, like an eager photographer determined to get a shot of her. When she approached it, the thing made no sign of retreating, but instead extended its neck so that its bug eyes seemed to get even bigger.

All this maneuvering gave Candy plenty of time to study the thing and appreciate its intricacies.

She should not have been surprised that a world which contained such a strange species as the Sea-Skippers should have insects as bizarre as this, but the more she looked at it, the more unusual it seemed. Its eyes had an unnerving *depth* to them, as if behind the layer of blue-green sheen was something more than insectoid intelligence.

In fact there was something almost *too* intelligent about the way it looked at her. Weren't bugs supposed to be stupid? Why then did this thing study her as though it had a mind of its own?

She tried everything to usher the creature out of the door, but it wouldn't go, so she decided to try Plan Two. When a bird got into the house (a rare event, but one that made Candy's mother become panicky), it always fell to Candy to get it out. She applied the same method now.

She went to the narrow pallet against the far wall, where apparently Izarith, her husband and Maiza slept, and picked up a sheet. When she turned, she found the creature had followed her across the room. Before it had time to work out what she was doing, she snatched up the sheet, threw it over the creature, and pulled it to the ground.

The dragonfly instantly began to flap wildly and give off what sounded remarkably like a baby sobbing, rising scales of complaint which the sheet did very little to muffle. Candy held on tight, attempting to capture the creature without hurting it. She gathered up the sheet beneath the insect and gently transported it to the door. But she had not counted on the violence of the creature's motion. It flapped so wildly—and its wings were so strong—that it began to tear the thin fabric open as if it were no more than a paper bag.

Candy hastened her trip to the door, but the creature was too quick for her. It tore out of the sheet and rose into the air again, hovering and turning on the spot seven or eight times. Plainly it wanted to ascertain who'd played this trick on it. When it fixed upon its captor, it defiantly flew closer than ever, and Candy saw the darkness behind its eyes close up like a mechanical iris.

"You're not *real*," she said to it, amazed and annoyed at the same time. Amazed because she'd been fooled by its perfection for so long, and annoyed for exactly the same reason.

The thing was spying on her.

"Damn thing!" she said, whipping the sheet around, as she would have done in the kitchen at Followell Street if she'd been in pursuit of a bluebottle.

The creature was so big (and perhaps a little dizzied by its own maneuvers) that she quickly caught it in the sheet and brought it down. It struck the ground very hard.

As soon as it hit the floorboards, she knew that her guess about its true nature was correct. The sound it made was undeniably metallic.

She pulled off the sheet. The thing was lying on its side, one of its wings flapping weakly, the other entirely still, and its six legs pedaled slowly as though somebody had just snatched a bicycle from between them.

But even now, wounded and dizzied, it turned its bug eyes toward Candy, and she heard a humming sound that the noise of its wings had hitherto disguised.

It was the noise of the creature's *mechanism* she could hear, and it was clearly badly damaged.

Even so, Candy didn't trust it. She'd seen roaches she was sure were dead and gone push themselves up off the ground and nonchalantly walk away. As long as this strange beast had life in it, it presented a danger.

She went to the hearth and picked up the iron rod

that was used to poke the fire. Then—keeping her distance from the thing—she touched the creature with the end of the poker.

What happened next came so fast that it caught Candy completely off guard. The creature suddenly flipped itself over, and crawled up the poker with the speed of a striking snake.

Before Candy had time to let go of the poker, the design beneath the bug's eyes opened up like the mouth of a crab, and a spike, about five inches long, emerged and jabbed Candy's hand in the cradle of flesh between her forefinger and her thumb. Blood ran out of the wound. Yelping, Candy dropped the iron poker.

She put the cut to her mouth immediately, tasting the tang of her own blood, and perhaps something of the creature's metallic innards, from whence the spike had come.

Meanwhile, the insect had dropped off the poker and was finally retreating. It *was* wounded, she saw; two of its legs were set awry and were being dragged behind it.

Even so, as it retreated, it underwent an extraordinary transformation.

Without missing a steady step of its speedy stride, its back opened up, two doors sliding out of sight. Its wings were then raised and folded and slid with perfect accuracy into the opening and its back closed up again. At the same time a host of other smaller changes were taking place in its anatomy. A telescopic tail appeared, almost doubling the insect's length when it reached its full measure, and a second rack of legs appeared along its abdomen. When its reconfiguration was complete it no longer resembled a locust or a dragonfly, but a huge centipede. Even its color seemed to have changed subtly, its bright greens bled of their intensity, so that now it was a sickly, mottled yellow.

It no longer tried to record Candy or her surroundings. All it wanted now was to be away as fast as possible, so as to avoid another attempt on its artificial life. Candy made no further attempt to stop it from escaping. It wasn't worth the risk.

The creature was now about two feet from freedom. And then, in walked Izarith. She failed to notice the thing scuttling beneath her feet. Good mother that she was, her eyes went first to her frightened daughter.

"Watch out!" Candy yelled.

Too late. Izarith had trodden on the tail of the creature, which cracked like the shell of a lobster.

Izarith looked down. The food she'd brought in with her fell from her hands. An expression of the most intense disgust came to her face.

She raised her foot to stomp on it again.

"Get it, Muma!" Maiza said, silent tears running down her cheeks.

"Be careful," Candy warned her, still trying to stop the blood flowing from her hand. "It fights back."

Izarith didn't seem to care; her house had been invaded and her child had been terrorized. She was furious. She stamped on it twice, bringing her heel down hard. The creature was fast, however. It tried to rush away between Izarith's legs. But she took a step back to stop it, and realizing the way was barred, the creature turned, its bug eyes scanning the wall to the right of the door. Picking up the poker that Candy had dropped, Izarith pursued the creature to the corner of the room.

But again the insect showed a remarkable turn of speed. It ran toward the wall, and *leaped*, driving its feet into the plaster. Then it made a zigzag ascent, evading each and every blow Izarith attempted to deliver. In a matter of seconds, it was out of her reach and heading across the ceiling to a place where the plaster had fallen away, exposing a sizeable hole. It disappeared through it and was gone. .

"*Hush,*" Izarith said to Nazré, who'd begun to cry out loud.

The child stopped crying almost instantly. Candy listened. She could still hear the creature's feet as it scuttled away. Eventually they grew so soft, Candy wasn't sure whether she was still hearing them, or imagining it.

Then they were finally gone.

Candy looked down at her hand. It was still bleeding. Not a lot, but enough to make Candy feel faintly sick. It was not just the blood that sickened her; Candy had a strong stomach. It was much more to do with the memory of the creature's scrutiny; the horrid intelligence in its stare.

"Do you know where that thing came from?" she asked Izarith.

Izarith picked up what looked like the remains of a child's shirt and tossed it over to Candy. "Here," she said, "it'll stop the blood."

"Well, do you?"

"No," Izarith replied, not looking at Candy. "There are things like that all over. But never before in my home."

"But it wasn't real, Izarith. It was a machine of some kind."

Izarith shrugged, as though the matter of its being real or not was completely irrelevant.

Candy tore the old garment she'd been given into two strips and bound it around her hand. It slowly stopped throbbing. As she tied off the knot, Izarith—who'd been silently working to calm and then feed her children—said, "I think you should go."

She still wasn't looking at Candy. Plainly the fact that she was ushering the girl who'd been so generous to her out of her house was an embarrassment. But her primary concern was her children's safety.

"Will others like that thing come to replace it?"

"I don't know," Izarith said, finally glancing up at Candy. The blood had gone from her face. Though she'd dealt with the insect efficiently enough, she was obviously deeply afraid. There were tears in her eyes, but she was fighting them bravely. "I'm sorry," she said. "I just think it's better if you go."

Candy nodded. "Of course," she said. "I understand. I hope things go well for you and your family."

"Thank you," Izarith said. "I hope things go well for you, too. But be careful. This is a dangerous time."

"So I begin to see," Candy said.

Izarith nodded, then she returned to the business of feeding her children, leaving Candy to make her own way out.

16

THE UNIVERSAL EYE

CARRION HAD NO LOVE of things Commexian. On the island of Pyon, where it was always Three O'clock in the Morning, Rojo Pixler had built Commexo City, his so-called city of Light and Laughter. It had been, many years before, the site of the Carrion Night Mansion. The Lord of Midnight had happy memories of the times preceding the fire that destroyed the Mansion; Hours when Pyon had been a place of play. He'd needed no magic then. He'd been the prince, his father's favorite. That was all he had needed in order to make the world glorious and Pyon a playground.

But after the fire he had never gone back. And when the man he'd thought was a harmless dreamer by the name of Rojo Pixler had offered to buy the land on which the ruins of the Night Mansion still stood, he'd readily sold it.

Only later did he discover that Pixler's representatives had been surreptitiously buying up other plots of land around Pyon, until he had enough ground to start the construction of his dream city; a place where night was to be permanently banished by a constant blaze of artificial light. What a mockery, that on the very site where the Carrion family had lived in a palace of shadow and enigma, was now a garish city whose every surface blazed. The dazzle and gaud of it could be seen at midnight, if you stood in certain spots along Marrowbone's Shore on the northwest where the wind off the Izabella thinned the red fogs.

Carrion had promised himself that he would personally extinguish those lights when his Night of Nights came. And Rojo Pixler would get a nightmare or two to replace his bright and wretched dream. Something plucked from Carrion's own cortex. Something that would leave the man a gibbering wreck, driven so far into madness he would be unable even to remember the name of his own damnable city.

But that was for the future. Until that happy Night came, it made sense to put the inventions that Pixler funded to use. Pixler was no fool. He had found a way to marry the ancient magical principles that had been practiced on the islands since the beginning of time with new machineries invented by the scientists he kept in gleaming laboratories in the towers of Commexo City.

Where had Pixler found those first magical principles? In books he had paid professional thieves to steal from Carrion's own library, among other places. Carrion had let it be known that he was aware of the theft and even of the price Pixler had paid the thief, a fellow by the name of John Mischief, for his illicit services.

Word had later reached him that Pixler—who was at heart a superstitious man—had become very agitated when he heard that his commissioned thefts were no secret. Fearing reprisal, he had casually offered the use of his "Sublime Verities," as he called his marriage of science and magic, to Carrion, should he ever have need of them.

Well, that time had come.

Immediately following his interrogation of Shape, Carrion had sent one of his trusted lieutenants, Otto Houlihan, the Criss-Cross Man, to Commexo City. He was sent with a very specific demand. He knew for a fact that, like any man of power—especially one who had risen suddenly, like Pixler—the King of Commexo City was not only superstitious, but paranoid. He feared for his life and for his city. And with reason. No doubt there were people on every island who hated Commexo City and all that it represented.

Being a practical man—a man who believed in finding solutions, not simply stewing in his fear— Pixler had instructed his magical scientists to use their Sublime Verities in the creation of spies that would take the shape of living things and would be dispersed through the islands to watch for and report any sign of rebellion against him.

Only a month before, the Criss-Cross Man had brought a dozen of these automaton spies to the Twelfth Tower for the Lord of Midnight's amusement. They were like exquisite toys to Carrion's eye; he had amused himself by having Houlihan blindfold them, then watched them batter themselves to pieces against the walls of his scrying room. Some of the finest he had turned over to his own scientists for closer analysis. One, an artificial meckle bird, he had caged and kept for himself, because it needed no nourishment, and it sang so fetchingly, even when blinded.

Now he had a new reason for Rojo Pixler's spying operations. He wanted to know if the girl who'd apparently been Mischief's accomplice had survived the waters of the Izabella, and if so, where she'd gone.

So he sent Houlihan to Commexo City; a short while later the man returned, not with information, but with one of Pixler's chief scientists, a certain Dr. Voorzangler.

The doctor appeared before Carrion dressed in a fine white linen suit, with white shoes and white tie; he wore one of the more peculiar ocular devices Carrion had ever seen. It had the effect of taking the image of his eyes and superimposing them, one over the other, in the middle of his face. Voorzangler's eyes were not a perfect match. One of them was a little bigger than the other, and one seemed to be a little slower in its motion than its companion, so the cyclopic eye the device created was seldom whole. One image was always trailing half an eye behind the other.

Whatever the reason for his wearing it, the thing didn't seem to impair Voorzangler's vision. He was studying the paintings on the walls of the gallery when Carrion came in.

His voice, when he spoke, was high-pitched and weaselly.

"I hear," he said, "that you are *searching* for somebody.

Is that right? Somebody who has conspired against you? And you need Mr. Pixler's assistance?" Before Carrion could reply, the doctor continued, his voice, after a few sentences, already annoying Carrion. "Mr. Pixler instructed me to tell you that he is more than happy to help a friend and neighbor. Could you perhaps supply me with a brief description of the miscreant?"

"No," said Carrion. "But I have somebody who can." He turned to Houlihan. "Where's Shape?"

"I brought him up from the kitchens as you instructed, sir. He's waiting in the next room."

"Fetch him."

While Houlihan went off down the length of the gallery to fetch Shape, Carrion turned his full attention on Voorzangler.

"So what have you brought to impress me with?" he said.

Voorzangler began to blink his one and a half eyes vigorously. "It was Mr. Pixler's desire that you be given access to our most secret spying device," he said. "The Universal Eye."

"I'm honored," Carrion replied. "May I ask why, if it is so secret, Mr. Pixler so honors me?"

"He looks to the future, Lord Carrion. He sees a time when—if I may be so bold—you and he may be more than distant neighbors."

"Ah," said Carrion. "Good. Then let me see what proof of his intentions he has sent."

"Here," Voorzangler said, bringing Carrion's attention to a dark gray box, about three feet square, which was standing a little way down the gallery. He took a small control unit out from his white jacket and touched it with his thumb.

The response from the box was instantaneous. It rose into the air on a quintet of delicate legs on which it had been squatting. Then, without any further instruction from Voorzangler, it began to open up like a geometric flower, so that it now presented sixteen screens, four facing each wall of the room. An instant later, they all flickered into life, the images bright.

Carrion smiled.

"Well, well," he said.

He started to move around the other side of the device, but as he did so it accommodated him by flipping around, so as to present him with four more screens. Some of the images were static, but more were moving, their motion sometimes chaotic, as the camera—wherever it was situated—went in pursuit of a particular suspect.

By now Houlihan had brought Shape in. He was still wearing the same shabby coat, except that it was now decorated with the remains of his meal in the kitchens. He looked embarrassed when Carrion called him to hobble forward and view the multiplicity of screens.

"I'm hoping we're going to find our little Candy somewhere here," Carrion said to him. He turned to Voorzangler. "What kind of creatures do this spying for you?" he asked.

"You saw some of them yourself, sir, a month ago." His cyclopic gaze became sly. "I believe you still keep the meckle bird in your private rooms."

The meaning of this remark was not lost on Carrion. Voorzangler was subtly telling him that even he, the Lord of Midnight, was spied upon.

Carrion filed the information away for another time, and simply pretended not to understand what he'd been told.

"How many reports do you have in this device?" he asked.

"Nineteen thousand, four hundred and twelve," Voorzangler replied. "That's just from the last two days. Of course if you want to go back further—"

"No, no," said Carrion. "Two days is fine. Shape?"

"Yes, Lord?"

"Doctor Voorzangler is going to show you a lot of pictures. If the girl is among them, I want to know. Otto? Come and find me when you're ready."

Carrion left them to it and went out into the midnight, his thoughts straying from Voorzangler's Sublime Verities to subjects more massive and remote.

It was the stars glimmering through the fog that were the present subject of his meditations.

He knew from his books that each one of those distant lights was a sun unto itself. And though their meager illumination did not disturb *him*, there were other creatures in the Abarat for which those little stars (not to mention the brightness of the noonday sun or the light of the pallid moons that hung over the islands) were a curse.

They were called the Requiax, these creatures, and their home was in the deepest trenches of the Sea of Izabella.

Their age and their capacity for evil were both beyond calculation. Such indeed was the scale of their wickedness and the extent of their age, that many learned men and women who'd made it their business to study the innumerable life-forms of the Abarat did not even believe they existed. Wickedness of such proportions was a mythic invention, they said. The Requiax could not be real.

But Carrion had it from a trustworthy source that the Requiax lived. And having that certain knowledge he had wondered many times how things would be for his enemies across the archipelago if the light of the sun, moon and stars were somehow to be blotted out for a little while.

In that time would the Requiax not rise up from their unfathomable trenches, forsaking the temples where they were still paid homage by the blind monsters of the deep, and turn their vast, depraved faces toward the lightless sky? Rise up and come where they had not ventured since the time when great clouds of ash had covered the sun and moon and stars?

What harm would they do, if they walked the islands again?

What cities would they bring down, what peoples would they erase?

It was beyond even Carrion's power to fully conceive of the devastation they would unleash.

But he knew one thing: he wanted to be there to witness it. And he wanted to be ready, when the Hour of Darkness passed, and the Requiax returned to their temples and their trenches. Ready with his masons and his priests, to lay down the foundations of a New World and rebuild it in his image.

"Lord?"

The voice that had disturbed his thoughts was not that of Houlihan, as he'd expected. It was one of his grandmother's many stitchlings, creatures sewn together from skin and leather and fabric, then filled with a living mud. This particular stitchling was called Knotchek, and he was a wretched piece of work in every way.

"What is it?" Carrion said to him.

"Your grandmother, Mater Motley, summons you, my lord. She needs to talk with you about the visitation you have had from Commexo City."

"She misses *nothing*, does she?" Carrion remarked.

"Little, m'lord," Knotchek agreed.

"Well, I cannot come now," Carrion told the stitchling. "I have too much urgent business."

"She told me . . . um . . ."

Knotchek was getting nervous. Plainly this was not a message he wished to deliver.

"Go on," Carrion said.

"She says . . . she *forbids* any further presence on Gorgossium of visitors from Commexo."

"She *forbids*?" Carrion said. There was a menacing undertow to his voice. The nightmares in the water around his head grew agitated. "*She* forbids *me*. That harridan? That *seamstress*?"

He caught Knotchek with one backward sweep of his gloved hand, so powerful it threw the stitchling ten yards.

"Go back to her!" Carrion shouted. *"And you tell her if she ever forbids me ANYTHING EVER AGAIN I will loose a pack of nightmares among her little tribe of stitchlings and drive them to tear down the Thirteenth Tower, till there is nothing left but a heap of rubble! DO I MAKE MYSELF CLEAR?"*

As he spoke, he moved toward Knotchek as though to strike him again. The stitchling drew itself up into a little ball of terror and waited to be brutalized.

But the blow never fell. Houlihan had emerged from the gallery, smiling.

"She's found!" he exclaimed.

Carrion waved Knotchek away. "Go. Tell her," he said.

Knotchek fled into the crimson mist and was gone.

"A problem, sir?" Houlihan said.

"Only my grandmother. She has too many fancy ideas about herself. One of these days she's going to go too far. So . . . you say you've found her? Show me."

Houlihan led Carrion back inside. The same image was now playing on all sixteen screens of Voorzangler's device. The white-suited cyclops had a smug smile on his face.

"She was in the Yebba Dim Day, in a house down on Krux Street, which is in the Fishermen's Ghetto. I must say, my lord, I can't see *why* you would have any interest in her. She doesn't look like much."

"I'll be the judge of that," Carrion said.

He approached the screens. The images before him were crystal clear. There was the girl, staring straight at the eyes of the spy, which moved to keep her centered and focused whenever she turned or backed away.

Carrion turned to Mendelson Shape. "Are you *absolutely sure* that this is the girl who was with Mischief?"

Shape nodded.

"No doubt?"

"No, Lord. None."

Carrion returned his gaze to the screens. "So . . ." he said quietly, staring at the girl. *"Who are you?"* He continued to stare at the image for several seconds, as though his eyes were attempting to interrogate the screen. Then he glanced around at Voorzangler.

"When did this happen?"

"Three hours ago. Maybe four."

"So she's probably still in the Yebba Dim Day. What do you think, Otto?"

"There have been some troubles there," Voorzangler said, before Houlihan had a chance to respond. "The dock collapsed. So there have been no boats getting out these last couple of hours."

"So she *is* still there," Houlihan said.

"What's the big deal?" Voorzangler said. "She's just—"

Carrion suddenly raised his finger to silence the doctor and stared with renewed intensity at the image on the screens. The stranger from the Hereafter had become angry, and her face—recorded by the very thing that was irritating her—had changed.

The girlishness had gone out of it. A young woman had been ignited by the fury she felt.

The change had Carrion entranced.

"Now what is this?" he said, so, so softly. He narrowed his eyes, taking off his glove and putting his naked hand on one of the screens as if wishing he could reach into it and seize hold of the girl herself.

"Do I know you?" he said, his voice even more mellifluous. "I do, don't I?"

The screen suddenly went blank. Carrion let out a little sob of pain, as though he'd been woken from a trance.

"It ends there," Voorzangler said.

Carrion didn't speak for a long while.

He simply continued to stare at the blank screen with an expression of profound bemusement on his face. Voorzangler opened his mouth to speak again, but Houlihan hushed him with a sharp look.

Finally, after fully two minutes, Carrion said: "Shape?"

"Yes, Lord."

"Go to Vesper's Rock and wait for me there."

"Am I to go after the girl?"

"Oh yes. You are to go after her. But not by glyph. I'm going to give you something a little more in keeping with the significance of your mission."

"I don't understand."

"Just *go*," Carrion said, still staring at the blank screen.

Shape hurried away.

"There is something in that face, Otto, that makes me think my enemies are wilier than I suspected. They play with dreams now."

"Dreams?" asked the Criss-Cross Man.

"Yes, Otto. I have dreamed that face. That innocent face. But who . . . ?" He glanced up and met Voorzangler's strange stare. "Oh, are you still here?" he said to the doctor. "You may go. Thank Mr. Pixler for his kindness, will you?"

"The Universal Eye," Voorzangler said. "I have to return to Commexo City with it."

"No," said Carrion, very plainly. "I'll keep it here for now."

"No, no, no, you, you, you don't understand," Voorzangler said, panic making his words skip. "The, the science of, of—"

"—is of *no* interest to me, Voorzangler. So don't fret yourself. I won't be stealing back any of your precious Verities. It's *her* I'm interested in. And until I have the real thing in front of me, I will keep your Universal Eye."

"It's, it's just not, just not—"

The doctor didn't get to finish his reply. Carrion was on him in a heartbeat, his hands at the man's throat. Voorzangler tried to drag Carrion's huge grasp away from his windpipe, but his own thin little fingers weren't equal to the job.

Carrion lifted him off the floor; his feet were dangling in the air.

"You were saying, Doctor?" Carrion said.

The life was rapidly going out of Doctor Voorzangler. His conjoined eyes were becoming glassy. His limbs were jangling as though he was having a fit.

"We might need Mr. Pixler's help in the future," Houlihan remarked casually.

Carrion chewed on this for a moment. Then he took his hands off Voorzangler. The man dropped to a gasping, sobbing heap at the Lord of Midnight's feet.

"Take him outside."

Houlihan hauled the doctor up and dragged him toward the door, pausing only to pluck the controls to the Universal Eye out of Voorzangler's pocket.

Once he'd deposited him outside the gallery door, he returned to await Carrion's next instruction. When it came, it was simple enough.

"Show me the girl again," Carrion said. "Then you can go."

Voorzangler's device was easy to work. The image of the girl from the Hereafter was soon called up onto the screen again, ready to be replayed and replayed.

"Arrange a glyph to take me to Vesper's Rock," Carrion said as he stared at the images of Candy. "I want five corpses there, waiting for me. The usual place. Get some off the gallows. But they have to be old. I'm going to need *dust*."

He stared at the screens.

"Dust for the girl from the Hereafter." He smiled to himself. "It's the least I can do."

17

ALMENAK

GIVEN HOW CLOSE TOGETHER the cottages were, Candy had fully expected to find a small crowd outside Izarith's door, drawn there by the noise of their fight with the insect. But there was far more interest in what was going on down at the dock; everybody was headed that way. So Candy made her way up the street, against the flow of the crowd. She was much more aware of the insect population now. Which of the numberless creatures buzzing around was a spy, like the one in Izarith's house? Every now and then something whined past her ear, and she swatted it away. None, she was pleased to see, came back.

The street had broad shallow steps, which made climbing a little easier. Even so, the labor of walking soon began to take its toll on her. The short sleep she'd had in front of the fire in Izarith's cottage had not been sufficient to fully restore her.

What she still needed, she knew, was some food. There were a number of stalls set out to the left and right of her on the steps, and they seemed to be selling a variety of edible goods: dried fish were hanging up on one stall (*not* her first choice); at another somebody was deep frying something that looked remarkably like a doughnut, especially when it had been dusted with sugar. She dug in the pockets of the little dress Izarith had given her and pulled out the six dollars she had kept. Perhaps it wasn't wise to use them, she thought. They marked her out as an alien here.

That left two options. She could either beg for food or steal it. Since she was in urgent need of sustenance, in her present situation morality didn't really enter the picture. She looked up the street a little way. One stall seemed to have been deserted by its owner, who'd probably gone down to the dock with the rest of the crowd.

As she started to make her way toward the empty stall there was a surge of noise behind her, and a portion of the crowd, along with a number of police officers, came back, all gathered around three or four people who had clearly been pulled out of the water.

"Make way! Make way!" one of the officers yelled. *"We've got injured people here!"*

That was, of course, precisely the wrong thing to say. As soon as the words escaped from his lips, more spectators appeared to swell the crowd, eager to see how horrible the injuries were. Many of them clogged the street ahead of the advancing throng. The officer began to yell again. But people wanted to see, and no amount of shouting from a police officer was going to stop them getting a glimpse.

It was a curiously familiar scene. Watching it,

Candy flashed on something that had happened four or five years ago, back home—or in the Hereafter, as she now thought of home. The family had been on a midsummer trip to see Grandma Hattie, Melissa's mother's mother, in Pelican Rapids. They'd been on Highway 94, and the trip had been going smoothly until suddenly the traffic had ground almost to a complete halt.

For the next hour and a half they had crawled along. The air conditioning in the car was not working properly so the heat was ferocious. It made everybody bad-tempered.

It had quickly become clear that the problem up ahead was a collision, and Candy's father had started to rage on about the fact that the real reason the traffic had come to a halt was because people were slowing down to see the wreckage.

"Damn *lookeeloos*! Everybody has to slow down and take a look! It's *sick*! Why can't people mind their own damn business?"

Of course, half an hour of sweat and curses later, when the Quackenbushes' car finally came up to the accident site, Candy's father had slowed down just like everybody else. In fact he had almost brought the line to a complete halt so that he could watch a body being brought out from under one of the seven vehicles— trucks, cars and an eight-wheeler rig—that were involved in the collision.

Candy should have known better, but her tongue had been quicker than her self-protective instincts. "I thought you told us it was sick, Dad?" she'd said.

Without missing a beat, Bill Quackenbush had leaned back between the seats and slapped her hard.

"Don't you give me cheek!"

"I just said—"

He slapped her again, harder.

"Enough, Bill," Candy's mother had said.

"I'll be the judge of that," came the reply, and just to show that he didn't care about his wife's opinion, he slapped Candy a third time, bringing tears to her eyes.

As she wiped them away, she caught sight of her mother in the mirror throwing an accusatory glance up at her husband. Bill Quackenbush had not seen the look: he was still staring at the bloody scene across the highway. But Candy had read the look clearly, and in the confusion of feelings she had for her father, it had given her a kind of sad satisfaction to see the cold loathing in her mother's eyes. But it wasn't enough. Why didn't she ever stick up for Candy—or herself? Why was she so weak?

All of this came back to Candy while she was watching the crowd come up the street, as clear as if it had happened yesterday. The heat of the car; the smell of her brothers' sweat and farts; her own discomfort and boredom. Then the horrible sight of the tangled wreckage; and the moment of regret when she'd spoken but it was too late to take the words back; followed by the slap and the tears and her mother's glacial stare.

That was the world she'd left. Boredom, violence and tears.

Whatever lay ahead of her here, she thought, it had to be better than that. It *had* to be.

She looked away from the crowd back up the street, to see that more than one stall had been deserted by their owners, who had all hurried down to see what could be seen.

She went up two or three steps, to a stall with a variety of pastries laid out on it. The display looked very similar to something she might have found in the supermarket in Chickentown, only tastier. Turnovers, croissants, sticks of bread rolled in dried fruit and a variety of small cakes.

She selected three very quickly: two turnovers and one huge scone; and then, greedily, went back for a croissant. Having got herself more than a meal's worth, she glanced up and down the street, just to check that the vendor wasn't making his or her return. It seemed she was free and clear. She hurried away, clamping one turnover between her teeth and pocketing the other three pastries. Then she went on up the street and found a low stone wall where she could sit and eat.

The pastry was doughy, perhaps undercooked, but the filling was extremely sweet, with an odd, almost peppery edge, which she didn't like on the first bite but quickly changed her mind about. While she ate, her eyes went to a large advertisement on the opposite side of the street. It showed a deliriously happy boy, drawn in a cartoony style, with baggy striped pants and a big curl of blue hair, like a wave about to break, in the center of his head. He was animated by carefully laid lines of neon light and was walking on the spot, waving as he walked.

Beside him, on the wall, was a sign that read:

The Commexo Kid says:
FOR EVERYTHING THAT AILS YOU,
FROM TOE-ROT TO TAXES,
TRY THE PANACEA.

Candy laughed, her mood—which had been darkened by her memories of the events on Highway 94—lightening again.

And then, from the corner of her eye a figure appeared. A man dressed in a blue coat, wearing a spotted all-in-one suit underneath, stepped into view.

"I saw you," he said.

"You saw me do what?"

"Take the pastries."

"Oh, dear."

"It's okay," the man said, sitting down on the wall beside her. "As long as you share."

He was smiling as he spoke, so it seemed the threat, such as it was, carried no weight. Candy pulled the scone out of her pocket and broke it in half.

"Here," she said, handing one half over to her new companion.

"Most generous," he replied, rather formally. "And you are?"

"Candy Quackenbush. And you are?"

"Samuel Hastrim Klepp. The Fifth. Here." He fished a little pamphlet, printed on coarse brown paper, out of his pocket.

"What is this?"

"*Klepp's Almenak*; first published by my great-great-grandfather, Samuel Hastrim Klepp the First. This is the new edition."

Candy took the pamphlet and flicked through its pages. It was rather chaotically designed, its illustrations in black and white, but it was packed to the margins with information. There were maps, gaming rules, a page or two of astrology, and a few pages of pictures of what the author described as *New Animals*, which was an interesting notion. Further pages listed Celestial Events (the times of meteor showers and eclipses), even a collection of recipes. And interspersed between these relatively commonplace pieces were articles with a rather more Abaratian twist: "The Cat's Hair Cathedral: Myth or Reality?" "The Dung-Jewels of Efreet: A Gatherer's Tale." And "The Golden Warrior: Alive or Dead?"

"So you publish this?" Candy said.

"Yes. And I sell it here in The Great Head and in Tazmagor and Candlemas and Kikador. But there's not much of a market for it any longer. People can get all the information they need from *him*." He jerked his finger, rather rudely, at the Commexo Kid.

"He doesn't exist, does he? I mean that kid?"

"No, not yet. But take it from me, it's only a matter of time."

"You *are* joking?"

"No, not at all," Samuel said. "These people over at Commexo City, Rojo Pixler and his gang, have *plans* for us. And I don't think any of us are going to like what they have up their sleeve."

Candy looked at him blankly.

"You don't know what I'm talking about, do you?"

"Not exactly, no."

"Where are you from?" Samuel said.

"Oh . . . here and there."

Samuel put his hand on her arm. "Tell me," he said. "I can keep a secret."

"I guess there's no reason why you shouldn't know," Candy said. "I came over from the other world. You call it the Hereafter."

A broad grin came over Samuel Klepp's face. "You did?" he said. "Well, isn't that something! I thought when I first laid eyes on you stealing those cakes: there's something about that girl . . ." He shook his head, his expression one of delight. "You see, a lot of people think the Hereafter is a myth, but I've *always* believed in it. So did my father and my father's father, all the way back to Samuel Hastrim Klepp the First. Tell me more, please. I want to know everything about the Hereafter."

"Really?" said Candy. "I don't think it's very interesting."

"Well, it might not be to *you*, because you were born there. But *my* readers need to hear about your world. They need to know the truth."

"But if people think it's all just a myth, how will you make anyone believe it?"

"Put it this way: I think it's better to *try* to get them to believe in new things than just to be content to have Commexo run their lives. *Curing everything from toe-rot to taxes!* I ask you! How ridiculous can you get?"

There was a new commotion from farther down the street, as more drowned or nearly drowned people were brought in from the docks. Klepp made a face.

"I'll never be able to hear you talking over that din and hullabaloo. Why don't you come back to the Press with me—?"

"The Press?"

"The place where I print the *Almenak*. I can show you a little of *my* world, while you tell me about *yours*. How does that sound?"

"Sure," said Candy. She was happy to get off the street, to be away from all the noise and confusion, so that she could gather her thoughts.

"Then let's depart, before the pastry cook comes back and counts her scones," Samuel said mischievously, and led Candy away up the long stairs to the heart of the city.

18

THE TALE OF HARK'S HARBOR

THEY PASSED SEVERAL MORE images of the Commexo Kid as they made their way to Klepp's Press. He was on a poster advertising his cinematic adventures: *The Commexo Kid and the Wardogs*, and there were several more advertisements for his Panacea. His face was on the T-shirts of children who ran by, and the toys they were playing with were plastic versions of the Commexo Kid.

"Do you have anything like this in the Hereafter?" Klepp said.

"Things like the Kid?"

"Yes. You can't escape him."

Candy thought about this. "Not *one* thing," she said. "Not like the Kid. He seems to be everywhere."

"He is," said Klepp grimly. "You see the Commexo Company has this promise: they will take care of you from the cradle to the grave, literally. They have Commexo Kid Maternity Hospitals and a Commexo Kid Funeral Service. And in between, while you're living your life, there's nothing they can't supply.

Food for your table. Clothes for your back. Toys for your children . . ."

"What does Commexo want?" Candy said.

"It's not Commexo, it's the man who owns Commexo: Rojo Pixler. It's what *he* wants . . ."

"And what's that?"

"Control. Of all of us. Of all the islands. He wants to be King of the World. He wouldn't use the word *king* because it's old-fashioned. But it's what he wants."

"And you think he'll get what he wants?"

Klepp shrugged. "Probably," he said.

They were almost at the top of the hill now, and Samuel paused to look up at a sculpted version of the Commexo Kid that was mounted on the building that awaited them at the end of their journey. It was huge.

"Behind that happy smile," he said, "is a very cold mind. Cold and clever. Which is why he's the richest man in the islands and the rest of us are left buying his Panacea."

"You too?"

"Me too," Klepp said, sounding almost ashamed of his confession. "When I get sick, I drink his Panacea like everybody else."

"Does it work?"

"Well, that's the trouble," Samuel said. "It does. It makes me feel better, whether I've got a bellyache or a bad back."

He shook his head despairingly and dug in his pocket, pulling out a bunch of keys. Selecting one, he led Candy to a little door, which was so dwarfed by the statue of the kid that she would have missed it if Klepp hadn't led her to it.

As he put the key in the lock he spoke again, his voice now the lowest of whispers.

"You know what I heard?"

"No, what?"

"Now this is just a rumor. Maybe it's nonsense. I hope it's nonsense. But I heard that Rojo Pixler has approached the Council of Magicians to buy the Conjuration of Life."

"What's that?"

"What does it sound like?"

Candy pondered on this for a moment. "The Conjuration of Life?" she said. "Well, it sounds like something that raises the dead."

"You're right. It's certainly been used for that purpose in the past. Though the results are unpredictable. And they can be grotesque, sometimes tragic. But no, that's not what Pixler wants it for."

"What then?" Candy said. Then her eyes grew wide. "No," she said. "Not the Kid?"

"Yes," said Samuel. "He wants to use the Conjuration to give life to the Commexo Kid. According to my sources, he was refused. Which, if any of this is true, is all good."

"What was his response?"

"Outrage. He flung a fit. He kept saying: *The Kid is a joy bringer! You can't deny him life! He could spread so much happiness.*"

"But you don't believe that? About being a joy bringer?"

"Here's what I believe," said Samuel. "I believe that if Pixler had the Conjuration of Life, we wouldn't just have *one* living, breathing Kid. There'd be *armies* of them! All of them wearing that idiotic smile as they took over the islands." He shuddered. "Horrible."

He turned the key in the lock and pushed open the door. The smell of printer's ink stung Candy's nostrils.

"Before you come inside, I should warn you," Klepp said, "it's chaos."

Then he swung the door wide. Chaos it was; from ceiling to floor. There was a small printing press in the middle of the room and dozens of unruly piles of *Klepp's Almenak* on every side. Clearly Samuel slept in the midst of his work, because there was an old sofa against the wall, with pillows and a couple of blankets strewn upon it.

But what immediately drew Candy's eye was a number of faded sepia photographs that were framed and hung up on one of the walls. The first in the series pictured the lighthouse where Candy's journey had begun.

"Oh, my . . ." she said.

Klepp came over to look at the pictures with her.

"You know this place?"

"Yes, of course. It's near my home in Chickentown."

She moved on to the next picture. It was a photograph of the jetty that had appeared from the ground when she'd summoned the Sea of Izabella. The picture had been taken at a busy and apparently happy time. There were people crowding the jetty from end to end, some dressed in what looked to be frock coats and top hats, others—the stevedores and the sailors—more simply attired. Moored at the end of the jetty was a three-masted sailing ship.

A sailing ship! In the middle of Minnesota. Even now, having walked on the jetty and skipped that sea, the notion still astonished Candy.

"Do you know when this was taken?" Candy asked Klepp.

"1882 by your calendar, I believe," Samuel said.

He moved on to the next photograph, which showed the other end of the jetty, where there were several two-story buildings, stores advertising ship's supplies and what looked like a hotel.

"There's my great-grandfather," Samuel said, pointing to a man who bore an uncanny resemblance to him.

"Who's the lady beside him?"

That's his wife, Vida Klepp."

"She was beautiful."

"She left him, the day after this photograph was taken."

"Really?" said Candy, her thoughts going for a moment to Henry Murkitt, who had also lost his wife when he'd turned his attention to the Abarat.

"Where did she go?" Candy said.

"Vida Klepp? Nobody knows for sure. She took herself off with a man from Autland and was never seen again. Whatever happened to her, wherever she went, it nearly broke my great-grandfather's heart. He only went back to Hark's Harbor once after that . . ."

"Hark's Harbor? That's the name of this place?"

"Yes. It was the largest of the harbors that served the Abarat, so that's where all the big ships came. The clippers and the schooners."

Of all things to think of at that moment, Candy pictured Miss Schwartz, instructing her class to find ten interesting facts about Chickentown. *Well, how about this?* Candy thought. What would the look on Miss Schwartz's face have been had Candy brought these pictures in to show the class? That would have been quite a moment.

"It's all gone now, of course," Samuel said.

"Not all of it," Candy replied. "That jetty—" She tapped the glass covering the photograph. "—is still there. And the lighthouse. But all the rest of it—these stores, for instance—they've all gone. I suppose they must have rotted away over the years."

"Oh no, they didn't rot," Klepp said. "Remember I said my great-grandfather went back there one last time?"

"Yes."

"Well, it was for the *burning* of Hark's Harbor."

"The burning?"

"Look."

Samuel moved on to the next to last photograph in the sequence. It showed a somewhat blurred image, perhaps the consequence of an old-fashioned plate camera capturing a scene filled with movement. The photograph was of the burning of the harbor. The buildings at the end of the jetty were all on fire, with smeared bright flames shooting out of the windows and through the doors. There was no attempt to put the fire out, as far as Candy could see. People were just standing along the jetty, watching the spectacle. She couldn't make out their expressions.

"Was it arson?"

"Well, it wasn't an accident," Klepp said. "But it wasn't strictly arson either. It was a piece of authorized destruction."

"I don't understand."

"As I told you, Hark's Harbor was the place where most of the business between the islands and the Hereafter was done. It was a very busy place. Sometimes there were as many as ten ships unloading and loading every day. There were cargoes of Abaratian wine and spices from the islands. And slaves, of course."

"And these people knew where the slaves came from?" Candy said, amazed by the idea. "People knew about the Abarat?"

"Oh yes, they knew," Klepp said. "But it wasn't common knowledge, you understand. There was a select circle of merchants from your world who liked doing business over here, and they did a roaring trade. Obviously they didn't want to have to divide the profit, so they didn't share the secret. And then of course there were merchants over here who imported art and plants and animals from the Hereafter, and made a fine business out of that."

"So why the burning?"

"Greed," said Samuel. "In the end everybody began to get greedy. The Abaratian merchants started to sell things that should never have been seen in your world.

Magical treasures that were stolen out of temples and dug up from burial sites, then sold in the Hereafter for enormous sums of money. Obviously, this couldn't go on. Our people were being soiled by the ways of your world, and probably vice versa. There were bitter disputes. Some ended in murder.

"No doubt there was fault on both sides, but my great-grandfather was of the opinion that the Hereafter was a place of infinite corruption. He said in the *Almenak* that it would wither the soul of a saint. Now he had a reason to hate the Hereafter: it had claimed his wife. But I believe he was probably right. The trade between the Hereafter and the Abarat corrupted everyone. The merchants, the seamen and probably the people who bought the merchandise in the end."

"That's sad."

Klepp nodded. "It's a tragic tale," he said. "Anyway, it was decided that the trade had to stop. No more selling of Abaratian slaves, or magic."

"So the harbor was burned down?"

"To almost nothing," Klepp said. He moved on to look at the last photograph in the sequence. It showed the gutted buildings, still smoking. And a row of people along the jetty, waiting to board a clipper ship.

"The last ship out," Klepp said. "My great-grandfather was on it. This is the final picture he took in your world."

"Amazing," said Candy. "But look." She pointed to the lighthouse, which was visible in the picture beside the clipper, clearly undamaged by the fire. "Why did they leave the lighthouse intact?"

Klepp shrugged. "Who knows? Maybe one of your people paid somebody to leave it there, in the hope that business would one day resume. Or perhaps they thought it would fall apart in its own time."

"Well, it didn't," Candy said. "Not completely."

"I'd like to see it one of these days," Klepp said. "Maybe get some photographs for the *Almenak*. Before and after, you know? That would sell a few copies! Of course a lot of people would probably say I'd faked it."

"People really don't believe my world exists, do they?" Candy said.

"It depends who you ask. The ordinary man in the street? No. He thinks the Hereafter is a story to tell his children at night."

Candy smiled.

"What's so funny?" Klepp said.

"Oh, just the idea that the world where I live is a story for kids. What do they say about it?"

"Oh, that it's a place where time goes on forever. And where there are cities the size of an island. That it's a place full of wonders."

"Well they'd be very disappointed if they knew the truth."

"I don't believe that."

"One day maybe I'll get to show you."

"I'd like that," said Klepp. "In the meanwhile, do you want a bird's-eye view of my world?"

"Of course."

"Come with me then."

He led her to a small door on the far side of the

room. It had an iron gate in front of it, which opened like a concertina.

"My private elevator," Klepp said, pulling the gate open. "All the way up to the top of the towers."

Candy stepped inside and Klepp followed, closing the gate behind him.

"Hang on tight," he said, turning an antiquated handle that was marked with two directions: *Up* and *Down*.

The elevator ascended with much creaking and complaint, sometimes passing an opening that gave Candy a tantalizing glimpse of the interior of the towers that were perched on top of The Great Head. Eventually, the elevator began to slow down and finally, with a loud grinding noise, came to a halt.

Candy could already smell the clean sea air, a pleasant contrast to the smoky interior of the Yebba Dim Day and the printing ink stench of the Almenak Press.

"Now, please," Samuel cautioned, "I urge you to be careful up here. The view is wonderful; however, we're very high up. I don't believe anybody comes up here but me. It's too dangerous. But you'll be fine as long as you take care."

His warning offered, Samuel opened the gate and led Candy up a narrow flight of steps. At the top was a grille, which he lifted up and threw back with a loud clang.

"After you," he said, moving aside to allow Candy to step out of the stairway and into the open air.

19

ON VESPER'S ROCK

MENDELSON SHAPE HAD BEEN to Vesper's Rock on several previous occasions, doing little pieces of grim business for Carrion. Its name was in every way deceptive. For one thing, it was a good deal more than a rock. It was a collection of enormous boulders, perhaps fifteen in all, the smallest of them the size of a house, all surrounded by a wide beach—if that was the appropriate term for something so charmless and uncomfortable—made up of millions of smaller boulders, rocks, stones and pebbles. Though Shape had once been told that if he listened closely he would hear the voices of sweet spirits singing lullabies as they circled the island, he had never heard anything so reassuring. Quite the contrary. The Rock was home to a species of malignant night bird called a qwat, and it was their relentless screeching out of the cracks of the boulders that greeted any visitor there.

Tonight, however, the qwat birds were as silent as those rumored spirit-voices, for Christopher Carrion was on Vesper's Rock, and even the most raucous bird was hiding its head rather than risk attracting the attention of the Lord of Midnight.

Carrion was working in a cavern formed by several boulders, a place he often used for conjurations, especially when he wanted to work out of sight of his grandmother. She had so many spies at Midnight, it was virtually impossible to do anything in secret. Vesper's Rock presented Carrion with the ideal spot for his private experiments, being close enough to Midnight for convenient travel and small enough that he could readily defend it with talismans.

Now, in his unholy place between the boulders, he had one of his grandmother's stitchlings at work pounding the remains of five mummified human cadavers to dust. The pounder's name was Ignacio, and he was one of Mater Motley's uglier creations, of which fact he was agonizingly aware. He hated the Hag (as he had dubbed her) for what she'd done to him, and though she often called him to service in the Thirteenth Tower, he escaped her summonings whenever he could to do odd jobs for Carrion.

"Are you done with the corpse dust yet?" Carrion said.

"Almost."

"Well, hurry. I don't have all night." Carrion allowed himself a smile. "Though one of these days," he murmured to himself, "I will."

"Will, *what*, Lord?"

"Have all night."

Ignacio nodded, not understanding, and continued to beat the bones. A cloud of human dust rose into his face. He sneezed, and spat out a wad of phlegm and dust. Then he hammered on for a minute or more just to be sure the job was properly done. Carrion was a perfectionist, and he wanted to please the Nightmare Man, which was Ignacio's secret name for the Lord of Midnight.

Eventually, he stood up, hammer in hand, and surveyed his handiwork.

"I always think they look better this way," he said.

"Everybody looks better that way," Carrion said, pressing Ignacio aside. "Go and alert Shape. He's down at the beach eating."

"Should we come straight back up?" Ignacio said.

He knew very well that some piece of secret conjuration was about to take place and was eager to witness it.

"*No,*" said Carrion. "You'll know when the work's done. Now get out of here."

Ignacio retreated, leaving the Lord of Midnight to crouch down and put his finger into the pounded bones, like a child about to make mud pies. The Nightmare Man paused for a moment, breathing in two lungfuls of the fluid that seethed around his head before he began the labors before him. Then, fortified by the horrible visions that filled his every fiber, he began to draw in the dust the outline of the thing he intended to raise from it.

Ignacio found Mendelson Shape, whom he knew a little from various labors they'd performed together for Carrion, sitting on the starlit beach beside a small cairn of pebbles. He was adding his own choice of stones to the pile.

"Done eating?" Ignacio said.

"I killed something, then I wasn't hungry," Mendelson said, glancing over at the immense overturned crab, its leg span fully six feet, which lay a little way down the beach. Mendelson had torn out its underbelly and begun to eat the cold meat of the thing, but hadn't got very far.

"May I?" said Ignacio.

"Help yourself."

"Pity to let it go to waste."

He went to the crab and proceeded to plunge his hands into its gray-green entrails, claiming two healthy fistfuls of its bitter guts, his favorite portion of the animal, in part because it was the most despised. He was one of the rare—perhaps blessed—stitchlings who ate. Most of his kind had no means of digestion and elimination. Ignacio was a happy exception. Two thirds of his body were still functioning as ordinary human anatomy. He was plagued by constipation, and consequently, piles, but it was a small price to pay for the pleasure of eating the meat of a crab that still had a couple of nervous twitches in it.

He glanced back up the beach at Mendelson.

"What are you here to do?" he asked.

"I'm here to ride whatever he's raising back there," Mendelson said gloomily. "And then I'm to fetch some girl for him."

"Is he thinking of getting married then?"

"Not to this one," Mendelson said sourly.

"You know her?"

"We've had our encounters. She comes from the Hereafter."

"Really?"

Ignacio seized the crab by one of its spiny legs and hauled the carcass up over the stones to where Mendelson squatted.

"You went to the Hereafter?" he said.

Shape shrugged. "Yeah," he said.

"And? What was it like?"

"What do you mean, what was it like? Oh. You mean: is it heaven?" He looked up at Ignacio, his beady eyes bright with contempt, even in the murk. "Is that what you think?"

"No," Ignacio said defensively. "Not necessarily."

"Angels guiding the souls of the dead to the immortal cities of light? The way the old preachers used to tell it?"

"I don't believe in all that nonsense," Ignacio said, concealing his true hopes on the matter, which had indeed been optimistic. He'd liked the idea that somewhere beyond the Sea of Izabella lay a world where a stitchling such as himself might be healed, his hurts melted away, his mismatchings erased. But much as he wanted to believe in what the preachers pronounced, he trusted Shape.

"So, this girl . . ." he went on, cracking the crab's huge claws and trying to sound indifferent to the news he'd just heard.

"Candy Quackenbush?"

"That's her name?"

"That's her name."

"She followed you here, and now you have to kill her?"

"I don't know if he wants her killed."

"But if he does?"

"Then I kill her."

"How?"

"I don't know yet, Ignacio. Why do you ask all these stupid questions?"

"Because one day I want to be doing what you're doing."

"If you think it's some great honor, it's not."

"It's better than digging up mummified bodies. You get to travel to the Hereafter."

"It's nothing special," Shape said. "Now help me up." He put out his arm so that Ignacio could haul him up onto his foot and stump. "I'm getting old, Ignacio. Old and tired."

"You need an assistant," Ignacio said eagerly. "I could assist you. I could!"

Shape glanced at Ignacio, shaking his head. "I work alone," he said.

"Why?"

"Because I only like the company of one person."

"Who?"

"Me, you fool. *Me!*"

"Oh . . ."

Shape looked back to the boulders where Carrion was working. He had noticed something that Ignacio, in the midst of his envious chatter, had failed to catch.

"The birds," he said.

The qwat birds, which had been silent in their crannies since Carrion's arrival on the island, had risen into the air above the Rock without uttering a sound, and were now hovering in a vast black cloud, wingtip to wingtip, overhead.

"That's something rare," Ignacio said, the wreckage of his stitched and overstitched face registering something close to wonder.

He had no sooner set eyes on the flock than from the place among the boulders where Carrion was working there came a flicker of dark blue-purple light, followed by another, this time orange-red, followed by a third, the hue of bone. The colors rose into the air above the rocks, driving the cloud of qwats still higher, and there colors broke into fragments, darts and slivers of light interlacing, performing an elaborate dance.

At this moment, the creator appeared from between the rocks, his hands raised in front of him as though he were conducting a symphony. Perhaps, in a sense, he was. Certainly the colors seemed to be responding to the subtle gestures he was making. They were becoming steadily more solid as he knitted them together.

Then, very gently he brought them down out of the air. At his silent instruction they settled on the long flat boulder that was the highest point of Vesper's Rock. There, finally, they began to cohere and form a recognizable shape.

"Is that what you're going to fly on?" Ignacio said, his voice barely more than a whisper.

"Apparently."

"Good luck," he said.

A vast *moth*, its hairy abdomen twelve feet long, and four or five times thicker than Shape's body, was now perched on the rock, its newly formed anatomy still shedding flecks of color.

Apart from its gargantuan size, it was close in appearance to a commonplace moth. It had long, feathery antennae and six long, fine legs.

But it wasn't until Carrion ordered it to *"Fly! Let me see you fly!"* that its true eloquence was revealed.

When it rose up above the island and spread its wings, the markings on them seemed to resemble a vast, screaming face, unfolding against the sky then folding again, then again unfolding. It was as though heaven itself was giving vent to its anguish, as beat upon beat the great creature ascended.

"Shape!" Carrion yelled.

"Yes sir! I'm coming."

Carrion was gesturing to the creature, summoning it back down onto the rock. Shape came to his side.

"Lord."

"Prettier than a glyph, don't you think?" Carrion said, as the moth settled on the long boulder.

"Yes, Lord."

"Climb on its back and fetch me that girl," the Lord of Midnight instructed.

"Does it know where to look?"

"It will take your direction. But I suggest you start at the Yebba Dim Day. And don't try and get clever with it. It may not have much of a brain, but I can *see* what it *sees*, and I can *feel* what it *feels*. That's why

I'm sending you on this, and not a glyph. So if you try to trick me in *any way*—"

"Trick you?" Shape protested. "Lord, why would I—"

"The girl is *mine*, Shape. Don't think you can fly away with her. You understand me? You bring her right back to the Twelfth Tower."

"I understand."

"There's something about her that makes me uneasy. I want to know why she was brought here—"

"I told you, Lord. It was an accident. I saw it all."

"I don't believe in accidents, Shape. Everything is working toward some greater plan."

"Really?"

"Yes."

"Do I have a place in that plan?"

Carrion gave Shape a hollow stare.

"Yes, Shape. Unlikely as it seems, I suppose even *you* have a purpose. Now *go*. The longer you wait the more chance that she's moved on."

"I'll find her for you," Shape promised.

"And—"

"Yes. I know. I'll bring her straight back here to Midnight. Straight back to you."

20

THE WORLD THROUGH
BORROWED EYES

OF ONE THING CANDY was absolutely certain: there was no sight on earth to equal the view from the top of the colossal head of the Yebba Dim Day. Wherever she looked from that high, windswept platform, she saw wonders.

She had help, of course. Not only did she have Samuel Hastrim Klepp the Fifth by her side to point out things (and to occasionally catch hold of her arm when a particularly strong gust of wind threatened to carry her over the edge of The Great Head), he had also supplied two very accommodating squid, which clung to their heads, and then so positioned their boneless bodies that their eyes—which were immensely strong—could be used as telescopic lenses.

Klepp's squid were his pets. One he had called Squbb and the other Squiller. At first Candy found it a little odd to be *wearing* a living creature, but she supposed it was like any animal that worked with a human companion: a horse, a dog, a trained rat. It was just one more reminder that she was *not* in Chickentown.

"If you want to get closer to something," Klepp said to Candy, "just say *'A little closer if you don't mind, Squiller.'* Or: *'A little farther away if you don't mind, Squiller.'* It's important you be precise and polite in the way you speak to them. They're very particular about the little courtesies."

Candy didn't have any difficulty getting the trick of this, and after only a minute or two Squiller had made himself so much at home on her head that it was no more peculiar than wearing a hat that had been left in a box of fish for a few days.

Certainly Squiller appeared to be eager to give Candy the best possible view of the Abarat. Half the time, she didn't even need to ask him to alter his focus. He seemed to know what she wanted instinctively; as though he was reading the brain waves coming off her skull. Candy didn't entirely discount the possibility. She'd read back at home that squid showed extraordinary means of communicating with one another; how much more likely was it that the equivalent species here would be blessed with some miraculous power? The whole world was filled with magic. At least that was the impression Klepp gave her as he named the islands of the archipelago and spoke of the miracles they contained.

"Every island is a different Hour of the day," he began by saying. "And on each island you'll find all the things that our hearts and souls and minds and imaginations connect with that Hour. Look there."

He pointed toward a place not far from the Straits of Dusk.

"You see that island wreathed in light and cloud?"

Candy saw it. The cloud rose in a rolling spiral around what looked to be a vast mountain, or perhaps a tower of gargantuan size.

"What is it?" Candy asked Klepp.

"The *Twenty-Fifth Hour*," he replied. "Sometimes called Odom's Spire. It's a place of mysteries and dreams."

"Who lives there?"

"That's one of those mysteries. Though I have heard the name Fantomaya associated with the place, I have no idea what it means."

Candy's new squiddy friend Squiller did his best to focus on the clouds around Odom's Spire, but for some reason the billowing spiral prevented her closer scrutiny.

"If you're looking for a glimpse of what's on the other side of the cloud," Klepp said, "don't bother. The light plays tricks with the eyes, somehow, and you just can't get a good grip on it. Then sometimes the clouds will part and give you the *illusion* that you're going to see something—"

"But you never do?"

"Not to my knowledge."

"So what would happen if you sailed a ship right into the clouds?"

"Oh, people have certainly tried that," Klepp said. "A few came out alive, but happily crazy. And of course completely incapable of describing anything they'd seen, while the rest—"

"—didn't come out at all?"

"You guessed it. One of them was my father . . ." He let this information hang in the air for a moment. Then he said: "You look cold, my dear."

"It's just the wind."

"Let me get you a jacket."

"No, I'm all right."

"I insist," Klepp said. "I don't want you getting pneumonia. I'll be back in a moment."

He headed for the elevator. Candy didn't protest. The wind was a lot chillier than she'd expected it to be.

"You stay away from the edge now!" Samuel said, and pulling the elevator gate closed, he disappeared from sight.

While he was gone, Candy and Squiller kept up their perusal of the islands. Samuel had named them all for her several times, and Candy now tested her memory by putting the names to the locations. Some she remembered easily, others she had to puzzle over for a while.

The island to the west of the Yebba Dim Day was called Qualm Hah, and its red-roofed city was called . . . Tazmagor. Yes, that was it: Tazmagor. To the southeast of it was a mountainous island called Spake, which stood at Ten O'clock in the Morning. At Eleven O'clock was the Island of Nully, and at Twelve Noon, the island of Yzil, which was bathed in the warmest, most magical light imaginable.

At One O'clock was either Orlando's Cap or Hobarookus, she couldn't remember which. At Two, conversely, was either Hobarookus or Orlando's Cap.

To the south-southeast lay another sun-drenched

island, which was the place, she remembered, where Samuel had said life was supposed to have begun: Three O'clock in the Afternoon, also called the Nonce.

At Four was Gnomon, at Five an island called Soma Plume, in the center of which was a vast Ziggurat. At Six, far to the east of the Yebba Dim Day, though separated by only two hours, was an island called Babilonium, where it looked as though life was fun all the time. There were several huge circus tents pitched in the middle of the island, and colored lights in their tens of thousands flickered in the branches of every tree. *I have to go there,* Candy thought to herself.

To the north of Babilonium was an island the name of which she could not remember, though she remembered the name of the still-active volcano at its center, which was Mount Galigali. The tide of evening then wound around the archipelago, ending up where she was standing, at Eight in the Evening, looking down on the Straits of Dusk.

And then, in the vicinity of the Yebba Dim Day, lay a second series of islands. At Nine in the Evening was a place called Hap's Vault. (She'd asked Samuel who Hap was, and he'd told her he didn't remember.) At Ten in the Evening lay the island of Ninnyhammer, which had on it a town occupied by a species called tarrie-cats. The town was called High Sladder.

The name of the island at Eleven had skipped her mind, but she remembered the name of the Midnight Isle: Gorgossium. *It's the most terrifying place in all the islands,* Samuel Klepp had said: *avoid it at all costs!*

There were six pyramids—some large, some

small—at One in the Morning, which was called Xuxux, and at Two, another island, wreathed in darkness, the name of which escaped her. Next door to it, however, lay the island that was the most attractive to her eye, despite all that Samuel had said about its architect.

The island was called Pyon, and covering it from one end to the other (and so bright with light it couldn't have mattered that it was the middle of the night there) was Commexo City. The towers and the domes of Commexo City were completely unlike anything Candy had ever seen before: huge and elaborate configurations that looked as though they'd been conjured from a geometry that didn't exist back home, then raised in defiance of physics.

By contrast, the island beside it was an ominous place, with an impenetrable-looking mountain range. It was called The Isle of the Black Egg, and it was one of the Outer Islands, she remembered, along with Speckle Frew, which was at Five in the Morning. Beside Speckle Frew were the two islands, joined by the Gilholly Bridge that stood at Six and Seven in the Morning. That left only Obadiah, at Eight in the Morning, and she'd come full circle to the little sunlit city of Tazmagor, perched on the eastern flanks of Qualm Hah.

"You're looking rather pleased with yourself," said Klepp, as he emerged from the elevator. In his hand he had a light green jacket, covered with small bright-red designs. She accepted it gratefully and put it on.

"I was just trying to remember the islands," she told

him as she pulled the collar of the jacket up. "There were a few I couldn't remember, but I think I made quite a good—"

She stopped talking.

A terrible look had appeared on Klepp's face. His eyes had grown huge, and he was no longer looking at Candy, but instead was staring *past* her into the sky high above her left shoulder.

"What . . . is . . . it?" she said, almost scared to turn, but turning anyway.

"*Run!*" he yelled.

She heard him, but her feet failed to obey her. She was too astonished, and appalled, at the sight that filled the sky behind her.

There was a moth swooping down on her, a moth with the wingspan of a small plane. And mounted on the back of this stupendous and terrifying insect was her old pursuer, Mendelson Shape.

"*There! You! Are!*" he yelled at her.

Now, finally, Candy's feet agreed to obey her panic.

She started to run toward the elevator, where Samuel Klepp was waiting to grab her and pull her to safety.

But even as she ran, some instinct deep in her gut told her she wasn't going to make it. The moth was coming down too fast. She could feel the freezing rush of its wings against her back, so fierce it almost threw her over. As she stumbled, the moth's immense and many-jointed legs closed around her body and plucked her up off the roof of the tower.

"*Got you!*" she heard Shape yelling triumphantly.

Then he spoke some incomprehensible order to his

mount, and the moth beat its vast wings and rose up into the air.

Candy caught a smeared glimpse of Klepp's horrified face as he reached up to try and snatch her out of the grip of the moth, but he was inches short of catching her hand.

Then she was carried up and away, over the edge of The Great Head of the Yebba Dim Day. She was terrified. Her heart became like a drum, thumping in her chest, and in her head. A trickle of sweat ran down her spine.

Poor Squiller was still attached to her face, clinging now more fiercely than ever. Candy was curiously thankful for his presence. It was like having a good luck talisman. As long as Squiller was with her, she felt, she would survive whatever lay ahead.

Moving tentatively, so as not to alarm the moth (she was now hundreds of feet above the waters of the Sea of Izabella; to be dropped from such a height would certainly bring her adventures in the Abarat to a quick end), she put her hand up to stroke the squid.

"It's going to be all right," she murmured to the trembling creature. "I promise I won't let anything happen to you."

It helped her to have another life besides her own to protect in this terrible situation. She had made a promise to Squiller. Now it was up to her to make good on that promise and bring them both through the adventures ahead alive, however dangerous the journey became, and however terrible the destination.

21

THE HUNT

UNDER MORE PLEASANT CIRCUMSTANCES, Candy might have enjoyed the journey that took her away from the towers of Yebba Dim Day. She had never suffered from vertigo, so she didn't mind the fact that they were a thousand feet up. The view was spectacular: the patchwork of glittering sunlit sea where the Hours of Daylight fell, and the dark waters where the Night Hours held sway.

But she could scarcely play the blithe sightseer in their present precarious position. Though the moth's hold on her was reasonably secure, it was clear to her that she was a burden that the creature's anatomy was not designed to support. Every now and again there would be a breath-snatching moment when its spindly legs scrambled to secure a better hold on her. Whenever this happened, Squiller automatically clamped himself more tightly to her head, like a climber clinging for dear life to a rock face.

Nor was her fear of being dropped her only concern.

Worse, in a way, was the threatening chatter of Mendelson Shape.

"I'm sure you thought you'd never see me again, eh?" he said.

She didn't reply.

"Well, you should know," he went on, "I'm not the kind of man who gives up easily. If Lord Carrion wants you, then Lord Carrion will have you. He is my prince. His word is law."

He paused, plainly hoping to get some fearful response from her. When none came, he continued in the same confident vein.

"I daresay he'll reward me for delivering you. He'll probably give me a piece of the Abarat when his Night of Victory comes, and Darkness takes everything under its wing. You realize that's what's going to happen? There's going to be an Absolute Midnight. And everyone in *The Sinner's Emporium* will be raised up on that Night, you'll see."

Candy had kept her silence thus far, but now her curiosity overcame her.

"What in God's name is *The Sinner's Emporium*?" she said.

"A place God's name is *not* written," Mendelson said, amused by his own joke. "It's a book, penned by my Lord Carrion's grandmother, Mater Motley, in which she lists the seven thousand greatest sinners in the Abarat."

"Seven thousand sinners. And are you one of them?"

"I am."

"It doesn't sound like much to be proud of," Candy commented.

"What would you know?" Mendelson Shape snapped. "You outrun me once and you think you have all the answers! Well, you don't, missy! I could have you dropped in an instant!" He leaned forward, and said: *"Cafire!"*

In response to this instruction, the moth twitched, *and let Candy go*.

She loosed a shriek as she slipped out of the creature's grasp and started to fall—

"Jazah!" Shape yelled. *"Jazah!"*

With a heartbeat to spare, the moth caught hold of her again, though its hold was precarious. Shape seemed to realize this. He barked out a third incomprehensible order, and this time the moth responded by gathering Candy back to its upper body and drawing her closer than ever; so close that the stiff black hairs of its thorax pricked her, despite the padding on the jacket Samuel Klepp had given her.

She felt a trickle of fluid running down the side of her face. Poor Squiller had obviously thought they were going to fall to their doom and had lost control of his squiddish bladder in his panic. She reached up and stroked him.

"It's all right," she whispered.

Her heart was beating furiously, her whole head throbbing. She glanced up at Shape, wondering if she shouldn't try to make some kind of peace with him, to prevent his playing that kind of lethal game again. Next time, the moth might not be quick enough to catch her.

But Shape's attention was focused upon something ahead of them. She followed the line of his gaze and saw a fleet of five or six air balloons appearing from a bank of moonlit cloud, perhaps a quarter mile away.

"What the *Nefernow* is this?" she heard Mendelson mutter to himself.

Nefernow, she thought; I think I just learned my first Abaratian curse word.

Apparently someone in the fleet had seen the moth, because the leading ship was changing direction and heading toward them.

"*Skrill! Skrill!*" Mendelson yelled.

The moth obeyed the instruction and began a vertiginous descent. It was so steep that Candy feared she and Squiller would slip right out through the loop of the moth's legs, so she reached up over her head and grabbed hold of the creature's thorax with both her hands, indifferent to the pricking of the hard hairs.

An island had come into view below them. If they fell now they would be dashed to death. She had to hold on. Her abductor was her only hope.

She glanced up again toward the fleet of balloons. They obviously had some other means of propulsion beside the wind, because in the ten or fifteen seconds since the moth had begun its descent, the ships had halved the distance between themselves and their quarry.

Candy heard a high-pitched whistling sound and something flew close to her face. A moment later came a second whistling, followed by a stream of Abaratian curse words. Shape had flattened himself against the body and head of the moth. It took her a moment to work out why. Then she understood: they were being *fired* at. There were hunters in the balloons, and they were obviously intent on bringing down the moth. Either they hadn't seen its rider and its captive, or else they didn't care what happened to Shape and Candy if their missiles hit home. Whichever it was, it scarcely mattered. The consequence for Candy and Squiller would be the same. She heard a third whistling now, which was followed by a thud. Then a traumatic shudder ran through the body of the moth.

"Oh, please . . ." she murmured. "Please don't let this be happening."

But it was too late for prayers.

She looked up at the insect's head to see that a crossbow bolt, fired by someone in one of the balloon's gondolas, had struck the insect directly between its huge eyes.

There was no blood spilling from the wound. Instead there came a spiraling stream of fragmented color that rose up into the darkened air. Apparently the insect was some kind of magical creation, which went a little way to explaining why it didn't die instantly, though it had surely been mortally wounded. Instead, it struggled to climb skyward again, its immense wings beating with a slow majesty as it attempted an ascent.

But it didn't get very far. A new round of shots came from the balloons, and the vicious bolts tore hole after hole in the delicate membrane of the moth's wings. Again, color streamed from the wounds, and as it discharged its myriad hues, the desperate beating of its wings began to falter. Then they stopped.

Their descent began a second time.

Candy looked back up at Shape. He was still bent close to the moth, desperately whispering to it in a panicked attempt to bring it out of its dive. But it was a lost cause.

Shot from the sky, the moth fell and fell and fell.

All Candy and her pursuer could do was hold on as the insect gathered speed and raced toward the unforgiving earth below.

PART FOUR

WICKED STRANGE

A soul of water,
A soul of stone.
A soul by name,
A soul unknown.

The hours unmake
Our flesh, our bone.
The soul is all;
And all alone.

—a verse, inscribed by
an anonymous hand, on a
boulder on Vesper's Rock

22

IN GALLOWS FOREST

Nobody—not even Christopher Carrion himself—knew every last secret of the Midnight Island. The place was a labyrinth, with its columns of black rock and its fathomless lakes, its mines, its forests, its steeps and its plains. It was the hiding place of countless ancient mysteries. Indeed he'd heard it said that every fear that had ever chilled the human heart was here on Gorgossium. All assembled at that terrible Hour when the past slips away from us and we are left in dark, not knowing what will come next. If anything.

Tonight, Carrion was out walking among Gorgossium's horrible splendors, meditating on what he had seen through the eyes of the moth he'd conjured out of human dust on Vesper's Rock.

He'd witnessed the flight to the Yebba Dim Day, and of course he'd seen the girl standing there on the tower of The Great Head, studying the islands. He'd taken pleasure in the look of terror on her face as his creation, guided by Shape, had swooped down to catch hold of her and carry her off. The journey back to Midnight had begun. Things had been going very well.

Then had come the appearance of the balloons and the attack on the moth. Carrion had watched the approach of the vessels in a state of impotent fury, listened in horror as their bolts flew. He'd heard Mendelson ordering the moth to descend, presumably in the hope of outmaneuvering their pursuers. But it was a lost cause. One of the bolts had struck home, wounding the moth's telepathic powers. The images in Carrion's mind's eye had gone blank.

He didn't care about the fate of the moth—it had been raised from dust and light and would now to dust and light return. Nor did Mendelson Shape's survival matter to him. All that concerned him was the moth's freight: the girl it had abducted from the towers of the Yebba Dim Day.

Though he'd only caught a brief glimpse of her—and her face had been obscured by some device she was wearing over her eyes—he had felt an extraordinary rush of *recognition* at the sight of her. She was somebody special; somebody important. Perhaps even somebody for whom he could feel love.

But even as his heart had quickened at the sight of the girl, his head had cautioned him to be careful. He had not had pleasant experiences where love was concerned. It could break your heart, if you weren't careful. It could make you feel so lost, so confused, and so worthless that life didn't seem worth living. This wasn't something he knew from books; these were the bitter lessons of his life.

He decided to think further on this, so rather than return to the Twelfth Tower he went walking, taking his favorite path through Gallows Forest. As he proceeded, his thoughts inevitably turned from the girl that he'd seen on the towers of the Yebba Dim Day to that *other* special one, the one who had caused him so much grief: his Princess Boa.

Though it was many years since she had hurt him, he still wore on his heart the scars she had left there.

In his eyes she had been beautiful beyond words, a creature of infinite charm and sweetness of nature. She had also been the daughter of King Claus, who ruled at that time an alliance of the Islands of Day. As such, she had been a perfect match for the Lord of Midnight. So he'd told her, in his letters to her.

"What a time of healing there would be," he'd written, *"if you would consent to marry me. You who love the Daylight Hours, and I, who love the Night. Wouldn't we be perfect together? For centuries the islands have been at war, sometimes secret hostilities, sometimes open struggle; but always a conflict that ended in a terrible loss of life, and in a stalemate which advanced the cause of neither side.*

"An end to all of that. An end to war, forever! If you would marry me, we would announce on our wedding day that all enmities between the Islands of Night and Day would henceforth cease; and that the old wounds would be healed away by the example of our love, and a new Age begin: an Age of Everlasting Love. The war-makers would be stripped of their weapons and made to turn their hands to some loving labor. On that

day too I would intend to free all my many stitchlings, who have worked to defend Midnight from attack. This would be an act of faith on my part. In doing this, I would be announcing to the world that I would rather die unarmed, and in love, than ever pick up another sword.

"And I would name you, my darling, as my inspiration. You, my sweet Princess, would be the loving soul that the Abarat would thank for your power to quell the anger in the heart of Night."

There had been many such letters, and many to him from the Princess Boa, in which she'd told him how beautiful his sentiments were, and how much she wanted to believe that Carrion's *Age of Love Everlasting* was something that could indeed be brought about.

"My father, King Claus, and my brother Quiffin have both advised me to accept your noble entreaties," the Princess had written, "but my lord, I am far from certain that I can do as you all desire me to do. If I fail to feel in my heart the depth of love that a union of our souls surely demands, things would never go well between us. Please understand that I wish you no discourtesy in speaking this way. I only desire to speak truthfully so that there be no misunderstanding."

Her letter, full of doubt (there was no outright refusal, at least not at the beginning) had hurt him. For long nights after receiving it he could not bring himself to eat, or to speak to anyone.

Finally, he had penned a response, begging her to reconsider.

"If you are concerned about my appearance, lady," he had said, *"please be reassured: my grandmother Mater Motley has promised to use her skills in the magical arts to erase the marks that a life of grief and loneliness have left upon me. Should you agree to a union between us—and though you say your soul is not touched by love for me, I yet dare hope I may earn that love—then your Midnight Prince would be made new again, as any lover should be: new in your eyes, new in my own, and new, finally, in the eyes of the world."*

But all his reassurances could not persuade the Princess Boa to change her mind. She wrote back to him with great tenderness, but there was always uncertainty in what she wrote. She wasn't saying *no*, outright, because her father agreed with Carrion and saw a great opportunity for peace between Day and Night if his daughter and the Lord of Midnight were to marry. But for her to say yes, she would have to be rid of all the questions that haunted her.

She had dreams, she had written, that did not reassure her.

He had written back, asking her what dreams these were.

The Princess Boa had not been specific in her response. She'd only said that the dreams frightened her, and though she did not doubt Carrion's good and honorable intentions toward her, she could not put these visions out of her head.

As he walked through Gallows Forest, the vultures and the ravens kept pace with him, the ravens flying from tree to tree overhead, the vultures hopping at his feet, fighting between themselves for the place closest to his heels. He remembered how he had labored over the letters he had written back to her, determined to convince her that the dreams she was having were of no significance, and that she should take comfort in his undying devotion to her.

"*I will protect you,*" he had written, "*from any power that threatens you. I will put myself between you and Death itself. Please, lady, be assured: there is no demon in air, earth or sea that can threaten you.*"

Whenever he had sent a letter to her there had always been a trial by hope while he had waited for her reply. And then a terrible moment when that reply had finally arrived and his fingers had become thick and fumbling with unease as he struggled to open the envelope.

The answer never satisfied him.

He pressed her, over and over, to stop punishing him with indecision. And finally, after much importuning on his part, the Princess had given him a clear answer. It could not, indeed, have been clearer. She *did* not love him, *could* not love him, and *would never* love him.

He'd almost drowned in the wave of self-hatred that had broken over him when he read that final reply. He knew *why* she was telling him no, and it had nothing to do with her nightmares. It was something else; something far simpler.

She hated him.

That was the terrible truth of the matter. However

tenderly phrased her refusal, he could read between the lines of her letter. She thought he was an ugly, scarred, nightmare-ridden grotesque, and she hated him with all her heart.

That was the beginning, the middle and the end of the matter.

His long, meditative amble through the trees had brought him into the heart of the forest now, where the great gallows of the past had been planted. Some still had rotted nooses tied to their beams, and a few of those nooses still supported the remains of executed men and women, mummified in their last, ghastly poses, mouths stretched grotesquely wide. Some had had their tongues plucked out by hungry ravens, and many of the birds in this vicinity had come to possess the voices of those whose tongues they ate. Now they chattered like men as they hopped around on the bloodred branches that had sprouted from the gallows.

"What a night to be hanged, eh?"

"I was hanged on a night like this. How my wife cried!"

"Mine didn't."

"Why not?"

"She was the reason I had a noose around my throat!"

"You killed her?"

"I surely did! She cooked the worst bread-pudding in Tazmagor!"

The Lord of Midnight put the absurdly grim gossip out of his head and let his thoughts go back to the girl he had seen through the moth's eyes on the towers of the Yebba Dim Day. Though she had fallen out of the air when the moth was killed, she was still alive; of that Carrion was irrationally certain. And sooner or later he would find her and speak to her.

Did he dare believe that perhaps this girl had come from the Hereafter as fortune's way of compensating him for what he'd suffered at the hands of the Princess Boa? Perhaps *that* was why he thought he recognized the girl: because she was a gift to him from circumstance.

The thought lifted his dark mood somewhat. He walked on through the trees, toward the cliff edge, where he would have a view toward the islands of the west. Including, of course, the Yebba Dim Day.

His route took him past a place among the trees where two masked men who'd been warders in his prison and had developed a deep enmity for one another were fighting with clubs. The pair were brothers, Wendigo and Chilek, and Carrion had amused himself some days earlier by casually sewing a seed of discord between the two (a rumor, no more, whispered in each ear, suggesting that one brother was attempting to become the prison's warden behind the other's back). It was a test, really, to see how long it would take for jealousy to overcome the once powerful love that the two brothers had borne one another. Not long, was the answer. Here they were now, fighting to the death over something that wasn't even true.

Unseen, Carrion watched from the shadows as the fight reached its grim conclusion. One brother slipped in the mush of rotted gallows leaves beneath their feet and went down in the dirt. The other man didn't give his brother a chance to beg for mercy. He raised his club and delivered the *coup de grâce* with a whoop of boyish glee.

The victor's moment of triumph didn't last very long. The whoop died away, and the surviving brother seemed to wake from his trance of envy and bloodlust. He shook his head and pulled off his mask. Then— letting both mask and club drop from his hands—he fell to his knees beside his sibling. Recognition of what he'd done flooded his face.

Carrion laughed, hugely amused. Hearing the laughter, Wendigo looked up from his brother's body and stared off into the shadows.

"Who's there?" he demanded of the darkness.

The sudden grief in his voice disturbed a flock of gallows ravens in the branches overhead. They too had been watching the fight, it seemed. Now they called to Wendigo as they swooped down around him.

"Murderer! Murderer! Murderer!"

He tried to wave them off, but they weren't about to be driven away.

Around and around they flew, some even daring to land on the man's head to hop there and laugh into his ears. He struck wildly at them, but they were up and away before he could catch hold of their black and spindly legs. Defeated, now alone with his crime, Wendigo sank down sobbing in the dead leaves.

Carrion left the ravens to their tormenting and Wendigo to his tears. His mood was improving by the moment.

As he walked, a wind came out of the west and passed through the forest, whistling between the rotted teeth of the hanged men and sighing out of their eye sockets. The nooses creaked as the corpses swung back and forth.

Carrion took off one of his gloves and put his bare hand up into the wind, his lips drawing back. They had been permanently scarred, those lips, by something that his grandmother had done to him many, many years before. Hearing him use the word *love*, Mater Motley had sewn his lips together, and left him that way, speechless and hungry, for the space of a day.

"*Where are you, child of the Hereafter?*" Carrion wondered aloud.

The wind carried his words away.

"*Come to me,*" he went on, as he walked through the swaying corpses toward the sea. "*I won't hurt you, child. I swear, on the tomb of my beloved.*"

And still the wind took his words. He let it. Perhaps his gift from the Hereafter would hear what he was telling her and do as he was asking.

"*Come to me,*" he said again, dropping his words to a whisper, imagining them finding their way into the ear of the trespasser. As she slept, perhaps, or as she stared out at the sea, just as he was staring out at the sea.

"*Do you hear me?*" he said. "*I'm waiting for you. Come to me. Come to me. Come to me.*"

23

THE MAN WHO MADE THE KID

THE GREAT MOTH, THOUGH it was certainly dead, did not fall from the sky like a stone. Its wings were so large that it spiraled down like a kite that had lost the wind. Candy held on to its thorax, praying aloud:

"Please, God, help me!"

But the words were snatched out of her mouth by the speed of their descent, which grew faster and faster.

She caught a glimpse of what lay below. It wasn't bare rock, but it wasn't a featherbed either: it was a stretch of what looked like moorland, with here and there a few scattered trees.

And then—as if things weren't bad enough—Mendelson Shape reached down around the body of the moth and began to shake her loose. Quite why he was doing this was beyond her; perhaps he was simply trying to lighten the load. Whatever his reasons, they were his undoing. In his attempt to throw Candy off, he lost his own grip on the animal and started to pitch forward over the moth's head. In desperation he snatched hold of the moth's antennae, but his body weight simply flipped the insect's whole cadaver over.

It was now Shape who started to pray aloud for help, though he did so in a language Candy didn't understand. His pleadings were no more efficacious than Candy's had been. She heard him clawing his way up over the moth, each breath a sob. But he was lost. His pleadings became more desperate than ever; then the wind gusted with particular force, and he was carried away. Candy glimpsed him as he swept past her. He plunged out of sight through the darkened air, leaving her lying face up on the belly of the insect as it too plummeted earthward. The spread of the moth's wings slowed its descent, which was about the only good news about Candy's situation. She held on tight, anticipating a massive blow when they hit the ground.

But she was lucky. The wind had carried the moth away from the rocks where Mendelson had fallen, and toward one of the copses. The insect's body landed in the canopy. Twigs and branches snapped, and the huge body threatened to continue its fall to earth, but the young trees had sufficient resilience to bear the moth's body up.

Leaves flew into the air and came spiraling down on top of Candy. She lay absolutely still, waiting for the last of the motion to subside. Then she gently rolled over onto her stomach and peered down through the creaking branches.

The ground was still twenty feet below her, perhaps more. She needed to proceed with extreme caution, she knew, if she was going to get down to *terra firma* without doing herself harm. As it turned out, it wasn't too much of a problem. The trees presented her with easy hand- and foot-holds. Though she still was shaky from the last few minutes of high drama, she managed to clamber down to earth without any further incident.

The first thing she did was to relieve Squiller of his duty by gently unknitting him from her head. The poor squid was trembling violently. She did her best to reassure him with soft words.

"It's okay," she told him. "We're perfectly safe now."

She would have to get him back to the water as soon as possible. Squiller had been serving her sight for an hour or more; she was surprised he was still alive.

Now that she was on the ground she took stock of the situation. What place was this? Or, more correctly, given that she was in the Abarat, what Hour?

It was dark here—darker than the Yebba Dim Day—but not yet deep night. Her guess was that this was Ten O'clock in the Evening, which she remembered from her lessons with Klepp was the island of Ninnyhammer.

There was a little chill in the air, and on the breeze, from some distance away, she could hear an orchestra playing some mournful music.

She ventured to the edge of the little stand of trees to see if she could discover the source of the music. She did so easily. As she peered out from the trees, two of the hunters set their balloons down gently, not fifty yards away from her, the floodlights on their gondolas illuminating the ground in every direction. Rather than step out into the light and make herself a potential target for the hunters she retreated into the cover of the trees again and watched while events unfolded.

First she heard the sound of the gondola doors being opened, and then—with a quiet hum—a set of steps emerged, so that these pampered hunters didn't have to jump the short distance from the doorway to the ground.

The three men who emerged were all wearing identical clothes: high-collared gray suits and highly polished gray boots. The leader—to judge by the way that the other two men fawned upon him—was not the oldest. He was a diminutive young man with a shock of orange hair that fell over his brow, and the perpetually narrowed eyes of one who was deeply suspicious of the world.

The other two—his bodyguards, perhaps—were almost twice his size, and they instantly proceeded to survey the territory into which their leader was wandering. Both carried guns.

Finally, bringing up the rear of this little group was a black man so tall he had to bend his head in order to get out through the gondola's door. He wore a pair of small silver glasses and he carried some kind of large electronic tablet, the screen of which gave off a pulsing glow that illuminated his face with light: sometimes white, sometimes turquoise, sometimes orange. He attended closely to everything the man with the orange hair said or did, and in response his long agile fingers moved restlessly back and forth over the tablet, missing no detail of whatever his boss said or did as he set it down.

The man with the suspicious eyes had already fixed his gaze upon the moth in the tree; and he approached the creature, talking as he went.

"Have you ever seen any life-form quite like this, Mr. Birch?" he said to the man in the silvered glasses. He didn't wait for a reply. "Doggett?" Mr. Suspicion said, now addressing the larger of the two bodyguards. "You'd better get some grappling hooks and ropes, so we can bring this thing down. I want it preserved for our collection."

"It's as good as done, Mr. Pixler," Doggett said, and left the little company to get the work underway.

Pixler? Candy said to herself. Was it possible that this little man was in fact the master architect of Commexo City?

"What do you make of it, Birch?" Pixler asked his companion.

The man came to Pixler's side. He was fully two and a half feet taller than his boss, and despite the insipid, functional cut of the pale suits they were all wearing, he wore his with a curious elegance. "I've been going through Willsberger's *Flora and Fauna of the Islands* and—"

"There's no entry for a giant moth?" Pixler said, gently patting his quiff to be sure it hadn't lost its shape.

"No."

"I'm not surprised," Pixler said. "It's my opinion that

this thing was made by magic. Look at the color flowing out of it, Birch. It was a conjuration that made this. And a powerful one." Pixler smiled. "It's going to take time to root out all the magic in these islands. We've got a lot of books to burn, a lot of spirits to break—"

Candy listened to the man speaking of book burnings and spirit breaking with a little smile of anticipation on his face, and it made her shudder. So this was the philosophy of Rojo Pixler, the great architect of Commexo City. It made grim listening.

"I don't want them going to their local shamans and witch doctors for their healing and their revelations. I want them coming to us. To me! If people want a taste of magic, let it be *our* magic. Sanitized. Systematized."

"Hallelujah," Birch said.

"You're not mocking me, are you?" Pixler snapped, reeling around on the man, his finger jabbed in the man's face.

Birch raised his hands in surrender, the tablet slipping from his hands. "Good Lord, no. Absolutely not, sir."

Pixler laughed out loud. "A joke, Birch. A joke!" he said.

"What?" said Birch, his expression empty.

"Where's your sense of humor?" Mr. Suspicion said.

"Oh. A joke."

"Come on, Birch, lighten up. I trust you."

Birch bent down and picked up the tablet he'd dropped. As he did so, he shot Pixler a glance that the boss-man didn't see, but Candy did. It spoke volumes. Under Birch's loyal manner lay a deep-seated contempt for his employer.

"Write this down for me, Birch," Pixler said. "I want to announce an amnesty on all books of magic. If they're turned over to us in Commexo City for burning in the next thirty days, I will personally guarantee that whoever hands the books over will be immune from prosecution."

"With respect," Birch said, "there are no laws, sir, forbidding the practice of magic outside Commexo City. And again, with respect, I think it would be very hard to get any of the Island Councils to agree to put such a law into effect."

"What if we told these two-bit councilors that they could never have any further dealings with Commexo unless they *did* create such a law?" Pixler said.

"That might work," Birch said. "But what about the big players? The Carrion family has a vast magical library, I hear. Probably the largest on the islands. How do we get them to give that up?"

"I'll find a way," Rojo said, his manner oozing confidence. "I always find a way, you know me."

"Wait," said Birch softly.

"What is it?"

"Would you mind, sir?" Birch said, handing his glowing tablet over to his boss.

"What's the problem, Birch?" Pixler said.

"None, sir," Birch said, taking a small step away from his employer, toward the copse, then another, then a third.

"Birch?"

At that moment Birch's steps became a long-legged dash into the undergrowth.

Too late, Candy realized that *she* was the target of his pursuit. She turned and started to run, but before she could get more than a yard, he had his hands on her.

"A spy?" Pixler yelled.

"It's just a girl," Birch said, as he pulled Candy out of the shadows and into the blaze of light from the balloons. She complained loudly about his manhandling of her, but she had no choice in the matter. He was considerably stronger than she was, and he didn't seem to care that he was bruising her in the process of holding on to her.

"Are you our moth maker?" Pixler said. "Did you do *that*?" He pointed to the dead moth, which was still in the trees, despite the attempts of Doggett and his team to bring it down.

"She's probably one of the local tribespeople," Birch said, still holding Candy tight. "Some of them are mute, I believe."

"Are you mute?" Pixler said.

"No," Candy replied.

"Ah. That's one theory that bites the dust," Pixler said.

"Then who are you?" said Birch.

"My name is Candy Quackenbush and for your information I was being abducted by that *thing* in the trees when you brave, clever gentlemen shot it out of the skies. You could have killed me!"

Pixler listened to this little outburst with a mildly amused expression on his face.

"I think you could probably let the young lady go now, Birch," Pixler said.

"She may be armed," Birch said, not releasing Candy.

"What have you got in your hand?" Doggett demanded.

"That's Squiller," Candy said, looking down. To her distress she realized that in the last few minutes—while she'd been listening to the book-burning non-senses Rojo Pixler was spouting—the life had finally gone from her little squid. Most likely it had been out of its native element too long.

"*Let me go!*" she raged, digging at Birch with her elbows to get him to release her.

"You heard what the girl told you," Pixler said.

Birch let go of Candy, but stayed within six inches of her in case she attempted to make a move on his boss.

"Shall I take that from you?" Pixler said, his hands extended to receive Squiller's body.

"No, you can't," Candy said. "I'll bury him myself. I want to say a little prayer."

"For a *squid*? My lord," said Birch, "you *are* a primitive lot on this island."

"Don't be so judgmental, Birch," said Pixler. His voice had become softer. "My sister Filomena used to bury all her pets in the back garden when we were young. We had quite a little cemetery back there. I used to dig the hole, and she'd write a little prayer.

These little rituals are important. Where are you from, child?"

"A long way away," Candy said.

She suddenly felt a deep tremor of sadness go through her, and she wished with all her heart that she could snap her fingers and be returned to her own backyard in Followell Street, where she could lay Squiller to rest beside Monty the canary and several deceased goldfish: the companions of her childhood. She could feel tears not that far off, and the last thing she wanted to do was weep in front of a couple of total strangers. So she said:

"If you'll excuse me, I'm going to bury Squiller in the woods. It's been nice meeting you, Mr. Pixler. And you"—she looked at Birch—"not so nice."

"Well, that's plain-speaking," Pixler said.

"We speak plainly in Minnesota."

"Minnesota?" said Birch. "What island is that?"

"Minnesota isn't in the Abarat, Birch," Pixler said.

"You mean—?"

"Yes," said Pixler. "Minnesota is in the Hereafter."

Leaving them to their discussion, Candy wandered off into the woods, making sure she kept well away from the area where the men were now at work under Doggett's supervision, bringing the dead moth down from the branches.

She found a place where the dirt looked relatively easy to penetrate and she proceeded to dig with her hands. When she'd got down a foot or so, she lay Squiller's little body at the bottom of the hole and threw a fistful of earth over him. She'd only been to one funeral in her life—her grandmother's—but she remembered a smattering of words from the ceremony.

"Ashes to ashes, dust to dust . . ." she murmured. Then she improvised: "Thank you for your company, Squiller. I'm sorry you're gone. I'm going to miss you." She began to push the remaining dirt over the squid's body as she spoke, covering it completely. "I hope wherever you've gone, it's a place you want to be." She sniffed hard, swallowing her salty tears. It wasn't just Squiller's impromptu funeral that had brought them on. It was thoughts of home, and of the great distance that lay between this place and the streets of Chickentown. "Now I'm alone," she said to herself.

"No, you're not."

She glanced over her shoulder. Rojo Pixler was standing close by.

"This is a private funeral," she said to him.

"Oh, I'm sorry," he said, sounding genuinely contrite. "I really didn't wish to intrude on your grief. It's just that back there you said something very interesting."

"I did?"

"When you told me that you came from Minnesota."

"Oh, that."

"Yes, that. Were you telling the truth?"

"Why?"

"Because I would be extremely thankful to you if you would lead me back there."

"To Minnesota?"

"Yes. To Minnesota."

Candy looked incredulous. "You wouldn't like it," she said.

"Oh but I think I would. I'm always looking for new markets for the Commexo Kid and his Panacea."

Candy didn't reply. She finished covering up Squiller and gently patted down the earth. Pixler had meanwhile squatted beside her.

"Here," he said. He had made a small cross of two pieces of twig, tied together with a length of grass.

Candy was a little taken aback by the simple gentility of the gesture, but then she thought, *Well, he's trying to be civil*, so she took the cross from Pixler and pushed it into the soft earth at the head of the grave.

"Thank you," she said.

"No problem. I want us to be friends. What's your name again?"

"Candy Quackenbush."

"Candy, I'm Rojo. I won't beat around the bush. The fact that you've come from the Hereafter is of the *greatest* possible importance to me."

"I don't see why," said Candy. "It's not as interesting there as it is here."

"Well, maybe not to *you*," Rojo replied. "But you're used to it. To me it's . . . new territory to explore. A new frontier. I've done all I can here. I need somewhere new to—"

"Conquer?" Candy said, standing up and looking down at Pixler.

"No," he protested mildly. "Do I look like a conqueror? I'm a civilized man, Candy. I build cities—"

"And burn books," she said.

He looked pained to have been caught in a lie. Before he could come back with another response, she had more to say: "And shoot down defenseless creatures."

"I didn't see you being carried by the moth, I swear. If I had, I wouldn't have fired."

"There was a rider on the moth too."

"Really?"

"Yes. His name was Mendelson Shape. He fell to his death."

Rojo looked genuinely distressed. "That's a tragedy. I am completely culpable. In the heat of the hunt I did something I shouldn't have done. Did you know him? The rider, I mean? If he has family I'll make whatever reparations I can."

"I don't know if he had any family. He worked for someone called Christopher Carrion."

"Carrion? *Really?*" Rojo glanced away from Candy toward the moth, which Doggett's men were seconds away from bringing down out of the trees. "So that was Carrion's handiwork, eh?" he said, his voice touched by awe. "Very impressive."

Candy followed his gaze toward the moth. Light and color were still pouring from it, dissipating on the air, illuminating the trees: blue and purple and yellow and red.

"So tell me—" Pixler said, "—what were you doing, taking a ride on Carrion's moth?"

"If you must know I wasn't taking a ride. Shape abducted me."

"Abducted?"

"Yes."

Rojo gave a little self-satisfied smile. "Well then," he said. "I saved you from some very serious trouble. You wouldn't have wanted to be Carrion's prisoner, believe me. He has the morals of the very Devil, that man. And if he ever found a way to get over to the Hereafter . . ."

"It's not that difficult," Candy said.

"To get there, perhaps. But to gain a foothold . . ." He passed his hand through his hair. "That's the challenge. Please listen to me, Candy. I truly believe we could be very useful to one another."

Candy was not convinced. "How?" she said.

"Think it through. I'm in need of somebody with a good working knowledge of the Hereafter, and you need somebody here to protect you from Carrion."

"I don't need protection."

"Oh, my dear, you don't have the first clue what this man will do to you if he takes it into his head to be cruel. He is a law unto himself, believe me."

"Even so, I don't care to tell you about the Hereafter," Candy said, backing away from him.

"Oh, now don't be difficult," Pixler said. "I realize we met under difficult circumstances. But I'm genuinely sorry about the moth. It was just an accident. It could have happened to anyone."

"Anyone who was out hunting," Candy said.

"I realize not everybody approves of it. But it relaxes me. And I have a huge collection of stuffed animals in Commexo City. Nineteen thousand specimens, from fleas to Kiefalent whales. I'd really like you to see it."

"Some other time, maybe," Candy said.

Pixler shrugged. "Believe me or not," he said, his tone hardening, "I don't really care. In the end, you're going to come begging to me, when Carrion's on your tail. Begging for me to hide you from him."

"Yes, well maybe . . ." Candy said. "But right now I'd prefer to take my chances."

"Please," Pixler said, making one last desperate attempt to convince her, "let me bring you back to Commexo City. It's not safe on half these islands. The inhabitants are savages. Totally uncivilized."

"I am *not* going back to Commexo City with you. That's final," Candy said.

In truth there was a little part of Candy that wanted to accept Pixler's invitation. He was polite enough, after all; he seemed more like an ordinary human being than many of the creatures she'd met on her travels, which right now she found reassuring. She was feeling very much alone, and very tired. She'd lost count of the time that had passed since she and Mischief had plunged into the Sea of Izabella (though she'd reset her watch when Mischief had told her to, it had stopped); now she felt the way travelers in the Hereafter felt when they'd traveled around the world and their body clocks had become confused. Her thoughts were sluggish and her limbs ached. The thought of going with Pixler to some civilized place where the showers were probably hot and the beds were surely soft was not without its attractions.

But then she'd effectively be in Pixler's control, wouldn't she? In *his* city, as *his* guest. Or his prisoner.

"I can see you're having second thoughts," Pixler said, reading the confusion on Candy's face. "You're thinking about a comfortable place to lay your head, no doubt."

Candy tried to block out his seductions by concentrating on something else. She turned her attention to the moth.

Off between the trees, Doggett's team was close to bringing down the creature's body. There was much shouting and a flurry of orders, then—sooner than any of the workmen had anticipated—the moth's corpse came crashing down out of the trees. As it struck the ground, it erupted in a brilliant shower of light and color.

But there was something else in the substance of the creature that was also set free as it flew apart. Candy saw four or five skeletal faces rise up out of the blazing remains of the moth and weave their way skyward.

The spectacle didn't just draw her attention. It drew that of Pixler and Birch too. Candy seized her moment. She cautiously retreated a step, then another, then another. Birch and Pixler hadn't noticed: the disintegration of the moth was like a fireworks display; it claimed all their attention.

After five backward steps Candy turned and ran.

It didn't take her long to get to the other side of the copse, and there she paused to take a backward glance. She could see Birch and Pixler, silhouetted against the brightness of the moth. By now they had both realized that she'd gone. They were looking around, obviously trying to locate her. But apparently they'd been staring into the blaze of the disintegrating moth for too long, and it was still blinding them. Or perhaps the darkness simply concealed her. Whatever the reason, when they looked in her direction—as now and then they did—they failed to see her.

Pixler yelled something at Birch, who immediately went back to the balloon's gondola.

He's gone for more men, Candy thought. *I'd better get out of here.*

She turned her back on the men and the moth and surveyed the starlit terrain in front of her. Ninnyhammer was an island of gentle hills; on top of one of those hills, perhaps two miles from where she was standing, was a building with a large dome upon it. There was light in its windows, so if it was a house, then somebody was at home, and if it was a religious building of some kind (which the dome made her think perhaps it was), then it was open for worship. Or sanctuary, which was what she needed right now.

She didn't look back now at Rojo Pixler, or the moth with its colors and its weaving ghosts. She simply started down the gentle slope that led away from the trees. Very soon, the copse was out of sight, and the men's voices had been carried away by the wind.

She was alone for the first time since she'd arrived in the Abarat. There were no hunters, no Sea-Skippers; no Izarith, no Samuel Klepp, no John Mischief and his brothers.

Just her, Miss Candy Quackenbush of Chickentown, under a heaven filled with alien stars.

From somewhere deep inside her a great—and unforeseen—surge of joy appeared.

Out of sheer pleasure she started to sing as she went. It wasn't a song from the Hereafter that came to her lips. It was the absurd little ditty she'd heard the Sea-Skippers sing.

> *"O woe is me!*
> *O woe is me!*
> *I used to have a hamster tree.*
> *But it was eaten by a newt*
> *And now I have no cuddly fruit.*
> *O woe is me!*
> *O woe is me!*
> *I used to have a hamster tree!"*

For some uncanny reason she remembered it perfectly, as though she'd known it all her life, which was of course impossible. Yet here it was, coming to her lips as easily as some rhyme she'd been taught at kindergarten.

Oh, well, she thought as she gave the song full throat, *there's another mystery.*

And content that somewhere on the journey ahead she would find the answer to that mystery—along with something to eat—she went on her way, singing of newts and hamster trees.

24

DIGGER AND DRAGONS

JOHN MISCHIEF HADN'T BEEN making an idle boast when he spoke of himself—or more correctly, of *themselves*, the brothers—as master criminals. During their long felonious career, they had stolen from all manner of places, coming away with all kinds of hauls. Only once had they been arrested, and slipped custody while being transported back to the Yebba Dim Day by throwing themselves overboard.

There were too many thefts for the brothers to remember every one, but there were some that they still liked to revisit in those idle moments of happy self-congratulation. Their burglary of the chateau of Malleus Nyce on Huffell's Hill, for instance, had been extremely profitable. They'd come away with every costume Nyce had ever worn to the Cacodemonic Carnivals on Soma Plume: sixty-one outfits, all set with precious jewels and sewn with Thread of Sirius. Just a year or so later, they had broken *into* the prison on Scoriae and stolen all the tattoos off the body of the gangster Monkai-Monkai, leaving him as naked as the day he was born.

Then there had been their picking of the locks on the door of the Repository of Remembrance, that contained one hundred and thirty-one rooms of treasures that had once belonged to the great and the good of the Abarat, going back to the time when the islands were twenty-four Tribal Territories.

Nothing in the Repository had been of any real value. There had been no jewels, no precious metals. But the rooms had contained objects of infinitely more value than wealth. Here, collected and cataloged on the Repository's shelves was a hoard of the heart: the nursery toys of kings, the playthings of princes, the mud pies that potentates had dreamed would one day be palaces. The potential purchasers of all these objects of lovely inconsequence were the people across the archipelago who still idolized their one-time owners; and the brothers had anticipated making so many millions of zem they would never have to steal another fork.

But it was not to be. Monkai-Monkai had broken out of prison two days later and had come after the brothers and the only way Mischief and his siblings had escaped with their lives was by handing over their booty from the Repository to him.

But the treasure the brothers had been most proud of stealing, because stealing it had proved so difficult, was a painting known as *The Beautiful Moment*.

It had hung in what was known as the Stone House, the possession of the sometime lord of the Islands of

Day, King Claus. Since the death of his daughter, Claus had become an obsessive eater, and weighed over a thousand pounds. He ate and slept in a vast clockwork car, and had chased the thieves in it when he'd awoken to find his painting being stolen.

That had been a close call. But the brothers had been proud of the job. And indeed so enamored of what they'd stolen that they had almost considered keeping it.

The Beautiful Moment was a lovely thing. Or more correctly, three things; for the artist, a man called Thaddeus George, had painted a triptych that, when laid side by side, portrayed the entire archipelago, immortalized in oils at a time when everyone had had high hopes for the future. King Claus had commissioned the work from Thaddeus six weeks before his daughter's wedding, taking him up in an air balloon so that he might see the Abarat spread out "at this beautiful moment."

The world Thaddeus had painted was very different from the Abarat of today. The islands had been very different sixteen years ago. There had been no Commexo City on Pyon. Babilonium had been a modest little collection of tents and fun-fair entertainments (a Ferris wheel, a hall of mirrors, a geek in a cage). The air traffic above the islands had been little more than a few million birds, and the odd balloon, and the sea traffic had consisted chiefly of sailing ships.

In the interest of his art, Thaddeus had also taken some liberties with the size and complexity of the islands. He had left out most of the towns and villages, and the smaller outcroppings, which did not count as Hours, like Vesper's Rock, had also been omitted.

But even in this much simplified form, Thaddeus's last known work had been his most ambitious achievement: to look at it was to feel as though you were a bird, hovering over the islands, borne aloft by a balmy wind.

The Johns had made a small fortune from that theft. They had sold the picture to Rojo Pixler. He had paid many thousands of zem, which Mischief assumed he had borrowed, for at the time Pixler had still been a traveling salesman, selling gaudily painted windup toys for children.

The fact that Pixler had probably used *The Beautiful Moment* as a way to plan his slow but apparently irrevocable takeover of the islands was not lost on the brothers. In the years since Pixler had bought the painting, Pixler's judgment (and his luck) had been flawless. He was now undoubtedly the most powerful nonmagical creature on the Abarat. Besides Commexo City, which was so vast it was practically a world unto itself, the sometime salesman also owned a controlling share of Babilonium, and was now planning the construction of a pleasure dome, as he described it, at Five O'clock in the Evening. There was even talk of his buying the Great Zigurrat at Soma Plume and deconsecrating it, then turning it into a second city the size of Commexo.

Despite the fact that his public face was the ever-smiling Commexo Kid, Pixler was by no means a sweetheart. Indeed, he had made it known when he purchased the painting that if John Mischief or any of his brothers ever whispered to anyone that the transaction had taken place he would arrange for the whisperer and his brothers to be silenced.

That was the real Rojo Pixler speaking.

So, Mischief and his brothers had kept their mouths shut, and the fact that the painting had gone missing didn't even make it into the news sheets. Still, there were plenty of other crimes for which the Johns were responsible which continued to be the talk of coffeehouse and mothercake stalls alike, years after they had taken place. It was widely thought that when Mischief and his brothers were finally tracked down and brought to trial, the punishment would be death.

All of which goes to explain why Mischief, exhausted by his travels though he was, and badly wanting to stay close to Candy so as to retrieve the Key she still carried, did not dare remain near the Yebba Dim Day.

Rather than enter The Great Head in pursuit of Candy and risk being recognized inside, he waited instead in the water close to the jetty until all the dramas there were over, and then dragged himself back onto the quay (or what was left of it) in the hope of finding a boat that would carry him away to a less busy island. Somewhere the brothers could relax for a few days and plan their next move.

He was in luck. He was sitting feeding flakes of buttered coa fish to Slop when he heard a woman clap her hands to get the attention of all who were on the dock and announce that: "We need someone who can dig!"

With one voice, his brothers all said: *"He can dig!"*

And not for the first time, Mischief found himself volunteered.

Five minutes later a two-masted sailing ship called *Belbelo* left the Yebba Dim Day and headed into the currents of the Straits of Dusk.

The man in charge of the vessel was one Captain Hemmett McBean, a bear of a man who had sea salt in his blood. There were four other occupants of the *Belbelo*, besides the eight brothers. First there was the person who'd called for a digger, a black woman-warrior by the name of Geneva Peachtree, who was obviously in charge of this mission, whatever its purpose. Besides her and the captain, there were two other diggers: one a creature who hailed from the Island of Spake, called Two-Toed Tom; the other a large, brutish fellow, bald but for three black curls, called "Kiss Curl" Carlotti. He had been a gambler of some notoriety, but had lost his tongue and his middle toes in a bet many years before and had sworn off gambling thereafter. The last member of this unlikely band—but by no means the least important—was a waiflike girl, no more than thirteen, with long, white-blond hair and dark, eloquent eyes. Her name was Tria, and she sat at the bow of the *Belbelo* most of the time, staring out over the waters of the Izabella.

Those waters soon became very much more turbulent, as McBean's little vessel left the Straits and headed out into the open sea. There were thunderheads moving down from the heights of Hap's Vault, and Hemmett had already warned his passengers that the storm was going to be ferocious. The clouds were now moving over the sea, spitting lightning down at the seething water.

The girl, Tria, seemed completely unperturbed by the way the *Belbelo* rode the increasingly violent waves. She simply gazed out toward the darkened islands ahead, and now and again whispered something to Geneva. The girl's instructions were in turn passed to McBean, who was piloting the vessel in whatever direction Tria's instincts indicated.

As they traveled, Two-Toed Tom, who boasted a fine array of spiral tattoos, sat on the starboard side of the boat, with a yellowed and much-folded map in his hands, studying its contents with a large magnifying glass. Geneva Peachtree stood in the center of the boat, occasionally giving orders, but most of the time scanning the horizon. Now and again she would go over to consult the map with Two-Toed Tom.

The Johns were far too curious not to wander across and ask what was so interesting about the document they were studying. As soon as they approached, Two-Toed Tom hurriedly began to fold the map up. Then Geneva said:

"It's all right, Tom, I know the brothers."

"You do?" said John Pluckitt.

"By reputation only," Geneva Peachtree replied with a smile so lovely that the Johns all fell a little in love at the same moment.

"Then if you know us," said John Moot, "you probably don't trust us."

"No. Quite the reverse," Geneva said to Moot. "The

only people I *really* trust are those who have nothing to lose."

"Ah," said John Pluckitt. "Then that's us."

"Nowhere left to run," said Fillet, rather wearily.

"Here's my promise to you, brothers," Geneva said. "If things go well on this expedition, I will give you a home where I promise you the law will never touch you. A place where you can start a new life."

"Where's that?"

"On the Isle of the Black Egg," Geneva replied. "It may not look like the most inviting of places. Four in the Morning is a dark time. The moon's gone down and the sun's nowhere near showing its face. But there's more to my island than darkness and death."

"Really?"

"Believe me. Sometimes when life looks to be at its grimmest, there's a light, hidden at the heart of things."

She looked away as she spoke, and John Mischief knew that she wasn't just describing the mysteries of her island. She was talking about the here and now: this voyage and its purpose.

This seemed as good a time as any to ask exactly what that purpose was.

"What have you got planned for us?" John Fillet asked. "Why do we need a digger, for one thing?"

"Tell them, Tom," Geneva said.

Two-Toed Tom looked a little reluctant.

"Go on," Geneva urged.

"I don't want to frighten them off," Tom said.

"I don't think John Mischief is the nervous kind

somehow," Geneva replied. "Nor are his brothers."

"If you say so."

"I say so," Geneva replied. Her words, however gently delivered, were indisputably an order. And having given it, she left Tom and the Johns to talk, and went to consult with Tria again.

The Johns watched her go.

"It happens quickly, huh?" Two-Toed Tom said.

"What?"

"Falling in love with Geneva. One look, really. That's all it takes."

The Johns all looked back at Tom. Sallow, Drowze and Pluckitt were blushing.

"Don't worry, she has the same effect upon everybody. Even me. Do you have a lady?"

"No," said Mischief. "You?"

"I have a strange household," Two-Toed Tom said. "Do you want to see?"

"Please," said Mischief.

Two-Toed Tom took out a much-thumbed photograph of five individuals. One was Tom himself, with a two-headed Idjitian Jenga curled up at his feet. Beside Tom stood a big, scarlet-skinned man with long braided hair, who had a miniature blossom pig in his arms.

"I see what you mean," Mischief said. "A strange household indeed. Do you miss them?"

"Of course; all of them. We've been together a long time. But this mission is important to me. They understand that I had to come." He very carefully put the picture away. "And they know I might not come back."

"What did he say?" John Pluckitt asked.

"*I* heard what he said," John Drowze replied. The whole horn on which Drowze grew leaned forward as he addressed Tom. "Let me get this straight," John Drowze said. "Are you saying we could get killed?"

"Oh, *hush*, all of you," John Mischief said, embarrassed by his brothers' show of cowardice. "We signed on for this trip and we're going to see it through to the bitter end."

"It would be nice to know exactly what all this was about, however," Sallow said, with his usual aplomb. "You know, just so that we can be prepared."

"Of course," said Tom, his earlier reserve now set aside. "Where do I begin? Well, let me start with Finnegan. Do any of you remember a man called Finnegan Hob?"

"Of course," said John Slop. "He was the poor fellow—"

"—who was going to marry the Princess Boa," said John Moot.

"But didn't get the chance—" said John Swallow.

"—because the Princess," said John Mischief, "was taken by a dragon at the altar."

"You have it right," said Tom. "Finnegan was a fine man. Indeed I believe he would have been a *great* man if he'd married the Princess and had a chance to come to power. Together they would have healed a lot of old wounds around the islands. Feuds that go back to the war between Night and Day."

"He wasn't of royal blood, was he?" said John Serpent.

"Well, that's the interesting thing about Finnegan," Tom went on. "His father was a Prince of Day. His name was Maffick Hob. His mother was of lowly birth, but had some extraordinary powers of her own. And she was a child of the Night. Her name was Mariah Capella, and she lived on Speckle Frew—"

"Interesting mix," Mischief observed. "Finnegan was quite a hybrid."

"That's an understatement," said Tom. "It was a forbidden union, this marriage between Maffick and Mariah. A Prince of Day and a witch from the Nightside; it was unheard of. So Finnegan was a rare man, in every way. I had the great honor of knowing him for a few months during his courtship with the Princess Boa. I was in charge of her stables, and I would arrange for them to go out riding together. It was a secret courtship, at first, of course. But it didn't stay secret for very long."

"Why not?"

"Because the love she felt for him poured out of her. Love that deep couldn't be hidden, not from people who knew her well, like her father. He soon saw through our little arrangements."

"And what did King Claus say when he found out?" John Moot asked.

"At first he was in a rage about it. How could the Princess contemplate falling in love with a man of such questionable birth? *'Half this and half that,'* I remember him saying. But that all changed very quickly."

"Why?"

"Because he met Finnegan." Tom made a small, sad smile. "You couldn't know Finnegan for more than two minutes and not see how good a man he was. How gentle. How compassionate. So certain in his opinions and so profound in his feelings . . ." He sighed heavily. These memories were obviously bittersweet. "So anyway, King Claus sanctioned the union and a wedding was announced. It was to be held on the Nonce, in the Old Palace of Bowers. Believe me, there was never a woman as happy as the Princess in those months leading up to the ceremony. Her love for Finnegan illuminated everything she said and did." Tears welled in Tom's eyes and, brimming, ran down his cheeks. "I have one consolation," he said, his voice raw with sorrow. "That she was the happiest soul in creation, until the last moment of her life."

"So you were there in the Palace when it happened?" Sallow said.

"Oh yes," said Tom. "I'm afraid I was. I was standing perhaps ten yards away from her when the dragon's tongue took her." He fell silent, as a picture of this horror entered his mind's eye. "It dragged her out through the Palace door before we even knew what was happening. Finnegan was the first to go after her. But he was too late. She was dead by the time he got outside. Ten, twelve seconds maybe, from standing at the altar with Finnegan at her side, to lying out in the dirt, gone from us. Even now as I think of it, after all those years, it scarcely seems believable."

A great roll of thunder shook the boards of the boat, and the first drops of icy rain started to splatter against their faces, mingling with the tears on Tom's face.

"What's all this got to do with this little fishing trip we're on?" John Mischief said.

"I'll tell you. For nine years after he lost his Princess, Finnegan went looking for the family of the dragon that had killed her. He needed answers, you see. He knew the murder of his beloved hadn't been the actions of a rogue worm—"

"Worm?" said John Serpent.

"Yes, sir: *worm*," Tom replied, with deep contempt. "Dragon is too noble a term for these *things*."

"Wait," said Mischief. "I don't think I'm quite following this. Are you saying that Finnegan was going after these dragons—these worms—to *interrogate* them?"

"Worms have tongues," Tom said. "And many of them are very eloquent. A few are poets."

"Really?" said John Sallow. "I never knew that."

"Any of it any good?" said John Moot.

"Ordure, muck, excreta," Tom replied.

"Just wondering," said Moot.

"So, Finnegan assembled a band of folks who were ready to help him find these worms," said Tom. "There were eleven of us back then. Twelve, including Finnegan. McBean, Kiss Curl, Geneva and myself are all that I know for sure are left of the band."

"Lordy," said Slop.

"Dragon hunting isn't a job for the people who are interested in living long lives."

"I assume Finnegan had already killed the dragon that murdered his beloved?"

"Oh yes. Finnegan killed it right outside the Palace. Climbed into its mouth and struck a sword blow to its brain. It was a famous worm too. Perhaps you heard of it? Gravainia Pavonine."

"That's impressive," said Mischief.

"They're entirely ridiculous creatures when you have them cornered," Two-Toed Tom said. "All that din and self-importance, and they have not a breath of love or honor in them."

"But intelligent?" said Pluckitt.

"Oh, certainly. Marvelously intelligent, some of them. But intelligence without love is an empty thing, I think."

"Well said," John Sallow remarked.

"Believe me, I've been nose to nose with several worms in my time, and they are a vicious, vain and cruel species. Even the crowned heads."

"You met royalty?"

"Oh yes. Gravainia Pavonine was fourth in line to the Scaly Throne. Only his brothers, Nemapsychus and Giamantis, and his sister, Pijirantia Pavonine, were before him. And all still alive, I'm afraid to say."

"What about Finnegan?" said John Moot. "You were telling us about him and you got lost with all this wormy talk."

"Ah yes. Finnegan. That's where *she* comes in," Tom said. He pointed to the small girl still sitting in the bow of the *Belbelo*, braving the waves. Geneva had put a coat around Tria's frail shoulders, but she seemed not to notice the downpour. "Our little friend Tria has an uncanny ability to *find* people; often people who've been missing a long time."

"And when did you all last see Finnegan?" Mischief asked.

"About six years ago," Tom replied. "He went off on his own."

"Why?"

"Because his quest for the family of Gravainia Pavonine had taken such a terrible toll of lives. He didn't want anybody else to die on his account, so he slipped away while we were on Efreet, leaving a note saying we should all get on and live our lives. Forget about him, he said. As if we could ever do that."

He glanced up at Geneva, who at that moment happened to be looking in his direction. She clearly knew by the expression on his face what tale he was telling, and with a little nod of her head encouraged him to finish it.

So Tom went on.

"We all tried to obey his instructions, for his sake as much as for our own. We went our separate ways and tried to live our lives. But Finnegan was never very far from our thoughts. How could he be? We had shared his quest and his company for years. We all knew he was out there somewhere among the islands alone." Tom shook his head. "We hated to think of that. We listened for news of him, and sometimes we'd hear something—he'd been seen here, he'd been seen there—but never anything certain. And then, about seven weeks ago, Geneva met Tria. And apparently the child knew immediately that there was somebody Geneva wished to find."

"So she knows Finnegan's alive?"

"So she says."

"For certain?"

"For certain. But she has a sense that wherever he is, he's *buried*."

"Ah-ha!" said Mischief. "So that's why you needed a digger!"

"You won't be alone, believe me," said Geneva, breaking into the conversation. "We'll all be digging beside you."

"I'm glad to hear it," said Mischief.

Geneva turned to Tom. "Will you try and persuade Tria to go below for a while? Maybe she'll listen to you. At least until this storm is—"

She was interrupted by the sound of something grating along the underside of the *Belbelo*. The vessel shook.

"Have we hit something?" John Serpent said in alarm.

"I knew we shouldn't have come on this trip!" John Pluckitt muttered. "Crazy . . ."

Mischief ignored his brothers and peered over the side of the boat, to see if they had struck a rock. But no; what they had struck—or rather, what had struck them—was *moving* through the thrashing waters. And it was no small object.

Tom looked up at Mischief, an expression of profound concern on his face.

"I think we found our first dragon," he said.

25

MISCHIEF UNDONE

A DRAGON IT WAS; A worm of the sea-going variety. It rose up twenty feet above the seething waters, the back of its head spread like the hood of a cobra, and lined with foot-long spikes. Its very appearance rocked the *Belbelo* so violently that it nearly capsized.

"*A'zo and Cha!*" Mischief said. "Look at that thing!"

"*Get the child!*" Geneva yelled.

Two-Toed Tom immediately raced up the length of the rocking vessel to claim Tria from the bow. Even the sudden arrival of the great serpent had not disturbed her from her meditations on Finnegan's whereabouts. But she put up no protest when Tom took her from her vulnerable position and brought her into the little cabin.

The dragon, meanwhile, was speaking.

"*These waters are mine,*" it said, its voice deep and smooth; its tone quite equitable. "*I demand a toll from anyone who sails through them.*" Its head swooped low as it scanned those upon the deck of the *Belbelo*. "*Today, I will be generous. In return for your trespass here, I will only take . . . let me see, what will I take?*"

It sniffed, its head skimming the creaking boards of the boat. *"I shall take a girl-child,"* it said. *"Where is she? Don't hide her away."*

The dragon's head drew closer to the cabin door.

"Bring her out!" the dragon demanded. *"Come on! Let me have her and I will guarantee you safe passage."*

He turned to Carlotti.

"What is your destination, sir?" the worm said, all politeness.

Carlotti shook his head.

"Don't deny me now," the dragon went on, its terrible teeth perilously close to poor Carlotti's head, as though in an instant it would behead him.

"You'll get no answers from him," said Geneva, glancing around to locate her sword. "He has no tongue."

"Ah," said the dragon, turning to Geneva. *"Then you tell me, woman. Where are you headed? To the Nonce is it?"*

"Maybe."

"I can work up a current with my tail that will get you there in half the time."

"I'm sure you can," said Geneva, pulling her sword out from the heap of garments where it lay.

"Just give me the girl-child," the dragon said, breathing so hard on the cabin doors they shook.

"Not a chance," said Geneva, poking the side of the dragon's throat with her sword, drawing its attention away from the cabin.

The beast threw its cadaverous gaze back toward her.

"Now don't incense me, woman," the worm said.

"Just let me have my toll."

"You heard me, worm," Geneva replied. "Not a chance."

"Damn thee, woman," the dragon said. *"Take this!"*

It made a foul retching sound and suddenly regurgitated the contents of its five stomachs in a noisome torrent that struck Geneva with such force it threw her across the deck. Her sword went out of her hand and spun across the boards.

Geneva pulled herself to her feet, her boots sliding in the slime of the dragon's stomach juices. Twice she slipped, but on the third attempt, she succeeded in standing upright. She had picked a new weapon—one of the bigger bones the worm had spewed up. Racing back across the deck she beat the bone back and forth against the snout of the dragon, and when the bone shattered, she picked up another, continuing to strike at the thing until that bone, like its predecessor, was smashed to smithereens.

"How long is this little game going to go on for?" the dragon said, putting on a show of weariness. *"I'm getting irritated."*

Mischief and the brothers were standing watching all of this, not knowing whether to hide or fling themselves over the side.

"I'm not going near that thing," John Serpent warned.

"You of all people, *Serpent*," said John Pluckitt, "should be happy in its company."

The exchange had drawn Geneva's attention.

"Mischief!" she yelled. "Distract it!"

"Do what?"

"You heard me: distract it!"

"How?"

"Use your imagination!"

So saying, Geneva went down on her knees in the stinking filth that had been expelled from the worm and searched for her missing sword.

"The grappling hook!" said John Moot. "Mischief! Listen to me! Get the grappling hook."

"Where is it?"

"Behind us!" said John Drowze.

"I don't see it!"

"On the cabin wall, Mischief!" John Moot yelled. "Are you blind?"

There was indeed a hook hanging in place against the wall of the cabin. Unfortunately, it was directly beneath the dragon, which had reared up to better assess the dispersal of its enemies.

"Don't worry," Drowze said. "It's not interested in us! We're beneath its notice."

"Famous last words," said John Serpent.

But Drowze was right. For the moment at least the dragon was uninterested in the John brothers. It was watching Geneva on her hands and knees, smiling with satisfaction at the sight of her humiliation.

Mischief ducked beneath the snaking neck of the beast and snatched the grappling hook out of its cradle. It was about six feet long, and it had an iron hook at its end, but it didn't feel like the most potent of weapons.

"It's going to break!" Mischief said.

"You've no choice!" John Drowze yelled to Mischief.

"I know," Mischief said. Then he hollered up at the great worm. *"Hey you!"*

The dragon glanced down at the brothers for a moment with a supercilious look, then it casually knocked them aside with its snout, as though they were a piece of bad meat that had somehow found its way onto its plate. With Mischief floored, it slid its huge spiked head past him to get to the cabin door.

"Girl-child!" it said. *"You can come out now."*

It pushed at the door, which flew open, its hinges wrenched from the frame.

Giddily, Mischief got to his feet. He heard Tom yelling to the beast to stay out. The creature drew a breath and expelled it. As it did so, all the windows in the cabin blew outwards, and a wave of smoky heat erupted from the interior. Coughing and blinded by tears, Two-Toed Tom and Tria stumbled out of the cabin, driven from their refuge by the heat.

Then the dragon opened its mouth, sliding its scaly chin over the ship's creaking boards to scoop up the child.

Before it could do so, Kiss Curl Carlotti came at it with a short sword and stabbed the tender flesh around its nostril. Dark blood sprang from the wound and hissed as it hit the *Belbelo*'s boards. The dragon's lip curled with anger and it opened its mouth horrendously wide, dislocating its bottom jaw so that its mouth gaped like a tunnel.

"Watch out, Carlotti!" Mischief yelled, scrambling over the wet deck to draw the dragon's attack away from the child.

He went straight for its eye, driving the grappling hook at the narrowed orb. The hook caught under the dragon's eyelid, more by chance than design.

"Pull!" John Serpent yelled.

Mischief did exactly that. The delicate membrane of the dragon's eyelid tore and a second spray of blood came from the beast. Some of it spattered on Mischief's bare arms. It stung ferociously.

The dragon shook its head, forcing Mischief to let go of his weapon. It reared up, letting out a bellow of narcissistic fury.

"My face!" it cried, its din making the vessel reverberate from end to end. *"My perfect face! My beautiful face."*

It shook its head, loosing the hook from its lid. More blood spouted from the wound, filling the dragon's eye.

"I think you did it!" John Moot said.

"I wouldn't be too sure," said Mischief, backing away over the blood-slickened boards.

Half-blinded, the dragon lowered its head to the deck again, opening its tunnel mouth and sliding its lower jaw over the boards to scoop Mischief up.

Weaponless now, all the brothers could do was retreat before the creature's vast maw, yelling for help as they did so.

"Geneva! Somebody! Please God, it's going to eat us alive!"

"I'm coming!" Geneva called back to him.

She was still digging through the vomitus, searching for her sword. Her endeavor was not helped by the violent rocking of the boat, which was escalating as the dragon's motion turned the waters around the *Belbelo* to a seething frenzy.

The dragon's maw was a foot or two from the brothers now. Having nowhere else to run, Mischief fled into the smoky cabin.

"Meat!" the dragon yelled, determined to devour its mutilators. *"You are all meat!"*

The spikes on the dragon's hood prevented it from getting through the door, but the maddened beast wasn't going to let a little detail like that stop it. It shook its head back and forth with such violence that the doorframe cracked and broke. Then it pushed its head in through the opening it had made and into the cabin.

The brothers were trapped.

"Kick it!" yelled Fillet.

"Punch it!" yelled Drowze.

With no hope of escape to left or right of the monster, and only the prospect of its hot-breathed throat ahead, Mischief went into a flailing frenzy, punching its snout, its lips, even its gums. But it availed him nothing. The worm thrust its head into the cabin and closed its teeth around the brothers' body. It did so with a curious gentility. No doubt it could have bitten Mischief in half if it had desired to do so, but it apparently wanted to torment him with a slow devouring, to which end it dragged the screaming brothers out through the smashed door.

On deck, everybody was yelling now, with the exception of Tria. Threats, demands, prayers: all were being offered up to keep Mischief from being eaten alive.

The dragon was unmoved. Slowly—almost

majestically—it lifted its head, the brothers' body hanging out of either side of its mouth, and began to sink back down into the frantic waters of the Izabella.

In one last act of desperation, Tom ran to the edge of the boat, reached out, and seized hold of Mischief's hand.

Somehow the worm managed to speak, even though it had a choice piece of meat between its teeth.

"Two for the price of one," it growled.

"Geneva!" Tom yelled. *"For A'zo's sake, help us!"*

"I'm here!" Geneva yelled back to him.

She had finally located her sword. Not waiting to wipe the slime off it, she raced over the pitching deck to strike the enemy afresh.

Tom had caught hold of the rail of the *Belbelo* with one hand, but his grip on the slick rail was tenuous; and every time the dragon pulled to loosen Tom's hold, its teeth sank more deeply into John Mischief's body.

He and his brothers were not bearing all this in silence. They were letting it be known that this was an agony; eight voices, all howling or sobbing or shouting, demanding that something be done to free them before it was too late.

Geneva yelled out to the dragon now, as she came to the side of the boat.

"Put them down, worm!" she demanded. *"Or I take your life. Down, I said!"*

The dragon looked at Geneva's sword from the corner of its blood-blackened eye. Then—seeing that if it held on to its quarry for another moment, Geneva would slash its throat—it did three things in quick succession. It let go of John Mischief, who lost his grip on Tom and fell into the water; it lifted one of its taloned forefeet and brought it down on the side of the boat, crashing through the deck and all the boards beneath to a spot well below the waterline. And finally it picked up Two-Toed Tom and threw him as far as it could from the *Belbelo*.

As the creature turned back, Geneva's sword slashed across the dragon's upper chest. The worm unleashed an agonized din; the pitch of its vibrations such that all the nails in the deck shot up out of the boards, leaving only the pitch that the shipwrights had used to seal the vessel holding the boards together.

Then it dived after Geneva with terrifying speed, its pursuit driving her back across the boat, her weight enough to crack the pitch and separate the boards.

In that instant the *Belbelo*—which had endured much, and mightily—became a doomed vessel.

"Hemmett!" Geneva yelled. The Captain had been at the wheel throughout the dragon's attack, attempting to keep his vessel from capsizing in the tumult the worm had created. *"Get Tria off the boat!"*

"But my ship—"

"There's no help for it, Captain! *Save the child!*"

As she spoke, the dragon's jaws snapped closed, three inches from Geneva's face. Its stinging, rancid blood, along with a wave of heat from its pierced lung, erupted from the wound she'd made in its chest, spattering her arms and neck, but she refused to let the pain drive her back. She held her ground, even though the wounded dragon snapped again and again, almost taking off her face. Luckily, with only one eye its spatial judgment was spoiled so that it repeatedly missed its target. But the sound when the teeth met was terrifyingly solid: like the din of an iron door slamming closed over and over.

Geneva took a deep breath and lifted her sword. She knew she would not have a second chance at the blow she was about to deliver. She would have to drive *down*, behind the solid breastbone, in order to pierce its heart. It would either find its way into the dragon's vitals and kill the damned thing, or she would miss and the worm would swallow her.

Making a silent prayer to the ninety-one goddesses of her homeland, she raised her sword.

The creature was preparing to snap at her again. She could hear the muscles of its jaws creaking like an immense spring as they opened.

Trusting to the goddesses and her instinct to guide her, she ducked down beneath the dragon's jaw and put the tip of her sword against its scaly throat. She met resistance immediately, as though she was pressing against bone. Cursing, she tried another place.

The dragon opened its mouth, expelling the stench of its stomachs.

This was it! She had to strike. It was now or never.

She *pushed*; and yes, the sword broke the armor of hard, gray-green scales and pierced its flesh.

She threw all her body weight against the sword. It was enough. The blade slid down behind the creature's breastbone.

She felt the worm's serpentine body shudder as the blade ran down into the cavity of its breast and pierced its vast heart. Its mouth, already gaping, opened a little wider still. And from deep, deep within the vile convolutions of the thing there came a noise like the growling of a thousand rabid dogs.

"*Die*," she said to it, just loud enough that it would hear.

Then she twisted her blade in its heart. The rabid din got louder, and the stench from its stomachs became foul beyond measure: the smell of death released from the entrails of the beast.

Slowly, the dragon's good eye slid to the left, so as to fix on Geneva one last time. It curled back its upper lip, baring its formidable array of teeth. But this was all an empty show. Its din was dying away. There was no real fury left in its wounded body.

The dragon trembled down to its stinking core. Then, putting both its front legs on the side of the sinking vessel, it pushed off.

Geneva let her sword slip out of her hands rather than risk being pulled into the sea as the dragon made its departure. She stumbled back onto the disintegrating deck, which was now six inches deep in water, scarcely believing that she'd bested the beast.

"Are you alive?" McBean yelled to her.

"Just," she said.

While Geneva had been fighting with the dragon, McBean had broken out the little red lifeboat and had launched it over the opposite side of the *Belbelo*. Now he was hurriedly depositing Tria—for whom the dragon had forfeited its life—in the boat.

Kiss Curl Carlotti was meanwhile attempting to salvage as much as he could from the sinking vessel. The precious map which Tom and Geneva had been consulting went into the Captain's hands for safekeeping. The rest—some food, some kegs of water, a few more weapons—were quickly stored at the bottom of the lifeboat.

Geneva drew a deep breath, thanked the goddesses for her survival, and started across the sinking vessel to the lifeboat. She scanned the waters as she did so, hoping against hope that the Izabella would give up the pair that she had claimed. The dragon had not yet sunk beneath the waves, she saw. Though weakened by blood loss—indeed barely able to lift its head above the waters—it continued to stay in the vicinity of the *Belbelo*, as though it hoped it might still claim its wounder. The Izabella was dark with its blood, and there was a yellowish steam rising off the waves, as if the mixture of salt water and the dragon's fluids were causing some kind of alchemical reaction.

"Do you see any sign of Tom or Mischief?" the Captain asked Geneva.

"No," she said grimly. "Nothing."

"Here . . ." said a frail voice from the railing.

Geneva looked over the side of the ship. There, barely keeping their heads above the churning waters, were John Mischief and his siblings. Some of the brothers looked to have slipped into unconsciousness. Two had their eyes rolled back in their sockets, as if they were dead.

"Oh, Lord," said McBean. "Let's get them in the lifeboat."

Together, Carlotti and Geneva hauled the limp body of Mischief and his brothers out of the water and into the lifeboat. Then McBean pushed the little vessel off from the sinking ship then proceeded to row away from the *Belbelo*, so that they would not be caught in the vortex when the vessel went under.

Tria went quietly to the bow of the little boat and took up her usual position.

"Emergency supplies?" Geneva said, gently easing Mischief's torn shirt out of his pants. The puncture wounds the dragon's teeth had left in his stomach and sides were ragged and deep. Blood was still oozing from them.

Carlotti went to the stern of the lifeboat and brought out the emergency first aid kit. He opened it up and started to select some bandages and gauze, while Geneva kept her hands pressed on the worst of the wounds, to prevent any further blood loss.

They were now a safe distance from the *Belbelo*, and McBean stopped rowing and put up the oars.

"I can take care of Mischief now," the Captain said to Geneva. "You look for Tom."

He pointed to his telescope, which was lying on the floor of the lifeboat.

"Go on," McBean said. Then, with a terrible sadness in his voice, "I may have lost the *Belbelo*, but I'm still Captain of this boat. Find Tom; please God, find him."

Geneva let McBean take over care of Mischief, and

she started to scan the waters in the general vicinity of the spot where Tom had been thrown by the worm.

Some distance from the little lifeboat the broken body of the *Belbelo* moaned eerily, as the waters of the Izabella rushed into her hold. The Captain didn't look up from tending to Mischief. This was not a sight he wished to witness. The noise of the vessel's demise grew louder. Its timbers burst; its mast cracked and fell into the water, throwing up a great wall of water. Then, just before the sea finally closed over her, the *Belbelo* stopped sinking for a long moment, and in the sudden eerie hush her bell could be heard tolling.

Six times it rang, and then the tolling ceased and the rushing of the water began one final time, louder than ever. There was one last, terrible crack from out of the depths, and Captain McBean's noble little vessel went down to join the tens of thousands of ships the Sea of Izabella had claimed over the centuries.

Not once through all of this did the Captain raise his eyes from his patients.

When the noise of the *Belbelo*'s sinking finally quieted, he said:

"Any sign of Tom?"

"Not so far," Geneva replied, still searching the water.

"And the worm?" the Captain said.

"Gone," Geneva replied. "Slipped out of sight when we weren't looking. How are the brothers?"

"Some, I think, are doing better than others," the Captain said grimly. "I've stopped the blood from flowing, but none of them are conscious." He dropped his voice, as though Mischief and his brothers might hear some of what he was saying. "It doesn't look good," he said.

At that moment, Tria piped up, her voice as pale as her skin.

"The Nonce," she said.

Geneva looked up from the melancholy sight of Mischief and his brothers to see that the girl was pointing off to the port side.

A quarter of a mile from them, the waters of the Izabella grew considerably calmer. The storm clouds thinned out, and shafts of sunlight breached them. They illuminated a golden shore, and beyond that shore, a rising landscape of tropical lushness.

Geneva had not been back to the Nonce since the tragic hour of Finnegan's wedding to the Princess Boa; and though she'd surmised, along with Tom, that this was indeed where Tria was leading them, her flesh tingled at the prospect of returning there.

"If there's any hope for Mischief and his brothers," Geneva said, "it's on the Nonce."

"What happens if one of them dies and the rest are still alive?" McBean said.

"We'll deal with that problem when we get to it," Geneva replied. Then more quietly, "Let's just hope we don't have to."

Suddenly there was a rapping on the side of the boat—for all the world like somebody knocking on a door, desiring entrance—and Geneva turned around to see a very welcome sight. Two-Toed Tom was hauling himself up over the side of the lifeboat. She went to help him. He clambered into the boat and collapsed, gasping, on the boards.

"I . . . was . . . afraid . . . you'd sail off and give me up for dead."

"We would have never done that," said Geneva.

"What about our digger?" Tom replied, looking over at Mischief.

"He's very badly wounded. We're heading to the Nonce, Tom. Let's hope we can get some help for him there."

"It's amazing he's even alive," Tom said admiringly. "He was in the dragon's mouth."

"That he was," said the Captain. "If the brothers live, they're going to have quite a tale to tell."

The current was on their side; it carried them swiftly toward the island of the Nonce. The condition of the wounded Mischief and his brothers did not deteriorate significantly as they went, and as the bright shore beckoned, and the smell of blossoms sweetened the air, Geneva's spirits began to rise just a little.

They were within perhaps six hundred yards of the beach when something nudged the little boat from below. Geneva went to the side of the vessel. She could see the reef below; the water was no more than fifteen feet deep. It was a beautiful spectacle: colored fish of every shape and size moving in shoals or happy solitude among the coral canyons.

And then, as she watched, panic seemed to seize them all. As a single animal they twitched and swam into hiding; gone in two heartbeats.

Geneva murmured the beginning of a prayer:

"Goddesses, hear me in my hour of desperation—"

That was as far as she got. At that moment, a midnight-black stain spread through the water beneath the boat.

Geneva took a cautious step back from the edge of the lifeboat.

"Get the child, Captain," she said, very quietly.

"Problem?" he murmured.

"Déjà vu," she said.

"I thought for certain it was—"

"Dead?" said the worm, as it rose out of the darkened waters. It was a truly grotesque sight. Geneva's sword was still lodged in its throat, and the creature's blood ran copiously from the wound, over the once pristine scales of its neck and upper body. Violent shudders passed through its body as though it was about to have a fit of titanic proportions.

"Do you have a gun, Captain?" Geneva murmured.

"Back in the *Belbelo* . . ."

"Something," she said. "Anything. Kiss Curl?"

Carlotti moved down the little boat to look for something that they could use to defend themselves. His motion attracted the gaze of the worm, and without hesitation the creature swooped down. Kiss Curl didn't have a chance. The dragon came up behind him, unhooked his jaw, and took Carlotti into its mouth whole.

"No!" Geneva yelled, flinging herself toward Kiss Curl to catch hold of him before he was swallowed. But the dragon threw back its head, like a bird taking a fish, and Carlotti slid out of sight into one of its bellies, as silent in death as he had been in life.

"Bastard thing!" Geneva said, tears of fury running down her cheeks.

The dragon made a terrible sound in its throat: a low joyless laughter. *"Who will be next?"* it said, scanning the survivors.

"McBean?" Geneva whispered.

"Yes?"

"Does the lifeboat have a flare gun?"

"I believe it does."

"Can you get it?"

"Surely."

"Very slowly, Captain. Take. Your. Time."

The Captain did as Geneva had instructed. With great caution he lifted the center seat of the lifeboat, where there was a compartment containing emergency rations, and—yes!—a flare gun.

The worm meanwhile twitched and reeled. It was obviously getting closer to collapse with every passing moment. But that didn't make it any less dangerous, Geneva knew. She had once seen a dragon take the lives of six people when it had all their swords driven into its head.

"Here," the Captain said, oh-so-softly, and put the flare gun into Geneva's hand.

It was a cumbersome thing, but Geneva knew she didn't need to have perfect aim: her target was large.

Had the worm seen what they were doing? It opened its mouth and loosed a ragged noise, but the sound was more of anguish than of rage; the death tremors in its serpentine body were increasing with every beat of its heart.

Geneva brought the gun into view. The worm's good eye flickered. There was a moment's stillness, then the worm said:

"Damn you, woman."

And Geneva fired the flare.

It left a smoky red trail, bright even in the light of the approaching day.

Though her aim didn't need to be good, it was. The flare flew straight down the dragon's throat, and for a moment the creature became the very image of its mythological self: the fire-breathing beast of the *Testaments of Pottishak* that Geneva had learned by heart at school.

"And yea, the Great Dragon Cascatheka Rendithius came upon the land like a plague, and fire came from its throat and blackened the living earth—"

She had scared herself many times as a child conjuring that image in her mind's eye. But seeing it now—made flesh, made smoke—it was not so terrible. It was just a worm after all: petty and sly and cruel.

Then the gunpowder exploded, and two columns of blinding white fire blew out the monster's eyes. The dragon *screamed*; a shriek that rose out of the inferno of its bellies and out of its throat and its pierced heart.

It lasted a little time, then it died away.

The dragon's body swayed, its eyes reduced to blackened holes, and without further sound the beast collapsed upon itself as though its spine had turned to jelly. It didn't fall to the left or right. It sank upon itself down into the bloodstained waters, descending so gracefully that it was gone from sight with scarcely a bubble.

"Thank you and good night," the Captain remarked bitterly.

"Worms," Geneva said, matching his bitterness. "I hate them with all my heart. And now they've taken Kiss Curl from us. I swear . . . I *swear* I will not be content until every dragon is wiped off these islands. And out of the waters too. Every last one." She looked sideways at Tom and the Captain. "Agreed?"

"Agreed," they both said.

They all stood in silence then, meditating for a time on their lost comrade.

And while they did so, the tide carried them gently to the beach, so that by the time their silent prayers were over, and they raised their heads, the hull of the lifeboat was gently nudging the soft white sand of the Nonce.

"We're here," said Tria.

"Finnegan is somewhere on this island?" Geneva said.

"Yes," the child replied.

Tom shook his head in disbelief.

"Back where it all started," he said. "Who would have thought?"

They said no more, but worked in thoughtful silence for the next little while, carrying the body of John Mischief and his brothers from the boat and up the sand to the cool shadows of the blossom-filled trees that lined the shore.

26

THE HOUSE OF LIES

CANDY WALKED ACROSS ROLLING hills, the route before her illuminated only by stars. As she went, she kept her eye on the strange domed house that was built on top of the hill. She was more tired and hungry with every step she took, and was desperately hoping she'd find a simple welcome there at the house; a place where she could finally lay her head down and sleep. Her limbs felt like lead, and her eyelids kept fluttering closed, so that it felt that she was actually sleepwalking.

She contemplated lying down right where she stood, making a nest for herself in the grass and napping until the worst of her exhaustion passed. But she rapidly argued herself out of that plan. She had no idea of what kind of animals lived on Ninnyhammer. For all she knew it could be an island of venomous toads, vampiric weasels and rabid snakes. Given the variety of strange fauna she'd encountered during her travels, anything was possible. So on she went, though her pace was slowing, step by exhausted step.

When she was about a mile from the house, she came upon a pillar topped with a little platform on which a well-fed fire was blazing. There were perhaps a dozen other such pillars, all topped with fires, which apparently marked the perimeter of the homeowner's property.

They certainly marked *something*, because once she had walked past the pillar, there was a subtle change in atmosphere. Though the pillar fires weren't particularly large, they cast a light with a strength out of all proportion to their size, multiplying Candy's shadow and making the solid ground appear to cavort beneath her feet.

She also sensed the presence of living creatures in her imminent vicinity, though for some reason she couldn't catch sight of them. Perhaps they were too quick for her weary eyes; or hidden in the long grass, or simply, given that this was the Abarat, *invisible*. But sometimes she felt them brushing her shins, or nudging the back of her legs.

After a while their teasing presence began to annoy her.

"Who are you?" she demanded finally. "Show yourselves, will you? There's nothing I hate more than games of hide-and-seek."

Her demand had an immediate effect. Two animals, twice as large as domestic cats but definitely of the feline family, emerged from behind a scattering of rocks close by. They had fur the color of brick and flame, with black stripes and vast, luminous eyes.

"You look hungry," she said to them. "But it's no

good looking at me. I don't have anything to give you."

By way of reply the scrawniest of the two cats let out a spine-tingling yowl, and within thirty seconds, half a dozen of its brethren had emerged from hiding. They all studied Candy with the same wide-eyed intensity as had the first couple.

Candy was just a little unnerved. Were they now sizing her up for devouring? If not, then why had they been following so closely on her heels, as though they were sniffing her raw flesh?

She halted a second time, turned back to them and said: "Will you just *stop* staring at me? Don't you know it's *rude*?"

If they understood, they didn't respond to the instruction. They just kept following her, staring, staring, as she strode along the narrow track that zigzagged up the slope toward the domed house.

In fact, the closer she got to the house the more agitated the cats' behavior became. Rather than being content to follow on her heels they ran ahead, weaving back and forth in front of her, as though they intended to trip her up. As they wove, they all let out the same caterwauling sound. It sounded like a chorus of damned souls, and it made Candy's stomach churn to hear it.

At last she could bear it no longer. She nimbly leaped over the backs of the animals in her path and made a desperate dash for the house. The cat-beasts came after her, their cacophony mounting in volume and disharmony the closer she got to the threshold.

She could feel their hot breath on the backs of her

legs as she ran, and she feared that at any moment the fastest of them would leap and dig its claws into her legs, immobilizing her. She managed to stay ahead of them, but the chase took its toll. By the time she reached the house, she was gasping for breath, her lungs and throat burning.

She banged on the door, and shouted as best her fiery throat would allow, *"Is there anybody at home?"*

There was no reply.

She banged again, yelling with fresh gusto. By now, the cats had caught up with her, but for some reason instead of attacking her they simply walked to and fro, two or three yards from the threshold, yowling.

"Will *somebody* please help me?" Candy said, hammering on the door yet again.

This time she heard the sound of somebody moving behind the door.

"Hurry," she implored.

After a few seconds the door was opened by an acidic-looking man in a bright yellow suit. He was short, but his height was increased by the fact that he wore not one unshapely hat on his head but several, all perched on top of one another. He also carried a hat in either hand, which he promptly added to the unruly pile. He then picked up a long staff that was propped just inside the front door and with a curt: "Stand aside, girl!" he charged past Candy and went after the cats with his staff.

"Get out of my sight, you repugnant specks of rabidity!" he hollered. *"You, girl: get inside!"*

The animals scattered until they were out of the

range of his staff. But once that was accomplished they began their to-ing and fro-ing afresh, accompanied by that same anxious yowling.

"Thank you," Candy said to her rescuer. "I was certain they were planning to attack me."

"Oh, they were," the man replied unsmiling. "I've no doubt of that. They were sent by the Devil himself to torment me, those damn tarrie-cats."

"Tarrie-cats, you call them?"

"Yes. Tarrie-cats. They have their own city on the other side of the island. It's called High Sladder. Why the hell they just can't *stay* there is beyond me. Did any of them get their claws in you?"

"No, they didn't touch me. I was just frightened because they were chasing me. And then there was that noise they were making . . ."

"Vile, isn't it?" the man said grimly, waving Candy aside so that he could bolt the door, top, middle and bottom. "Believe me when I tell you there's reason to be afraid of those creatures. Every single one of them has taken an innocent life."

"No?"

"It's God's honest truth! Children have been smothered by fur balls. Babies have been bled dry by tarrie-cat fleas the size of my thumb. You're lucky you had the energy to outrun them. If you'd slipped and fallen, they would have been on you in a heartbeat. I saw you from my big window"—he pointed up the stairs to what was presumably the dome of the house—"and I sent down a little incantation for you, to speed your heels. I hope it helped."

"Well, it must have worked, because here I am."

"Here you are indeed. And I'm happy to see you." He set the stick down and turned to clasp Candy's hand. "I'm Kaspar Wolfswinkel: philosopher, thaumaturgist and connoisseur of fine rums. And you are—?"

"Candy Quackenbush."

"Quackenbush. Quack. En. Bush. That's not an Abaratian name."

"No . . . no, it's not. I'm a visitor, I suppose you'd say."

Kaspar's deeply lined and gnomic face was a perfect portrait of fascination.

"Indeed?" he remarked casually. "A visitor? From . . ." His finger noodled about in the air. "The *other* place, perhaps."

"The Hereafter? Yes."

"Well, well," Wolfswinkel said. "That's quite a journey you've taken. All the way from there to . . ."

"Here?" Candy prompted.

"Yes. Quite so. There to here. That's aways." He smiled, though the expression sat uncomfortably on a face made for scowls and gloom. "You know, you really don't know how wonderful it is to have you in the house with me."

"Are you all alone?"

"Well, more or less," Kaspar said, leading Candy into his living room. It made Samuel Klepp's press-room look tidy by contrast. Books, pamphlets and papers lay on every surface but one, the comfortable green leather chair into which Wolfswinkel now lowered himself, leaving Candy to stand. "Most of my

family and friends are deceased," he went on. "Victims
of the war waged upon us by those wretched *kitties*."
He sighed. "It was paradise here on Ninnyhammer till
the tarrie-cats built that shantytown they call a city. I
mean, I'm an older man. Semiretired. This was going
to be the perfect Hour for me to spend my twilight
years. I planned to sit and sip my rum and ruminate on
my life. Things done, things left undone. You know
the way it is. I regret nothing, of course."

"Oh," said Candy. "Well I suppose that's good." She
was a little lost for words on the subject of regret so
she moved on to a subject she did know something
about. "It must be lonely," she said.

"Yes," Kaspar said. "It gets lonely, to be sure. But
what's worse than the loneliness are the memories."

"Of what?"

"Of how Ninnyhammer *used* to be, before the tarrie-
cats came. They turned this perfect island into a
nightmare. They really did. Every now and again I get
a supply of fuel for the fires—"

"The fires on the poles?"

"Yes, they at least allow me to *see* the enemy. But I
live in fear of the time when I run out of fuel and—"

"—the fires will go out."

"Exactly. When that happens . . . well . . . I fear
that'll be the end of me and Kaspar Wolfswinkel will
be a memory too."

"Surely there must be some way to *catch* the cats,"
Candy said. "Back home in Chickentown—"

"I'm sorry? Chickentown? What exactly is a
Chickentown?"

"It's the town where I live. Or where I *used* to live."

"What a perfectly ridiculous name for a place," Wolfswinkel commented.

His tone brought out a little defensiveness in Candy. "It's no weirder than *Ninnyhammer*," she remarked.

Wolfswinkel's eyes grew narrow and sly. "Well, of course this island isn't my real *home*," he said.

"No? So why do you stay here?"

"It's a very long story. Maybe I'll tell you later. Why don't you sit down? You look tired."

Candy glanced around the room for a place where she might take up his invitation. Wolfswinkel, seeing that all the chairs were occupied, muttered something under his breath and threw a simple gesture toward one of the smaller chairs. The pile of books perched upon it flew off the seat like a small flock of startled birds.

"Now *sit*," he said.

"May I take off my shoes?"

"Be my guest. Allow me to get you something to eat. Make yourself at home."

"My feet are killing me."

"I knew somebody who had feet like that. They'd walk all over him. Archie Kashanian was his name. He used to wake up with footprints all over his chest, all over his face. It was the death of him, finally."

Candy wasn't sure whether Kaspar was making a joke or not. So rather than insult him by laughing she kept a straight face, though the idea of somebody being stomped to death by his own feet seemed utterly nonsensical.

Once again Candy changed the subject.

"Back in the Hereafter," she said, "we have people who catch stray animals and find new homes for them. Or if they can't do that, then they have them put down."

"Homes?" Wolfswinkel said, his tone incredulous. "Who would give a home to any one of those *monsters*? The Infernal Regions is the only home the tarries deserve. Anyway, they can't be caught. They're too quick. They have to be tricked. Poison! That's the way. You see that plate of fish on the table by the door? It contains enough scathrassic acid to kill a whole pack of them. If only I could just get them to *eat* it. But they're suspicious of me." He paused, then he snapped his fingers. "Wait a minute," he said. "Maybe *you'd* have more luck! Yes. I believe you would."

"Me?" said Candy.

"Yes, *you*! If they saw you putting out the food— you, whom they don't really know—they'd be fooled into taking it." He looked smugly satisfied with his little plan. "You just need to be very casual—" He started to get up from his armchair.

"Wait!" Candy said. "I don't want to disappoint you, Mr. Wolfswinkel, especially as you've been so kind and all, but I'm not going to poison cats for you."

"If they were just cats I'd understand your moral dilemma, Miss Quackenbush. But they're not. They're hellspawn. Trust me on this. *Hellspawn*. After all the harm they've done—not just to me, but to poor, innocent people right across Ninnyhammer—scathrassic acid is kinder than they deserve, believe me. If there were any justice in heaven, they'd be struck down by lightning, every last one of them!"

Before Candy could reply to this outburst from her host, there was a sound from an adjacent room.

"What was that?" she said.

"Oh, it was just the wind," Wolfswinkel replied hurriedly. "Take no notice."

"It didn't sound like the wind," Candy said, getting up out of her chair. "It sounded like a voice. Like somebody crying."

"Oh! Crying! Well, yes. Of course there's crying! I didn't want to depress you when you first arrived, but there are several mourners here in the house with me."

"Mourners?"

"One of my friends—a dear, dear friend—was killed by the tarrie-cats just yesterday, and we're having a wake on his behalf. You know, gathering to toast his memory and tell tales of what a fine fellow he was."

"Really?" Candy said. Something about this explanation didn't quite ring true. "If there's a wake going on," she said, "then why are you wearing a bright yellow suit?"

Wolfswinkel glanced down at his jaundiced ensemble, then feigned a look of surprise. "This is *yellow*?" he said. "Are you sure?"

"Yes."

"Oh, dear," he said pitifully. "Poor Kaspar. The blindness is getting worse."

"You're saying you didn't realize that was a yellow suit?" said Candy, more and more certain that her suspicions were correct, and that this strange little man was for some reason deceiving her.

"Yes," Kaspar said, putting his hand to his brow, as though the drama was too much for him. But Candy wasn't convinced by his hammy theatrics. Her real interest now was to discover who had made the grieving sound she'd heard.

She got up from her chair and went to the adjoining door, through which the sound of sobbing had come.

"Where *are* all these mourners then?" she said, as she went. Kaspar moved to stop her, but he wasn't quick enough. Candy stepped through the door into the next room.

Just as she'd suspected, there was neither a casket here, nor a corpse, nor so much as a single mourner. There was simply a dark, cluttered room, one of its walls dominated by a huge portrait of Kaspar sitting on an animal that looked like a cross between a giant armadillo and a camel.

"There's no wake going on in this house!" Candy snapped. "You were lying to me. I can't bear liars!"

Kaspar had followed her through the door. "So what if I was?" he replied, nonchalantly. "It's my house. I can lie in my house if I want to. I can run around in the nude yelling hallelujahs if I so desire."

"Didn't anybody ever tell you it was rude to lie?"

"*Maybe* I can't help it," Kaspar said. "*Maybe* I've got an incurable disease that *makes* me lie. Poor Kaspar."

"Oh," Candy said. "And do you *have* such a disease?"

"Maybe I do. Maybe I don't."

"Oh, *stop* it," Candy snapped, her temper stretched to breaking point. "Can't you simply tell me the truth?"

"Well . . . yes, I suppose I could. But where would the fun be in that?"

"You know what?" Candy said. "This is a ridiculous conversation. And you are a ridiculous little man."

She turned on her heel and started to walk back toward the door she'd just walked through.

"I wouldn't go out there if I were you. The tarrie-cats are still out there."

"So what?" said Candy. "I'd prefer to take my chances with them than stay in here another—"

Before she could finish, Kaspar stepped into the doorway, blocking her path.

"What are you doing?" Candy said. "Get out of my way."

He didn't reply to this. He simply raised his arm, put his stubby-fingered hand over Candy's face, and shoved.

Candy stumbled backward, her foot catching on a rucked-up rug. Down she went, on her tailbone. It hurt, and she yelped.

"I think you should stop being so judgmental, little missy," Wolfswinkel said, every little trace of kindliness abruptly gone from his face. He stood over her and looked her dead in the eye. "Believe me, I've done worse than lying in my life. A whole lot worse."

"I believe you have," Candy said softly.

She started to scramble to her feet. Wolfswinkel

neatly kicked the legs from under her, and down she went for a second time. She was beginning to get a little scared of Wolfswinkel now. He might look like a clown, with his stupid hats and his yellow suit, but then she'd always been a little afraid of clowns.

"I want to leave now," she told him.

"Do you indeed? Well, I'm afraid you're not going to. You're going to stay here with me."

"You can't *keep* me here. I'm not—"

"—a child? You are to me. To me you are an infant. A baby with no one to protect you. I'd lay a bet that nobody even knows you're here."

Candy didn't reply, but her silence was all the confirmation Wolfswinkel required.

"I didn't lie about one thing," Kaspar said.

"What was that?"

"I *did* whisper an incantation when I saw you. I prayed you'd make the mistake of ignoring the tarriecats who were trying to warn you about coming up here. Lo and behold, my supplications were answered! Into my hands you came, like a stupid little fish."

"One minute I'm a baby, the next minute I'm a fish," Candy snapped. "Make up your mind!"

She was feeling more afraid of Wolfswinkel by the moment, but she wasn't going to show it.

"My error," Kaspar said. "You're not a baby, and you're not a fish. You're a hostage."

"A *what*?"

"You heard me: a hostage. I'll bet there are people out there who would pay a few thousand zem to have you in their hands."

"Well, you can forget that," Candy said. "I don't have any friends in the Abarat."

"*Now* who's lying?" Wolfswinkel said, bending down to poke Candy. "Of course you've got friends. A pretty girl like you? You've probably got half a dozen boys pining away for you."

Candy laughed out loud at the preposterousness of this.

"Then you have family."

"Not here I don't," Candy said, thinking, while she spoke, of how quickly she could squirm out from between Wolfswinkel's legs and get to the door. "My parents are—"

"—in Chickentown."

"Yes."

"Hmm," said Wolfswinkel. "Well give me time. I'll find *somebody* here who wants you. Somebody who'll pay a price. Malingo? Where are you? *Malingo!* Present yourself before me *right now*, or I'll have your hide for boot leather."

"I'm here," said a voice from above, and there—hanging upside down from a roof beam—was a creature that resembled a Halloween mask come to life. His skin was a mottled orange, the pupils in his dark-rimmed eyes dark slits. There were four knobbly horns on his head, and two large fans of leathery skin spread from either side of his head, where ordinary folks would have had ears. He was wearing a dirty T-shirt and an even dirtier pair of pants.

He would have made a fearful sight if he hadn't worn such a pitiful expression on his face. Seeing him,

Candy thought back to the weeping she'd heard when she'd first come into the house. This Malingo was surely the source of that unhappiness.

"Come down here and catch hold of this wretched child for me," Wolfswinkel told him. *"Now!"*

"I'm coming, I'm coming."

Malingo began to clamber down out of the rafters.

But before he could reach ground level, Candy was away. She gave Kaspar a two-handed shove in the belly and then she raced back to the door between the rooms, darting through to the front room. Malingo was on the ground now. She could hear the slap of his bare feet as he raced over the tiled floor in pursuit of her. He was fast. She was barely halfway across the room when he caught hold of her.

"Don't struggle," he said softly. "It'll be worse for the both of us if you fight him, believe me."

Hearing the delicacy in Malingo's voice, Candy looked up and met his gaze. There was a sweetness in his eyes she had not expected to find there, the Halloween horror of his face concealing something far gentler.

"Bring her back here," Wolfswinkel yelled. "And be quick about it."

Malingo duly pulled Candy away from the front door and into the second room, where Kaspar was standing in front of a long mirror, rearranging the ridiculous tower of hats on his head.

"I suggest you take Malingo's advice," Wolfswinkel said. "You really don't want to be on my bad side."

Candy ignored him, struggling to free herself from

Malingo's grip. But it was a lost cause. The creature was considerably stronger than she was. And to add to his physical strength, he gave off a dizzying smell, a bittersweet mixture of cloves and cinnamon and rotted limes.

"Now listen, my dear," Wolfswinkel said, "you have to calm down. You're only going to exhaust yourself, struggling like that. I'm not going to do any harm to you as long as you behave."

He turned away from the mirror and walked across to the other side of the room, where a large square of tile on the floor had been painted an eye-pricking blue. At each corner of the square was a short, fat candle.

"Candles, illume," Kaspar said, and with a little sound like a snatched breath each of the candles ignited itself.

"Brighter!" he instructed them, and the flames grew longer, the illumination they threw up making every other lamp in the room inconsequential.

"Now," said Kaspar, turning his attention back to Candy. "Let's see what secrets you're keeping from me, shall we? Malingo, you know what to do."

Malingo pushed Candy toward the blue square. "Don't worry," he whispered. "It doesn't hurt."

"I heard that," Wolfswinkel said. "I don't know why you're trying to curry favor with this girl. She can't be of any use to you."

"I'm just—"

"Shut up!" Kaspar snapped. "Put her in the light! Go on!"

Malingo gave Candy a second little shove and she

stumbled forward into the square. As she did so, she felt her body pass through an invisible barrier. Within the square, she felt a peculiar pressure on her, as though the air inside the design was heavier than the air outside, and it was pressing against her body from every side. It was not by any means a pleasurable sensation. The pressure made it harder for her to draw breath, and her head ached furiously.

Not only that, but being in the painted box sealed her off from the outside world. Now—though she could see Wolfswinkel giving orders to Malingo—she could not hear his voice. Clearly there was now some kind of invisible wall around her. She tested the thesis by extending her hand. It was like pushing her fingers into cold fat. The thickened air congealed against her skin, and the sensation was so disgusting that Candy withdrew her hand before she even reached the limits of her persistence.

Wolfswinkel, meanwhile, was waving his staff around as though he were writing letters in the air.

The candles flickered; the cell convulsed around Candy.

And then, much to her horror, she felt something *pulling* at her. Not at her hand or arm, but at some place in the center of her head. It didn't make her headache any worse, but she still felt somehow invaded by the sensation. It was as though Wolfswinkel was reaching inside her to pull something out. She saw strange smears of images appearing in the air at the end of Wolfswinkel's staff, and as they settled and focused she realized that these images were recognizable to her.

Ten, twenty, thirty pictures appeared, all plucked out of her memories. There was 34 Followell Street, where she'd stood so often, dreaming of the far away. There was her bedroom, and her mother's face, and the schoolyard, and Widow White's house, with its front lawn covered in colored pinwheels.

Apparently none of these images was of the slightest interest to Wolfswinkel, because he erased them with an irritated wave of his staff.

He gathered his strength for a second summoning, and a new wave of images emerged from Candy's head, these more recent. First there was the lighthouse, and the ramshackle jetty of Hark's Harbor. Then there was Mischief and Shape and the turbulent waters of the Sea of Izabella; then the Sea-Skippers, and the Yebba Dim Day.

In the midst of all these familiar sights, however, was one Candy didn't recognize. It was a shape made of blue-green light that looked like a short length of braided ribbon which had been put in the deep freeze. There were tiny crystals glinting on it, and from one end spilled a trail of brightness that broke into tiny pinpoints of intense luminescence before they melted on the air.

At the sight of it Wolfswinkel paused, the color rising in his already ruddied cheeks. There was a look of shock on his face, of disbelief.

"Will you look at that?" he mouthed.

An ugly, avaricious smile had begun to creep onto his face. He left his staff to stand by itself, and he spat onto his palms, rubbing them together before wiping them on his trouser legs. With his hand thus prepared, he reached forward to take hold of the strange object that he'd conjured from out of Candy's mind. Though it wasn't solid (how could it be, when it was made of pure *thought*?) it nevertheless seemed to gain a measure of solidity as his hands closed around it.

Candy felt a terrible wrenching pain in her skull as Wolfswinkel's fingers took possession of the object. There were flashes of white at the corners of her eyes, which rapidly spread, so that in a matter of moments they washed out her sight completely.

Her legs grew suddenly weak beneath her. She toppled forward against the invisible wall of her square blue cell, and then collapsed to the tiled floor.

The last thing she remembered was the sound of Malingo's voice, breaking through from the other side.

He didn't speak her name. He simply let out a cry of distress. It echoed in Candy's throbbing head for a moment. Then it faded away, and she was lost to blissful unconsciousness.

27

WORDS WITH THE
CRISS-CROSS MAN

CANDY WOKE WITH THE worst headache she'd ever experienced in her life, but at least she was no longer in the cell in which Kaspar Wolfswinkel had imprisoned her. She was lying sprawled on a decadently overstuffed velvet chaise lounge, tossed there along with a load of old books. She sat up, her hand going up to her throbbing brow. She felt mildly feverish, and her eyes burned behind her lids when she blinked.

Wolfswinkel was talking in the next room, sounding half crazy with excitement.

"Yes . . . yes . . . I *know* what I have, believe me! This is the Pyramid Key, right here in my hand. Somebody had put it in her thoughts, but I've got it now."

Candy got to her feet, fighting her giddiness, and went to the door between the rooms. As she approached it, however, something dropped into view in front of her. It was Malingo. He was hanging upside down from the rafters, with one long, orange and partially bent finger pressed to his lips. Candy pointed through the door, indicating that she wanted to see Wolfswinkel, but he waved her away. Candy did as instructed. Bizarre though Malingo was, there was something about his gaze that not only endeared him to her, but also made her instinctively trust him.

He climbed over the ceiling and, still inverted, clambered down the wall, using minuscule cracks in the plaster as toe- and finger-holds. Then he flipped over and dropped lightly to the ground three or four yards from Candy, his expression and his posture tentative, as though he was nervous in case all he earned for his troubles was a blow.

"It's all right," Candy whispered. "I'm not going to hit you. You don't have to be frightened of me."

Malingo sidled up to her.

"You have to get out of here," he whispered. "My master's a very cruel man."

"What are you two talking about?" Wolfswinkel yelled from the other room. "Show yourself, child! *Now!*"

Candy knew it would be wiser to obey this petty despot rather than argue with him. So she went to the door and stepped into view.

Wolfswinkel was sitting in his leather armchair with the receiver of an antiquated telephone in his hand.

"I'm talking to somebody who has some considerable interest in you," he said.

"Oh, really?" she replied with a little shrug.

"It seems you're quite the celebrity, Candy

Quackenbush. At least that's what I'm hearing." He returned his attention to the person at the other end of the line. "Yes, I've got her here right now. She's standing right in front of me, as plain as day. Oh, she's about five-three, five-four.

"So, what am I to do with her, Otto? What's she worth on the open market?" Clearly the man he was talking to became agitated at this remark, because Wolfswinkel's next words were: "Calm down, Otto. That was a joke. I know Carrion wants her. But be reasonable. If he wants both the Key *and* the girl, then I'm going to be expecting something substantial by way of recompense. That's only right and proper, isn't it? Ninnyhammer? No, I don't want Ninnyhammer. When all this is over I never want to see this wretched little rock ever again. No. I want to be Lord of Babilonium! Or Commexo City! Anywhere but here. I'm sick of living in a place where everybody's half asleep!"

Again, the person at the other end of the line had something to say in response. Wolfswinkel listened, drumming his stubby fingers—like the fingers of a chicken slaughterer, fat with blood—on the threadbare arm of his chair.

"Have you quite finished, Houlihan?" he said finally. "You seem to forget that *I'm* the one with the cards at this table. I've got something Carrion wants *badly*. No, no, not the girl. The Key! I've got the Key! I don't know how she got hold of it, but I'd stake my hats on the fact that it's the real thing. I know what *power* feels like. And this is it."

He raised his right hand, which held the aforementioned key, and casually studied the object. He wore a smug smile as he listened to the reply from the fellow he was speaking to.

Finally, he said, "Candy? Get over here, will you? I'm speaking to a friend of mine called Otto Houlihan. He's a . . . deal maker and he wants to speak with you." Wolfswinkel beckoned to her, his gesture impatient. "Hurry up, girl! And be polite. He just wants to know you're the real thing." Candy kept her distance. *"Come on,"* Wolfswinkel muttered, his face reddening with fury.

"Go," Malingo murmured behind her. "He loses his temper in a heartbeat."

Very reluctantly, Candy went over to Wolfswinkel.

"Here she is, Otto," Wolfswinkel said. He handed Candy the receiver. "Like I said, you be nice. Otto Houlihan's a very old friend of mine. We were at school together."

Candy took the receiver from Wolfswinkel and put it to her ear.

"Hello . . . ?" she said.

"Am I speaking to Candy Quackenbush?"

The voice at the other end was silky smooth. She imagined she was talking to someone closely related to a snake, which—given the variety of people she'd met so far—was not beyond the bounds of possibility.

"Yes, I'm Candy Quackenbush."

"Well, you're a very lucky young lady."

"Am I?" Candy said. She didn't feel very lucky at the moment. "Why's that?"

"Well, carrying that Key around could have been the death of you."

"Really?" she said. She didn't believe a word of it.

"Agree with him," Wolfswinkel mouthed.

"I didn't realize I even *had* a key," Candy said. She remembered how passionately Mischief had impressed on her the need to deny that she had it.

"You tell me the truth now," Houlihan was saying. "It'll be better for you if you tell the truth than be found out later."

"I *am* telling the truth."

"I won't warn you again," Otto Houlihan said, his voice losing its silkiness. "Where did you steal it from?"

"I didn't steal it," Candy said. "I told you: I didn't know I had it."

"Wolfswinkel tells me he found it in your thoughts. Are you telling me he's a liar?"

"No," Candy said. "If that's what he says, then I guess he must have found it there."

"But you don't know how it *got* there?"

"No. I don't." The line went quiet for a moment. "Can I go now?" Candy said. "I really don't have anything else to tell you."

"Oh, I think you've got plenty more to tell me," Houlihan said, his voice now entirely bereft of its silken quality. There was now a subtle element of threat in his words. "But we'll have plenty of time to talk when I come to fetch you. Put Kaspar back on. I'll be seeing you very soon."

"He wants to talk to you again," Candy said, passing

the receiver over to Wolfswinkel.

"Are you finished with her?" Wolfswinkel said to Houlihan.

The answer was apparently *yes*, because Wolfswinkel now waved Candy away. She retreated into the next room, relieved that the interrogation was over.

Perhaps she might get out, she thought, while Wolfswinkel was occupied by his telephone call. She went over to the window and tried the handle, but it was locked. Outside, rain was falling. It pattered against the little panes of glass.

"There's no way out. At least not that way."

She looked around. Malingo was hanging upside down from the rafters. She wandered over to him.

"Can I trust you?" she said. It was a silly question, of course; if she couldn't, he wouldn't confess to it. But still he nodded, as if he knew what was coming next.

"You have to help me," she whispered to him. "I need to get out of here."

A pitiful expression crossed Malingo's inverted face.

"It's impossible," he said. "You think I haven't tried over the years? But Kaspar always catches me. And when he catches me, he beats me with his stick. You don't want to have that happen."

"I'll risk the beating," Candy said. "This fellow Otto Houlihan is coming to get me. And I really don't want to be here when he arrives."

Malingo looked even more distressed. Rocking back and forth from the rafters he sang a little rhyme:

> *"Houlihan, Houlihan,*
> *The Criss-Cross man,*
> *The Criss-Cross man.*
> *Fetch yourself a holyman*
> *Do it fast*
> *Fast as you can,*
> *Because here comes*
>   *Houlihan,*
> *The Criss-Cross man—"*

"Well that's not very useful," Candy said. "I need help and you hang upside down, singing songs like a crazy man."

"I'm not crazy," Malingo protested. "I'm just tired of being beaten all the time. When I sing my songs it makes me feel better."

He started swinging again, his arms wrapped around his body, a perfect picture of despair.

"Listen to me," Candy said, putting her hand on his shoulder to slow his swinging. "We both want the same thing. You want to get out of here and so do I."

"What are you two *yabbering* about in there?" Wolfswinkel yelled from the next room.

"Nothing," Malingo said plaintively.

"Nothing? Nobody yabbers about nothing, unless they're witless spit-for-brains fools. Is that what you are, Malingo?"

"Y . . . y . . . yes, sir."

"Well, say it out loud so we can hear you! What are you?"

"I've . . . forgotten, sir."

"A spit-for-brain fool. Say it! Go on! Say: I'm a spit-for-brain fool, sir."

"You're a spit-for-brain fool, sir."

Wolfswinkel slammed down the telephone.

"WHAT DID YOU SAY?"

"I mean: *I'm* a fool, sir. I! Me! I'm the spit-in-his-eye fool, sir."

"You know what I'm doing, Malingo?"

"No, sir."

"I'm picking up my stick. And you know what that means . . . don't you?"

Candy watched as two tears formed in Malingo's eyes and ran down over his forehead, then dropped to the carpet.

"Come here, Malingo."

"Leave him alone!" Candy protested. "You're frightening him."

"Keep your mouth shut, or you'll be next! Malingo? *Come here, you little rat-spasm!*"

Candy went to the door. "Please. It was me who was doing the talking, not him."

Wolfswinkel shook his head.

"Why are you standing up for him?" he said. "Oh, *I* know. You're trying to get him to *help* you, aren't you?" He smiled, showing his mostly rotted teeth. "Well let me explain something to you. Malingo's a geshrat. And geshrats are cowards, even the best of them. And Malingo makes most of his breed look like heroes. Come here, Malingo. *Right now!*"

Candy heard a soft thump as Malingo dropped from

the rafters. A few seconds later he appeared at the door.

"Please sir, no sir," he said, the words becoming one pitiful appeal.

"*I said here!* NOW! If I have to wait *one more second*—"

Malingo didn't attempt to seek clemency any longer. He started to walk toward Wolfswinkel, casting a forlorn glance at Candy as he went, as though being beaten in front of her made the prospect even worse.

"On your knees," Wolfswinkel said. "NOW! Come to me on your knees. Bare back!"

Malingo went to his knees and shuffled over to the wizard.

"Please—" Candy began.

"You want to make it worse for him?" Wolfswinkel said, coldly.

"No," said Candy. "Of course not."

"Then *shut up*. And watch. You could very well be next. I have absolutely no compunction about beating a member of the fair sex, believe me."

I bet you haven't, Candy thought. At that moment she couldn't imagine despising anyone with the heat of the hatred she felt for Wolfswinkel. But she didn't dare speak her mind. Not with Malingo at the bully's feet, about to be beaten for the crime of speaking.

"Fetch me a glass of rum, girl," Wolfswinkel said. "And smile, girl, *smile!*"

Candy made a pitiful attempt to look cheery.

"Now, get me my libation! It's on the dresser in the living room. *Go!*"

Candy turned her back and returned to the room where she'd conversed with Malingo.

There was a large, elaborately carved dresser set against the far wall. On it sat a crystal decanter of liquor and a small glass.

She took the stopper from the decanter. As she did so, she glanced up at the row of five paintings lined up on the wall above the dresser. They were all portraits: two women and three men. Underneath the portraits were the names of those portrayed: Jengle Small, Doctor Inchball, Hetch Heckler, Biddy Stuckmeyer and Deborah Jib. There was nothing about the group that suggested they were related or in any way connected, except perhaps for one detail. They were all wearing hats. The same style of hats—no, the same hats, *the very same*—that were now piled somewhat absurdly upon Kaspar Wolfswinkel's head.

As she took notice of this oddity, she heard the sound of Wolfswinkel's stick whistling through the air and landing on Malingo's back. She winced. A second stroke came quickly after the first, then a third, and a fourth and fifth. Between the blows she heard the soft sound of Malingo's sobs. She understood those heart-wracking tears; she'd shed them herself, when her father was done with her. Tears of relief that it was all finished, for now. And tears of fear that it would happen again when she least expected it. Her father hadn't used a stick to strike her, but he'd had his own ways to cause pain.

Trembling with anger and frustration, she poured the glass of rum—silently wishing the wizard would choke on the stuff—put the stopper back in the decanter and started to carry the liquor back to Wolfswinkel. The blows kept falling as she walked in, but as she entered they stopped.

Malingo was curled up in a little ball of pain and tears at Wolfswinkel's feet like a punished animal. The magician was out of breath. There was a catarrhal rattle in his chest.

"The rum! The rum!" he said, beckoning to Candy.

He took the glass from Candy's fingers.

"Out of my sight!" he shouted.

Malingo scuttled away on all fours, up the wall, through the top of the door, and back—Candy assumed—to his favorite hanging place. Back to his rocking and his song about Houlihan and the holyman.

Wolfswinkel downed the rum in one gulp.

"More! More!" he said, proffering the empty glass. "Where's the decanter, girl?"

"I didn't bring it."

"Didn't bring it, you maggoty clod? *Well, get it!*"

Candy ducked just in time.

He swung his staff in her direction. It missed her nose by precious inches.

She backed away from the sweating Wolfswinkel before he could aim a second blow at her, and she retreated out of his range.

Then—cursing the little man under her breath, using a few choice adjectives she had picked up from her dad—she headed into the next room for the rum decanter.

28

A SLAVE'S SOUL

SHE HAD GUESSED CORRECTLY about Malingo.

He was indeed rocking from the rafters, his tears running down his brow and soaking the carpet beneath him.

"We've got to get out of here," Candy mouthed.

He shook his head, his expression one of bottomless despair.

Candy picked up the rum decanter and returned to the front room. As she arrived at the door, the telephone rang. Wolfswinkel picked up the receiver, thrusting the empty glass at Candy to have it refilled.

He had put down his staff, she saw. It lay across the arms of his chair.

What if she threw the decanter at Wolfswinkel, and while he was busy trying to catch it, picked up his staff and made a break for the front door? No; that was no good. Even if she made it out there—and who knew what traps Wolfswinkel had laid around the house to prevent escapees?—she'd be leaving Malingo behind.

She couldn't do that. Though they had had no more than two minutes' worth of conversation, she felt responsible for him. They had to get out together.

She poured the wizard some more rum. Wolfswinkel wasn't even noticing what she was doing. Whatever he was being told on the telephone had him absurdly excited.

"He wants to talk to *me*?" he said. "Really?"

He downed the glass of rum and thrust it toward Candy to be refilled. She obliged happily. She knew from experience what alcohol did to sharp minds. It dulled them, stupefied them. A drunk magician, she reasoned, was a sluggish magician, which was exactly what she wanted right now.

Wolfswinkel emptied the third glass of rum with the same speed as he had the first two. And demanded a fourth. Before he could get it to his lips, however, his whole demeanor changed, and a look of strange reverence came over his face.

"My Lord Midnight," he said. "This is indeed an honor, sir."

Lord Midnight? Candy thought. He's speaking to Christopher Carrion, the Dark Prince himself. And what was the subject under discussion? Apparently *she* was.

"Yes, my lord, she's here," Wolfswinkel said. "She's here right beside me." There was a pause. "Well, if I may be so bold, sir, she doesn't seem to me in any way an extraordinary creature. She's . . . just a girl, you know. Like most girls: something and nothing." There was another pause while Wolfswinkel listened. "Oh, yes sir, I spoke to Otto Houlihan. He's on his way to collect the Key." Another pause. "And the girl, too? Oh yes, of course. She's yours."

He drank the rum and again thrust the glass out to have it refilled. But the decanter was empty. Irritated, Wolfswinkel gestured that Candy should go find some more. She got the impression—judging by the slight trembling in his hands, and the twitches under his eye and at his mouth—that though he was honored to be speaking with the Lord of Midnight, he was also intimidated to his cowardly core.

Candy went next door in search of the liquor. She didn't have to look far. There was a bottle in the dresser. As she wrestled to unscrew it, her eyes went up to the portraits again.

"Who are these people?" she murmured to Malingo.

It took the beaten geshrat a moment to come out of the trance of unhappiness he was in. But when he did, he whispered:

"They were all friends of his. Members of the Noncian Magic Circle. But then he swore allegiance to *King Rot*—"

"Who?"

"Carrion."

"Oh. King Rot. I get it. What did he do, once he'd sworn allegiance?"

"He murdered them."

"What? He murdered his own friends?"

"Rum!" Wolfswinkel roared.

"Why?"

"RUM!"

Wolfswinkel was at the door now, with his empty glass. His face was flushed red with liquor and excitement, like a shiny tomato balanced on top of an overripe banana.

"*That*," he said, with an expansive gesture, "was Lord Midnight himself. My liberation, you see, is imminent. All thanks to you." He smiled lopsidedly at Candy, displaying his ill-kept teeth. "It was quite a moment, missy, when you came knocking at my door. You changed my life. Fancy that, huh? Who'd have thought a little ferret's dung-hole like you would be the cause of Uncle Kaspar's Liberation?"

He walked over and pinched Candy's cheek, as if she were a little child and he the indulgent relative.

"Give me another glass of rum, girl," he said. "Keep me happy till Otto arrives, and maybe I won't beat you black and blue."

Candy took the top off the bottle and poured another brimming glassful. As Wolfswinkel put the glass to his lips, Candy took her life in her hands and deliberately let the bottle slip from between her fingers. It smashed on the floor between them, releasing a pungent stench of rum.

"You idiotic—"

Candy didn't give Wolfswinkel time to finish his next insult. Instead, she pressed her hands against his chest and *pushed*. The rum had made Wolfswinkel unsteady on his feet. He staggered to regain his balance, and while he did so she slipped through the door into the next room.

There, still lying across the armchair where he'd left it, was his staff.

Without giving herself time to question or doubt the wisdom of what she was about to do, Candy picked it up.

The thing vibrated in her grip, as though it resented being handled by a stranger. But she refused to let the staff intimidate her. She held onto it and waited for the inevitable reappearance of its owner.

Somehow, he knew what she'd done, because he yelled: *"Put that down!"* even before he appeared at the door.

The staff's vibrations became still more violent at the sound of its master's voice. But Candy refused to release it.

Wolfswinkel was at the door now, pointing at her.

"I said *put that down*," Wolfswinkel said, his voice slurred with alcohol. "Put it down, or I'll—"

"Or *what*?" Candy said, wielding the stick like a baseball bat. "What will you do? Huh? You can't kill me because then you won't have anything to hand over to your lord and master."

Wolfswinkel wiped away the sweat that had popped up all over his forehead and was threatening to run into his eyes.

"Malingo!" he yelled. *"Get in here! RIGHT NOW!"*

Malingo dutifully crawled in, upside down, around the top of the door.

"Seize that wretch!" Wolfswinkel demanded. "And give me my staff!"

Malingo hesitated, his despairing eyes on Candy.

"I said—"

"I heard what you said," Malingo replied.

Wolfswinkel took a moment to consider what his slave had just said, or rather the tone of it. There was something new in Malingo's voice. Something Wolfswinkel didn't like at all. It called for a new order of threat.

"Do as I say, geshrat. Or so help me I'll break every bone in your body."

"With *what*?" Candy reminded him. "I've got your little magic stick."

"But you don't know how to use it, missy," Wolfswinkel replied, and before Candy could evade him he caught hold of the end of the staff.

Even drunk on rum, he had a supernatural power in his grip. He twisted the stick to the left, then to the right, then to the left again, attempting to wrest it from Candy's grip. But the more violently he twisted, the harder she held on.

"If you don't let go—" he hollered at her, his unpretty face made uglier still by his rage.

"Hot air. That's all you are," Candy said. "Hot air in a banana-skin suit."

Wolfswinkel's lip curled with fury, and he hauled his staff toward him. There was a short scuffle, and in the heat of the moment they both lost their grip on the staff.

It fell to the floor between them and rolled off across the boards.

Both Candy and Wolfswinkel made a lunge to

reclaim it, but before either could reach it Malingo dropped from the ceiling and neatly snatched it up.

A smug smile appeared on Kaspar Wolfswinkel's face.

"Good boy," he said to Malingo. "You are a very, very good boy. I will think of some way to reward you for this." He wiped his sweaty brow with the arm of his yellow jacket. Then he put out his fat hand. "Now give it back to Uncle Kaspar," he said.

The beaten Malingo looked at his master like a creature mesmerized by a poisonous snake. But he didn't move to return the staff.

"Didn't you hear me?" Wolfswinkel demanded. "*GIVE ME MY STAFF.* I'm going to beat this wretched girl till she's yelping. Won't that be fun?"

There was a long, long moment in which nothing happened. Then, slowly—very, very slowly—Malingo *shook his head.*

"Candy . . ." he said quietly, not for a moment taking his eyes off the man who had once been his master. "You'd better go. Quickly, before Houlihan gets here."

"I'm not leaving without you."

At this, Malingo shot her a glance, filled with a mixture of fear and exhilaration.

"Oh, how sweet this is," Wolfswinkel remarked, "how touching." Then, putting on a smile, he beckoned to Malingo. "Come on now, boy. Joke's over. You've had your moment. Let's stop all this playacting. You know you don't have the guts to leave me."

His tone was all milk and honey, and it was frighteningly credible.

"You *belong* to me, Malingo," he went on. "Remember? I bought you in an honest transaction. I have the papers. You can't walk away. I mean, goodness gracious, where would the world be if every slave just upped and walked away when they got the inclination?"

The smile went from his face. Wolfswinkel had exhausted his supply of sweetness.

"Now," he said, "for the last time: give me back my staff and I promise you, *I promise you*, I will not hurt you."

Malingo didn't move. He didn't even blink.

"Oh now, wait a moment," Wolfswinkel went on. "I know what you're thinking. You can smell freedom, can't you? And it's rather tempting. But think, geshrat. You don't know how to *live* out there in the world."

"Take no notice of him," Candy said.

"You've got a slave's soul, geshrat. And you'll never change that."

"There's nothing to be afraid of out there," Candy said. Then revising her opinion in the interest of honesty, she said: "Well, nothing worse than this. Than *him*. And I'll be with you—"

"Oh no, you won't," Wolfswinkel said, snatching hold of Candy's wrist.

His grip was like fire. She cried out in pain and struggled so hard to be free of him that his hats, all carefully perched upon one another, slid sideways from his sweat-slickened head.

A look of panic crossed his face, and he let go of Candy so as to catch the falling hats and push them back into place. She stepped out of his range, her hand numb with pain. As she rubbed it back to life, the paintings of the five murdered magicians came into her mind's eye. And with them, a simple thought:

His hats. Part of his power is in those idiotic hats.

She had only a moment to register this notion. Then Wolfswinkel was closing on Malingo, his hands reaching out to reclaim his staff.

"Give it to me," he said to Malingo. "Come on. You know it's mine."

There were flecks of yellow-white spittle on his lips. He looked as though he was about ready to explode with fury.

Malingo raised the staff.

"Good boy," Wolfswinkel said, a slight smile returning to his sweaty face.

Malingo looked his master straight in the eyes. Then he lifted his leg, and taking the staff in a two-handed grip, he brought it down across his knee.

Wolfswinkel let out a howl as the staff broke in half. Splinters flew in all directions, and the crack of the breaking staff echoed off the walls.

Malingo lifted the pieces of the staff and showed them to Wolfswinkel.

"You'll never beat me with this again," he said.

Then he threw the two halves down on the floor, on the very spot where he'd been bruised and humiliated just a few minutes before.

Wolfswinkel looked down at them, his body shaking.

"Well, now . . ." he muttered. "Aren't you a brave little rebel?"

Now it was he who lifted his hands, locking his fingers together above his head.

Then, muttering something that was incomprehensible to Candy's ears, but still sounded profoundly threatening, he unknotted his hands and began to slowly, slowly ease them apart. There was a form made of seething darkness between his palms, which grew as he parted his hands. It resembled a fat, five-foot-long maggot armed with tentacles, each one of which ended in a cruel red hook. It had two heads, one at either end of its body, their faces resembling Kaspar. Their teeth were as sharp as a shark's teeth.

"Lovely," Wolfswinkel said, looking up at this foul thing that he'd conjured. "You like my little eeriac?"

Then, without waiting for a reply, he dropped his hands in front of him and released the creature.

The eeriac, though solid, seemed to be able to defy gravity, for it instantly rose high above the heads of those in the room, twisting and turning like a rope that had an ambition to knot itself.

It made an inverted curve of its body and turned both its grotesque faces down to look at its creator.

Wolfswinkel nodded to the thing. "Are you ready?" he said. It opened its mouths and let out a hiss from the depths of its throats. "Good," said Wolfswinkel. He pointed at Malingo and uttered these words:

"Kill my slave."

The eeriac didn't hesitate. It threw itself down from the heights of the room and flew toward Malingo.

Luckily, Malingo was quick. He was used to climbing over the rooms. He knew every rock and cranny.

Before the eeriac could reach him, up he went, like a spider on the wall. The creature pursued him, the hooks on its numberless tentacles striking sparks off one another, bright enough to flood the room with a rancid light.

Wolfswinkel was pleased with the spectacle he'd created. He applauded like an egotistical child as the chase set the chandelier swinging. A dry rain of dust and dead moths came down off the crystals as they twinkled and shook.

"Get out!" Malingo yelled down to Candy. *"Go!"*

The moment that he took to beg her to leave was his undoing. The creature closed the distance between them in a heartbeat and clamped both sets of jaws upon him.

Candy couldn't bear to look. She averted her eyes, her gaze going instead to Wolfswinkel. He was totally engrossed by the spectacle overhead. Surely she could creep up on him and not be noticed.

Did she dare? Yes, of course she dared. Anything to save Malingo from Wolfswinkel's monster.

She glanced up once to see how Malingo was faring. Not well was the answer. The eeriac was wrapped around Malingo, its hooks seeking to catch his skin. But he wasn't quite as vulnerable as a human being. Though doubtless his skin was tender from the beating he'd endured, the hooks did not wound him.

Even so, he was in dire jeopardy: not from the hooks but from the eeriac's teeth. He did his best to hold the beast's two mouths away from his face with his hands, and for a while he succeeded. But the eeriac was strong. It was only a matter of time before the monster's needle teeth pierced him.

Candy waited no longer. As Wolfswinkel continued to applaud the horrible spectacle, Candy moved behind him. Then she pitched herself at his back.

Wolfswinkel turned at the last moment and raised his hand to strike her, but he was too late. She threw herself at him, and with a backward sweep of her hand, she knocked all of his hats off his head.

Wolfswinkel unleashed a howl of fury and went down on his knees in a desperate attempt to pick up the fallen hats. Candy did her best to prevent him from doing so by kicking them out of his hands.

From overhead there came a din like the sound of an enormous firecracker exploding.

Candy looked up to see that the eeriac was no longer threatening Malingo. With Wolfswinkel's power suddenly removed, the eeriac was diminishing. It had let Malingo go and was bouncing back and forth around the room like an over-filled balloon that had suddenly had the air let out of it. As it struck a solid object—a wall of books, the chandelier, a table, the floor—it erupted in a shower of black sparks, its body getting smaller each time it did so. Candy watched it for a moment, then she called up to Malingo, who was still hanging on the ceiling.

"Come on! Quickly!"

He dropped down to stand in front of her.

"Are you all right?" she said.

"It didn't hurt me." He smiled. "It tried, but—"

Candy smiled and caught hold of his clammy hand.

"We have to get out of here!" she said, and they ran toward the front door.

As they reached the door the beast slammed into the wall above it and released one last stinging rain of black sparks. Then it dropped to the ground between them. It was deflated to a tiny version of its former self. It writhed on the floor, its minuscule mouths still loosing that throaty hiss.

"Look away," Malingo said.

"Don't worry, I'm not squeamish," Candy said.

Malingo stamped his heel down on the eeriac, grinding out the last of its magical life. When he lifted his foot, the creature was no more than a dark stain on the carpet.

"*Now* we go," Malingo said.

He pulled open the top bolt of the front door. Candy took the middle and the bottom. "Wait. What about the Key?" she said to Malingo, as she threw open the door.

"This isn't the time to be worrying about that," Malingo said, as Kaspar's din became louder behind them.

Candy agreed with a little nod, and hand in hand they pitched themselves over the threshold.

They didn't look over their shoulders.

They just stumbled away from the house into the early night of Ninnyhammer, leaving Kaspar Wolfswinkel to roar his threats and his frustration at their backs.

29

CAT'S EYES

"*I'M FREE,*" MALINGO YELLED as they ran. "I can't believe it! I'm free! *I'm free!*"

Suddenly he stopped running and picked Candy up in his arms, hugging her so tightly she could barely catch her breath.

"Thank you, thank you, thank you," he said, swinging her around. "You gave me the courage to do it! Whatever happens to me after this, I'll always be grateful to you."

Then he planted a loving, leathery kiss on her cheek and set her down again.

Candy was a bit flustered by all this. She couldn't remember the last time she'd been hugged or kissed. But she quickly regained her composure and turned the conversation back to practical matters.

"We're not out of the woods yet," she pointed out. "We need to put as much distance as we can between us and Ol' Banana Suit."

Malingo laughed. "Agreed," he said. "Do you have a boat?"

"No. And I don't suppose you have a luxury yacht in the vicinity?"

"No. 'Fraid not. How did *you* get here, by the way?"

"Well, there was this giant moth, you see—" she said.

"Giant moth?"

"Sent by Christopher Carrion."

"So the Lord of Midnight has been after you for a while. What's he so interested in?"

"Well, I had this Key—" Candy began. Then she stopped herself. "But that can't be why he was after me. He didn't even know I *had* the Key until Wolfswinkel found it."

"Do you know what this mystery key is for?"

"No, I don't. I don't think I was ever told."

Candy had no sooner spoken than she heard the voice of Kaspar Wolfswinkel. He was somewhere nearby, to judge by the way he whispered.

"Oh the *Key*," he said. "You want to know what the Key is for . . ."

Malingo turned to Candy, the joy stripped from his face, terror replacing it. *"He's here!"* he said.

"It's all right," Candy murmured. "He's not going to hurt us."

As she spoke, she looked around for some sign of Wolfswinkel in the murk. But despite the eerie intimacy of his voice, he was nowhere to be seen.

"For your information," the magician went on, "the Key opens the Pyramids at Xuxux."

"Really?" Candy said, hoping to keep the chat

going while she tried to locate Wolfswinkel. "The Pyramids, huh? Very interesting." She leaned close to Malingo. "Let's stand back to back," she said. "That way he can't creep up on us."

Malingo did as she suggested and carefully stepped into place, his back against Candy's.

"Believe me," Wolfswinkel went on boastfully, "I will be massively rewarded for what I did this Hour. I will have power on a scale that would be unimaginable to the likes of you—"

"*Where is he?*" Candy whispered to Malingo. "He's close. I know he's close. Why can't we *see* him?"

"It's driving you *crazy*, isn't it?" Wolfswinkel said. "You're wondering if your pitiful senses are finally giving out? Perhaps you're going crazy. Have you thought about that? What is it the poet says? *The mind cannot bear too much reality.* You poor thing. It's the madhouse for you."

Malingo seized hold of Candy's hand. "You are *not* going crazy," he said.

"Then why does he sound so close to us?"

Malingo was trembling violently. "Because he *is* close," he said. "He's very close."

"But I don't *see* him," Candy said, still inspecting the landscape around them.

"Those hats of his give him a lot of powers," Malingo whispered. "He's just made himself invisible."

"So . . . so he could be anywhere?" Candy said.

"I'm afraid so."

Armed with this new information Candy studied the landscape around them for some sign, however subtle, of their enemy's presence. A bush shaking as Wolfswinkel brushed past it; a pebble cracking beneath his invisible heel. But in the flickering, deceptive light from the fire-poles, it was difficult to be sure of anything. Was that Wolfswinkel moving through the grass off to her left, or just a trick of the light? Was that his breath, close to her ear, or simply the wind?

"I hate this," she whispered.

She'd no sooner spoken than there was a loud slapping sound, and Malingo stumbled forward, crying out. He instantly let go of Candy's hand and swung around, raising his fists like an old-fashioned boxer.

"He's *right here*!" Malingo warned. "*He's right here*! He just hit the back of my—"

He didn't finish. There was another smack, and then a third, this one so violent that it threw Malingo to the ground. He put his hands over his head to protect himself from any further assault.

"Run, Candy!" he yelled. "Get out of here before he starts on you."

At this point Candy felt Kaspar's arms catching hold of her, and she was lifted up into the air. It was a supernatural strength Wolfswinkel was displaying: the source of it, of course, those ridiculous hats of his. Candy flailed around, hoping by chance to knock them off his head again, but he had her held in such a position that she was powerless to do so.

"You're coming back to the house with me," he said. "*Right now*."

Candy continued to struggle, but the man's strength was simply overwhelming. She started to yell for help, hoping there might be somebody out there on the murky slopes that could save them.

"It's a lost cause, I'm afraid," Wolfswinkel said, his invisible mouth inches from Candy's ear. His breath stank of rum.

Before Candy could reply, there was a lot of motion in the grass around them, and out of the darkened landscape came a number of tarrie-cats. It was not a small assembly. One minute the place was deserted; the next the beasts seemed to be all around them, their ears pricked, their eyes incandescent, watching Candy intently as she struggled in the arms of her invisible captor.

As they approached, she remembered the horrendous crimes Wolfswinkel had claimed the cats had been responsible for. Had any of what he'd told her been *true*? Had the tarrie-cats come here now to commit some new atrocity? To leap on poor Malingo while he lay on the ground and scratch out his eyes? Or to climb up her body and smother her?

As if their situation wasn't bad enough, it had now become incalculably worse.

Or so she thought.

But as the tarrie-cats advanced upon them, she felt Kaspar's hold on her weaken a little, and a few muttered words escaped his lips.

"You stay away from me . . ." he warned them.

The tarrie-cats ignored him. They simply continued their approach, their scrutiny frighteningly intense.

"Don't look at me that way," Wolfswinkel said to them.

Look at me? Candy thought. What did he mean by *look at me*? He was invisible, surely. How could they possibly be seeing him? Suddenly it was clear to Candy.

"They can *see* you," she said to Kaspar.

The magician made no reply. But he didn't need to. His body was answering for him. He'd begun to shake, and his grip on Candy had weakened so much that she was able to slip free of him. She went immediately to tend to Malingo, who was still curled up on the ground.

"It's all right," she reassured him. "The tarrie-cats are here."

"That's *good*?" he said, turning over to look at her. There was blood and fear on his face.

"Oh, yes, it's good," she said.

"How so?"

"Because the tarries can *see* him, Malingo."

"They can?"

They both looked up.

The animals' eyes were all focused on the same spot, just a few feet from Candy and Malingo. And from that exact place came Wolfswinkel's voice.

"You keep your distance, you spit rags!" he wailed at the tarries. "Stay away, I'm warning you, or I'll set fire to your tails. I mean it. You don't know the things I can do to the likes of you!"

A few of the tarries exchanged anxious glances at Wolfswinkel's outburst, but none of them were intimidated enough to retreat.

"He's bluffing," Candy said to them. "Do you understand me? He's *afraid* of you."

"You be *quiet*, bug-rot!" Wolfswinkel yelled, his voice shrill now. "I'll deal with you later."

Malingo, meanwhile, had got to his feet. The blood was running down the side of his face from the wound on his brow, but he seemed indifferent to his own hurt. There was a strange new confidence about him.

"You know all you *ever* do is threaten people," he said, striding toward the place where the many stares of the tarrie-cats converged; in other words, the spot where the wizard stood. Wolfswinkel said nothing more—presumably hoping to keep his ex-slave's hands from touching him. Then he beat a rapid retreat. Candy and Malingo could hear the dirt his heels kicked up, and they could see the collective gaze of the tarries moving up the slope, following the magician as he fled for the sanctuary of his house.

Malingo wasn't about to let him get there. He chased Wolfswinkel up the slope, glancing back at the animals now and again to confirm that he was indeed running in the right direction.

He was twenty yards shy of the front door when he pounced.

There was a loud, profoundly outraged yell from the murk.

"Unhand me, slave!" Wolfswinkel yelled.

"I am not your slave!" Malingo yelled back.

Clearly Wolfswinkel fought to be free of Malingo's hold. It looked as though Malingo was wrestling with two armfuls of invisible eels, all slathered in fat.

Threats and curses poured from Wolfswinkel.

Tired of the wizard's endless mouthing, Malingo shook his prisoner back and forth.

"Show yourself," he demanded.

He had grabbed Wolfswinkel's neck, as far as Candy could guess, and was threatening to choke him.

"Take the hats off and show yourself!" he demanded.

A moment later a flickering form began to appear in Malingo's arms, and an irate Kaspar Wolfswinkel came into view. He had taken off his hats, and he was clutching three in each hand. By the expression on his face, he would gladly have murdered every living thing on Ninnyhammer at that instant—starting with Candy and Malingo, then going on to the tarries.

"So now, Kaspar," said a voice behind Candy, "you should perhaps go back to your house and stay there. You know you're not supposed to be running around."

Candy turned, wondering who the speaker was, and found herself face-to-face with a two-legged creature who had clearly some familial relationship with the tarries. Its wide face was covered with a subtle down of reddish-brown fur. Its luminous eyes were decidedly feline, as were the whiskers that sprouted from its cheeks. It had apparently wandered up the hill to see what was going on.

"She started all this, Jimothi!" Kaspar said, pointing at Candy. "That damnable girl. Blame *her*, not me."

"Oh, for A'zo's sake, be quiet, Wolfswinkel," the creature said.

Much to Candy's surprise, Wolfswinkel did exactly that.

The creature returned to its gaze to Candy. "My name is Jimothi Tarrie."

"I'm very pleased to meet you."

"And you, of course are the famous—or is it infamous?—Candy Quackenbush."

"You know of me?"

"There have been very few visitors to these islands whose presence has been so widely discussed," Jimothi said.

"Really?"

"Oh, certainly." He smiled, showing his pointed teeth. "I've been out among the islands these last two days, and it seems every second soul I met knows of you. Your celebrity grows by the Hour. People who can't possibly have met you claim they have."

"Really?" said Candy.

"Believe me. Did you buy a slice of Furini from the cheese maker in Autland?"

"No."

"Well, he says you did. What about the shoes you ordered from a cobbler in Tazmagor?"

"I've never even *been* to Tazmagor."

"You see how famous you are?" Jimothi said.

"I don't understand why," Candy said.

"Well, there are several good reasons," Jimothi said. "One, of course, is your origins. You're the first soul to have come through from the Hereafter in quite a while. Then there's the fact that you seem to have left consternation wherever you traveled. Admittedly, none of this was of your doing. Others were causing trouble by pursuing you with such vehemence. But trouble is trouble."

Candy sighed, still confused.

"And then," said Jimothi, "there's the matter of *when* you arrived."

"Why's that so important?"

"Well, because a lot of people, from street-corner elegiacs to the most respected bone-casters in the Abarat, have been saying for a long time that some transforming force was imminent. A force that would somehow upset the sad order of our lives."

"Why sad?" said Candy. "What's so sad about things?"

"Where do I begin?" Jimothi said softly. "Put it this way. We do not sleep well these days."

"We?"

"Those of us who care to wonder where our lives are going. And what our dreams are worth. We wake with the taste of Midnight in our throats."

"You mean Christopher Carrion?"

"He's part of it. But he's not the *worst* part of it," Jimothi said. "After all, the House of Carrion has had its place in the balance of power since there were historians to write these things down. Darkness has always had its part to play. Without it, how would we know when we walked in the light? It's only when its ambitions become too grandiose that it must be opposed, disciplined, sometimes—if necessary— brought down for a time. Then it will rise again, as it must. In the end, following the Dark Road is no less honorable than following the Light, as long as it is done with a clear purpose."

Candy was not sure she entirely understood what she

was being told, but she was sure when she thought it all over that Jimothi's observations would come to make sense. Anyway, she had no chance to ask the tarrie-cat questions. Jimothi was continuing to talk about the state of the Abarat, and Candy drank it all down.

"The *real* trouble is Commexo," he said. "Rojo Pixler and his Kid. He buys holy sites and builds restaurants on them. And nobody seems to care. They're too busy drinking his Panacea. It makes me sick. Hour by Hour, Day by Day, we're letting him take the magic out of our lives. And what do we get in exchange? Soda and Panacea." He shook his head in despair. "Do you begin to understand?" he said.

"A little," Candy said.

"And now, here you come, out of the Hereafter. And the moment you arrive everybody starts to talk, everybody starts to wonder . . . is *she* the one?"

"The one?"

"To cure our ills. To save us from our own stupidities. *To wake us up!*"

Candy had no answer to this, except to say *no, she wasn't the one; she was a nobody*. But Jimothi didn't want to hear that, she knew. So she kept her silence.

"You're an extraordinary spirit," he said to her. "Of that I'm certain."

Candy shook her head. "How can that . . . ? I mean . . . me?" She sighed, the words failing her, just as she knew she would fail Jimothi's high hopes for her. How could she wake up anybody? She'd been asleep herself until a few days ago, doodling in her dreams.

"Take courage in your purpose," Jimothi said.

"Even if it isn't yet clear."

Candy nodded.

"It's amazing that you've survived your journey thus far. You do know that? Somebody must be taking care of you."

His observation brought to mind all that Candy had faced in the hours since she'd met John Mischief: narrowly avoiding death at the hands of Mendelson Shape, and nearly drowning in the Sea of Izabella; the bolts of Pixler's hunting party whistling past her head; then falling out of the skies, clinging to the corpse of the great moth. Finally, of course, there'd been her encounter with Wolfswinkel. Everywhere she looked there was jeopardy.

"This all began with a key," she said, trying to make sense of what had brought her to this moment. "And Wolfswinkel took it, out of my mind. Can you get it back from him?"

"Unfortunately there's nothing I can do about that. Although Wolfswinkel is a prisoner and I am his warden, I have no authority to take back what he has taken from you, any more than I can confiscate his hats."

"Why not?"

Here Wolfswinkel, who had once again set his hats upon his head, spoke up:

"Because I'm a great magician, and a Doctor of Philosophy, and he's just a flea-bitten tarrie, who happens to stand on two legs. He can't do *anything* to me, except prevent me from getting off this wretched island. And all of that will change when Otto Houlihan gets here."

"Houlihan!" Candy said. She'd been so engrossed in listening to Jimothi she'd forgotten Houlihan.

"What business does that wicked man have with you?" Jimothi asked.

It was Wolfswinkel who replied.

"Arrangements have been made to have him take her to the Lord Midnight, along with the Key she stole."

"Go back to your house, wizard," Jimothi said, waving Wolfswinkel away. "I don't want to hear any more of you. Brothers and sisters, *take him*." The cats, which had followed Wolfswinkel up the hill, gathered around him now, yowling as they pressed him back toward his prison.

"Damnable creatures," Kaspar said. Then, calling back to Candy: "Why couldn't you just have poisoned them when I asked you to?"

The cats set up a chorus of yowling that blotted out whatever else he had to say.

"He's a lunatic," Candy said.

"Maybe," Jimothi replied, though he sounded doubtful. "I'm sorry you had to deal with him. But in the end he's a very small player in a very large game."

"Who's organizing the game?" Candy wanted to know. "Christopher Carrion?"

"I'd rather not talk about him, if you don't mind," Jimothi said. "I believe the more you talk about death and darkness, the closer it comes."

"I'm sorry," Candy said. "This is all my fault."

"How so?"

"Because I let that man have the Key. I should have fought him harder."

"No, lady," Malingo said, speaking for the first time since this whole exchange had begun. (*He calls me lady*, Candy thought, *like John Mischief. That's nice*.) "You're not responsible," Malingo went on. "He had a Spell of Revelations on you. Nobody could have resisted something like that. At least, nobody who was not a magician."

"He's right," Jimothi said. "Don't blame yourself. It's a waste of energy."

Up on the hill Wolfswinkel slammed the door to his house. His threats and inanities were finally silenced, and so was the barrage of yowling that the tarrie-cats had set up to drown him out.

All that remained was the moan of the wind in the long grass. Its sighing put Candy in mind of home, of the tall-grass prairie around Chickentown. She suddenly felt a pang of loneliness. It wasn't that she necessarily wanted to be back in the confines of Followell Street. It was just that the distance between this windy place and that modest little house seemed so immeasurably immense. Even the stars were different here, she remembered. Lord, even the stars.

Whatever this world was—a waking dream, another dimension, or simply a corner of Creation that God had made and forgotten—she was going to have to find herself a place in it and make sense of why she was here. If she didn't, her loneliness would grow and consume her in time.

"So what happens to me now?" she said.

"A very good question," Jimothi replied.

30

"COME THOU GLYPH TO ME"

"OUR FIRST PRIORITY," JIMOTHI said, "is to get you both off this island before Otto Houlihan arrives. I don't want to see you taken to Christopher Carrion."

"Do you happen to have a boat?" Candy asked him.

"Yes, I do," Jimothi said. "Cats hate to swim. But I'm afraid the boat's way off over on the other side of the island. If we tried to get you to it, Houlihan would have caught up with you before you were halfway to the harbor."

"I . . . I have an idea," Malingo put in tentatively.

"You do?" Jimothi said.

"Go on," Candy said. "Let's hear it."

Malingo licked his lips nervously. "Well . . ." he said. "We could leave the island in a glyph."

"A glyph?" Jimothi said. "My friend, it's a fine proposal, but who among us has the knowledge to speak a glyph into creation?"

"Well . . ." said Malingo, looking modestly down at

his oversized feet, "*I* do."

Jimothi looked frankly incredulous. "Where in the name of Gosh and Divinium does a geshrat learn how to conjure a glyph?"

"When Wolfswinkel used to pass out from drinking an excess of rum," Malingo explained, "I would read his books of magic. He has all of the classics up there in the house. *Saturansky's Grimoire*; *The Strata Pilot's Guide*; *The Wiles of Gawk*; *Chicanery and Guising*. But it was *Lumeric's Six* that I really studied."

"What are *Lumeric's Six*?" Candy asked.

"They are seven books of Incantations and Profound Enchantments," Jimothi said.

"If there's seven books, why are they called *Lumeric's Six*?"

"It was Lumeric's way of helping a true magician to quickly discover if they were dealing with a false one."

Candy smiled. "That's clever," she said.

"There is another way," Malingo said.

"What's that?" Jimothi wanted to know.

"Just ask whether Lumeric was a man or a woman."

"And what's the right answer?" Candy asked.

"Both," Malingo and Jimothi replied at the same moment.

Candy looked confused.

"Lumeric was a Mutep," Malingo explained. "Therefore both a *he* and a *she*."

"So . . ." said Jimothi, obviously still a little suspicious of Malingo's claim to the skill of glyph-speaking. "You've read the books. But have you actually done any of the magic?"

Malingo made a little shrug. "Some small spells," he said. "I got a chair to sit up and beg, one time." Candy laughed, amused by the image. "And I made fourteen white doves into one . . . uh . . . one very big white dove."

"Ha!" said Jimothi, apparently suddenly convinced. "I've seen that dove of yours. It's the size of a tiger-kite. Enormous. That was your handiwork?"

"Yes, it was."

"You *swear*?"

"If he says it's his work, Jimothi, then it's his," Candy said. "I believe him."

"I'm sorry. That was remiss of me," Jimothi replied. "Please accept my apologies."

This was plainly the first time Malingo had been offered an apology. "Oh," he said, looking at Candy, his eyes wide. "What do I do now?"

"Accept the apology, if you think he means it."

"Oh . . . yes. Of course. I accept the apology." Jimothi offered his hand, and Malingo shook it, plainly delighted at this new proof of his advanced position in the world.

"So, my friend," Jimothi said. "I believe you have it in you to make a glyph. Go to it."

"I did tell you I've never actually done this before?" Malingo pointed out.

"Just give it a try," Candy said. "It's our only way out. No pressure of course."

Malingo offered her a nervous smile. "You'd better both stand back then," he said, spreading his arms.

Jimothi took a small telescope from his jacket pocket, opened it up and wandered away to scan the skies.

"Don't be nervous," Candy said to Malingo. "I have faith in you."

"You do?"

"Don't sound so surprised."

"I just don't want to disappoint you."

"You won't. If it works, it works. If not—" She waved the thought away. "We'll find some other escape route. After all that you've done in the last few hours, you don't have to prove anything."

Malingo nodded, though he looked far from happy. To judge by his expression, Candy guessed that a part of him was regretting that he'd spoken up in the first place.

He stared down at the ground for a moment, as though recalling the spell.

"Please stand away," he said to Candy, without looking up. Then he raised his arms from his sides and clapped them together above his head, three times.

> *"Ithni asme ata,*
> *Ithni manamee,*
> *Drutha lotacata,*
> *Come thou glyph to me.*
> *Ithni, ithni,*
> *Asme ata:*
> *Come thou glyph to me."*

While he spoke these words, he walked in a circle about six or seven feet wide, grabbing hold of the air and appearing to throw what he'd caught into the circle.

Then he began the words of the ritual afresh.

> *"Ithni asme ata,*
> *Ithni manamee.*
> *Drutha lotacata,*
> *Come thou glyph to me."*

Three times he made the circle, throwing the air and repeating the strange words of the conjuration.

> *". . . Ithni, ithni,*
> *Asme ata:*
> *Come thou glyph to me."*

"I don't want to hurry you," Jimothi said, glancing back at Candy, his eloquent eyes flickering with anxiety, "but I can see the lights of three glyphs coming this way. It must be the Criss-Cross Man. I'm afraid you don't have much time, my friend."

Malingo didn't break the rhythm of his invocation. He went on, around and around, snatching at the air. But nothing seemed to be happening. From the corner of her eye, Candy caught sight of Jimothi making a tiny, despairing shake of his head. She ignored his pessimism and instead went to stand with Malingo.

"Is there only room for one cook in this kitchen?" she said.

He was still circling and snatching, circling and snatching.

"The pot looks pretty empty to me," Malingo said.

"I need all the help I can get."

"I'll do what I can," Candy said, stepping into the circle behind Malingo, copying his every move and syllable.

> *"Ithni asme ata,*
> *Ithni manamee . . ."*

It was remarkably easy, once she'd done it one time through. In fact, it was eerily easy, like a dance step she'd forgotten but remembered again immediately the music began, though where she'd heard the music of this magic before she could not possibly imagine. This was not a dance they danced in Chickentown.

"I think it's working," Malingo said hesitantly.

He was right.

Candy could feel a rush of kindled air coming out of the middle of the circle, and to her amazement she saw a myriad of tiny sparks igniting all around them: blue and white and red and gold.

Malingo let out a triumphant whoop, and his happiness seemed to further fuel the fire of creation. Now the sparks began to trail light, forming a luminescent matrix in the dark air. The glyph being conjured was a complex form, dominated by three broad strokes, between which there was a filigree of finer lines. Some rose up to form a kind of cabin. The rest swept down behind the craft where they knotted themselves together forming something that might have been the glyph's engine. Moment by moment it looked more solid. In fact it now seemed so substantial it was hard to imagine that the space it now occupied had been empty just a little time before.

Candy looked over at Jimothi, who was staring with naked astonishment at what Malingo had achieved.

"I take it all back, my friend," he said. "You are a wizard. Perhaps the first of your tribe to speak a glyph into creation, yes?"

Malingo had stopped circling. He now also stood back to admire the vehicle that was being called into existence.

"We are *both* wizards," he said, looking at Candy with a stare that contained surprise and delight in equal measure.

Jimothi was once again consulting the skies through his telescope. "I think it's time for you to go," he said.

"There's still more to do," Candy said, looking at the unfinished glyph.

"It *should* finish itself," Malingo told her. "At least that's what Lumeric writes."

Lumeric the Mutep knew its business. As Candy watched, the glyph continued to become more and more coherent, the lines of light running back and forth, knitting the matter of the vehicle, refining its form. But it was taking its own sweet time, and that was the problem.

"Is there no way to hurry it up?" Jimothi said.

"Not that I know of," Malingo replied.

Candy glanced in the direction of the approaching enemy. She could now see the glyphs Jimothi had spoken of; all three considerably more elaborate than the vehicle that she and Malingo had conjured. But a craft was a craft; as long as it could carry them, it scarcely mattered what it looked like.

As she watched, Houlihan's trio came in to land on a ridge perhaps four hundred yards from them. There they sat, looking like predatory animals.

"Why did they land over there?" Candy asked Jimothi.

"Because Houlihan is a military man. He sees traps and ambushes everywhere. He probably thinks we've got an army of ten thousand tarrie-cats hiding behind the hill. How I wish we had them. I'd tear him and his *mires* to pieces."

"Mires? What are mires?"

"The creatures he brought with him. They're a particularly brutal breed of stitchling."

Candy was just about to ask Jimothi if she could take a look through his telescope to see these mires when a voice they all hoped had been silenced—at least for a while—echoed across the island.

"There's nothing to be nervous about, Houlihan! There's only three of them. And a few cats."

It was Wolfswinkel, of course.

Candy glanced around at the house. The wizard had appeared in the dome, which functioned as a giant magnifying glass, grotesquely distorting Wolfswinkel's face and body. It was as though he was being reflected in a vast fun-house mirror. His head bulged, and his body looked dwarfed, so that he resembled an infuriated fetus dressed in a banana-skin suit.

"Come and get them, Houlihan!" he screamed, pounding his tight red fists against the glass. *"They're*

weaponless! Kill the geshrat! He's a mutinous slave! And beat that girl! Teach her a lesson."

"I really hate that little man," said Candy.

"There's a lot worse than him, I'm afraid," Jimothi replied.

"Such as . . . ?"

"Try the Criss-Cross Man," Jimothi said. "The list of his crimes is so long we could be here till the sun comes up over Ninnyhammer."

Candy licked her parched lips and went back to studying the glyph. It was still polishing itself, much to her frustration. Malingo was also staring hard at it, as though he was trying to will it to finish its autocreation.

"What about you, Jimothi?" Candy said to the tarrie-man. "If we get away, what happens to you?"

"I'll be fine and dandy," Jimothi said. "Houlihan won't touch me. He knows where to draw the line."

"You're sure?"

"I'm sure," said Jimothi. "Don't worry about me. Oh, A'zo. He's coming."

Candy returned her gaze to the ridge. Houlihan and his gang of mires had vacated their glyphs and were approaching, confident—thanks to Wolfswinkel—that they had nothing to fear. Houlihan wore a long purple coat with a blood-red lining; his face was faintly jaundiced, and there seemed to be a checkerboard design tattooed upon his cheeks. The seven mires that followed on his heels were all bigger than he was, the largest nearly twice his size. Like all their vile species they were patchworks of flesh and fabric, all crudely sewn together. Their heads, however, were of inhuman design: like the skeletal remains of devils, with horns and snouts and vicious teeth. They all carried elaborately configured blades; three of them carried one in each hand.

All in all, it was a terrifying spectacle.

"How much longer?" she asked Malingo.

"I don't know," the geshrat replied. Then, with a little puff of pride: "It's my first." He glanced up at the approaching posse. "I suppose we could get in it now, but I'm afraid it would decay, and we'd fall out of it."

At this juncture, there came a shout from Houlihan.

"Candy Quackenbush?" he hollered. *"You are under arrest, by order of Christopher Carrion."*

Jimothi laid a light hand on Candy's shoulder. "I'll get the tarries to do what we can to delay him," he said. "Safe voyages, lady. It is my sincerest hope that we meet again when matters are not so . . . rushed. Good-bye, Malingo. A pleasure, truly."

So saying, he started away, then returned to tell Candy: "If you should get caught—now or at any time—take courage. I don't believe Carrion wants your life. He has some other purpose for you."

He didn't linger for a reply. There was no time. Houlihan was no more than thirty strides away.

"Brothers and sisters," Jimothi called. "Come to me. Come."

At his summons the tarrie-cats appeared from the gloom and followed on his heels. They were only a dozen or so at first, but then, miraculously appearing from the long grass, came two or three dozen more.

Jimothi Tarrie positioned his feline soldiers directly in Houlihan's path.

The Criss-Cross Man raised his hand and brought his mires to a halt.

"Jimothi Tarrie," he said. "Surprise, surprise. I didn't expect to meet the scum of High Sladder here. I thought they'd rounded up all you strays and put you out of your misery."

Jimothi ignored the insult.

He just said: "You can't have her, Houlihan. It's as simple as that. She's not going to Carrion. I won't let you take her."

They spoke, Candy thought, like the most ancient of enemies, their words steeped in the curdled blood of old feuds.

"She's a trespasser, Tarrie," Houlihan replied, "and a thief. And the Lord of Midnight demands that she be delivered directly to him."

"You don't understand, Houlihan. The girl is not going with you."

"No, it's you who doesn't understand, animal. *This is the law.* She's under arrest."

"Under what warrant?"

"Midnight's warrant."

"Ninnyhammer isn't part of Carrion's empire, Criss-Cross Man. You know that. His laws mean nothing here. So you go back to him and tell him . . . whatever you like. Tell him she slipped away."

"I can't do that," Houlihan said. "He wants her. And he won't be denied. So stand aside, or I'll have to take her by force."

"Tarries!" Jimothi yelled suddenly. *"Take down the mires!"*

The animals needed no further instruction. They surged through the grass like a striped tide and leaped upon Houlihan's faceless crew, climbing their bodies by digging their claws into their coats and attacking their hooded heads. The mires let out no sound in response, but they used their swords with terrible efficiency. Several of the bravest tarrie-cats dropped into the grass, slaughtered within seconds. It was a horrible sight. The fact that her presence had brought this battle about tore at Candy's heart.

"I have to stop this," she told Malingo. "I won't let this go on. I'll just let Houlihan take me."

"No need," Malingo said. "Look."

He pointed to the glyph. The process of its construction was finally completed. The vehicle was steaming lightly in the cool evening air, warm from the fever of its creation.

"Come on," Malingo urged. "Climb in!"

As Candy climbed into the vehicle, she yelled to Jimothi Tarrie. "Call the tarries off, Jimothi!"

He instantly threw back his head and let out a high-pitched yowl. The cats, having done their brave work, and having in several cases paid the ultimate price, now retreated from the battlefield.

Houlihan led the mires unopposed toward the glyph, his teeth bared, his eyes blazing.

He pointed straight at Candy as he approached.

"Don't move, girl!" he roared.

"Quickly, lady!" Malingo urged. "Say the words!"

"What words?"

"Oh, yes. *Nio Kethica*. It means: Answer My Will."

"And then what?"

"It will answer. Hopefully."

"I have you, girl!" the Criss-Cross Man was yelling. *"I have you!"*

Houlihan was ten strides away, but one of the mires, whose headpiece resembled some monstrous bird, had moved ahead of him, clearly intending to stop Candy and Malingo. Luckily, he had lost his weapon in the short battle with the tarrie-cats, but his arms were enormous, like claws, in fact, with curled, silvery talons.

There was no response from the glyph.

"Nio Kethica," Candy said. "Nio Kethica! NIO KETHICA!"

The mire was almost upon them. Reaching out—

Suddenly, the glyph shuddered. A noise escaped its engine, like the sound of an asthmatic taking a painful breath.

Candy saw the mire's talons inches from her ankle. She lifted her leg to avoid its grip, and as she did so the glyph miraculously obeyed her instruction. It shuddered and began to rise slowly into the air. The mire threw itself forward and caught hold of the craft as it ascended. In a matter of seconds the vehicle was twenty, thirty, forty feet off the ground. But the mire wasn't about to let go. It hung on tenaciously, throwing its body back and forth in a deliberate attempt to unbalance the craft.

"He's trying to overturn us," Candy said, grabbing hold of the glyph's armrests.

Malingo seized her arm. "I won't let you fall," he said.

It was a sweet promise, but in truth it was little reassurance. The mire was throwing its body around, making the vehicle rock back and forth more violently by the moment. It was only a matter of seconds before its assault succeeded and the craft flipped over.

"We have to shake him loose," Candy said to Malingo.

"What do you suggest?" Malingo replied.

"First we have to get that wretched helmet off him. He's on my side, so you hold on to me."

She leaned over the edge of the vehicle and grabbed hold of the vicious beak of the mire's headpiece. The creature could do nothing to fend her off. All it could do was cling to the glyph as it tipped and rolled like some lethal fun-fair ride.

"*Pull!*" Malingo yelled.

"I'm doing my best!" Candy yelled back. "I need to go farther over the side."

"I've got hold of you," Malingo reassured her, grabbing her even more tightly.

Candy leaned as far out of the reeling, rocking glyph as her balance would allow. She was now farther out of the vehicle than she was in it. Meanwhile the glyph continued its unchecked ascent, the wind steadily moving it away from the spot where it had been conjured into being. Wolfswinkel's house was coming into view below.

The wizard had apparently witnessed the vehicle's whole giddying climb, because his bizarrely magnified head was pressed against the glass dome, his expression demented.

Candy ignored Wolfswinkel's wild stare and concentrated on trying to wrench the spiked hood off. Besides its savage beak, the headpiece had countless tiny barbs on its surfaces, which pricked and stung her palms. But she refused to let go. She was fighting for their lives here. The mire seemed to comprehend this too and was apparently prepared to kill itself in order to bring the glyph down. It thrashed around with incredible violence. But its appetite for destruction was to Candy's purpose. When the mire twisted to the right, she wrenched the headpiece to the left, and when it pulled left, she wrenched right.

Finally, as the glyph moved directly over Wolfswinkel's house, there was a series of strange noises from the mire's skull. First there came a cracking sound, as though a heavy seal were being broken, then a loud, sharp hissing.

When Candy pulled the spiked head toward her, there was a third sound: a wet, glutinous noise, like a foot being pulled out of a sucking pit. And finally the mire's headgear came away in her hand. It was heavy, and she let go of it instantly. It dropped from her hands and tumbled away toward the roof of Wolfswinkel's house, turning over and over until it struck the glass dome below.

Now Candy was looking at the mire face-to-face. The shape of the creature's head was the same shape as its headpiece: the snout and horns were identical. It had no features, no coloration. It was precisely the same gray as its headpiece, except that it glistened horribly, like a fresh wound.

"Mud," Candy murmured to herself. "It's made of mud."

"What?" Malingo yelled over the din of the wind.

"It's made of mud!" Candy yelled back.

Even as she spoke, the mire's head began to lose the shape of its mold. Clots and globs of mud began to detach themselves and fall back through the air toward the dome.

The mire stopped struggling, as its body—which was entirely made of mud, Candy guessed, all encased in hood, suit, boots and gloves—began to lose its coherence. Its head collapsed completely, releasing the vile reek of putrefaction. Gobs of mud spattered the dome of Wolfswinkel's house, as though a vast passing bird had defecated on the glass.

Headless now, its body full of little shudders and twitches, the mire had little strength left to resist Candy. She began to pry its talons off the edge of the glyph, one by one, and finally the mire's grip on the vehicle slipped. Candy let out a whoop of triumph as the creature fell away, trailing mud from the open wound of its neck.

In the shiny glass dome below, Kaspar Wolfswinkel saw the mire's body tumbling toward him and began to retreat from the glass, a look of fear crossing his rage-flushed face. He had barely begun his retreat when the great bulk of the mire smashed into the glass. One moment Wolfswinkel was a huge, leering presence, his face massively magnified. Then the leaking body hit, and as the glass shattered, Candy and Malingo saw the tyrant as he truly was: a ridiculous little man in a yellow suit.

Even his voice, which had echoed across the slopes earlier like the voice of a tyrant, was reduced to a petulant shriek as glass rained down on him.

Candy watched as the mire's body hit the tiled floor and broke open, like a watermelon dropped from a tall building. Its swampy contents were splattered in all directions. There was no anatomy to speak of. No blood, no bones, no heart or lungs or liver. As she had guessed, the mire was made of mud from head to foot. And although the fleeing Wolfswinkel had attempted to avoid being hit by the contents of the mire's suit, he hadn't retreated fast enough. His yellow jacket was covered in mud and his long blue shoes were similarly bespattered, their heels slip-sliding under him.

He did his best to keep his balance, but he failed. Down he went, falling hard on his backside, his humiliation complete. There was no further for Kaspar Wolfswinkel to fall.

The last sight Candy had of him, before the glyph carried them away from the shattered dome, was Kaspar Wolfswinkel as the silent comedian, struggling to get to his feet and falling down again, his face now as besmirched as his suit and shoes.

The sight made her laugh, and the wind carried her laughter away over the darkened slopes of Ninnyhammer.

* * *

Jimothi Tarrie, who was kneeling in the long grass giving the last rites to one of his dying sisters, heard the girl's triumphant laughter, and despite the fact that he had lost five of his dearest in the battle with Houlihan's monstrous crew, managed to make a little smile.

Otto Houlihan heard the laughter too, as he sent his surviving mires back to their glyphs to give chase. He had left three of his creatures on the battlefield, their hoods clawed off them by the tarrie-cats, the stinking mud running out of their suits. He wasn't optimistic that the mires pursuing the girl and the slave in their makeshift glyph would catch up with them. Mires were fearless fighters, but they didn't have brilliant intellects. They needed close instruction or they rapidly lost their grasp on their purpose. More than likely the clouds over Ninnyhammer would conceal their quarry from them, and after a time they would forget why they were up there and begin circling around. Unless they received fresh directions they would simply continue to circle and circle and circle, until their glyphs ran out of significance and crashed.

But Houlihan—though he was sorely tempted— could not afford to give chase personally. The girl was important to Carrion, and the Key was more important still. His priority was to go back up to the house and get Wolfswinkel to hand the Key over. The girl would have to wait. It wouldn't be difficult to find Candy Quackenbush again. She was noticeable, that one. There was something about the eyes; something about the bearing. She'd find it hard to hide.

He ascended the little hill on which Wolfswinkel had built his domain and stepped into the chaotic ruins, calling the wizard's name. There was no immediate reply so he went through the living room and up the stairs to the dome. He'd seen the glass shattering of course, so he knew what to expect when he got up there. What he didn't anticipate was the sight of Kaspar Wolfswinkel standing in his underwear, socks, and mud-smeared blue shoes, staring up at the star-filled sky through the gaping remains of his precious dome. His dirtied clothes lay in a heap on the floor.

His near-nakedness was not a pretty sight.

"The Key," Houlihan said.

"Yes, yes," Wolfswinkel said, going to his pile of muddied vestments and searching through the pockets. "I have it here."

"You will be rewarded," Houlihan said to him.

"I should hope so," Wolfswinkel said, handing the Key over to Houlihan. He was trembling, the Criss-Cross Man saw.

"What's troubling you?" Houlihan said.

"Oh, besides all *this*?" Wolfswinkel said, spreading his arms and circling on the spot. "Well, I'll tell you what's troubling me. That girl."

"What about her?"

"Her presence here is no accident, Otto. You do realize that?"

"It's occurred to me. But what's your evidence for this?"

"She finds it too easy, Otto."

"Easy?"

"Being here," said Wolfswinkel. "Back in the old days, before the harbors were closed—"

"You weren't even born, Kaspar."

"No, but I can *read*, Otto. And all the books agree: it took visitors from the Hereafter days, weeks, sometimes months to become acclimatized to being in the Abarat. If you tried to speed up the process, people went crazy. Their fragile imaginations couldn't take it."

"Well, they're weak," Houlihan said.

"You're missing the point, Otto, as usual. I'm talking about the girl. This *Candy Quackenbush*. For her, being here is nothing. She's doing magic as though she was born to it. *Born to it, Houlihan!* What does that tell you?"

"I don't know," Houlihan said.

"I'll tell you what it tells *me*."

"What?"

"*She's been here before*."

"Huh. Well that's something for Carrion to puzzle out," Houlihan said, plainly not interested in debating the subject with Wolfswinkel.

"What about me?" Kaspar said.

"What about you?"

"I found the Key. And the girl."

"Then lost her. You let her slip away."

"It wasn't my fault. That was your damn mires. They could have had her. Anyway, two minutes ago you were telling me I'd be well rewarded."

"That was before I had the Key in my hand."

Wolfswinkel's lip curled. "You—"

"Now, now, Kaspar. No foul language. Accept your error. She was in *your* charge."

"What could I do? She turned my slave against me. He broke my staff."

"That seems rather careless of you," Otto said. "What was he doing with your staff in the first place?"

"I was outnumbered by them," Wolfswinkel protested.

"By a girl and a geshrat?"

Wolfswinkel paused. Then, narrowing his eyes, he pointed his fat forefinger at the Criss-Cross Man. "I know what you're doing, Otto," he said.

"And what's that?" Houlihan replied.

"You're going to try and take all the glory for yourself and leave me with all the blame."

"Oh, Kaspar. You are so paranoid."

"That is what you're going to do, isn't it?"

"Very possibly," said Houlihan, with a little smile. "But you can't tell me you wouldn't do the very same thing if you were in a similar situation."

Wolfswinkel was defeated. He drew a deep, anguished breath. "At least tell Carrion I languish here," he said, pitifully. "We used to be friends, Otto. Do *something* for me. Please."

"I'm afraid our Lord Midnight is a practical man. He has what he needs from you. So now? You're forgotten. It's on to new business."

"That's not fair!"

"Life's not fair, Kaspar. You know that. You had a slave for—how long?"

"Twelve years."

"Did you treat him *fairly*? No, of course not. You beat him when you were in a bad mood, because it made you feel better, and when you felt better you beat him some more."

"You think you're clever, don't you, Houlihan?" Wolfswinkel said, bitter tears of frustration and rage spilling into his eyes. "But let me tell you: the Hour of your undoing will come. If you don't let me track this girl down and kill her, she'll make such trouble for you—" He looked around at the ruins of his precious dome. "This is just the beginning, believe me."

Houlihan went to the door.

"You like playing prophet of doom, don't you? You always did, even back in school."

Wolfswinkel reached out for this last, fragile hope. "Ah, school. Otto, do you remember how close we were back then?"

"Were we?" Houlihan said. Then, considering the forlorn figure before him, he managed a scrap of compassion.

"I'll do what I can for you," he said. "But I'm making no promises. These are unruly times. Crazy times."

"All the better. In times like these a smart man profits."

"And which of us is the smart one?" Houlihan said, smiling. "The one standing in his underwear covered in mud, or the man with the Key to his Master's heaven in his pocket?

"Never mind, Kaspar," Houlihan said, walking away from the door, leaving Wolfswinkel in the filth and chaos, unable to cross the threshold without having tarrie-cats on his throat. "All you can do is hope your chance for revenge comes around again, eh?"

"That would be something to look forward to, at least," Wolfswinkel said.

"Then I'll leave you with this thought, Kaspar. If I *do* secure your freedom—"

Kaspar turned, the light of hope rekindled in his eyes.

"Yes?" he said. "What?"

"Then you must swear now that you will serve me. Be my cook, if I so desire. My knife washer, my floor scrubber."

"Anything! Anything! Just get me out of here!"

"Good. Then we understand each other," Houlihan said, turning away.

"Good night to you, Otto."

"Good night to you, Kaspar," said the Criss-Cross Man. "And sweet dreams."

31

THE TWENTY-FIFTH HOUR

THE TRIO OF HOULIHAN'S glyphs came chasing after Candy and Malingo at considerable speed, but with a little maneuvering Candy left them behind in a bank of purple-blue cloud. Though she'd never driven a vehicle of any kind (besides her bike, which didn't really count), she found the task of piloting the glyph remarkably easy. The craft responded quickly to her will and moved with a grace that pleased her greatly.

Once she and Malingo were convinced that their pursuers were not going to put in another appearance, she slowed their frantic pace and guided the glyph down so that they were just skimming the curling waves. That way if anything unpredictable were to happen to the glyph—if, for instance, it were to decay for some reason—they would not have more than a few feet to fall.

It was time for a little mutual congratulation.

"The way you conjured this thing!" Candy said. "It was amazing. I had no idea—"

"Well, I wasn't really sure I could do it," Malingo said. "But I guess in a tight squeeze you find out you can do all kinds of things you didn't know you could do. Besides, I couldn't have done it without your help." He grasped Candy's hand. "Thank you."

"My pleasure," Candy said. "We make a good team, you and me."

"You think so?"

"I *know* so. I'd be on my way to Midnight if it weren't for you."

"And I'd be a slave if it weren't for *you*."

"See? A team. I think we should stick together for a while. Unless of course you've something else you need to do?"

Malingo laughed. "What would I have to do, that was more important than keeping you company?"

"Well . . . I thought, now that you're free you'd want to go back and see your family."

"I don't know where they are. We were all split up when we were sold."

"Who did the selling?"

"My father."

"Your father sold you to Wolfswinkel?" Candy said, scarcely believing what she was hearing.

"No. My father sold me to a slave trader called Kafaree Skeller, and *he* sold me to Wolfswinkel."

"How old were you?"

"Nine and three quarters," Malingo said, with the precision of a child who'd been asked the same question. "I don't blame my father. He had too many children. He couldn't afford to keep all of us."

"I don't know how you can be so forgiving," Candy said, shaking her head. "I wouldn't be able to forgive *my* father if he did that to me. In fact, there are some things nowhere near as bad as that that I can't forgive my father for."

"Maybe you'll feel differently when you get back home," Malingo said.

"If I ever *get* back."

"You will if you want to," Malingo said. "And I'll help you. My first responsibility is to you."

"Malingo, you don't have any responsibility to me."

"But I owe you my freedom."

"Exactly," said Candy. "*Freedom*. No more being ordered around, by me or anybody else."

Malingo nodded, as though the notion was very slowly beginning to make sense to him.

"Okay," he said. "But what if I *want* to help you?"

"That would be nice. As I said, I think we make a very good team. But it's your choice. And I think I should warn you that it isn't always safe being around me. Ever since I arrived in the Abarat, it's been one thing after another."

"I won't let anything happen to you, lady," Malingo said. "You're too important."

Candy laughed. "Me? Important? Malingo, you don't understand. A few days ago I was a lost schoolgirl from a place called Chickentown."

"Whatever you were back there, lady, it's not what you are here. You can make magic . . ."

"Yes. That *is* strange," said Candy, bringing back to mind her strange familiarity with the working of spells. "So many times on this journey I've felt as though . . . I don't know . . . almost as though I'd been here before. Yet I know that's impossible."

"Maybe it's in your blood," Malingo suggested. "Maybe a relative of yours came here, in the distant past?"

"That's a possibility," Candy replied.

She pictured the faded photographs lined up on the wall of the Almenak Press: the old jetty of Hark's Harbor, with its row of stores and the great vessel moored at the quayside. Was it possible that one of the people in that crowd had been a relative of hers?

"Wolfswinkel's grandfather used to trade with your people all the time. He made a fortune from it."

"Selling what?"

"Abaratian magic. Copies of *Lumeric's Six*. That kind of thing."

"Surely that must have been forbidden?"

"Oh certainly. He was selling some of the most precious secrets of the Abarat. Anything for profit."

"Which reminds me," Candy said. "What was it with the hats? Magic doesn't always come in the form of headgear, does it?"

Malingo laughed. "No, of course not, it can be in any form: a thought, a word, a fish, even in a glass of water. But you see it was a tradition of the Noncian Magic Circle that you kept most of your power in your hat. I don't know how it started; probably as a joke. But once it began, it stuck. And then when Wolfswinkel killed all the other magicians and he wanted to transfer their power to something more convenient, he couldn't. They'd all put their power in the hats when they were a circle, and once the circle was broken—"

"He was stuck with the hats."

"Exactly."

"How very undignified for Ol' Banana Suit."

"Oh yes, he was in a fine state when he found out. He went crazy for a week."

"Changing the subject—"

"Yes?"

"Do you have any idea where we are?"

They had entered a patch of dense shadow, cast by mountainous peaks of clouds that were passing overhead. In the sea below them an enormous shoal of fish, possessed of some exquisite luminescence, moved into view. Their brightness seemed to turn the world on its head: light spilling up from below, while darkness was cast down from the sky.

"Where did you intend to take us?" Malingo asked Candy.

"Back to the Yebba Dim Day. I know a man at The Great Head called Samuel Klepp. He could give us some advice about how to—"

Before she could finish speaking, the glyph, which until now had been proceeding forward effortlessly, did a very peculiar thing. It made a sideways motion, as though something was tugging on it. For a moment it zigzagged wildly, and Candy had to use all her will-power to stop it from veering off in another direction.

She finally brought it back on course, but the swerve had unnerved her.

"What *was* that?" she said. "Is the glyph deteriorating?"

Malingo slapped the side of the vehicle with the flat of his hand. "I don't think so," he said. "It feels solid enough."

"Then, what— oh no, Malingo, it's happening again!"

The glyph veered a second time, much more violently than it had the first, and for a moment it seemed that they were about to be pitched into the sea. Malingo slid from his seat, and would have fallen had Candy not caught hold of him at the last possible moment and hauled him back to safety.

The glyph, meanwhile, was gathering speed. It seemed to have elected a new destination and was simply racing toward it, all previous instructions forgotten. All Candy and Malingo could do was hang on for dear life.

"Can't you slow it down?" Malingo yelled to Candy over the rushing of the wind.

"I'm trying!" she hollered. "But it doesn't want to listen to me. Something's got hold of us, Malingo!"

She glanced over at her companion, who had an expression of raw astonishment on his face.

"What?" she said.

"*Look.*" His awed voice was so low she didn't hear the word; she only saw its shape replied on his lips. She saw too the shape of the words that followed:

"*The Twenty-Fifth Hour,*" he said.

Candy looked up.

Straight ahead of the hurtling glyph was the vast

column of spiraling cloud that Samuel Klepp had pointed out to her. It was indeed the Twenty-Fifth Hour, the Time Out of Time.

"Something in there must be pulling us," Candy yelled.

"But what?" said Malingo. "And why?"

Candy shook her head. "I guess we're going to find out very soon," she said.

There was no doubt of that. The vehicle was moving so fast that the sea and sky were virtually a blur. Candy had relinquished all mental control over the vehicle. There was no purpose in wasting energy fighting a power so much greater than her own.

But as the glyph rushed toward the cloud she could not help but remember the stories she'd been told about the travelers who had entered the Time Out of Time. Most had never returned, Klepp had told her. And those who *had* come out of the cloud had returned crazy. Not a happy thought.

"Maybe we should throw ourselves out?" she yelled to Malingo over the whistling of the wind.

"At this speed?" he yelled back. *"It would be the death of us!"*

He was probably right. But then what would happen when they hit the wall of cloud that concealed the wonders—or the terrors—of the Twenty-Fifth Hour? Wouldn't that be equally suicidal?

And then—all in one sudden moment—it became *too late* to pitch themselves out.

The glyph threw itself over and over, three hundred and sixty degrees, flipping so fast its passengers remained in their seats. Candy heard poor Malingo yelling in mortal terror beside her, then all the sounds that were filling her head—Malingo's cries, the rushing of the wind, the crash of the glyph as it came to a violent halt—all of them disappeared.

She was plunged into a sudden and absolute silence, and a darkness just as sudden, just as absolute.

She couldn't feel the glyph beneath her; nor, when she reached out, could she feel Malingo at her side. She seemed to be floating in blank space, her body removed from all physical contact.

Then, of all things, she heard rain.

It was distant, but it was reassuringly real. Whatever this lightless place was, it rained here. Seconds later another sound came to find her. No, not one sound, two.

Two *heartbeats*.

Somebody was here in the darkness with her. And whoever it was, they were very close.

She tried to shape a question, a simple: "Who's there?" But for some reason her mouth wouldn't obey the instruction. All she could do was wait and listen, while the twinned hearts beat on, and the downpour continued.

For some reason she wasn't afraid. There was something reassuring about the mingling of heartbeats and rain.

And finally, there came a third sound. The last sound she expected to hear in this mysterious place: her mother's voice.

"Please don't be long, Bill," Melissa Quackenbush said. *"I can't wait long."*

Her voice sounded remote from Candy, dulled not by distance but by something placed between them. A wall of some kind.

"Did you hear me, honey? I don't like being here on my own."

Here? Candy thought. What did her mother mean by that? Was Melissa Quackenbush in the Twenty-Fifth Hour with her? Surely not. Besides, there was something about the way her mother sounded that made Candy think that it was a younger woman who was speaking. It wasn't the tired, sad woman she'd last seen making meatloaf in the kitchen in Followell Street. How long, for instance, had it been since she'd heard her mother call her father *honey*? Years.

And now—astonishment upon astonishment—she heard her father's voice replying.

Like Melissa's voice, Bill Quackenbush's speech was muted. But again, it was a gentler, more loving version of her father Candy was now hearing.

"I promise I'll be quick, sweetheart. You just hold on. I'll be back in just a few minutes."

"Maybe I should come with you . . . " Melissa said.

"In your condition, baby?" Bill Quackenbush replied lovingly. *"I don't think that would be too smart. It's cold out here. You stay in the car and keep that blanket wrapped up tight around you, and I'll be back so fast you won't even know I've gone. I love you, Lambkins."*

"I love you too, Nachos."

Lambkins? Nachos? Candy had never heard her parents exchange pet names, not even when she was very young. Perhaps she'd forgotten, but she doubted it. Lambkins and Nachos she would have remembered. She felt slightly uncomfortable, as though she was spying on a secret part of her mother and father's life. A part that belonged in some distant Once Upon a Time when they'd both been young and happily in love. Probably before—

"Before I was born," Candy murmured to herself.

This time, for some reason, her mouth obeyed her instruction, and the words came out.

She even got an answer.

"That's right," said a woman, somewhere in the darkness ahead of her. It wasn't her mother who replied to her. This woman had subtle Abaratian inflections in her words, her tone warm and reassuring. *"You haven't been born yet,"* she said to Candy.

"I don't understand."

"We just wanted to give you a hint of your past," said a second woman, her voice slightly lighter than that of the first speaker. "You need to know who you were before you became who you're going to be."

"How do you know who I was?" Candy said. "Or who I'm going to be? Who are you, anyway?"

"Questions."

"Questions."

"Questions."

A third woman laughed along with the other two, and as they did so there was a gentle blossoming of light in Candy's vicinity. By it she saw all three women. In the middle of the trio, standing a little closer to Candy than her companions, was a woman who looked to be extraordinarily old. Her face was deeply etched with lines, and her hair—which was woven into navel-length braids—was pure white. But she still carried herself with great elegance, even in her antique phase. Nor did she seem weakened by age. There was a dark energy that flickered in the delicate veins of her face and hands.

The women who stood to the right and left of her were somewhat younger than the old lady, but there was nothing fixed about any of the trio. Their faces, despite the welcoming expressions they offered Candy, seemed to be full of subtle hints of transformation.

The youngest of the three—her black hair cropped to her skull—carried a glimpse of something feral in an otherwise benign expression, a beast that was just out of sight behind her lovely bones. The other woman, who was black, had the strangest gaze of the three. When her long hair—which was filled with hints of bright color—parted and showed Candy her eyes, they had the glory of a night sky in them.

So there they were, three protean souls: one carrying lightning, one carrying sky, one touched with wilderness.

Candy felt no fear in the presence of these three: just mystification. By now, of course, she was used to experiencing that particular feeling here in the Abarat. And she'd learned what she should do in the face of mystery. She would watch and listen. The answers to her questions would probably make themselves apparent, after a time. And if they *didn't*, then she wasn't meant to know those answers. She'd learned that too.

The women now started to identify themselves.

"I'm Diamanda," said the old woman.

"I'm Joephi," said the wild one.

"And I'm Mespa," said the one with the night sky in her eyes.

"We are Sisters of the Fantomaya," said Diamanda.

"The Fantomaya?"

"Ssh! Keep your voice down," said Joephi, though it hadn't seemed to Candy that she'd spoken any more loudly than the other three. *"By law we shouldn't have brought you into the Twenty-Fifth. But one day you'll be coming here with work to do of your own. Great work—"*

"So we felt you should get a taste of it—" said Mespa.

"That way," said Diamanda, *"when you come back you'll be prepared. You'll know what it's like."*

"You sound very certain that I'm coming back," Candy said.

"We are," Diamanda said. *"You will have things to do here, in the future—"*

"If we are reading the future right," said Mespa. *"Sometimes it's hard to be sure."*

Now Candy thought about it, the idea didn't seem so very unlikely. If the Twenty-Fifth Hour had let her in once, then why not again, when she better understood who she was, and what purpose she had in this strange world?

"I want to see more of this place," Candy said, staring into the darkness that surrounded them.

"Do you indeed?" said Mespa.

"Yes."

The three women exchanged tentative looks, as though to say, are we ready to do this, or not?

It appeared that they were, because the air suddenly quickened with life around Candy, and in it, like tiny silver fish being carried in a fast-flowing river, she saw glimpses of extraordinary things. At first the images moved past her so fast she could make only the most rudimentary sense of them: a white tower, a field of yellow blossom, a chair sitting on the blue roof of a house, and a man in gold sitting upon it. But as her eyes grew accustomed to the way the shoal of pictures were flowing past her, she in her turn became more able to snatch hold of one for a few moments; like a hot coin, caught in the palm of her hand, that she had time to turn over and examine on both sides before the discomfort obliged her to let it go.

And there was an undeniable discomfort in seeing many of these images. They were so powerful, their shapes and their colors so full of strangeness that it hurt her head to catch them and hold them, even for a moment.

It wasn't just the intensity of each image that ached, it was the fact that there were so *many* of them. For every coin that she caught and flipped, there were a thousand, no ten thousand, that tumbled by, glittering and unexamined.

What did she see?

A woman walking upside down, fish in the sky above her, birds at her feet.

A man standing in a moonlit wasteland, his head flowering like an oasis of thoughts.

A city of red towers, under a sky filled with falling stars; another city, made in perfect miniature, and raised up on legs, with a blue bird—surely vast, even monstrous, to the city's inhabitants—wheeling overhead.

A grotesque mask singing as it floated in midair; a creature the size of a lion, with the head of a human being, vast and bearded, sitting on the lip of a volcano. A shore of some tropical island, with a tiny red boat in the bay, and a single star hanging over the horizon.

And so on. And on. And on. The images kept flying.

Sometimes there would be a sound attached to the scene, though it didn't always seem to fit, as though—just like lightning preceding thunder—the images came more quickly than the sounds, so that they were out of step with one another. Sometimes she glimpsed things that she recognized, albeit briefly. The Yebba Dim Day, rising from the misty waters of the Straits of Dusk. The Gilholly Bridge being crossed by an army of people with bright white fire springing from their heads. Even Ninnyhammer, in the midst of a storm so violent that its young trees were being plucked from the earth and carried away.

At last—just as the flow of images came close to overwhelming her—the shoal of fish began to thin out, and between the occasional flash of strangeness, the relatively reassuring vision of Diamanda, Joephi and Mespa began to reappear.

Candy was left breathless.

"What . . . ?" she gasped.

"What was all that?" Mespa said.

"Yes."

It was Diamanda who replied.

"An infinitesimally small piece of a tiny fragment of a virtually invisible fraction of what is here at Odom's Spire. The past and the present-past and the future-present. They're all in this place, you see. Every particular of every thing in every moment of forever."

"And you?"

"The Fantomaya?"

"Yes. What do you do with the images?"

"We study them. We immerse ourselves in them. We protect them."

"From who?" said Candy.

"From any and all. These are not things a common soul needs to see."

Candy laughed.

"What's so funny?" said Joephi.

"Well . . . aren't *I* a common soul?" said Candy.

"Good question," said Diamanda. *"The fact is you are many things, my dear. Many, many things. One of them is Candy Quackenbush of the town of Murkitt—"*

"You mean Chickentown?"

"Oh. Yes, of course. I mean Chickentown. Back when I was there, it was called after my husband's grandfather."

"Wait a moment," Candy said, a little smile of

realization creeping into her face. "I *knew* I'd heard the name Diamanda before. *You're Diamanda Murkitt.* You were married to Henry Murkitt."

The old woman nodded slowly, staring at Candy with fresh intensity. *"I am that woman. Much changed, but in many ways the same."*

"Amazing," said Candy.

"Is it?" Diamanda said. *"I mean, am I? Why?"*

"Everything's coming full circle."

"Please explain," said Diamanda.

"Well, my journey began with Henry Murkitt," Candy said. "You see, I wrote something about him."

"About Henry?" said Diamanda, speaking her husband's name with no lack of tenderness. *"You wrote about Henry?"*

"Just a few pages," Candy said. "I was in the room where he . . . committed suicide."

"Ah," said Diamanda softly. *"So that's what happened to him."*

Candy nodded. "I'm sorry to be the one to tell you."

"No, don't apologize. It's better I know than not. I knew I'd have to make my peace with the truth sooner or later. I ran out on Henry, you see. He had so few dreams."

"Yes, I heard," Candy said. "Not about the dreams, but about you running out on him."

"He thought I went to Philadelphia, but why would I do a thing like that, when I knew about the Abarat? No . . . I caught the first ship out of that wretched world . . ."

"You did the same, yes?" said Joephi.

"Yes. I did the same. I didn't have a ship to carry me. I came by Sea-Skipper." Candy smiled at the memory; it seemed so long ago.

"But my, you got here quicker than we expected," said Mespa. *"A lot quicker."*

"Well sisters," said Diamanda, unbraiding her hair as she spoke, *"it seems we will have to be very careful about laying our plans in future. A new and highly unpredictable element has entered our sphere. And she changes everything. It will be impossible to guess the future with any of the old confidence."* She looked back at Candy. *"All we know is that we've got our hands full."*

"What's changed?" said Candy. "Please explain. There's so much I want to know. I feel as though I *belong* here for some reason. That this is really my home."

The three women didn't make any attempt to dissuade her of this.

Apparently they believe I belong here too, Candy thought. The realization made her eyes sting with happy tears. The women's smiles and silence were confirming something she hadn't dared to believe until now. *She had a reason to be here. Even if nobody yet knew what it was, she still belonged.*

"If I really do have some purpose here," Candy said, "I mean, if I'm more than just some dumb sightseer, then can you help me understand what that purpose is?"

"We'd be happy to," said Joephi.

"But I'm not sure we understand ourselves," Mespa

went on. The starlight in her eyes trembled. The woman wasn't afraid, Candy thought; but filled with a curious excitement.

"Something's going to happen to me, isn't it?" Candy said.

"My dear, something already has," Diamanda replied. *"You're not the same girl who threw herself into the Izabella, are you?"*

Candy took a moment to think about this. But no more than a moment.

"No. No, I'm not." Then she said: "I'm somebody else. I just don't know who that somebody else *is* yet."

"Well that's what journeys are for," Diamanda Murkitt said. *"Remember, I made the same trip myself. Looking for something I didn't have. And trust me, Candy, wherever you think you're going, the real destination is . . . right here."* She tapped her chest, directly above her heart.

"Will I ever go back to the Hereafter?" Candy said.

The three women exchanged anxious looks.

"What's wrong?" said Candy, reading the discomfort in their eyes. "Do you know something about this?"

"We've had glimpses . . ." Diamanda said, *"only glimpses."*

"There isn't much to tell," Joephi said.

"But the news is bad?" Candy said.

"Not for you," Mespa said.

"Then who for?"

Joephi and Mespa both looked at Diamanda, as though seeking some guidance from their elder.

"I'm not going to start making prophecies on the basis of glimpses," Diamanda said. *"But you should know, my dear, that from now on there is jeopardy at every step. For you. For those who travel with you. And even for the places you choose to go. You may bring down cities before you have solved all the mysteries that lie ahead of you."*

"That sure sounds like a prophecy to me," said Mespa.

"Well, what do you suggest we tell her?" the old lady said, a little irritated.

"We could begin with the stories we've been hearing about Finnegan."

"Who's Finnegan?" Candy said, thinking halfway through the question that perhaps somebody on this journey had already told her, because the name rang a bell. Or did she maybe know a Finnegan in Chickentown?

"Oh, you'll like Finnegan," Diamanda said, with a teasing little smile.

"That she will," said Mespa.

"Then there's the Requiax," said Joephi, moving on before Candy had time to ask about Finnegan.

"Who are the Requiax?" Candy asked, determined to get an answer this time.

There was silence for a moment. Candy looked from face to face. "Please," she said. "I need some help here."

Mespa began: *"The Requiax are the worst of the worst,"* she said.

"They're the enemies of love," Diamanda went on.

"The enemies of life. Wicked beyond words . . ."

"And where are they?"

"Right now," said Joephi, *"they're deep in the Izabella, and let's hope they stay there."*

"Doubtful," Diamanda went on. *"We hear all manner of rumors about the Requiax being on the move. And there are those who say that when they surface, it will be the end of the world as we know it."*

"You're scaring me," Candy said.

"I forbid you to be scared," Diamanda replied, gently. *"She was never scared, so you shouldn't be."*

"She?" said Candy. "What do you mean, *she*?"

Curiously enough, all three women opened their mouths to reply to this, but before any of them could answer, there came the sound of a series of doors closing—maybe ten in all—the smallest of which sounded like the noise of a doll's house door, the largest a solid oak door, slamming somewhere nearby.

"He's coming," cried Joephi.

"We've got to be off, Candy," Diamanda said. *"Abraham Hollow, the Keeper of the Twenty-Fifth Hour, doesn't approve of anybody from the outside world being brought into the Time Out of Time. If he knew you were here, he'd have the Fugit Brothers tear you from limb to limb."*

"Nice," said Candy. "What do I do with all the questions I've still got?"

"Keep them for another time," said Joephi.

"But I have so *many*," Candy said.

The women were clearly preparing to make a hasty exit, gathering up their robes, glancing around nervously as they did so. Obviously they did not want to encounter this Abraham Hollow.

"*We'll find one another again,*" Diamanda said. "*Don't you worry about that. There is so much to tell, on both sides. Thank you for the news about Henry, by the way. You've shamed me into an apology.*"

"But . . . he's dead," Candy said.

"*A matter of little consequence here,*" said Diamanda.

"Why?"

"*Because this is the Twenty-Fifth Hour. Everything is Here. Everything is Now. Even Yesterday.*"

"I don't—"

"*Will you hurry up, Diamanda Murkitt?*" said Mespa, catching hold of the old woman's hand. "*I hear Old Abraham coming.*"

"*Yes, yes,*" said Diamanda. "*I'm coming. I just wanted her to understand—*"

"*We don't have time,*" said Mespa.

"*No time?*" said Joephi, laughing. "*That's the one thing we surely have in abundance. Time and more time and time again.*"

"*Don't get clever,*" Mespa snapped. "*I don't want Abraham finding us. Any of us. NOW COME ON.*"

She was pulling on Diamanda's arm now.

"*I'm sorry,*" the old lady said to Candy, "*there's so much more I wanted to show you here. And we won't get another chance to sneak you in, I'm afraid. Even this little peep took a lot of maneuvering—*"

"*Will you stop gabbing?*" Mespa said.

"*Yes, yes. Coming.*"

The light that had first revealed the women was brightening all around them. In a few seconds they would be gone. But before the sisters were eroded by the brightness, Diamanda reached out and touched Candy's arm.

"I envy you," she said.

"You do?"

"The journey ahead of you . . . it's going to be quite something. The things that are out there waiting to be discovered . . ." She smiled and shook her head. *"You cannot imagine,"* she said. *"Truly . . . you cannot imagine."*

Then her fingers drew back from Candy's arm, and the three women vanished into the flux of light.

As they disappeared, Candy caught a glimpse of the door slammer: Abraham Hollow, the Keeper of the Time Out of Time. He was no more than ten yards away, standing on the threshold of a door that he had just closed, and staring down at something at his feet. He was dressed in voluminous scarlet robes, and his thin face was possessed of that smoothness and translucence that sometimes comes with extreme old age. He wore tiny round black-lensed spectacles, which concealed his eyes, and had a matted mop of white hair on his head.

"There you are, Tattle," he said, addressing a large piebald Abaratian rat, which had appeared from between his feet. With great effort Hollow bent down and offered the sleeve of his robe to the rat. The animal instantly scampered up the sleeve and ran along Hollow's stooped shoulder to his ear, as though whispering into it. Indeed, perhaps the rat was doing just that, because the old man then muttered to himself:

"An interloper, eh? I should maybe summon the brothers . . ."

He opened the door behind him and called back through it.

"Tempus! Julius!"

Time to go, Candy thought, *before I'm caught trespassing*. But in which direction should she run? There was darkness everywhere except for the light on the threshold where Abraham Hollow and his telltale rat stood. She decided the best thing to do was simply turn her back on the old man and run in the opposite direction.

She did exactly that, racing off into the darkness, and silently cursing the three sisters for heading off without taking her with them.

"There!" said Abraham Hollow. *"I hear our trespasser's feet. Over there!"*

Candy glanced back over her shoulder. The door at which Hollow and Tattle stood had been flung wide, as had the door behind it, and the door behind that door. And through them came the Fugit Brothers.

Candy had been warned, of course, about the dangers of the Twenty-Fifth. She'd been told how all the people who'd ventured here over the years had either disappeared, or been driven mad. One glimpse of the Fugit Brothers and she understood why. They had the faces of clowns: white skin, gaping mouths and pop eyes. But that was the least of it. What was truly distressing was the fact that their features—their eyes, their mouths, their noses, their ears, and even the three little tufts of red hair they sported, were moving around their faces like the hands of crazy clocks. Despite the fact that their mouths were on the move, they still spoke:

"*I see her, Brother Julius!*" said one of the brothers.

"*Me too, Brother Tempus. Me too!*"

"*I say we tear out her heart, Brother Julius!*"

"*I say we make her crazy first, Brother Tempus!*"

So that was the way of it, Candy thought. One vote for lunacy, one vote for murder. Either way, if these two caught her, she would never live to learn from what she'd seen in the Time Out of Time.

She didn't wait to hear any more of their chatter. She fled into the darkness, which enveloped her completely. She could see no sign of a way out in any direction: no door, no window. Not so much as a sliver of light from the outside world.

There was nothing to be lost from yelling for help, she thought. After all, these clock-faced clowns knew where she was. So she called to Malingo, in the vain hope that he would hear her.

"Malingo? I'm over here!" (Wherever *here* was.) "Please, if you can hear me, yell back."

She got an answer, but it wasn't the one she wanted. It was an echo of what she'd just yelled, but the walls it had bounced off of had rearranged the words, and made nonsense of them.

"You can if me. Yell back here, hear? I'm over Malingo."

Even the *echoes* had their own tricks in this place.

As the words died away, she heard two soft voices, horribly close.

"*I believe we should take her, Brother Julius.*"

"*I believe we should, Brother Tempus, I believe we should.*"

They sounded as though they were two or three yards away. She didn't wait for them to get any nearer. She headed off into the darkness again, not caring where she went, just determined not to allow the Fugit Brothers to catch up with her.

She couldn't run forever, she knew. It was only a matter of time before the clowns on her heels caught up with her. And then what? Well, they'd already laid out their options. Even if she escaped their clutches, the echoes, and the memory of her pursuers' circling faces, would take their toll. Whatever wonders she had witnessed here would be erased by insanity.

No! She couldn't let that happen. She ran on blindly, determined she was not going to be numbered among those who'd escaped the Twenty-Fifth too crazy to tell their tale.

32

MONSOON

THE EXHAUSTED SURVIVORS OF the sinking *Belbelo* spent their first day on the Island of the Nonce at the beach where they'd been washed ashore. Every time the tide came in it would bring more pieces of the wreckage up onto the sand: splintered timbers and rope, mostly. They didn't expect to have to build fires on the island (it was warm at Three O'clock in the Afternoon; what need would they have of fire?) so the timber was of very little use. But every now and again a box of supplies was washed up, including a box of emergency rations.

Unfortunately there was no medication for Mischief and his brothers, who were still in very poor condition. Though their wounds had stopped bleeding, there was no sign of consciousness returning. All Geneva, Tom, the Captain and Tria could do was to work together to build a small shelter out of branches and leaves, and lay the brothers in it, away from the heat of the midafternoon sun.

Luckily both Tom and the Captain still had their

copies of *Klepp's Almenak*, and each had a different edition, so they were able to consult the pamphlet on a wide variety of matters.

"It isn't always reliable information," Geneva cautioned them, as Tom proposed to make a stew of berries he'd found when he'd ventured a little deeper into the island. "We could very well poison ourselves."

"I doubt there'd be a recipe in the *Almenak* which produced poisonous food," Tom said.

"So you say," Geneva said, plainly unconvinced. "But if we all get sick—"

While they'd been arguing about this, Tria had been picking up the berries, one by one, and sniffing them. A few, particularly the smaller, greenish berries, she tossed away. The rest she left in the bag in which Tom had collected them, and declared with her usual strange confidence: "These are all right."

The stew was duly cooked, and it proved to be delicious.

"We still could have got sick from the green ones," Geneva reminded Tom and the Captain, "if Tria hadn't stopped us from eating them."

"Oh, for goodness sake, Geneva," McBean said, "let it go. We've got more important things to worry about without arguing over stew."

"Such as?"

"Such as him." McBean glanced in the direction of Mischief. "I mean them," he said, correcting himself. "I'm afraid they're slipping away from us."

"I don't know where we go for help," said Tom. "According to the *Almenak*, there aren't any towns on the island, so if there are any doctors around, they're living in the wild. There are a lot of churches, but Klepp describes most of them as abandoned."

"There's the Palace of Bowers," Geneva said. "Perhaps there's still some people there . . ."

"How far is the Palace from here?" Captain McBean asked Tom.

"See for yourself," Tom said, proffering his edition of *Klepp's Almenak* so that all of them could see it. He pointed to a bay on the north-northwesterly side of the island. "I believe we're *here*," he said. "And the Palace is way over *here*. It's probably two days' walk, maybe more if the landscape between here and there is hilly."

"Which it is," said Geneva. "The whole island is hilly. But we can still carry Mischief between us."

"Is moving them a wise idea?" McBean asked.

"I don't know," Geneva replied, shaking her head. "I'm no doctor."

"That's the problem; none of us are," said Tom. "If I had to guess, I'd say moving them would be fatal, but maybe waiting here is an even worse idea."

At that moment, everybody stopped staring at the map and looked up. The wind had suddenly risen, making the great blossom-filled banks of foliage in whose shadows they sat churn and sigh. And carried on that wind there came the sound of hundreds of voices, all singing a wordless song.

"We're not alone," said the Captain.

The music was both majestic and serene.

"Snakes," said Tria.

"Snakes?" said the Captain.

"She's right," Tom told him. "There's a red-and-yellow serpent on the island called the vigil snake. They sing. It says so in the *Almenak*."

"I don't remember snakes on this island," Geneva said.

"Yes you do," said Tom. "They were requested by the Princess—"

"For the wedding."

"Exactly. Finnegan had them brought over from Scoriae, which is their natural habitat. Apparently they liked it here. Klepp said they all escaped in the confusion after . . . all that happened at the wedding. And they have no natural enemies here on the Nonce. So they bred and bred. Now they're everywhere."

"Are they poisonous?" Tria asked. It was perhaps the first time that any of them had heard her voice any fear about the natural world.

"No," said Tom. "Very mild-mannered, as I remember. And very musical."

"Amazing," said the Captain. "What are they singing? Is it just nonsense?"

"No," said Tom. He read from the *Almenak*. "*'The song that the Vigil Snake sings is in fact one immensely long word; the longest in the ancient language of the species. It is so long that an individual can sing it for a lifetime and never come to the end of it.'*"

"That sounds like a Kleppism to me," Geneva said. "How would they ever *learn* it?"

"Good question," said Tom. "Maybe they're born with it, like a migration instinct?"

"Born with a song," said Geneva.

Tom smiled. "Yes. Don't you like that idea?"

"Liking it and having it be true aren't the same thing, Tom."

"Huh. Sometimes you need to let things strike your heart and not your head, Geneva."

"And what's that supposed to mean?" snapped Geneva.

"Never mind."

"No, tell me Tom," she said, bristling. "Don't make sly remarks and then—"

"It wasn't sly."

"Well, how else would you—"

"I resent being called—"

"And I resent—"

"Stop it," said Tria. "Both of you." The girl had sudden tears in her eyes. "Look at them."

While the argument between Tom and Geneva had been mounting, Mischief and his brothers had started to breathe in a most terrible fashion, a rattle in their collective throats that did not bode well.

"Oh Lord . . ." Tom threw aside the *Almenak* and went over to the little bed of leaves and blossoms where they'd laid the brothers. "This doesn't sound good at all."

He went down on his knees beside Mischief and laid a hand on his brow. Mischief's eyes were rolling back and forth wildly behind his lids, and his breathing was getting quicker and shallower with every passing moment.

At the same time, as though there was some strange synchronicity in the air (the argument, the singing, the wind and now Mischief's anguish all happening within seconds of one another), the Captain looked skyward and announced: "I think we should get our stuff under cover."

He didn't need to explain why. A vast thunderhead moved over the sun as he spoke, and the wind in the trees grew suddenly stronger, stripping some of the more fragile blooms of their petals.

There was a sudden burst of activity as everyone did as the Captain had suggested. But fast though they were, they weren't fast enough to move everything before the rain began. There were a few scattered drops, and then—in a matter of seconds—the drops became a torrential downpour, the rain coming down with such vehemence they had to shout to make themselves heard.

"You and me, Tom!" the Captain yelled. "We'll take Mischief together!"

"Where are we going?" Tom hollered.

"Up there!" McBean said, pointing up a small slope between the trees. The rainfall was so powerful that rivulets of sandy-brown water, carrying a freight of dead leaves, twigs, blossoms and the occasional dead rodent, were running down the slope. The area around Mischief's makeshift bed was already an inch deep in water.

There was a flash of lightning now, followed by a roll of thunder; the rain came on with fresh attack, as though it wanted to wash the world away.

"Let me carry him!" Tom said, having to yell until his throat was a roar over the noise of cracking boughs and rolling thunder.

The Captain didn't have an opportunity for argument.

Tom simply picked up Mischief in his arms and, putting his head down so as not to be blinded by the rain, proceeded to climb to higher ground. The others followed, all carrying what they could rescue from their little encampment.

And still the rain came on, with mounting power, until the world was reduced to a deafening gray-green blur.

Step by step Tom climbed the slope, until he was two thirds of the way to the top. Then out of nowhere a large log came down the slope carried by the force of the flood. Tom tried to move aside to avoid being struck, but the weight of the brothers slowed him. The log caught him a heavy blow, knocking his legs out from under him. Down he went, and Mischief slipped from his arms. They were both carried back down the slope, knocking everybody else over as they descended.

When they reached the bottom, it was like being thrown into the midst of a fast-flowing river. Geneva caught hold of Tria to stop the child from being swept away down the beach and out into the sea. McBean in turn caught hold of Geneva with his right hand and grabbed a tree with his left, holding on for dear life until the monsoon had exhausted itself.

And still it mounted, beating down on their heads. It was as if the skies had opened and unleashed a hundred years of rain.

And then, just as abruptly as it had begun, it all ceased. It was as though a faucet had been turned off. The sun broke through the exhausted clouds, and it illuminated a battered world. Every single blossom

had been stripped of its petals by the force of the rain.
The smaller leaves had been pulled off the twigs, the
larger ones shredded. Bushes had been uprooted and
carried down onto the beach and into the surf, which
was no longer white but tinted reddish brown by the
mud that had been washed into it.

Weary from the relentless assault of the rain,
McBean, Geneva, Tria and Tom stood ankle deep in
mud and debris. Unable to speak, they stared up at the
sky, watching the patches of blue grow between the
thinning clouds.

As the warmth of the sun pierced the bruised
canopy and touched the greenery around the survivors,
they were all witness to a phenomenon that Klepp had
failed to mention in his *Almenak*. Apparently he had
never been on the Nonce when a rainstorm had been
unleashed, because if he had the ensuing miracle
would surely have been reported in his *Almenak*'s
pages.

Everywhere around them, the wounded plant life
was beginning to grow again. Roots, many of which
had been exposed by the force of the water, stretched
down like gnarled fingers into the muddied ground.
From broken twigs and cracked boughs new growth
sprang up, healthy and green, buds fattening and bursting in front of their astonished eyes. Vines curled and
climbed from the remains of their rain-beaten elders
like eager green children, while ferns sprang up,
uncoiling their tender shoots at such speed they were
grazing the lower boughs of the trees in seconds.

"Oh. My," Tom said.

"Have you ever seen anything like this before?" Geneva asked the Captain.

He slowly shook his head.

"Never," he said.

This spectacle of growth would have been extraordinary enough in itself; but there was more. The monsoon had awoken dormant elements in the greenery, parts of its blossoming anatomy that did not entirely resemble plants. Wasn't that an eye surreptitiously opening in the head of a flower? And something uncannily like a mouth, gaping in the moisture-fattened bulbs of a plant that sat half in the earth and half out, like a bright green onion?

On all sides there were signs of this uncanny life: cracklings and mutterings and stretching and yes, even something like laughter, as though the plants were hugely amused by the sight of their own protean lives.

It was Tria who first said: "Where's Mischief?"

Everybody looked around. The John brothers were not to be seen. The Captain sent everyone in different directions, telling them to look quickly, as this was a matter of life and death.

"If they're lying facedown in water, they could be drowning right now!"

His words gave urgency to everybody's search. There were large, shallow pools of muddy rainwater at the bottom of the slope; they went through them from end to end on their hands and knees, desperately hoping to find Mischief before too much time passed.

Meanwhile, the greenery continued to become more active and more fruitful around them, the buds bursting like popcorn, releasing the sweet fragrance of new flowers. Some of the plants were so eager to be fruitful that they were already releasing clouds of pollen that filled the air like soft golden smoke.

The survivors, of course, noticed none of this. They were concerned about Mischief.

Nothing was said, but everyone was beginning to fear the worst. Perhaps the force of the water had carried him down the slope of the beach and out to sea. If not, *where was he*?

It was Tria—the ever-observant Tria—who pointed out what had happened to the *rest* of their belongings. The things that they'd attempted to save from the monsoon, and had successfully carried back up the slope, only to lose them again when they'd tumbled back down, were all in one spot. They had been gathered together, it seemed, by the large, serpentine tendrils of an enormous plant that sat in regal solitude at the bottom of the incline.

They went to examine it. The plant was continuing to grow and thrive, its huge seedpods shiny green with health. They creaked as they grew, and gave off the pungent smell of all green growing things. The plant was like a little grove unto itself, its outer layer a knotted thicket of freshly sprung and interwoven flora. It was here that articles from their encampment had been brought by the water. Now they were part of the elaborate network of tendrils, as though some ambitious intelligence in the plant was attempting to turn them into bizarre blossoms.

Beyond the thicket—at the heart of this miniature

forest—the foliage grew considerably denser. So dense, in fact that it *almost* hid from sight an enormous seedpod, dripping with the juices of its recent creation.

"Will you take a look at that?" said Tom, parting the veil of tendrils.

"There," Tria said. "He's in there."

"Mischief?" Geneva asked her.

Tria nodded.

The other three exchanged confounded looks.

"Here, Captain," Tom said. "Lend me a hand, will you?"

They began to pull at the outer layer of the thicket, and the tendrils uncoiled and wrapped around their hands and arms, around their legs too. They were too thin—perhaps too playful—to do any real harm, but they still slowed the men's advance.

"I wish I had a knife," the Captain said.

"Oh, let me at it!" said Geneva. "You two will be fighting that stuff all day!"

She stepped between them and started to pull at the tangled mass. Now all three of them were in the midst of the green coils, and pieces of flora were flying in all directions.

But Geneva was a better tactician than the other two. She ducked down under the great mass of thicket, and then—once she was on the other side—pushed it out, like two enormous doors, which Tom and the Captain grabbed hold of, creating a passageway into the heart of the grove.

They were all breathless now, fragments of the leaves stuck to the sweat on their faces and caught on their eyelashes and in their hair.

They stood aside as Tria entered through the opening they'd made and approached the pod that all this foliage had been protecting.

"Be careful," Tom said to her.

He'd no sooner spoken than the pod—which was hanging from a great looping network of vines—began to move. Small tremors ran through it, as though something inside was having a little fit. Its seam began to split with a sound of tearing canvas, spitting gobs of sweet juice as it did so.

Tria turned and looked at the adults.

"See?" she said, an expression of delight on her face, a rare sight indeed.

The top of the pod now flew open like the lid of a casket. And there, lying in a mess of mud and water, but cushioned by the leaves and the coiled tendrils that lined the pod, was John Mischief and his brothers.

Their eyes were still closed, but something—perhaps the light suddenly falling on their upturned faces when the lid rose—now stirred them.

John Moot was the first to open his eyes. He blinked hard. Then he frowned and let out a little laugh.

"What happened?" he said.

"You're awake . . ." said Tom.

John Drowze piped up next. "So am I!"

It was like watching the stars come out at night, as now—one by one—the John brothers opened their eyes and the light of full consciousness returned into their puzzled faces.

Mischief himself, however, remained comatose,

even though in a short time every other one of his brothers was awake.

"We should lift you out of here," Tom said to them, "before the greenery thinks about swallowing you up again."

"Don't bother," said Serpent. "We'll wake him, and then he can climb out himself."

"You might have difficulty," said Geneva, peering closely at Mischief. "He's showing no sign of stirring."

"Don't worry—" said John Sallow.

"—we do it all the time when he's dozing," John Slop said. Then, looking at his brothers, "Is everybody ready?"

There were murmurs of affirmation from both antlers.

John Serpent took the countdown:

"Three. Two. One—"

And as a single voice, the Johns all yelled:

"MISCHIEF?"

At first there was no response, absolutely none. They held their breath; Fillet, Sallow, Moot, Drowze, Pluckitt, Serpent and Slop included. Then there was the tiniest of twitches in Mischief's left eyelid and a moment later his eye opened. His right eye followed a heartbeat later.

"What am I doing lying in this plant?" was the first thing he said, and rolled out of it, onto the rain-sodden, root-covered ground. He winced as he fell.

"Damn fool, Mischief," John Serpent said. "Will you be more careful? This body of ours is *wounded*, remember?"

"The dragon . . ." John Mischief said.

"You remember?" said Geneva. Mischief nodded. "Well, that's good."

"Of *course* we remember," John Serpent said. "A thing like that you don't forget."

"I just don't know how I got from *there* to here," Mischief said.

"Well, that's for us to tell and you to listen," Geneva replied with a smile.

"Give me a hand up, somebody," Mischief said, offering his arm to Tom.

"I've got you," Tom said, hauling the brothers to their feet.

The greenery was still burgeoning on every side, so they all stumbled out of the grove together, picking pieces of tendril and shredded leaf out of their hair and from inside their clothes. The sun was bright and warm; there was not a cloud in the sky. Even the deepest of the puddles was rapidly soaking into the ground.

"Welcome to the Nonce," said Tom to the Johns. "You were as close to death as anyone could get and still come back."

"We're not going anywhere," John Mischief said, carefully stretching in the warmth. "We've got a lot of adventuring to do. Dragons to fight. Finnegan to find."

"What *is* that music?" John Sallow said.

"It's the snakes of the Nonce singing," Tom replied.

A broad grin spread over John Mischief's face. "See?" he said, making a tiny shake of his head. "That's another thing we've got to do. We've got to listen to the snakes sing."

33

ALL THINGS IN TIME

CANDY RAN, AND KEPT running, without daring to look back over her shoulder at the Fugit Brothers. She didn't need to. They kept up an almost ceaseless exchange as they came after her.

"She doesn't know where she's going, Brother Tempus."

"Nor she does, Brother Julius, nor she does."

"She could trip at any moment, Brother Tempus."

"Flat on her face, Brother Julius, flat on her face."

They were like a couple of bad comedians—all talk and no punch line. In fact, their chatter was so irritating she was half tempted to turn around and tell them to shut up. But then she thought of their vile unfixed features circling and circling—and her appetite for confrontation faded. Better to just run. There had to be some way out of here. After all, she'd got *in*, hadn't she?

But no matter which way she looked, there was no sign of an exit. Just the same featureless darkness in all directions. And she was getting tired. Her chest was tight, and her throat was raw. Sooner or later, she knew, she was going to stumble. When she did her talkative pursuers would be on her in a heartbeat.

"She's slowing down, Brother Julius."

"That I see, Brother Tempus. That I see."

Just to prove the pair wrong, Candy put on an extra spurt of energy. As she did so she remembered the chaotic moments that had preceded her entrance into this dark place. How the glyph had turned over, flinging her out.

Ah, she thought, *maybe that's the answer to my problem.*

Here she was looking for a door, assuming there was no way out except *through* a door. But she hadn't come in that way, had she? Maybe her best escape route was to throw herself into the darkness, and trust to fate.

She glanced over her shoulder. The brothers were no more than a few strides behind her. If she was going to try and escape them, it was now or never.

She counted to three.

"One—"

"What did she say, Brother Julius?"

"Two—"

"I didn't catch it, Brother Tempus."

"Three—"

And with that she pitched herself forward, almost as though she were diving into a pool of water. It worked. The moment her body was free of the ground, the darkness around her seemed to convulse. She was instantly released from its grip, and she felt herself tumbling over and over. A moment later, there was light! And she fell heavily among the rocks on the shore of the Twenty-Fifth.

She landed so hard that her breath was knocked from her. For a few moments she lay there gasping and bruised, listening to the sound of the waves and the din of the seabirds squabbling over some piece of fish that had been washed up.

Then, from nearby, there came a reassuring voice.

"Lady?"

Seconds later Malingo's face came into view, upside down.

"You're here! You're alive!"

Candy was still in a mild state of shock. She opened her mouth to answer Malingo, but at first all that would come out was a trail of disconnected words. "Running. Clocks. Faces. Tempus Fugit. And Julius. Horrible. Two. Horrible."

"Oh my poor lady," Malingo said. "Did they make you crazy in there?"

"I'm *not* crazy!" Candy said, pushing herself up into a sitting position. She took a deep breath and tried to construct a more coherent sentence. "I've got a few bruises," she said. "But I'm sane. I swear I am. And I'm alive."

"Alive you are," Malingo said, with a bright smile.

Candy laughed. She'd done it! She'd actually escaped the Twenty-Fifth Hour!

She got to her feet and embraced Malingo. "The things I've seen," she said to him. "You wouldn't believe some of the things . . ."

"Such as?" said Malingo, eyes gleaming with curiosity.

Candy opened her mouth, intending to describe her adventures inside the Twenty-Fifth. But then she decided against it.

"You know what?" she said. "Perhaps it's best not to do it here."

She stared at the wall of roiling mist that separated the beach from the secret world on the other side. Anybody could be on the other side, she reasoned. Listening; or worse, ready to pounce and drag her back in.

"We should get out of here first," she said to Malingo, "before the Fugit Brothers catch up with us."

"Who are the Fugit Brothers?" Malingo said.

Before she could offer a reply, Candy caught sight from the corner of her eye of something emerging from a crack between the stones. She looked around and focused on it. The thing moved sideways, like a crab. But it was no animal. It was a mouth. A mouth with legs.

"Oh no . . ." she said softly.

"What's wrong?" said Malingo.

"Where's the glyph?" Candy said.

"The glyph?"

"Yes, the glyph!" Candy said, as an eye with legs appeared from under the rocks and blinked up at her.

This time Malingo followed her gaze. "What are they?"

"They belong to the Fugit Brothers," Candy said, catching hold of Malingo's arm and pulling him away from the spot. If a mouth and eye were here, could the brothers that owned them be far behind?

"They live in the Twenty-Fifth," Candy said hurriedly. "And if they get hold of us—"

She didn't have a chance to finish. The rocks nearby had started to shake, their motion gentle at first, but quickly becoming stronger. It wasn't hard to guess what was going on. Tempus and Julius had somehow burrowed out, under the stones, and they were planning a surprise attack from below. They would have succeeded in their surprise, too, if their wandering features hadn't given their sneaky game away.

"We have to get out of here!" Candy said.

Malingo was still staring at the stones, which were rattling together.

"Where's the glyph, Malingo?"

"That's an eye on legs!"

"Yes. I know. Malingo. Where's the glyph?"

He pointed back down the beach, without looking at where he was pointing. She followed his finger, and yes, there was the craft, lying on the stones. It was overturned, but at least it looked to be intact. The impact of striking the wall of the Twenty-Fifth hadn't smashed it to smithereens.

"Come on!" she said to Malingo, pulling on his arm again. He didn't move, however. The strange lifeforms on the stones had him entranced.

"We can't wait around here," Candy said. "Or we're dead."

The rocks were being rolled aside now—the smaller ones thrown into the air—as the Fugit Brothers prepared to make their entrance.

"I never saw anything like that before," Malingo said, his voice filled with fascination.

"Can we please *go*?"

Before they could take a step however, a dark voice rose from the crevices between the rocks.

"You won't escape us, Candy Quackenbush," said one of the brothers.

"Nor will your flap-eared friend," said his sibling.

The sound of the Fugits' voices punctured Malingo's curiosity. Now it was he who backed away from the spot where the rocks were shaking.

"You're right," he said to Candy. "We should go."

"Finally."

There was no more hesitation. The two of them raced together over the slimy stones toward the beached glyph.

"Let's just hope it still works," Candy said to Malingo, as they ran.

"What do we do if it doesn't?"

"I don't know," Candy said grimly. "We'll worry about that if it happens."

They had reached the vehicle now, and they instantly got to work pushing it back into an upright position. Something rattled as the glyph rocked back into place, which didn't sound particularly optimistic.

"Get in!" Candy said.

As Malingo slipped into his seat, Candy dared a momentary glance along the beach. One of the brothers—Candy didn't know whether it was Julius or Tempus—had now dug himself clear of the stones. But there was no sign of the other. Still, she thought, one of them could do plenty of damage.

He started to stride along the beach toward Candy and Malingo, pointing toward them as he did so.

"You will not leave this island!" he yelled as he approached. *"Do you hear me? You will not leave."*

Even as he spoke he proceeded to pick up his speed, his stride quickly breaking into a run.

Now it was Malingo who was urging Candy to get into the glyph. "Hurry!" he said.

Candy put one foot into the glyph.

As she lifted her other leg, an arm was thrust up out of the stones beside the glyph and seized hold of her calf.

She let out a yelp of shock. The stones rolled away as the second Fugit Brother pushed himself out of the ground, using Candy to haul himself up.

"Hold her, Brother Julius!" Tempus yelled as he came racing down the beach.

"Help me!" Candy yelled to Malingo.

She reached down and tried to unknot Julius' fingers, but his grip was cold and strong.

Malingo put both his arms around Candy and pulled hard on her. Desperation gave him strength. Candy's clothes tore, and Fugit's grasping hands were left holding two pieces of shredded fabric.

Freed of the monster's grip, Candy looked straight down into Julius' face. His crawling features had assembled now. His eyes were wide and hungry. His mouth wore the contented smile of a hunter who believed he had his prey trapped.

"You're not going anywhere," he said, and reached

up to catch hold of Candy again. Without hesitation she put her foot down on the middle of Julius' face, putting all her weight behind it. The creature let out a cry of rage and frustration, and slipped back down into the darkness.

Tempus, meanwhile, was no more than twenty strides away, racing over the stones.

"Halt," he yelled. "Both of you. Halt!"

Candy ignored him. She climbed back into the glyph, her thoughts entirely focused on the next challenge: getting the craft into the air.

"What are the words?" she said to Malingo.

"Nio Kethica."

"Of course. That's it."

Candy took a deep breath and closed her eyes, picturing the glyph rising into the air. Then she spoke the words: "Nio Kethica."

The response from the glyph was instantaneous. The vehicle's engine made a strangled choking sound, and for a moment it seemed the craft was going to ascend. It rocked and shuddered, but unfortunately there was no upward movement. Candy looked up. Tempus was getting closer by the moment.

"Nio Kethica!" she said again. "Come on, glyph! Nio Kethica!"

There was more noise from the craft's engine, but it wasn't promising.

"It's a lost cause!" Malingo said, his eyes on the approaching Fugit Brother. "We should get away—"

Before he could finish, Julius Fugit made another lunge from the hole beside the glyph. He failed to catch hold of Candy, but his hands seized the craft. The vehicle started to tip over. Candy let out a yell as she slid from her seat toward Julius' grinning face.

Malingo caught hold of her arm and pulled her back, scrambling to get them both out of the craft. As he did so, Candy tried one last cry of *"Nio Kethica!"* in the hope of awakening the glyph's engine. But it didn't work.

"Come on!" Malingo yelled, hauling her over the side of the toppling machine. He was just in time. As Candy stumbled backward into Malingo's arms the glyph fell over, trapping Julius Fugit beneath its weight.

"Help me, brother!" Julius yelled.

Tempus was two or three strides away. *"I'm coming for you, brother!"* he yelled, and threw himself on the craft, tearing at its decaying structure to reach his sibling.

"Don't make me wait, Brother Tempus!"

"I'm doing the best I can."

"I'm sure you are, brother. I'm sure you are."

"We're in trouble . . ." Malingo murmured to Candy.

He was right. It would take Tempus only a minute or two to free his brother, then the two of them would come in pursuit of their quarry with fresh zeal. And where were Candy and Malingo to go? The beach offered nothing by way of hiding places, and they couldn't outrun the Fugit Brothers for very long.

Candy shook her head in desperation.

"It can't end this way," she said to herself.

For all the grimness of their prospects, she couldn't believe it was all going to end here. After the journeys she'd taken, and the visions she'd seen she couldn't die on a deserted beach at the hands of a couple of crazy brothers. It wasn't right! She knew in her heart that she had more journeying to do, more visions to see. Wasn't that why the three women had allowed her that glimpse into the mysteries of her life before she was even *born*? They were preparing her for something, telling her to be ready to solve some major secrets.

The Fugit Brothers weren't going to put a stop to all that. She wasn't going to let them.

"It can't end here," she said aloud.

"What can't?" Malingo replied.

"Our lives. *Us.*" Malingo looked startled by the fierceness in her voice, and in her eyes. *"I won't let it."*

She'd no sooner spoken than a breath of wind came from off the sea, as though it were somehow answering her heartfelt plea. The gust cooled the sweat on Candy's face.

Despite everything, she managed a smile.

"We'd better start running," Malingo said. He pointed back toward the glyph.

The Fugit Brothers were now clear of the glyph's wreckage and were coming toward Candy and Malingo. Their features were on the move again, their grinning mouths racing around their faces like runners circling a track.

"Our friends appear to have nowhere left to run, Brother Tempus."

"So it would seem, Brother Julius. So it would seem."

There was another gust of wind from the sea, and its coolness made Candy unglue her gaze from the approaching assassins and chance a look toward the water. The wind had thinned the colorless mist that hung over the waves. And through it came a patch of bright red.

Red.

"A boat!" Candy yelled.

"What?"

"Look! A boat!"

The mist parted, and a simple little vessel, with a single mast and much mended sail, came into view. It had neither captain nor passengers.

"Ha!" said Malingo. "Will you look at that?"

They raced down to the water and strode into the mild surf. The wind was coming in stronger and still stronger gusts. It filled the patchwork sail until the ropes creaked under the strain.

"Get in!" Candy said to Malingo. "Quickly! *In!*"

"But the wind's just blowing the boat back to shore!" Malingo said. "Back to them!"

The Fugit Brothers had followed them down to the water's edge. They too had read the direction of the wind, and had apparently decided they had no need to get their feet wet. All they had to do was wait. The boat would come to them.

Candy glanced back at them as a large wave came in, wetting her all the way up to her neck. She let out a little yelp of shock, much to the amusement of the brothers.

"Please," she said to Malingo. "Just get in. Have a little faith."

"In what?"

"In me."

Malingo stared at her for a moment, then shrugged and clambered in a rather ungainly fashion into the boat. Candy stole a moment to offer up a little prayer to the women of the Fantomaya. Surely it had been they who'd sent the boat. But what was the use of a boat without the right wind?

"Help me," she murmured.

And as she spoke the sail of the boat snapped like a flag in the wind, and Candy looked up to see the women—all three of them—standing in the boat. It was a vision intended for her eyes only, it seemed. Neither the Fugit Brothers nor Malingo responded to the sight.

Malingo offered his hand to Candy. She caught hold of it, and he hauled her onboard.

She had no sooner set foot on the timbers of the little boat than Diamanda lifted her hands into the air. They were clenched tight, Candy saw. White-knuckled fists.

"Travel safely," the old lady said.

Candy nodded. "I will."

"And don't breathe a word of any of this," said Joephi.

"I won't."

"What is this *I will, I won't* stuff?" Malingo said. "Are you talking to me?"

Luckily Candy didn't have any need to tell a lie, because at that instant Diamanda unclenched her fists. As she did so the wind abruptly shifted, swinging around so fast that Candy could feel it move over her face: blowing against her left cheek one moment, and two seconds later blowing hard against her right.

The boat shook from bow to stern. The ropes creaked. And the old patched sail filled with a fierce wind that now came from the landward side, a wind so strong that its gusts fattened the canvas to near-bursting point.

Candy looked back over her shoulder at the Fugit Brothers, who were now wading into the frenzied surf in pursuit of the escapees. But the waves broke against them with no little force, slowing them down. Tempus lunged forward, attempting to catch hold of the boat before it was beyond his reach, but he was too late. The wind bore the little vessel away at such a speed he missed his grip and fell facedown in the water.

Candy smiled up at the women. They did not linger more than another moment. Just time enough to return Candy's smile. Then they were gone, their delicate forms blown away by the very wind Diamanda had summoned.

"That was a close call," Malingo said. He was watching the diminishing figures of the Fugit Brothers, neck high in the surf. They were hoping, presumably, that the wind would veer and carry their quarry back to them.

But theirs was a lost cause. The gusts quickly drove the little vessel away from the island, and very soon the mist that always hung around the Twenty-Fifth Hour covered the sight of the rocky shore.

Exhausted but happy, Candy turned her back on the island and faced the open sea. There would come a time when she would think very closely about all that had happened to her in the labyrinths of the Twenty-Fifth Hour. About what the women had said and shown her: the visions of tomorrow, the mysteries of yesterday. But she was too tired to think such weighty thoughts now.

"Do you have any clue where we're heading?" she asked Malingo.

"I just found this old copy of *Klepp's Almenak* in the bottom of the boat," he said, proffering the sodden pamphlet for Candy to study if she wished. She shook her head. "I think there's a sea chart in here somewhere," Malingo went on. "The trouble is, half of the pages have rotted together." He delicately worked to tease the pages apart, but it was a nearly impossible task.

"I guess we're just going to have to trust to the Izabella," Candy said.

"You make her sound like a friend of yours."

Candy trailed her hand in the cold water and splashed some up onto her face. Her eyes were heavy with fatigue.

"Why not?" she said. "Maybe she *is* a friend of mine."

"Just as long as she treats us nicely," Malingo said. "No twenty-foot waves."

"We'll be fine," Candy replied. "She knows we've been through some hard times."

"She does?"

"Oh sure. She'll carry us somewhere nice." Candy lay her head on her arm and let her hand trail in the water. "Like I said: have faith, she'll bring us where we need to go."

34

DIFFERENT DESTINIES

ONCE BEFORE, AT THE beginning of her adventures in the Abarat, Candy had been told to entrust herself to the care of Mama Izabella. On that occasion she'd needed some extra help to survive her journey. This time, however, safe aboard the nameless boat that had come to find her on the shore of the Twenty-Fifth, she let the sea carry her where it wished to; and all was well. There were some provisions on the boat, plain but nourishing. And while she and Malingo ate, the wind carried them away from the Time Out of Time, and off between the islands.

As they traveled—having no idea of where the tide was taking them, nor any fear that it would do them harm—there were people across the archipelago who would have significant parts to play in Candy's destination who were about their own business.

At Midnight, for instance, Christopher Carrion was wandering the mist-shrouded island of Gorgossium, plotting, endlessly plotting.

He was like a ghost haunting his own house. People were afraid of encountering him, because lately the nightmares that moved in the fluids were more active than ever, lending him an even more terrible appearance. Nor was there any way to predict where he might next appear. Sometimes he was seen in the Gallows Forest, feeding scraps of rotted meat to the vultures that assembled in stinking flocks there. Sometimes he was seen down in the mines, sitting in one of the exhausted seams. Sometimes he was spotted in one of the smaller towers, where Mater Motley's seamstresses worked on creating an army of stitchlings.

Those who did have the bad luck to encounter him in one place or another were always closely interrogated by those who did not. Everybody wanted to know what the likely mood of their lord might be. Did he look angry, perhaps? Not really, came the reply. Did he look distracted, as though his thoughts were elsewhere? No, not distracted either.

Finally, some brave soul asked the question that everybody wanted an answer to, but all were too afraid to voice. *Did he look demented?*

Ah now, came the reply, yes perhaps *that* was it; perhaps he did act a little crazily. The way he talked to himself as he wandered among the gallows, or sat in the tunnels, speaking softly as though he imagined that he was talking to someone very dear to him. A friend, perhaps? Yes; that was it. He spoke as though he was sharing secrets with a friend. And sometimes, as he talked, he would reach into the seething fluids that he breathed and he would fish out a nightmare, and proffer it, as if to his invisible guest. The gift of a nightmare.

Was all this evidence of insanity? In any man other than Christopher Carrion the answer would surely have been *yes*. But Carrion was a law unto himself. Who could judge the depths of his thoughts, or of his pain?

He kept no councils; partook of nobody's advice. If he was planning a war, then it was not with the assistance of his generals. If he was planning murder, then he did not look to the advice of assassins.

The only clue to the subject of his present meditations was a name he was several times heard to mutter; a name that did not yet mean anything much to those who heard it, but very soon would.

The name he spoke was *Candy*. He said it to himself not once but many times, as though repetition would somehow summon up the owner and bring her near to him.

But she did not come. For all his power, Christopher Carrion was alone at Midnight, having nothing for company but the vultures at his heels, and the nightmares at his lips, and the echoes of that name he spoke, over and over again.

"Candy."

"Candy."

"Candy."

His behavior did not go unnoticed, or unreported. There were creatures in the shadows all around the island, watching what Carrion did, and bringing reports of it to the top of the Thirteenth Tower, where the Lord of Midnight's grandmother, Mater Motley, sat in her high-backed rocking chair, sewing stitchlings.

It was her perpetual labor; she never stopped. She didn't even sleep. She was too old to sleep, she'd once said. She had no dreams left to dream. So she sewed and rocked and listened to the stories of her grandson's lonely vigils.

Sometimes, when the skins of the stitchlings had piled up around her, and she was filled with a strange dementia of her own, Mater Motley *also* talked to herself. Unlike her grandson, she did not call out for company. She spoke in an ancient language known as High Abaratic, which was incomprehensible to all those who listened to the old woman. But the listeners didn't need to comprehend her words to understand what Mater Motley was debating with herself. One look at the army of stitchlings she was assembling provided the answer to that question.

War was her subject; war was her obsession. She was sewing the skins of soldiers together, and planning their deployment as she labored. Over the years the old woman and her seamstresses had created tens of thousands of warriors. Most of them, having only mud for muscle, needed neither to eat nor breathe. She had them assembled in great labyrinths beneath the island, where they waited in the darkness for the call to arms.

And while they waited in the bowels of Gorgossium, Mater Motley waited too. Waited, sewed and chatted to herself in the language of the Ancients about the great coming time when Christopher Carrion would declare war upon the islands of light, and her army—her vast, soulless army of mud and thread and patches—would march to war in the name of Midnight.

As for the architect of Commexo City, Rojo Pixler, he had labors and ambitions and meditations of his own.

At the heart of his silver city, hidden away from the busy citizens that filled the streets of that metropolis, there was a great circular corridor. A hundred feet in height, it was lined from floor to ceiling—on both of its walls—with screens. This was the place to which Pixler's tens of thousands of spies, the voyeuristic children of Voorzangler's Universal Eye, sent their reports.

It had become a place that Rojo Pixler frequented more and more often, circling the corridor for hours on end, inspecting the numberless screens. In truth, he was not really interested in the information that came from Tazmagor or Babilonium or the Yebba Dim Day. It was those reports that came up from the depths of the Izabella that had lately caught Pixler's attention.

Hour upon Hour he would traverse the Ring on his flying disc—his hands locked behind his back, his feet set wide apart—studying the screens for news from the deepest trenches of the Izabella. And why? Because there was *life* down there. His fishy spies, wandering deeper than they usually went, had sighted vast claw marks on the walls of the crevices, indisputable evidence that there was some order of creature in the depths of the Izabella that demanded his study.

When he had consulted the grimoires he'd had stolen, searching their heavy pages for some clue as to the nature of these beasts, he had found more than he expected.

In the seventh volume of *Lumeric's Six*, he'd discovered an apocalyptic text that described all too well the occupants of the abysses of the Izabella. They were a race of creatures called the *Requiax*—beasts of sublime wickedness that lived, according to Dado Lumeric *"in the profounde entrailes of the Mother Sea."*

They would not always remain there, Lumeric prophesized. There would come a time when these creatures would rise out of the depths.

". . . they have long hungered," Lumeric wrote, *"for that time when darkness fell upon these many islandes of ours, erasing the lighte of sunne, moone and starres. In that terrible Midnighte, when all lighte hath passed away, they will come like a great pestilence; and commit such crimes against life as will change the order of thinges forever.*

"This I, Dado Lumeric, tell to be a thruthfulle prophesie, and count myself gladde to my soul's core that I will not be upon the living stage to witness these sightes, for it will be beyond the wittes of men to endure. The great cities will go to duste, and the great men and women also, and all be carried away by the winde. . ."

Pixler took Lumeric's words to heart, especially the part about the crumbling cities. To see Commexo City wiped away? Erased as though it had never even existed? It was unthinkable.

He had to be ready for this *"terrible Midnighte,"* when the Requiax rose into view. Plans had to be laid; defenses strengthened. If the Requiax appeared, as Lumeric predicted, he and his dream city would be ready to defy the prophecy, and stand against the darkness.

Meanwhile, the architect of Commexo City rode the Ring, around and around, studying the screens, watching for some sign of movement in the uncharted depths of Mama Izabella. . . .

It was snowing in Chickentown. Or so it seemed.

Candy stood in the backyard of 34 Followell Street while fat flecks of white swirled around her and carpeted the brown dirt and the gray grass.

But there was something odd about this blizzard. For one thing, it seemed to be happening in the middle of a heat wave. Candy's hair was pasted to her forehead with sweat, and her T-shirt glued to her back. For another thing, the snow was spiraling down out of a perfectly blue sky.

Strange, she thought.

She reached up and caught hold of one of the snowflakes. It was soft against her palm. She opened her hand. The flake had a drop of blood on it. Suspicious now, she examined the snowflake more closely. Despite the warmth of her hand, the flake wasn't melting. Before she could examine it more closely however, a gust of wind came along and carried it away, leaving a fine trail of scarlet across the middle of her palm.

She reached out and snatched at another flake. Then at another, and another. They weren't snowflakes, she now realized. They were *feathers*. Chicken feathers. The air was filled with a blizzard of chicken feathers.

She felt them brushing against her face, some of them leaving little trails of blood. Horrible. She tried to wipe them off with the heels of her hands, but the storm of feathers seemed to be getting worse.

"Candy?"

Her father had come out of the house. He had a beer bottle in his hand.

"What are you doing standing out here?" he demanded.

Candy thought for a moment, then shook her head. The truth was that she didn't *know* what she was doing out here. Had she come to look at the snow? If so, she didn't remember doing so.

"Get back inside," her father said.

His neck was flushed, and his eyes were bloodshot. There was a mean expression in his stare that she knew to be careful of: he was close to losing his temper.

"You heard me," he said. *"Go back in the house."*

Candy hesitated. She didn't want to contradict her father when he was drunk, but nor did she want to go inside. Not with him in his present mood.

"I just want to take a little walk," she said softly.

"What are you talking about? You're not taking no walk. *Now get the hell inside.*"

He reached out and caught hold of her, gripping her

neck close to her shoulder so tightly she let out a yell.

As though in response to her cry there was an eruption of din in the yard around her: the clucking of countless chickens. The birds were everywhere, filling the yard in all directions. She felt a kind of revulsion at the sight of so many chickens. So many beaks, so many bright little eyes; so many heads cocked so that they could look up at her.

"How did they get here?" she said, gently reaching up to free herself from her father's grip.

"They live here," he said.

"What?"

"You heard me!" her father said, shaking her. "God, you are *so* stupid. I said: they live here. *Look*."

Candy turned her sickened gaze toward the house. He was right. There were chickens on the roof, carpeting it like beady-eyed snow; chickens at the windows, lining the sills; chickens squatting all over the kitchen. On the table; on the sink. She could see her mother standing in the middle of the kitchen with her head bowed, weeping.

"This is crazy," Candy murmured.

"What did you say?"

Her father shook her again, harder this time. She pulled herself free of him, stumbling backward as she did so. Somehow she lost her balance and fell down on the hard dirt, the bitter stench of chicken excrement filling her nostrils. Her father started to laugh; a mean, joyless laugh.

"Candy!" somebody said.

She had covered her face with her hands to keep the

chickens' claws from scratching her, so she didn't see who it was, but somebody was calling her. Somebody in the house, was it? She peered between her fingers.

"Stupid girl," her father said, reaching down to catch hold of her again.

As he did so, the voice came a second time.

"Candy?"

Who's voice was that? It obviously wasn't her father. She cautiously let her hands fall from her face, and looked around. Was there somebody else in the vicinity? No. Just her father, laughing. And her mother, weeping in the kitchen. And the chickens. The endless, ridiculous chickens.

None of this made any sense. It was like some horrible . . .

Wait, she thought.

Wait! This is a dream.

As she formed this thought the voice that had been calling to her called again.

"Please, Candy," he said. "Open your eyes."

That's all I have to do, she thought to herself. *All I have to do is open my eyes.*

The idea was so simple it made her weep. She could feel the tears pressing between her locked lashes and running down her cheeks.

Open your eyes, she told herself.

"You're a great disappointment to me," her dream-father was saying to her. "Did you know that? I wanted a daughter who'd love me. Instead I get you. You don't love me. Do you?" She didn't reply to this. "ANSWER ME!" he yelled.

She had no answer to give—or at least none that he wanted to hear—so she simply looked up at him and said:

"Good-bye, Dad. I gotta go."

"Go?" he replied. "Where the hell are you ever going to go? You're going nowhere. *Nowhere.*"

Candy smiled to herself.

And smiling, she opened her eyes.

She was back in the single-sailed boat that had carried them away from the shore of the Twenty-Fifth Hour. It was rocking gently, like a cradle. No wonder she'd been lulled to sleep. Malingo was kneeling beside her, his leathery hand laid lightly on her shoulder.

"*There* you are," he said, when her eyes focused on him. "For a minute I didn't know whether to wake you or not. Then I decided you weren't enjoying your dream very much."

"I wasn't."

She sat up, and the tears she'd shed in her sleep ran down her cheeks. She let them fall. They seemed to have washed her sight clean, in a curious way. The world around her—the Sea of Izabella, and the sky filled with light-shot clouds, even the round-bellied sail—looked more beautiful than she had words to describe.

She heard what she thought was laughter from the side of the boat, and looked over to see that a school of fish the size of small dolphins, only covered in scales that had a golden sheen to them, were swimming beside the vessel, taking turns to leap into the bow wave and feel its foam seethe over their backs.

The noise they were making was like laughter. No, she thought, it was not *like* laughter. It *was* laughter. And it was a sound that went well with the whole bright world that she'd woken to: sea, sky and sail. There was laughter in all of it at that moment.

She got to her feet, the wind at her back. Its insistence reminded her of being in the lighthouse, what seemed an age ago; feeling the light pressing against her back as it summoned the Sea of Izabella.

"I'm *here*, aren't I?" she said to Malingo, holding onto the mast to steady herself.

Malingo joined the laughter now. "Of course you're here," he said. "Where else would you be?"

Candy shrugged. "Just . . . somewhere I dreamed about."

"Chickentown?"

"How did you guess?"

"The tears."

Candy wiped the last of the wetness from her cheeks with her free hand.

"For a minute—" she began.

"You thought you were stuck back there."

She nodded.

"Then when I woke up I wasn't sure for a moment which one was real."

"I think they probably *both* are," Malingo said. "And maybe one day we'll catch the tide and go back there, you and me."

"I can't imagine why we'd ever do that."

"I can't either," Malingo said. "But you never know. There was a time, I daresay, when you couldn't have imagined being here."

Candy nodded. "It's true," she said.

Her eyes had gone again to the laughing fish. They seemed to be competing with one another to see which of them could leap the highest, and so gain her attention.

"Do you think maybe a part of me has always been here in the Abarat?" Candy asked Malingo.

"Why do you say that?"

"Well . . . it's that this place feels as though it's home. Not that other place. *This*." She looked up. *"This sky."* Then at the water. *"This sea."* Finally she looked at her hand. *"This skin."*

"It's the same skin here as it was there."

"Is it?" she said. "It doesn't feel that way some-how."

Malingo grinned.

"What are you laughing at now?"

"I'm just thinking what a strange one you are. My heroine." He kissed her on the cheek, still grinning. "Strangest girl I ever did meet."

"And how many girls have you met?"

Malingo took a moment or two to make his calcu-lations. Then he said: "Well . . . just you, actually—if you don't count Mother."

Now it was Candy who started to laugh. And the leaping fish joined in, jumping higher and higher in their delight.

"Do you think they get the joke?" Malingo said.

Candy looked skyward. "I think today the whole world gets the joke," she said.

"Good answer," Malingo replied.

"Look at that," Candy said, pointing up into the heavens. "We must be moving toward a Night Hour. I see stars."

The wind had carried all the clouds off toward the southwest. The sky was now a pristine blue, darkening to purple overhead.

"Beautiful," she said.

Staring up at the pinpricks of starlight, Candy remembered how she had first noticed that the constellations were different here from the way they were in the world she'd come from. Different stars; different destinies.

"Is there such a thing as Abaratian astrology?" she said to Malingo.

"Of course."

"So if I learned to read the stars, I'd maybe discover my future up there. It would solve a lot of problems."

"And spoil a lot of mysteries," Malingo said.

"Better not to know?"

"Better to find out when the time's right. Everything to its Hour."

"You're right of course," Candy said.

Perhaps a wiser eye than hers would be able to read tomorrow in tonight's stars, but where was the fun in that? It was better not to know. Better to be alive in the Here and the Now—in this bright, laughing moment—and let the Hours to come take care of themselves.

Journey to the end of day,
Come the fire-fly,
Come the moon;
Say a prayer for God's good grace
And sleep with love upon your face.

So Ends
The First Book of Abarat

APPENDIX

SOME EXCERPTS FROM
KLEPP'S ALMENAK

FOR A TRAVELER IN THE ABARAT there can be few documents as useful, or as thorough in their contents, as *Klepp's Almenak.*

It was first published some two hundred years ago, and it is a stew of fact and fiction, in which the author, Samuel Hastrim Klepp, writes one moment as a practical explorer, the next as a mythologist. There are significant errors on every page, but there is some reason to believe that Klepp knew that he was playing fast and loose with the truth. He speaks at one point of his "leavening the flat bread of what we *know,* with the yeast of what *we dream may come to pass.*"

However questionable its value as a work of truth, there is no doubting the hold *Klepp's Almenak* has on the hearts of the people of the Abarat. The *Almenak* is updated yearly by the current descendant of Klepp, Samuel

Hastrim the Fifth. He has kept the contents of the pamphlet much the same as it always was: it chronicles holy days around the archipelago; carries tables of tides and stars; lists all manner of event, mythical and actual. It carries the rules of two of the Abarat's favorite sports: Mycassian Bug Wrestling and Star-Striking. It also lists Celestial Events, both Benign and Apocalyptic, carries news of appearing islands, and for those with a taste for grim inevitability, it chronicles the steady—if infinitesimal—sinkage of other islands. Besides these, contained within the *Almenak*'s pages are news of Extinctions, Migrations, Emancipations and Redefinitions of the Infinite, while for those seeking more practical information it contains maps of every island, and of every major city, including those that have been destroyed by time or calamity.

It is, in short, the essential guide to the archipelago. Even if (as one Jengo Johnson once calculated), no less than fifty-seven percent of its information is for some reason or other questionable, every sailor and traveling salesman who crosses the Abarat, every pilgrim and pig farmer about the business of worship or gelding, has a copy of the *Almenak* within reach, and each finds in its contradictory pages something of value.

I would, if I could, reproduce it all here. But that's of course impossible. I will limit myself instead to Klepp's eloquent descriptions of the major Hours, including the Twenty-Fifth, with a few references to what the author dubs "Rocks of Some Significance" (though it is necessarily incomplete; small islands appear and disappear in the Sea of Izabella all the time; a complete listing would be out of date the moment it was printed).

I will list the Hours, as Klepp did, beginning at Noon.

However, I strongly urge anyone tempted to use the information that follows as a *literal* guide to the islands to proceed with extreme caution. It is worth remembering Samuel Klepp the First died having become lost on one of the Outer Islands. He was found, dead from exposure, with a copy of *his own Almenak* in his hand. According to a detailed map in the *Almenak* that he *himself* had drawn, there was supposed to be a small town that bore his name on the very spot where he had perished; he had no doubt been looking for the town when exposure overtook him. As it happened, no such town existed.

But since his death a town *has* been founded at that place, to service the sightseers who come to see the spot where the great *Almenak* maker perished. And yes, it is called Klepp.

His map, then, was correct. It was simply *premature*.

Such things happen often in the archipelago, especially on those islands closest to the Twenty-Fifth Hour. So be warned.

Here, then, are some brief excerpts from Klepp's descriptions of the Twenty-Five Islands of the Abarat.

"Of the island of *Yzil*, which is *Noon*, let me say this: it is a place of exceptional beauty and fruitfulness. Furthermore it does a soul good (sometimes) to stand with the sun directly over his head. Here at Yzil, a man hoping for fame might be reminded to live in the moment and not care too much where his shadow may fall tomorrow, but rather concern himself with where it lies today.

"The island is temperate and lush. A gentle breeze passes constantly through the thick foliage, and there are creatures of every shape and size being wafted through the greenery. It is said their singular source is a Creatrix of very ancient origins, called the Princess Breath, who makes her home here on Yzil, and is in the infinite and rapturous process of conjuring life-forms from her divine essence, which the breeze carries through the canopy and out across the Sea of Izabella. There caught by this tide or that, they are carried out across the islands to populate them with new kinds of life.

"At *One O'clock*, which lies to the south-southeast of *Yzil*, is the island of *Hobarookus*. Traditionally this has been a haunt of sea bandits and buccaneers. One O'clock being my lunching hour I have many times sought a healthy repast upon this island, and may happily report that whatever fiendish piratical types haunt the island, their presence has not deterred the cooks of Hobarookus from becoming fair geniuses of their craft. I will tell you plainly, there is *no* better food to be had at any Hour.

"The topography of the island of Hobarookus is unattractive. It's mostly rocky, though there are areas of the interior where the ground becomes unpredictably swampy. These areas, which the Hobarookians call the Sinks, are the habitats of kalukwa birds, which species reportedly hatch downy human babies from their eggs every ninth year. These children—if saved from being pecked to death by juveniles of the previous year's hatching—are often saved by the pirates and raised as their children. This means the island, far from resembling a vile enclave of thieves and murderers, resembles instead an island of wild children watched over fondly by that aforementioned vile enclave of thieves and murderers, like mothers watching over their errant (and occasionally lightly feathered) children.

"At *Two* lies *Orlando's Cap*, which is not an island I know well. An asylum for the insane is located here—so placed because its founder, Izzard Coyne, believed Two in the Afternoon to be an Hour that promotes a healing balm in the soul.

"The island, however, is so ill-favored that it's hard to imagine those prone to irrationality being much comforted there. The island's name, by the way, comes from its caplike shape. I can find no evidence of who Orlando was, nor, I suppose, do the sorrowful occupants of the island much care.

"It should be noted, for those interested in either the products of the insane mind or in art (and how often are those things one and the same!), that Coyne's healing methodologies included allowing his patients the means to *create*. Thus, scattered across Orlando's Cap are artifacts that his patients fashioned. Some are of humble ambition, but others seem to be entire fantastic *worlds* carved from stone or wood and often painted in hallucinatory colors.

"When we look at the way the islands are arranged in the Sea of Izabella, there seems to be a designing hand at work, which conspires with nature to unseat our expectations. Thus close beside the island of Orlando's Cap, which is a place of dour scenery (albeit enlivened by the creations of Coyne's patients) there lies *the Nonce*, which is to my eye the most beautiful of all the islands. How is it that they can be so different from one another, when they are divided by a passage of water so narrow you might skip it with a stone?

"*Three* in the Afternoon—the island of the Nonce—is a dreamy time. The labors of the day are more than half over, and our thoughts turn to what pleasures the twilight Hours may hopefully provide. Personally I enjoy a siesta around this time, and I can testify to the fact that those who doze in the Nonce do not conjure ordinary dreams. They imagine the Beginning of the World. I have done so myself several times: slept there and dreamed of some Edenic place where there was no enmity, nor division, between plant and animal, angel and man. This suggests to me that there is some validity to the claim (which was made in the highest of metaphysical circles) that the Nonce is the island where life on the archipelago began.

"So, on to *Gnomon*, which lies at *Four O'clock.*

"Here, I wish to interlude with a little piece of autobiography. Some years ago I lost my wife. Literally lost her, in a maze on Soma

Plume. I was, needless to say, much distressed by this (I was uncommonly fond of her), and taking the advice of my brother-in-law I went to Gnomon in search of an oracle who might enlighten me as to my wife's whereabouts.

"Despite the bland reputation of the Hour (there's nothing very mystical about Four in the Afternoon) the place is littered with the ruins of temples and other oracular sites. In some parts of the island the air is filled with whispering voices, like the scraps of a thousand unfulfilled prophecies. Personally I find it a rather unsettling place, its most distressing location being the North Shore, from the cliffs of which a visitor may look across the Straits of Limbo toward the island of Midnight. There is nothing of that despicable Hour visible at such a distance, of course, except for sheer rock and veils of roiling crimson mist. But it's more than enough to get the most impoverished of imaginations feeling clammy. Anyway, back to my story . . .

"The oracle I spoke with on Gnomon did indeed give me some information that finally led to the retrieval of the missing Mrs. Klepp. But while searching for the oracle I discovered an extremely strange phenomenon: Gnomon has upon it a number of roads that seem to have no destination. The theory I offer for this is that Gnomon was once part of the adjacent island of Soma Plume, which is twice its size. What cataclysm caused the land between the two islands to sink can only be guessed at, but it would certainly explain the mystery of the roads, because their destination would then be the Great Noahic Ziggurat on *Soma Plume*.

"The Ziggurat has been, since time immemorial, a place of burial, and for that reason there are many who dub themselves explorers and gazetteers who have not dared venture there. Pah! to their cowardice, I say. In my travels I have never had dealings with the deceased that were ever less than pleasant. (This is particularly true of the long-since dead; those recently deceased can be irritable on occasion.) Anyway, I urge you not to be put off by the rumors about the Noahic Ziggurat. It is an astonishment.

"Travelers by ship—especially those who are piloting their own vessels—should be warned that the next leg of the trip, the passage from Soma Plume to *Babilonium*, which lies but an Hour away at *Six O'clock*, can be treacherous. Not because the waters of the Izabella are particularly choppy thereabouts, but because there is always such a convergence of happy souls about the Hour of Six that navigation between the hundreds of boats which throng the straits is difficult. I've witnessed countless collisions and capsizings in the narrow band of water, even, I'm sorry to say, an occasional fatality, marring otherwise joyful expeditions.

"What need I tell you about Babilonium? If you know even a little about these islands of ours, then the reputation of this pleasurable Hour will be perfectly familiar to you. If you are tired of Babilonium, so the saying goes, then you are tired of life, for among its tents and its stages, its hippodromes and its arenas, is every species of frolicsome thing that can be devised by masker, menagerist, musician, mountebank or magician. I have never left that island but with a sense that I have taken only a sip of its pleasures, and promising myself I will return there soon.

"Perhaps the heaviness of my heart is increased because of the sight that lies ahead: the Island of Lengthening Shadows, *Scoriae*. You will forgive me if I don't linger over the details of that ashen place overmuch. Scoriae depresses the soul.

"Scoriae is not, of course, the only island of the Abarat that can so readily overshadow a man's natural capacity for joy. So, as I've said elsewhere, does Midnight. So too, for different reasons (which I'll come to later) does The Isle of the Black Egg, which stands at Four in the Morning; and even Speckle

Frew, which stands at Five. But there is much about Scoriae which invites a particular mournfulness. It is bleak, of course: a sprawling mass of laval rock and black dust, with the open wound of the volcano, Mount Galigali, at its center. Galigali's spewings and ragings have, over the ages, claimed three magnificent cities: Gosh, Divinium and Mycassius. To wander in the ruins of any of the three is a melancholy business. All were noble cities, filled with fine and loving souls. Not one of these souls, to my knowledge, survived Galigali's tantrums. Only the signs of their lives remain to us, clotted in volcanic ash: their temples, their racetracks, their nurseries.

"I remarked earlier that I have never met a dead fellow whose company I did not enjoy. I should except some of the ghosts of Gosh, who were—on one occasion some years back—rude enough to drive me out of their city with their howlings and their batterings. But I should add this: that I had just reached the safety of my boat when Galigali gave a growl and belched a rain of liquid rock, which fell where I had been exploring mere minutes before. The ghosts, in short, had meant me no harm with their assault. They simply didn't want to add my name to the toll of Galigali's victims.

"Now we must make a journey from one side of the Abarat to the other, moving in a south-southwesterly direction. The journey, of course, still takes an hour, for we are going to *Eight O'clock* in the Evening, to the *Yebba Dim Day*.

"The island of Yebba—The Great Head, as it is colloquially called—is carved in the likeness of its sometime owner, Gorki Doodat, and is a warren of tunnels and tiny, ramshackle habitations. Perched on Doodat's stone cranium (an addition only made after the potentate's passing) are half a dozen towers occupied by those personages rich enough for such lofty apartments. Reportedly some of these towers contain inhabitants of immense age: the ancients of the Aeph Nation, who were the first architects of the islands. I cannot confirm or deny these rumors.

"Over the years the Yebba Dim Day has become the informal capital of the Inner Islands, and much bureaucratic work is done in the labyrinths of Gorki Doodat's head. Here an Abaratic may obtain birth papers, death papers, sea charts, maps and the like. The price list is on the wall close to the entrance to The Great Head. In many cases the price of maps and charts has remained at a zem or two in all the years that I've been exploring the islands. My own modest printing press is here at Eight O'clock, a small office at the base of the towers.

"The Yebba Dim Day marks the last hurrah of daylight. By the time we reach *Huffaker*, which stands at *Nine O'clock* in the Evening, every last trace of sunlight has departed from the skies. Huffaker is an impressive island, topographically speaking. Its rock formations—especially those below ground—are both vast and elaborately beautiful, resembling natural cathedrals and temples. The greatest of these is *Hap's Vault*, discovered by one Lydia Hap. Even if it were simply a cavern it would be notable enough for the uncanny precision of its symmetries. But it is not. It is Miss Hap who was the first to suggest the Chamber of Skein.

"The Skein? How do I begin to describe the Skein?

"The word, of course, has humble origins. It means a length of yarn or thread that has been wound on a reel. But the *Abaratic Skein*, as Lydia Hap describes it, is something far more significant. It is the thread that joins all things—living and dead, sentient and unthinking—to all other things. According to the persuasive Miss Hap, the thread *originates* in the Vault at Huffaker, appearing momentarily as a kind of flickering light before winding its way invisibly through the Abarat, to begin the task of connecting us, one to another. I have twice visited the Vault, and on both occasions saw phenomena that could well fit Lydia Hap's theory: fine lines of light crisscrossing the cavern. Perhaps what I saw was an optical illusion, and the idea of Infinite Connectedness is pure sentimental invention. But what we want to believe and what *is* true are, I think, more closely related than the Rationalists would sometimes have us believe. Personally, I do not doubt that some power connects us to everything else in our archipelago. Even if we would wish it otherwise—for we are not just joined to what pleases our eyes and our morals, but also to what is shameful and ugly—we are indisputably a part of a greater system than ourselves. Until somebody comes along with a better idea, Lydia Hap's Skein will do very nicely.

"From the grandiose scale of Huffaker, we move on to *Ten O'clock*, and the more modestly scaled *Ninnyhammer*, an island which boasts very little that's noteworthy, excepting perhaps the small town of High Sladder, which is occupied by a tribe of feral tarrie-cats. On a hill to the northeast of the island is a house of odd construction with a dome that, when approaching the island by boat, can in some lights resemble an eye. I believe it has been the domicile of wizards over the years. I have little else to say about the island, having been sworn to secrecy on the matter of wizardly goings-on.

"Close by, however, is a Rock of Some Distinction, called *Alice Point*. It is a tiny place, but it was for some years the best spot from which to see Odom's Spire, which stands at the Twenty-Fifth Hour. A viewing platform was built on the Point, and large telescopes were brought to the island. A tempest of unusual ferocity brought the structure down after a time, however, and there is a body of opinion that believes this tempest originated in the Spire, because those who occupy the Twenty-Fifth Hour have no wish to be spied upon. I have heard these entities referenced to as the Fantomaya, but who or what these creatures might be is beyond me. The remains of the viewing tower, by the way, can still be seen if you sail close to Alice Point. But the Rock itself no longer has human occupants.

"On then, to *Eleven O'clock*, and the island of *Jibarish*. This is truly a place of paradoxes. Though most of the island is bare rock, there is a curious mutability in the air here. You look away for a moment and that rock, which seemed so solid a moment ago, seems to have *flowed* into some new configuration. It's easy to become lost here, though the island isn't large; no path remains in the same place for long.

"A tribe of women has traditionally occupied Jibarish, and it is their appetite for making the island unpalatable for visitors—especially male visitors—that is largely responsible for the protean nature of the landscape. Over the centuries these extraordinary women have caused the elements of Jibarish to defy the laws by which those elements conventionally live. Rock is *fluid* here; fire burns *cold*; water is like *iron*; and the air—which we expect to serve our needs invisibly—is here a sovereign *power* in its own right. The very name of the island is derived from the means by which the air continues to alter the very words a visitor may speak, turning sense into nonsense or 'jibberish.'

"What comes next, of course, is the island of *Midnight*, also called *Gorgossium*. What few observations I will offer here must be prefaced with the confession that I have never set foot on that Hour, nor have any wish to do so.

"Gorgossium is wreathed in red mists, which seem to have a serpentine life of their own. The old fortress of *Iniquisit*, with its thirteen towers, dominates the heights of Midnight and looks down with frightful authority on the joyless landscape below. The Carrion family has of course occupied Gorgossium since the beginning of written history, and what attributes the island may or may not possess (all this information is third or fourth hand) is their handiwork. A forest of gallows; a morbid garden that contains every harmful plant in creation; a collection of machines devised to torment and murder: all these are rumored to exist on the island.

"But these are the least. There is a great deal more, which I will not sully the pages of this *Almenak* by relating. Instead I will move on, as one might move on past a fetid cadaver, in the hope of discovering some sweeter sight.

"We are now, of course, in the very dead of night. The skies are star-pricked overhead. There is a great quiet. And there is no quieter place in the Abarat than at *One O'clock* in the Morning, where the six *Pyramids of Xuxux* rise out of the dark and uncannily placid waters of the Izabella.

"Not far from here, visible across the Straits of Segunda, is the Noahic Ziggurat on Soma Plume, which I have previously described. The silhouette of the Ziggurat is of course remarkably close to that of the Xuxux Pyramids, and there are those who have suggested that all seven structures were designed by the same hand and built by the same masons. I disagree. The tombs at Soma Plume are, as I stated earlier, calm and curiously reassuring places. The six Pyramids at Xuxux, however (perhaps owing to their proximity to Midnight), are sites of mystery and tragedy. Four of the six have been broken into and gutted by thieves, but the two largest remain unpenetrated, their locks beyond the wits of even the most ambitious master criminal. There is little doubt that they are occupied, however. Something lives and breeds in the great Pyramids; I do not claim to know what.

"Moving on to the northwest, we come to *Idjit*, which is (in the opinion of this explorer) an island of immense charm. I have never visited the island sober, I will admit, so my view may be somewhat influenced by that fact. But Idjit is an island that encourages excesses, a kind of happy foolishness.

"This is at first glance an unlikely place for clowns. It shares with neighboring Gorgossium a spiky, barren topography, and storms rage perpetually about the landscape. It has been calculated that a visitor to Idjit is more likely to be struck by lightning than a man on the Roosts of Efreet is to be hit by bird excrement. I can personally testify to this. I have been struck three times while climbing the heights of the island. The experience is quite refreshing, akin to taking a plunge in icy water. Yes, it certainly takes the breath away. But when it's over, one is left either dead or invigorated. An extreme choice, I grant you, but life untouched by such extremes would be dull indeed.

"Leaving Idjit and taking now a northeasterly course, we approach *Pyon*, with its instantly recognizable arch. Pyon was once a quiet island, but no longer. The work of an entrepreneur by the name of Rojo Pixler has transformed the island utterly. It was Pixler's dream (some have said folly) to build the biggest city in the archipelago on Pyon, its lights so bright that the darkness of the Hour would be a grand irrelevance. Using funds built up through his titanically successful household products, Pixler has created his own dream city. By bringing together the genius of wizards and the skills of more conventional architects (all touched by their own genius) Pixler has not only transformed Pyon, but may eventually (and to the mind of this writer, regrettably) transform the entire archipelago. Nobody is safe from the Panacea, or from its relentlessly happy salesman, the Commexo Kid.

"Pixler's flying machines are now venturing far from the skies over Pyon, while his burrowings beneath the seabed, where he intends to build a second city, three times the size of Commexo City, have dug through layers of rock which is filled (so I'm told by friends who are experts in their fields) with never-to-be-duplicated evidence of our earliest beginnings.

"But it is probably fair to say that a man like

Rojo Pixler has no interest in the past. He looks only toward tomorrow. A life lived in perpetual expectation may be a fine thing for a time, but it's a young man's game. Mister Pixler has apparently yet to be touched by the shadow of his mortality. When that happens, I venture, he may be more respectful of all that lies quietly in the earth, as he will one day be its fellow.

"I apologize for such dark ruminations, but they come to me naturally when I contemplate the gaud of Commexo City. Nor is there much comfort to be discovered in the so-called Outer Islands—of which Pyon was once a member. Now there are only four in that group: The Isle of the Black Egg, Speckle Frew, Efreet and Autland. They are unquestionably the least pretty, the least charming, the least seductive of the archipelago. But that is not to say that they don't possess a considerable degree of drama.

"At *Four O'clock*, on *The Isle of the Black Egg*, for instance, lie the Pius Mountains, a range of needle-sharp crags that are the tallest *natural* phenomenon in the islands. (In fact the top of Odom's Spire, at the Twenty-Fifth Hour, is closer to Heaven. But there is nothing natural about the Spire, I would submit. It is surely the work of some less than divine architect.) The Pius Mountains, despite their inaccessibility, are not unpopulated. In the early days of the Abarat, during the Celestial Wars, guerrilla forces hid there and used their aerie as a base for devastating attacks on the fleets of the Empress Deviavex. The descendants of those rebels still have communities in Pius Heights (as they call the mountains), and there live a life of blameless and uncommon purity.

"As to the Black Egg, which gave the island its name, I can say only this: I have discovered to date two hundred and seventeen explanations for the name, each contradicting the next. As I cannot distinguish the value of any one explanation over any other, and it seems arbitrary to simply pick one for retelling here, I'd prefer to simply state that nobody knows how the island got its name and leave it at that.

"Moving on west, along the line of the Outer Islands, we come to *Five O'clock*, and *Speckle Frew*. It is geographically an uneventful island; the earth sandy and covered with fine, sharp-edged grass, the wind always howling. Though the terrain is scarcely varied, the island is home to a wide variety of species, most of them dangerous. The Naught, the Scab-Faced Snouter, the Rife—all have their habitats in the undulating grasslands of Speckle Frew. And when ground is contested, or eggs are trampled or stolen, the ensuing battles can be brutal and bloody. In short, Speckle Frew is less an island than it is a bestiary, and it is not to be trespassed lightly.

"The next of the Outer Islands is *Efreet*. Unlike its neighbor, Speckle Frew, which has always been a wild spot, Efreet was once an island of great sophistication. The city of Koy, considered to have been the most cultured city in the Abarat, was built on the lower steppes of the island, which lies to the northeast. Opinions vary as to how long Koy stood, and why it fell, but what remains of the city—rows of pillars, archways, frescoes—testify to a site of elegance and learning. In recent times the ruins have become the haunt of lost and unhappy souls, and it seems impossible, visiting its mournful shores, that there was once a bright world here. Efreet's Hour, I should add, is *Six* in the Morning.

"At *Seven* lies *Autland*, which is joined to Efreet by the Gilholly Bridge. There is a palace on Autland, built for Queen Muzzel McCray, to a design that appeared to her in a dream, or so local legend dictates. The Queen's husband was a creature called Nimbus, Lord of the tarrie-cats. He still lives in McCray's Palace, inside the dream—so to speak—of the woman he loved.

"Just a few islands remain to be described. At *Eight O'clock*, as the day brightens, stands

Obadiah, an island of extraordinary flora. Here a visitor will find strange and sometimes aggressive plants growing in virtually inexhaustible profusion. Some have called Obadiah the Elegiac's Garden, and suggested it may have been a kind of laboratory in which the mythic Creators of Abarat, A'zo and Cha, experimented with life-forms. Some even claim to have seen the one-eyed A'zo wandering the plant-thronged slopes of Obadiah, his presence causing the flowers to open long dormant eyes and reach toward him as if to catch his gaze and share some secret of the earth.

"At *Nine* in the Morning we arrive at the island of *Qualm Hah*. It is a puzzling place to explore, because it has two distinct faces. At the western edge of the island stands the busy seaport of *Tazmagor*, where the food is good, the people happy and the air filled with the din of extemporized songs. (Tazmagorians hold festivals regularly, in which competitors create epic songs on the spot, from subjects chosen by the crowd. Its reigning champion is one Sally Sullywart, who at the last festival beguiled the audience with a nine-minute song on the subject of fish gutting.)

"Outside the bounds of Tazmagor, toward the eastern end of the island, the land is empty. Nobody builds there; not so much as a shack. This is peculiar, given how crowded

Tazmagor has become of late. But nobody I spoke to would tell me why.

"Onward, then, to *Spake*, which is an island I always take the greatest pleasure in visiting. It is a splendid, green place, with many cypress trees on its lower slopes. On its heights, above the trees, stands a simple stage, which has been used for performances of every kind—circuses, slapsticks and High Tragedy— since the beginning of known time.

"It may seem curious to a visitor that a drama would be performed in the open, at *Ten* in the Morning. But in fact the actors who first performed here, Norta Geese and Arlo Godkin, chose well. By a strange miracle of the island's location, Geese and Godkin's Theater is every three days shrouded in a mist that blows from the southeast, and surrounds the hill in a dark blanket. Tiny flames—like the sloughings of stars—litter this dark fog, and magically illuminate the dramas that are performed on the heights of the hill.

"Onward, then, to *Nully*, at *Eleven*. Topographically speaking, the island merits little study, but it is the location of one of the Abarat's most extraordinary buildings: the *Repository of Remembrance*. From the outside the Repository is a large but commonplace building. Inside, however, it is anything *but* commonplace. Its rooms (which number over a hundred) are filled to capacity with objects that were once loved by the mighty. The toys of emperors, the rag dolls of queens; the stuffed crocodile which the great warrior Duke Lutherid of Skant was devoted to in his old age; the seventeen thousand porcelain mice Prince Drudru played with as a child. Room after room, cabinet after cabinet, shelf after shelf: the Repository is filled with bric-a-brac loved to distraction by people whose devotion at times suggests a touch of madness.

"I have described some twenty-four Hours and twenty-four islands, plus, of course, the occasional Rock. Only the Twenty-Fifth Island remains to be described, though I know already that its mysteries will outwit my pen in a heartbeat. I will therefore keep my description simple.

"The *Twenty-Fifth Hour* lies at the center of the archipelago. It is called, among other things, Whence and Lud and the House of the Fantomaya. But it is most frequently referred to as *Odom's Spire*. When it comes to the history and purpose of the island's spire—or to an evocation of its undeniably sentient mists, or the strange music the Sea of Izabella makes when she breaks upon its shores, utterly unlike any other sound her waters make, breaking on sand or stone—all this is beyond me. No doubt the claims of the Righteous

Bandy (a criminal who ended up on the shores of the Twenty-Fifth by chance, and who escaped a poet) are correct. 'Every mystery of the Abarat,' he said, 'has its solution here; every enchantment its source, every prayer its destination.'

"Beyond that neither he, nor I, can say much more. There are no books about the Spire, for no writer that I know of—except Bandy—has gone there and returned. There are, however, innumerable paintings, though not one of them resembles any other. Odom's Spire, it seems, possesses a very particular glamor: no two witnesses, sailing past it, will see quite the same sight. What this may indicate about the nature of the island's interior may only be imagined."

Here, then, is a brief taste of *Klepp's Almenak*. As noted at the beginning of this Appendix, the information offered here should *not* be taken as definitive, but may be usefully consulted both by those who wish to explore the Abarat on foot, and those braver adventurers who wish instead to close their eyes and dream their voyages.

S. H. K.

HUNGER

Here is a list of fearful things:
The jaws of sharks, a vulture's wings,
The rabid bite of the dogs of war,
The voice of one who went before.
But most of all the mirror's gaze,
Which counts us out our numbered days.

—Righteous Bandy,
the nomad Poet of Abarat

OTTO HOULIHAN SAT in the dark room and listened to the two creatures who had brought him here—a three-eyed thing by the name of Lazaru and its sidekick, Baby Pink-Eye—playing Knock the Devil Down in the corner. After their twenty-second game his nervousness and irritation began to get the better of him.

"How much longer am I going to have to wait?" he asked them.

Baby Pink-Eye, who had large reptilian claws and the face of a demented infant, puffed on a blue cigar and blew a cloud of acrid smoke in Houlihan's direction.

"They call you the Criss-Cross Man, don't they?" he said.

Houlihan nodded, giving Pink-Eye his coldest gaze, the kind of gaze that usually made men weak with fear. The creature was unimpressed.

"Think you're scary, do you?" he said. "Ha! This is Gorgossium, Criss-Cross Man. This is the island of the Midnight Hour. Every dark, unthinkable thing that has ever happened at the dead of night has happened right here. So don't try scaring me. You're wasting your time."

"I just asked—"

"Yes, yes, we heard you," said Lazaru, the eye in the middle of her forehead rolling back and forth in a very unsettling fashion. "You'll have to be patient. The Lord of Midnight will see you when he's ready to see you."

"Got some urgent news for him, have you?" said Baby Pink-Eye.

"That's between him and me."

"I warn you, he doesn't like bad news," said Lazaru. "He gets in a fury, doesn't he, Pink-Eye?"

"*Crazy* is what he gets! Tears people apart with his bare hands."

They glanced conspiratorially at each other. Houlihan said nothing. They were just trying to frighten him, and it wouldn't work. He got up and went to the narrow window, looking out onto the tumorous landscape of the Midnight Island, phosphorescent with corruption. This much of what Baby Pink-Eye had said was true: Gorgossium *was* a place of terrors. He could see the glistening forms of countless monsters as they moved through the littered landscape; he could smell spicy-sweet incense rising from the mausoleums in the mist-shrouded cemetery; he could hear the shrill din of drills from the mines where the mud that filled Midnight's armies of stitchlings was produced. Though he wasn't going to let Lazaru or Pink-Eye see his unease, he would be glad when he'd made his report and he could leave for less terrifying places.

There was some murmuring behind him, and a moment later Lazaru announced: "The Prince of Midnight is ready to see you."

Houlihan turned from the window to see that the door on the far side of the chamber was open and Baby Pink-Eye was gesturing for him to step through it.

"Hurry, hurry," the infant said.

Houlihan went to the door and stood on the threshold. Out of the darkness of the room came the voice of Christopher Carrion, deep and joyless.

"Enter, enter. You're just in time to watch the feeding."

Houlihan followed the sound of Carrion's voice. There was a flickering in the darkness, which grew more intense by degrees, and as it brightened he saw the Lord of Midnight standing perhaps ten yards from him. He was dressed in gray robes and was wearing gloves that looked as though they were made of fine chain mail.

"Not many people get to see this, Criss-Cross Man. My nightmares are hungry, so I'm going to feed them." Houlihan shuddered. "*Watch*, man! Don't stare at the floor."

Reluctantly, the Criss-Cross Man raised his eyes. The nightmares Carrion had spoken of were swimming in a blue fluid, which all but filled a high transparent collar around Carrion's head. Two pipes emerged from the base of the Lord of Midnight's skull, and it was through these that the nightmares had emerged, swimming directly out of Carrion's skull. They were barely more than long threads of light; but there was something about their restless motion, the way they roved the collar, sometimes touching Carrion's face, more often pressing against the glass, that spoke of their hunger.

Carrion reached up into the collar. One of the nightmares made a quick motion, like a striking snake, and delivered itself into its creator's hand. Carrion lifted it out of the fluid and studied it with a curious tenderness.

"It doesn't look like much, does it?" Carrion said. Houlihan didn't comment. He just wanted Carrion to keep the thing away from him. "But when these things are coiled in my brain they show me such delicious horrors." The nightmare writhed around in Carrion's hand, letting out a thin, high-pitched squeal. "So every now and then I reward them with a nice fat meal of fear. They love fear. And it's hard for me to feel much of it these days. I've seen too many horrors in my time. So I provide them with someone who *will* feel fear."

So saying, he let the nightmare go. It slithered out of his grip, hitting the stone floor. It knew exactly where it was going. It wove across the ground, flickering with excitement, the light out of its thin form illuminating its victim: a large, bearded man squatting against the wall.

"Mercy, my Lord . . ." he sobbed. "I'm just a Todo miner."

"Oh, now be quiet," Carrion said as though he were speaking to a troublesome child. "Look, you have a visitor."

He turned and pointed to the ground where the nightmare slithered. Then, without waiting to see what happened next, he turned and approached Houlihan.

"So, now," he said. "Tell me about the girl."

Thoroughly unnerved by the fact that the nightmare was loose and might at any moment turn on him, Houlihan fumbled for words: "Oh yes . . . yes . . . the girl. She escaped me in Ninnyhammer. Along with a geshrat called Malingo. Now they're traveling together. And I got close to them again on Soma Plume. But she slipped away among some pilgrim monks."

"So she's escaped you twice? I expect better."

"She has power in her," Houlihan said by way of self-justification.

"Does she indeed?" Carrion said. As he spoke he carefully lifted a second nightmare out of his collar. It spat and hissed. Directing it toward the man in the corner, he let the creature go from his hands, and it wove away to be with its companion. "She must at all costs be apprehended, Otto," Carrion went on. "Do you understand me? *At all costs.* I want to meet her. More than that. *I want to understand her.*"

"How will you do that, Lord?"

"By finding out what's ticking away in that human head of hers. By reading her *dreams*, for one thing. Which reminds me . . . *Lazaru!*"

While he waited for his servant to appear at the door, Carrion brought out yet another nightmare from his collar and loosed it. Houlihan watched as it went to join the others. They had come very close to the man, but had not yet struck. They seemed to be waiting for a word from their master.

The miner was still begging. Indeed he had not

ceased begging throughout the entire conversation between Carrion and Houlihan. "Please, Lord," he kept saying. "What have I done to deserve this?"

Carrion finally replied to him. "You've done nothing," he said. "I just picked you out of the crowd today because you were bullying one of your brother miners." He glanced back at his victim. "There's always fear in men who are cruel to other men." Then he looked away again, while the nightmares waited, their tails lashing in anticipation. "Where's Lazaru?" Carrion said.

"Here."

"Find me the dreaming device. You know the one."

"Of course."

"Clean it up. I'm going to need it when the Criss-Cross Man has done his work." His gaze shifted toward Houlihan. "As for you," he said. "Get the chase over with."

"Yes, Lord."

"Capture Candy Quackenbush and bring her to me. Alive."

"I won't fail you."

"You'd better not. If you do, Houlihan, then the next man sitting in that corner will be you." He whispered some words in Old Abaratian. *"Thakram noosa rah. Haaas!"*

This was the instruction the nightmares had been waiting for. In a heartbeat they attacked. The man struggled to keep them from climbing up his body, but it was a lost cause. Once they reached his neck they proceeded to wrap their flickering lengths around his head, as though to mummify him. They partially muffled his cries a little, but he could still be heard, his appeals for mercy from Carrion deteriorating into shrieks and screams. As his terror mounted the nightmares grew fatter, giving off brighter and brighter flashes of sickly luminescence as they were nourished. The man continued to kick and struggle for a while, but soon his shrieks declined into sobs and finally even the sobs ceased. So, at last, did his struggle.

"Oh, that's a disappointment," Carrion said, kicking the man's foot to confirm that fear had indeed killed him. "I thought he'd last longer than that."

He spoke again in the old language, and—nourished, now, and slothful—the nightmares unknotted themselves from around their victim's head and began to return to Carrion. Houlihan couldn't help but retreat a step or two in case the nightmares mistook him for another source of food.

"Go on, then," Carrion said to him. "You've got work to do. *Find me Candy Quackenbush!*"

"It's as good as done," Houlihan replied, and without looking back, even a glance, he hurried away from the chamber of terrors and down the stairs of the Twelfth Tower.

PART ONE

FREAKS, FOOLS AND FUGITIVES

Nothing

After a battle lasting many ages,
The Devil won,
And he said to God
(who had been his Maker):
"Lord,
We are about to witness the unmaking of Creation
By my hand.
I would not wish you
to think me cruel,
So I beg you, take three things
From this world before I destroy it.
Three things, and then the rest will be
wiped away."

God thought for a little time.
And at last He said:
"No, there is nothing."
The Devil was surprised.
"Not even you, Lord?" *he said.*
And God said:
"No. Not even me."

—From *Memories of the World's End*
Author unknown
(Christopher Carrion's favorite poem)

1

PORTRAIT OF
GIRL AND GESHRAT

"LET'S GET OUR PHOTOGRAPH taken," Candy said to Malingo. They were walking down a street in Tazmagor, where—this being on the island of Qualm Hah—it was Nine O'clock in the Morning. The Tazmagorian market was in full swing, and in the middle of all this buying and selling a photographer called Guumat had set up a makeshift studio. He'd hung a crudely painted backcloth from a couple of poles and set his camera, a massive device mounted on a polished wood tripod, in front of it. His assistant, a youth who shared his father's coxcomb hair and lightly striped blue-and-black skin, was parading a board on which examples of Guumat the Elder's photos were pinned.

"You like to be pictured by the great Guumat?" the youth said to Malingo. "He make you look real good."

Malingo grinned. "How much?"

"Two paterzem," said the father, gently pressing his offspring aside so as to close the sale.

"For both of us?" Candy said.

"One picture, same price. Two paterzem."

"We can afford that," Candy said to Malingo.

"Maybe you like costumes. Hats?" Guumat asked them, glancing at them up and down. "No extra cost."

"He's politely telling us we look like vagabonds," Malingo said.

"Well, we *are* vagabonds," Candy replied.

Hearing this, Guumat looked suspicious. "You can pay?" he said.

"Yes, of course," said Candy, and dug in the pocket of her brightly patterned trousers, held up with a belt of woven biffel-reeds, and pulled out some coins, sorting through them to give Guumat the paterzem.

"Good! Good!" he said. "Jamjam! Get the young lady a mirror. How old are you?"

"Almost sixteen, why?"

"You wear something much more ladylike, huh? We got nice things. Like I say, no extra charge."

"I'm fine. Thank you. I want to remember this the way it really was." She smiled at Malingo. "Two wanderers in Tazmagor, tired but happy."

"That's what you want, that's what I give you," Guumat said.

Jamjam handed her a little mirror and Candy consulted her reflection. She was a mess, no doubt about it. She'd cut her hair very short a couple of weeks before so she could hide from Houlihan among some monks on Soma Plume, but the haircut had been very hurried, and it was growing out at all angles.

"You look fine," Malingo said.

"So do you. Here, see for yourself."

She handed him the mirror. Her friends back in Chickentown would have thought Malingo's face—with his deep orange hide and the fans of leathery skin on either side of his head—fit only for Halloween. But in the time they'd been traveling together through the islands, Candy had come to love the soul inside that skin: tenderhearted and brave.

Guumat arranged them in front of his camera.

"You need to stand very, very still," he instructed them. "If you move, you'll be blurred in the picture. So, now let me get the camera ready. Give me a minute or two."

"What made you want a photograph?" Malingo said from the corner of his mouth.

"Just to have. So I won't forget anything."

"As if," said Malingo.

"Please," said Guumat. "Be very still. I have to focus."

Candy and Malingo were silent for a moment.

"What are you thinking about?" Malingo murmured.

"Being on Yzil, at Noon."

"Oh yes. That's something we're sure to remember."

"Especially seeing *her* . . ."

"The Princess Breath."

Now, without Guumat requesting it, they both fell silent for a long moment, remembering their brief encounter with the Goddess on the Noon-Day island of Yzil. Candy had seen her first: a pale, beautiful woman in red and orange standing in a patch of warm light, *breathing out* a living creature, a purplish squid. This, it was said, was the means by which most of the species in the Abarat had been brought into Creation. They had been breathed out by the Creatrix, who had then let the soft wind that constantly blew through the trees and vines of Yzil claim the newborn from her arms and carry them off to the sea.

"That was the most amazing—"

"I'm ready!" Guumat announced from beneath the black cloth he'd ducked under. "On the count of three we take the picture. One! Two! Three! Hold it! Don't move! Don't move! *Seven seconds.*" He lifted his head out from under the cloth and consulted his stopwatch. "Six. Five. Four. Three. Two. One. That's it!" Guumat slipped a plate into his camera to stop the exposure. "Picture taken! Now we have to wait a few minutes while I prepare a print for you."

"No problem," Candy said.

"Are you going down to the ferry?" Jamjam asked her.

"Yes," said Candy.

"You look like you've been on the move."

"Oh, we have," said Malingo. "We've seen a lot in the last few weeks, traveling around."

"I'm jealous. I've never left Qualm Hah. I'd love to go adventuring."

A minute later Jamjam's father appeared with the photograph, which was still wet. "I can sell you a very nice frame, very cheap."

"No, thanks," said Candy. "It's fine like this."

She and Malingo looked at the photograph. The

colors weren't quite true, but Guumat caught them looking like a pair of happy tourists, with their brightly colored, rumpled clothes, so they were quite happy.

Photograph in hand, they headed down the steep hill to the harbor and the ferry.

"You know, I've been thinking . . ." Candy said as they made their way through the crowd.

"Uh-oh."

"Seeing the Princess Breath made me want to *learn* more. About magic."

"No, Candy."

"Come on, Malingo! Teach me. You know all about conjurations—"

"A little. Just a little."

"It's more than a little. You told me once that you spent every hour that Wolfswinkel was asleep studying his grimoires and his treatises."

The subject of the wizard Wolfswinkel wasn't often raised between them: the memories were so painful for Malingo. He'd been sold into slavery as a child (by his own father), and his life as Wolfswinkel's possession had been an endless round of beatings and humiliations. It had only been Candy's arrival at the wizard's house that had given him the opportunity to finally escape his enslavement.

"Magic can be dangerous," Malingo said. "There are laws and rules. Suppose I teach you the wrong things and we start to unknit the fabric of time and space? Don't laugh! It's possible. I read in one of Wolfswinkel's books that magic was the beginning of the world. It could be the end too."

Candy looked irritated.

"Don't be cross," Malingo said. "I just don't have the right to teach you things that I don't really understand myself."

Candy walked for a while in silence. "Okay," she said finally.

Malingo cast Candy a sideways glance. "Are we still friends?" he said.

She looked up at him and smiled. "Of course," she said. "Always."